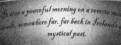

It was a peaceful morning on a remote mountain summit, somewhere far, far back in Ireland's ancient mystical past.

Faltauragh & the Ivy Castle

Glenariff

Witches Forest

Slough Neagh

Slemish

Ancient Pine Forest

ORAN
and the
Dragon Crystal

ORAN

and the
Dragon Crystal

By

A.J. Clinton

Grosvenor House
Publishing Limited

The right of A.J. Clinton to be identified as the author of this
work has been asserted in accordance with Section 78
of the Copyright, Designs and Patents Act 1988

Cover design and concept by A.J. Clinton and Martin D. Hale © A.J. Clinton.
ajclinton2017@yahoo.com

All artwork and original illustrations by Martin D. Hale © A.J. Clinton.
mdh1982@hotmail.co.uk

This book is published by
Grosvenor House Publishing Ltd
Link House
140 The Broadway, Tolworth, Surrey, KT6 7HT.
www.grosvenorhousepublishing.co.uk

A CIP record for this book
is available from the British Library

ISBN 978-1-78623-371-4

The author does not hold copyright to information obtained from
freely available articles on the internet regarding the history/legends
of the Danu, Banshee and Children of Lir.

Dedicated to the three most important and influential women in my life.

To my late grandmother, Mary, and her sister, Ellen - both of whom I dearly miss, and wish were still here to share this with. Also, to my wonderful mother, Rosemary, who has taken everything that life has thrown at her and come out the other side a lovely person - a person who supports, advises, and encourages me... and who was first to learn of this story.

For "Danwell"

Contents

CHAPTER ONE: Unlikely Allies   1

CHAPTER TWO: Myth or Fact   21

CHAPTER THREE: First Encounters   36

CHAPTER FOUR: Incarceration and Inquisition   54

CHAPTER FIVE: A Bargain for Life   69

CHAPTER SIX: Into the Outworld   85

CHAPTER SEVEN: The Dance of Light   101

CHAPTER EIGHT: The Messenger of Death   115

CHAPTER NINE: The Witch's Forest   132

CHAPTER TEN: The Veil of Mist   153

CHAPTER ELEVEN: The Children of the Waters   180

CHAPTER TWELVE: The Unseen Dragon   200

CHAPTER THIRTEEN: The Boy Changeling   222

CHAPTER FOURTEEN: Behold! Slieve Mish   238

CHAPTER FIFTEEN: The Ascent   253

CHAPTER SIXTEEN: Rydian Versus Rydian   271

CHAPTER SEVENTEEN: The Joining   285

CHAPTER EIGHTEEN: Homeward   306

CHAPTER ONE
Unlikely Allies

It was a peaceful morning on a remote mountain summit, somewhere far, far back in Ireland's ancient, mystical past. Nothing here stirred, except for the long grasses that swayed and waved gently in the cold winter's morning breeze that now drifted across the bare, rolling landscape that was the Balveeran mountain range. The mountain was older than history itself and had stood sentinel for millennia over a land that was filled with myth, legend and folklore, and was called Faltanragh. Here, on the summit, almost four thousand feet above sea level, the views were stunning and took in almost the entire northern territories of Ireland. From here, you could see clear across to the mountains of the Inishowen Peninsula; beyond Lough Foyle to the north and north west; then round, eastward, past a glimpse of blue-green ocean to the Antrim Hills over in the east; and even those of Galloway and Arran of Scotland, far in the distance behind them, on a clear day such as this one. Further round lay the solitary old, long extinct volcano known as Slieve Mish, or Slemish, as it is now called, in the south east; the great vastness of Lough Neagh and the majestic Mourne Mountains toward the south; and lastly, round to the Balveeran and Sperrin Mountains, where they spread out to the south west and west.

The sun was just rising over the hills, far off to the east by the coast, casting its eerie winter glow from the summit to half way down the sparsely forested slopes below, as it had done for millions of years before. For now, everything looked much as it always had done on Faltanragh, which had remained un-spoilt by human touch thus far.

No-one lived this far up into the glen, or even within several miles of the summit of Faltanragh, as it was considered by all who knew of it as unfit for farming of any crops, and very inhospitable and dangerous in winter, what with the howling winds and the drifting snows. The nearest village or settlement was that of Glenarran, roughly translated as meaning *Glen of the Eagles*, which was visible roughly five miles away to the south east, and a good three thousand feet lower than the summit in altitude. There was ample fishing and hunting in the rivers and forests of the lowlands surrounding the village, which meant that there was no real need for the villagers to stray too far from their home down there anyway. In fact, the only visitors to stray near, or onto, the summit, were those of the four-legged variety, or those that could fly.

On this morning, as with every other, people were stirring in the village below as, with the onset of daybreak, there was work to be done, and lives to be lived. Faint plumes of smoke could be seen rising through the clear morning air, and the distant sounds, both of farm animals and of metal clanging - probably the village blacksmith - drifted up here on the breeze. On a rare occasion, one of the village folk might cast an unwitting glance in this direction, only to admire the majesty, then carry on busily about their day. Most of the locals considered the summit so barren and desolate that there was no good reason for anyone to venture up here, as there was nothing to see or do here except admire the views... or so they all thought, at least.

A small, stone-built house with whitewashed walls, a thatched roof, and an occasional tiny window here and there, sat by a babbling stream near the northern-most edge of the village, in an area of Glenarran known locally as Esslan. It lay nestled in the shade of a giant old Sycamore tree, whose branches, the leaves now stripped by autumn and winter, oddly resembled skeletal, outstretched arms and fingers. Inside the house, the old stone walls and exposed thatched roof fought to keep the heat of the fire in, and the bitter chill of the winter out. The inhabitants of this house, the MacBrien family, were just normal, everyday people like you would find in any village during these times, and they were going about the business of breakfast, as any other family would probably also be doing right about now.

The living room, where they were presently gathered around a roughly made wooden table, was small and served as the kitchen and dining room as well. It was dimly lit by the morning sun peering in through the one tiny window at the back where the house faced east, and by two old oil lamps, one of which stood in the middle of the table at which they sat. The room was filled with the aroma of peat, or turf, which was burning in the big open fire where breakfast had just been cooked. A black and white collie dog lay stretched out on the floor in front of the fire, enjoying the heat bathing her body from the flames behind her and the warm stone floor beneath her. They had named her

Holly, after the tree near the back of the house which she was born under three years earlier.

At one side of the table, furthest from the warmth of the fire, sat Dara, father, husband and head of household. He was a handsome young man in his mid-twenties, tall and lean with long dark hair and the bluest eyes you could imagine. His face was thin with high cheek bones, and he wore a faint smattering of stubble on his lower jaw. Dara was gentle in his ways, and always thoughtful and considerate toward others. He was also a bit of a dreamer, as somewhere in the back of his mind, he secretly believed in all the legends and the folklore of his people, which he had heard many times as a child, and hoped that someday during his lifetime, he might actually see evidence of some of it, but as of yet, hadn't. He was a hard worker, which he needed to be, as he had a wife, Mary, and two young daughters named Ellen and Rosemary, the other occupants of the table, to look after and provide for. To this end, his days were spent fishing, hunting and tending their small farmstead while Mary looked after their children, cooked for them, and washed and mended their clothes.

Mary was his childhood sweetheart and they had happily grown up together, married and then started a family, but a year or so back, she had gradually started to become noticeably weak and showed signs of a strange illness. It was almost more than she could manage these days to look after the two girls and do the cooking and cleaning, with her illness weakening her to the point where she was unable to do more, as it now exhausted her.

Although she never complained of her illness and the occasional pain in her breast, suffering in silence all the while, the local community knew, or feared, that she was dying slowly, of course. At least they assumed so, as did Dara, and all were fairly certain, sadly, of what lay ahead of her. All of their friends and family did what they could to assist Mary and Dara, wherever and whenever possible, but this was a time before effective medical treatment and hospitals, and there wasn't much else they could do but help out, comfort and wait for the inevitable, regrettably.

This morning, as with every other, Dara was readying himself to set out with his faithful sheepdog on his daily check of their small flock of sheep that roamed the lower slopes of the eastern side of their neighbouring mountain, the majestic Faltanragh. After, he'd go hunting for rabbit, or maybe even a deer if he got lucky. He finished the breakfast of potato, bread, black pudding and eggs, which Mary had prepared for them on the fire, and rose to his feet, being careful not to tread on Lucy, the big grey and black tabby cat that was sprawled out amongst their feet on the floor below the table. He walked round to behind his beloved wife, placing a hand gently on her shoulder.

"I'll be off now, Mary love. Look after yourself and the girls, and I'll see you in the evening," he stated in his soft voice, as he bent to kiss her softly on the cheek.

She looked up at him and smiled, warning, "Wrap up warm now, Dara love. It's bitter cold out there today."

He moved round to the side of the table where his two daughters were sat and kissed each gently on the top of their heads in turn and whispered to them, "Love you," to which they giggled. Then he walked to the corner of the room where he kept his heavy coat and his hat. As he put them on, Mary bravely beamed at him, "Try to bring something nice for the dinner, my dear."

He gave her a courageous smile and a nod as he walked to the door, somewhat reluctantly, and said, "Holly, come now girl," tossing the dog a scrap of black pudding at the same time.

Dara reached for the longbow and quiver of arrows hanging on the peg to the side of the door and slung them over his shoulder, then pushed his big hunting knife down into the sheath on his belt. He turned and gave his family an almost forced smile, then drew back the heavy bolt and lifted the iron latch. Swinging the heavy wooden front door open, he reluctantly stepped outside with a "*Brrr*", closing the door quickly behind himself and Holly again.

Outside, the January air felt crisp as Dara drew his coat in around his waist tightly and adjusted his hat so that it covered his ears from the biting chill, as best he could. He reached down to pat Holly on the shoulder affectionately, then walked down the rough stone steps, away from the door, and set off across the little wooden bridge and along the lane heading south-west out of the village, following the stream as far as the waterfall, then turning westward. His heavy boots crunched through the frozen mud as he walked in the direction of the mountain, where he expected his sheep would be, bidding good morning to the one other person whom he passed on his way.

It wasn't long until they were in open country, as his house was near the northern-most edge of the village. Off in the distance, he could just make out the tiny white dots that were sheep, grazing on the mountain's lower slopes just near the Gorran Forest's southern-most edge. As they walked, he thought to himself that, despite the cold, it was a beautiful sunny morning, with not a cloud in sight. He also thought, with a heavy heart, about his beloved Mary, and worried what would become of her, as always. What would he do if he lost her due to her illness, and how would he explain her passing to his daughters of just four and six years of age? He desperately wished that he knew of some way to make her well again, or that he could find *someone* who could make her well again, but resigned himself to the fact that there really wasn't much chance of either happening.

Dara now, with some difficulty, forced these thoughts to the back of his mind and tried to lift his spirits by whistling his favourite song, as he trudged onward through the icy mud and grass, Holly busily sniffing her way along at his side. The grass was relatively short here, harvested at the end of summer to provide feed for the villagers' cattle throughout the winter months, then shortened even more by the sheep grazing since. Its shortness afforded the dog the opportunity to stretch her legs, and off she sprinted ahead of Dara until he called her back by his side with a sharp whistle after some moments. After an hour or so walking, they reached the lower side of the forest and turned left to follow the tree line around to where he hoped his flock would still be, as the forest blocked his view and he could now no longer see them.

The smell of larch and pine filled his nostrils as he took a deep breath through his nose, then slowly let it back out as he closed his eyes. He loved the smell of pine, and had done ever since his childhood. He had used trees from this very forest to fashion most of the furniture in the house that he and his family shared - the house left to him by his late parents. At this point, he could have taken a short cut through the forest, for certainly it would have saved him time, but he decided wisely against it. Others from the village may have laid traps for hunting, so it was risky for Holly, as well as himself, and he thought better of it.

Rounding the edge of the forest now at its most southerly corner, he worked his way up the gradual slope, with Holly faithfully by his side as they began to ascend the mountain. At one point, he stopped to catch his breath and slowly tilted his head back to look skyward. A large bird circled high above him against the blue backdrop of the clear sky, gliding effortlessly in whatever air currents it was using. He wondered what it was and what it was like to be up there, soaring on the breeze, but it was so high above that he couldn't tell if it was a buzzard or an eagle. Either way, it wasn't interested in them, he was sure, and so he made his way onward and upward in search of his flock.

An hour or so later, and they were on the upper side of the forest now, walking some hundred yards out from the tree line so that he could take in the views that this altitude afforded him. Below in the distance, just a few miles away, he could make out the village, with his little house by the stream on the side nearest him. He thought to himself that it looked so peaceful and for a second, he wished that Mary had come with him, but she was too weak for the journey, sadly.

Dara had been walking on the upper side of the forest for half an hour now, still with no sign of his sheep, and he was growing evermore concerned.

"Where are you hiding?" he asked out loud, even though he knew there would be no answer.

He turned and looked back in the direction he had come, in case they'd gotten around him somehow - through the trees, maybe - but there was no sign of them back there. So, he decided to turn north-west and head further up the mountain, just in case they'd ventured that way. He found himself wishing that there had been some snow - just a little on the ground; enough to show animal tracks, which would have made his task so much easier. Unfortunately for him though, there had been no snow this winter - not yet. He kept walking, on and up, passing a solitary old hawthorn tree that had been forced to grow at an almost forty-five-degree angle by the prevailing winds up here, but still no sign. Then, a thought suddenly occurred to him...

"I think this may be the farthest up this mountain that I've ever been," he said out loud again, to Holly this time.

He wondered if anyone he knew of had ever been this far up the mountain, but doubted it. Maybe old man McKinney had, as he was the oldest in the glen, Dara thought.

Suddenly, it occurred to him that he must be only a mile or so from the summit at this point, but he still couldn't see it yet. Nor could he see his sheep, worryingly.

The mountainside undulated somewhat here, like giant steps cut into the now steeper slope. Every time he thought he could see the top, as he climbed, it turned out to be just the top of yet another giant step or ridge, and there lay another beyond it, and another, and so on, for more than an hour. At one point, as he negotiated a particularly steep slope, Dara slipped and fell, and landed face down in the icy grass with an "Umph!" Holly immediately got the idea that it was some kind of game and darted to his side, shoving her cold, wet nose in his ear, and barking playfully.

"Off, Holly. Stop it now," Dara said calmly, as he patted her head affectionately and dragged himself back onto his feet. He quickly brushed the front of his clothes down, using only his hands, and set off again, onward and upward.

As they approached the top of the next ridge, he thought that there would be yet another one of these steps or ridges, to climb, but he was surprised as he came over the top, when into view, about half a mile in the distance, lay what appeared to him to be the very summit of the mountain, as he could see no higher point anywhere nearby. Fortunately, he could also see his sheep, a hundred or so yards in the distance ahead.

Dara let out a sharp, high pitched whistle. That was the signal for Holly to go to work, and she set off at speed toward the sheep, sprinting around behind them and gathering them together as they protested, *baa*-ing loudly, then driving them back toward her master. As she did this, Dara momentarily stared in awe at the summit and the surrounding lands below, far off in the distance. He found himself thinking of the legends and folklore he'd heard as a child about an ancient people known as the Danu - or was it Duan, he wondered - who once supposedly ruled over the entire kingdom of Ireland using ancient magical powers which they possessed. He wondered if they'd ever really existed, and if so, what had become of them, and where they were now?

Suddenly, the flock thundered past with Holly in pursuit, bringing Dara back to his senses as he calmly turned and began to follow them back down the slope.

He'd only walked a hundred yards or so when, suddenly, he heard a faint, but audible, strange sort of buzzing or crackling noise in the distance behind him, the like of which he'd never heard before. Almost fearfully, he began to turn around slowly, worried as to what on earth could be making it...

Not very far away, meanwhile, a boy named Oran sat slumped on a very large, ornately carved wooden chair near the centre of the great room at the heart of a castle which had stood here secretly, concealed from all by magic, on the summit of Faltanragh for hundreds of years. The early morning sunlight filtered in through the three tall, narrow stained glass windows to his rear, colourfully illuminating the walls of the room around him. The two end walls either side of him were lined with book shelves that were stuffed with very old books of varying size and thickness, bound in all colours. In the middle of each of these walls stood a large, round-topped wooden door, both of which were currently shut. The longer walls of the room to his front and rear were home to vast murals and tapestries depicting the ancestry and history of the castle's very unique inhabitants. The wall to his rear showed scenes of what appeared to be gods or angels and other winged creatures descending to earth from what seemed to be some manner of great floating air-ships. On the other wall, to his front, was a great battle scene which featured, at its centre, a fire breathing dragon with a rider on its back.

Spaced evenly on the black granite floor along each of these longer walls stood a total of six life-sized white marble statues. There were three on each side, all of which faced the centre-line of the room. On one side were three men and on the other, three women, all with names inlaid in gold on the base of each. On the side hung with the tapestries depicting gods and magical creatures to Oran's rear, the women's names read Eriu in the middle, with Banba and Fódla either side. On the side depicting the great battle scene to his front, the men's names read Nemed in the centre, with Nuada and Lugh either side. Thirty or so feet above, the vaulted ceiling was an ornate, wooden beamed affair, the entirety of which was decorated with ancient Irish symbols and designs. Near either end of the room, two large wrought iron chandeliers hung from it, adorned by dozens of tiny oil lamps which glowed dimly.

Oddly, there was a hole which measured about twelve inches across right in the centre the ceiling or roof, through which could be seen the bright blue sky. In the exact centre of the room, just in front of Oran and directly below the hole in the ceiling, stood a round grey stone structure, some four feet in diameter and three feet tall, which had a shallow pool of water in the top. In this pool of water sat, perched on its end, what appeared to be a rather large, egg-shaped, bluish object, some twenty inches tall.

The room was completely quiet, except for the faint sound of Oran's breathing - or rather, snoring - as he was currently fast asleep.

In fairness, most ordinary folks' houses would fit into this rooms vastness quite easily, several times perhaps. The room was *not* ordinary though, and Oran was certainly *not* an ordinary boy, not by any stretch of the imagination. Certainly, at first glance, he had all the appearance of a normal boy, albeit a strikingly handsome boy. He had, in fact, the appearance of a youth in his very early teens and was of roughly the same height and slight build of a boy that age, in spite of his many, many years.

He, himself, wasn't actually sure how old he was - no-one here was - but he had been here for almost one hundred years, since the time when they had discovered him, then just an infant, abandoned just outside the castle's entrance one summer's morning. They had found him by chance, nestled in the long grass and heather, peacefully asleep and wrapped in several heavy blankets, one of which bore the name *Oran,* embroidered in gold at one corner. Cocooned inside the blankets, he wore nothing but a slightly ill-fitting, although extremely ornate, silver bracelet, which was adorned with various coloured gemstones.

To this day, no-one had ever figured out how he had gotten inside the protective time cocoon generated by the dragon crystal that morning, and all had since passed it off as some divine or magical intervention of some sort. Perhaps it was the bracelet, perhaps not, and up until now in fact, none were even aware as to the full extent of the bracelet's secrets, nor the magical gifts concealed within it. Despite the strange circumstances surrounding his being there, they took him in as one of their own, calling him Oran from that day onward, in the belief that someone, perhaps a parent, had stitched it into the blanket so that whomever found him might know his name.

He was dressed now in a heavy purple robe, the breast of which was embroidered with an intricate Gaelic design in gold thread on the left side, and which was tied at the waist with a heavy gold cord. He wore a pair of white sheepskin slippers on his feet and, of course, the silver bracelet on his right wrist, which he had been found wearing all those years before, and which neither he, nor anyone else, had ever removed. He sat leant, or rather slumped, to one side in the big wooden chair, with his head tilted to the right and his cheek leant on his upturned right palm, his right elbow supported by the arm of the chair and his left leg crossed over his right. His dark hair was cropped quite short, except for a long, thin tail at the back which was currently draped over his left shoulder and down across the middle of his chest, reaching almost to his waist. On closer inspection, as well as his unusual age, there was also the very unusual pair of slightly pointed ears that would set him apart from a normal teenage boy - well, a normal human teenage boy anyway. For now, he was still fast asleep, although he *really, really* shouldn't be.

Elsewhere in the castle, most of the rest of its few hundred inhabitants were fast asleep also, as they would normally be at this time of morning. They were now, sadly, the only surviving people of the Danu race, or *Tuatha Dé Danann* in old Irish, translated as *"The people of the goddess Danu,"* who were also previously known as *Tuath Dé,* which meant *"tribe of the gods."* Myth and legend say they themselves were gods, or the offspring of the gods, who had arrived in Ireland somewhere near Connaught sometime around 2000 B.C., in great airships which blotted out the sun for three days. It is said that after they landed, they burned their mighty ships, having no intention of ever leaving Ireland.

The legend goes on to describe them as possessing striking beauty, unbelievable longevity of over one thousand years (possibly even immortality) and magical powers which they had used to rule over all of Ireland for centuries. Over time, they had fought off many invaders in great battles - firstly on arrival in Ireland under King Nuada, a direct descendant of a previous ruler of Ireland named King Nemed, defeating and displacing the then native tyrant, Fir Bolg. The second battle, where King Nuada lost his life and was succeeded by his champion Lugh, took place against their old rivals the Formorians, a malevolent race who practiced dark magic, sorcery, and who represented everything destructive and harmful in nature. A third and final battle took place against a race called the Milesians of Iberia, which they again survived, but only just. Over the centuries, with each battle, they suffered many losses despite their victories, and now, all who remained lived a peaceful, secluded and very secret life here in this hidden castle.

No human had seen them for centuries and to the current population of Ireland, the Danu were all but forgotten. All that existed of them now were the muddled stories handed down from generation to generation, over the hundreds of years that had passed since their disappearance. Different people told the myths and legends in their own way and stories changed as they were passed down through many families and generations. Some told the story that the Danu were a fierce, powerful and tyrannical race who stopped at nothing to get what they wanted, murdering and pillaging down through the ages. Others told a kindlier tale of them, saying they were a peaceful, benevolent, magical people who helped mankind of older times with the use of their magic, and that they had made the lands fertile and bountiful for everyone in Ireland.

The truth is more along the lines of the latter story and that they were, in fact, a kind race who were blessed with all manner of good magical abilities, known to some as "light" magic, who peacefully co-existed with and helped mankind where and when they could. They all possessed magical gifts or abilities of varying degrees and types. Some had more than one gift, which were mainly to do with life or nature, or both - for example, the ability to control fire or water, or even plant life.

A few very accomplished magicians could even manipulate the very earth itself and conjure wondrous creatures out of it and its elements. Others could control and command various types of animals or insects and a small number had evolved into what became known as the Aos Sí, or Fairies, and were capable of flight.

When the last battle, against the Milesians, ended several hundreds of years ago, the three hundred or so surviving Danu fled here on the orders of King Lugh to share in a secret - a well-kept secret which now sat on the stone plinth directly in front of Oran.

The secret was, in fact, the bluish crystal object - an unhatched Fire Dragon's egg, or dragon crystal, which sat in the now almost completely evaporated pool of water on top of the old stone plinth; a secret which had been kept by this mythical race for hundreds of years and which was now, oddly, turning slightly orange in colour.

All Fire Dragon eggs possess a little-known "magic trick" of their own, you see, and from the time they are fertilised until the time they hatch, they magically encase themselves in the hardest crystal known, and then envelope themselves and their surroundings in a time cocoon for protection and to avoid unwelcome discovery. Unfertilised eggs don't possess the ability to produce the time cocoon, because if they could and were "hidden in time", then the male dragons would be completely unable to locate them in order to fertilise them, if they couldn't see them in the first place.

The time cocoon allows the egg to be just a few moments ahead in time and engulfs everything around it for a few hundred yards, for safety's sake. When the embryo inside nears maturity, it gets warmer and warmer, hotter and hotter, then when it is about to hatch, heats up to the point where it bursts into flames, then emerges from the crystalline shell, at which point the Fire Dragon is born and the time cocoon ceases to exist.

Now, the time cocoon may seem an odd concept, but think of it this way... you're walking through a woodland and one tree is a few moments ahead in time - of the time that the rest of the forest and you, yourself, currently occupy - but you don't even notice as you walk past it, because to your eyes, it's not there, and never was. You're not expecting it to be there and therefore, it doesn't seem unusual or out of place. You would only notice its absence had you known that it was there before, you see. That's how the cocoon works. It makes what it's protecting - in this case, the castle - skip a few moments ahead in time, so that it appears not to be there at all. Simple really, and very effective.

The leader of the Danu, King Lugh, knew of this secret and had, by virtue of a bargain with the now sole surviving Fire Dragon, come to possess this fertile egg with the express intention of using its abilities to hide his people from the rest of the world. He had been fortunate enough to be, for one thing, "Commander of Dragons" amongst the many magical gifts he possessed, and rode on their backs commanding their every move as they flew through the skies, throughout all the great battles. At the end of the last fight, he made a solemn pact with her. He offered her not only her freedom, but also immortality, if she would give him one egg and she, known as Rydian, accepted and agreed.

So, the Danu fled here from almost total defeat, having lost hundreds at the hands of the Milesians on the plain near the north coast, although the Milesians suffered great losses too. They were banished to live underground forever by the Milesian ruler, although Lugh had other intentions for his people. The fearless Fire Dragon, Rydian, flew with King Lugh astride her shoulders to this spot he had chosen on the summit of this mountain called Faltanragh, meaning *"ancient peak"*. Here, on this summit, she laid the precious egg once the rest of the Danu had arrived and were present, as they must all be within the range of the magical time cocoon when the egg was laid and fertilised, else they would be separated by time forever. Then, in order to fertilise the egg, an elder named Murchad the Wise used an ancient incantation to transform her to a male dragon briefly, upon which she, or he, swiftly hovered over the lone egg, providing the required fertilisation. That done, and as the time cocoon developed, she turned to Lugh and bowed her great spiny head to him and said, simply and solemnly,

"It is done, my King."

Lugh simply nodded, knowing that it would, sadly, be the last he would ever see of her, as Rydian turned her back to them all and with a mighty whoosh of her giant leathery wings, rose gracefully into the air, at the same time returning to female status, and with her new gift of immortality, flew off towards the east. Now laid and fertilised and, at last, under the dragon crystal's protection, the Danu built their magnificent, beautiful castle in two days, using only their magic, and have existed peacefully here within its walls - a well-kept secret ever since.

There was one problem, however, with using a dragon crystal as a means to keep the castle hidden. It must never be allowed to heat up and hatch, or the time cocoon would be lost forever and the castle and all within it would be exposed to the world. This meant keeping it cool at all times, and at all costs, thus preventing it from maturing and hatching.

Now, this may sound odd, or even slightly absurd, but for Oran and his peers, this meant half of some days and nights spent taking turns at fetching cold water from the mountain spring in the castle courtyard nearby and dousing the egg with it periodically to keep it cool, thus prolonging the cocoon indefinitely - as Oran was now charged with doing on this very night. You may also be wondering why it is that the Danu can't just use their magic to stop the egg from hatching, and the answer is that the crystal sheath serves a purpose. It protects the egg from the magical spells of others amongst other things and besides, Lugh thought that the task of keeping it from hatching was a good way of teaching the younger elves discipline and responsibility.

Oran was still fast asleep, despite what was taking place in front of him, but he would wake soon - very soon. At first, as he slowly stirred from the deep sleep, he thought he was dreaming the strange buzzing, crackling sound. Suddenly, he realised that he couldn't possibly be dreaming because he wasn't allowed to fall asleep and therefore, couldn't possibly be having a dream. The noise was getting quite loud and suddenly he became aware that he *had* fallen asleep. *Oh no!* he thought. *No, no, no!* He woke with a jump, panic-stricken, his heart pounding in his chest, and snapped open his eyes as he bolted upright in the chair. "No!" he gasped, then wailed again, "Nooooo," at what he thought he saw in front of him.

He was still half asleep as his nostrils filled with an awful burning smell and he rubbed frantically at his vivid green eyes with both hands, trying to see, no, trying to rub away the sight in front of him that was the source of the noise that he really wished he was *not* hearing right now.

"I'm in *so* much trouble," he cried aloud...

CHAPTER TWO
Myth or Fact

Dara continued to turn around slowly, fearful of what he might actually see, and of what was making the strange noise, which he could now hear quite clearly. He stopped turning and stood facing the summit, rooted to the spot with fear, having forgotten about the sheep already, and almost about Holly too... but not quite.

"Holly! Here, girl... come!" he yelled, coming to his senses once more. He tried desperately to see what was making the awful noise, but still he couldn't quite tell, or see, where it came from or what was making it.

The sheep were still galloping down the mountainside in the direction in which they had just been chased by Holly, as she now returned to Dara's side, sat down by his feet and looked up at him blankly. He didn't return the look but instead, stared directly and intently ahead, still trying to see what on earth was making this strange, awful noise. Whatever it was, it appeared to be just out of sight, over the top of the ridge which they had just come down over.

He then looked down at Holly - maybe for inspiration and maybe for courage - who was still looking up at him, her tongue hanging out one side of her open mouth as she panted, waiting for his next command. He found no inspiration from her, but somewhere, deep inside himself, he found the smallest little bit of courage - enough to make him want to walk in the direction from which it seemed the noise originated.

"You stay here now. Good girl! I'll be back in a minute or two," he commanded, as he wagged his index finger at her.

He patted her on the head then put one foot forward, slowly, never taking his gaze from the ridge in front. Then he put another, and another, until he got to the point where he could almost see over, and that's when he turned to look back at Holly. She was still sitting obediently where he'd left her, some hundred yards or so back, still waiting for her master to give the next command. Suddenly, Dara felt the need for company, for he felt somewhat scared too, so he beckoned her to his side again with another sharp whistle. Holly darted up the slope and was sat next to him in no time, at which Dara felt a welcome sense of relief.

From where he stood now, he felt that he need only walk a few more yards and he would be over the top of the ridge and surely be able to see the source of the noise, which was now getting even louder. With that in mind, he thought it best to get down on his belly and crawl to the top of the ridge - for his own safety, in case there was something, or someone, that would have the desire to attack them. As he lay down on the ground, he winced at the unpleasant damp chill penetrating his clothes from beneath him, then wriggled himself forward slowly. Holly followed along closely behind in her own similar canine version of his crawl.

Upon nearing the top of the ridge, something to his front-left, toward the summit, caught his eye briefly. It was like a bright flash in the sky, it seemed, like lightning, but then not. Well, it couldn't be lightning, he told himself. Firstly, there wasn't a cloud in the sky, and secondly, it was winter, so how could it possibly be lightning? Then, he wondered if he had gone mad. He shuffled himself round a few degrees to his left, still on his belly, so that he was directly facing where he thought he had seen the flash just before. This way, if it happened again, he was sure he would be looking in the right direction and have a better view of it next time.

Dara didn't have to wait long as, within a few seconds of repositioning himself, what appeared to him to be another bolt of lightning originated from a point in mid-air, a couple of hundred feet above the mountains summit. It shot straight up, not down, into the heavens above and with it there came an audible, crackling sound. As he continued to focus his gaze in the direction of the summit, which was now just under half a mile away, he became aware of something else, which he understandably hadn't noticed before.

Just below the point where the lightning bolt had emanated from in mid-air, there appeared to be a haziness, or distortion, in the very air itself, which expanded as it reached down toward the summit. Farther below, at ground or summit level, it appeared to extend several hundred feet in either direction and was really only noticeable by the way it distorted what you were seeing, like heat haze does in summer. As Dara carefully studied the haze, he worked out that it formed a type of giant, dome-like shape.

Just then, another bolt of lightning shot up into the sky above, with another loud crackle which startled him briefly. He focused his eyes on the spot in mid-air now, directly below where the lightning had originated from, noticing now that, floating in the air, there appeared to be swirling mist which had a faint, bluish tinge to it, slightly darker than the blue of the sky around it. The swirling patch of bluish mist appeared to Dara to be something in the region of several feet across and hung in mid-air, at the top of what he was now telling himself was a giant, transparent dome that shot out lightning every so often. *What manner of magic or trickery must this be?* he puzzled.

He lay there motionless, on his belly, with Holly at his side and continued to watch intently. As he did so, it appeared that, slowly and steadily, the dark blue swirl grew larger in diameter and now formed a large ring, and also appeared to be descending slowly through the air as it expanded, approaching the ground below at a slow but steady pace. He kept watching, never taking his eyes off the strange sight in front of him as it sank lower and lower in the sky. After another ten minutes or so, the swirling ring of blue mist had grown to about two or three hundred feet in diameter and was now just over a hundred feet off the summit.

As the ring of mist continued to descend toward the ground, Dara observed, astonished and in complete disbelief, as what seemed to be four shimmering, white stone turrets appeared to rise out of it. They seemed evenly spaced - about two hundred feet apart, he guessed - and he also guessed correctly that they formed the four corners of a large building, or more specifically, a castle. Dara was so in awe of what he was witnessing that he hadn't even noticed that his heart was now racing madly. His mind was also racing with thoughts of what was unfolding in front of him, and questions. What could it be? Who could it be? Was it real, or a strange dream?

The great, shining, white stone castle continued to reveal itself over the next few minutes or so, as the swirling ring of mist continued to descend. When the mist was only a foot or so from the ground, and the castle now fully revealed, there was a final loud crackle, accompanied by a bright blue flash, as the ring of mist vanished and then, there was only silence...

Without even thinking, Dara rose to his feet to get a better view, throwing caution to the winds now in the process. He was completely speechless following the events that had just occurred and looked down at Holly, who was still lying on her belly beside him, staring back up at him with what appeared, if possible, to be a surprised look on her face. Dara was now the one with his mouth hanging open.

At this point, curiosity got the better of the dreamer in him and his fear was almost completely overcome. He could see no obvious signs of life or danger anywhere, and the castle appeared to be uninhabited, from where he now stood. He took a deep breath and started to slowly walk in the direction of the vast structure.

As he walked, he took in every detail of the castle. The four turrets, first revealed, were almost a hundred feet tall and thirty or so feet in diameter, and were distanced evenly, as he had suspected, so the castle formed a perfect square. They were connected by walls of almost the same height, which appeared to curve outward slightly as they rose from the ground and then curved completely inward at the top with no apparent edge, like the hull of some great ship. The entire structure appeared to be made from the same white, shimmering, marble-like stone which appeared to be somewhat reflective, as he could see both the ground and the blue sky around reflected clearly in its surfaces. Both the walls and the turrets were crenellated along their tops and the only openings appeared to be small archers' slits dotted here and there on the walls and turrets, and several small windows here and there, near the tops of the turrets. He wondered now if anyone was watching him from one of these windows but thought it unlikely - or at least, hoped not.

He carried on slowly, forward, toward the formidable structure, noticing that within the ramparts sat a tall, circular tower, which protruded well above the walls as it stood taller than everything else around it. It was some thirty to forty feet in diameter and had a conical, slate type roof. The uppermost dozen feet or so of the tower appeared to be entirely made of glass and around the lower edge of this were what appeared to be ornately carved stone birds, set into the walls every few feet. He assumed that the entrance must be on another side as he was unable to see any way in from where he stood.

As he neared the castles' perimeter, now only about fifty yards away, he lost sight of the tower due to the sheer height of the walls. Oddly, he thought to himself, there were still no signs of any life as of yet. Perhaps the castle was abandoned many years earlier, he pondered. He pressed on slowly, one second looking down at his feet and the ground ahead so he didn't trip, then up at the walls and turrets.

Holly was once again by his side as they both now approached the castle from the south-east together. As he stared up at the turret nearest them, he noticed what he assumed was a statue, set into a niche in the turret wall about three quarters of the way up. It appeared human in form and size but seemed to have a pair of large wings folded across its front and was the same colour as the rest of the stone from which the castle was made. He looked once more at the ground to check his footing briefly, then back up at the turret, but thought he was imagining things or had gone mad again, as the statue that was white only a moment ago was now the blackest of blacks.

Suddenly, there followed an ear-piercing shriek, which could only have come from the direction of the castle, and which made Dara think that an eagle was swooping on Holly. He quickly turned to his side, briefly looked down at her and saw that she was safe, and then turned to look back at the castle in front but did not for one second expect what he now saw before him.

The black statue, which was once white, was now no longer a statue it seemed and was stood directly in front of him, no more than five feet away, swaying hypnotically from side to side slightly, with wings folded across its front as before. His heart suddenly leapt into his mouth and fear gripped him inside, rooting his feet to the spot where he now stood. It was all Dara could do to mumble the word, "Huh?"

He noticed that the creature, if that was indeed what it was, was extremely unusual, in that it seemed to have a glossy, almost liquid kind of skin, if such a thing were possible. He also noticed its rather disturbing lack of any facial features, despite the human like head, and small bump that resembled a nose on what *would* be its face if it were human. There was no mouth, deep sockets with no eyes, and no ears, it appeared, and it was completely naked and completely hairless and smooth all over.

Suddenly, it stopped swaying in front of him and in the blink of an eye, fully extended not one, but two pairs of wings with a somewhat loud, ruffling noise. One pair of wings was set slightly lower than the other, he observed, and were slightly smaller in size, and both pairs were similar in shape to those of a bat. The creature started to sway again but this time fluttered, or shook, its wings as it did so, and Dara wondered, oddly, if it was doing some kind of dance perhaps. He was too scared to ask - too scared to say anything, in fact - and he then realised that he too was shaking, but in his case, it was from sheer terror. He was just about to look down at Holly again to check that she was alright when suddenly something wrapped itself around him from behind, gripping tightly and restricting his arms and legs. In fact, it was such a firm grip he couldn't move at all and could just about breath.

It was then that he realised that there had been another one of these creatures behind him all along and that the one in front had served the sole and specific purpose of distracting, or mesmerising, him while others moved stealthily into position behind him, just out of sight. He then looked either side and discovered that there were two more of these creatures stood several feet away on either side and just behind him as well, so there were four in total. Then, it dawned on him - one for each turret, they were guards or look out sentinels, he presumed.

They were in fact called Shawan, and were formidable creatures, no less, conjured up by Danu magic using animated minerals from the earth such as oil, tar and limestone amongst other things. They possessed amazing strength and blinding swiftness in flight and were very adept in combat. Their most useful trait, however, was that they could not die, as they were not living things, thus meaning that they could not be slain on the battlefield.

The one directly behind Dara had almost completely engulfed his arms, torso and legs in its lower pair of wings, making it virtually impossible for him to move. He tried to turn his head to get a look at it, then thought better of it, based upon what he could see either side and in front of him. They all looked identical. He looked directly at the creature in front and as he did so, it tilted its head slightly to the left and a wry kind of smile, lined with dozens of tiny white, needle-like teeth, appeared across its face where there was no mouth before.

Seconds later, as he was still staring at the creature to his front, there came a strange, loud whoosh directly behind him. The next thing Dara felt was the particularly odd sensation of himself being jolted or lifted upward. His immediate reaction was to look down - maybe because he could no longer feel the ground under his feet, or perhaps because the creature in front was now disappearing below him. And yet, the ground was still there, it was just getting further away, and he suddenly came to realise he was being flown through the air.

"Arrghh!" he screamed out in terror, as they flew swiftly toward the castle wall...

Meanwhile, inside the castle, Oran stopped rubbing his eyes and removed his hands from them quickly, at the same time staring in horror at what was happening in front of him. What *had* been a large, bluish coloured, egg-shaped crystal was now an amber to almost red egg-shaped crystal, with very little blue remaining.

The crystal was now so hot that it was in the process of boiling the water in which it was sat. He realised to his horror that, as he had somehow fallen asleep, he had allowed the egg to heat up. Now, it was going to hatch, and they would lose the time cocoon forever, he feared.

He jumped to his feet, frantically grabbed the pitcher of water on the floor and swiftly began pouring it onto the egg, but soon acknowledged that his efforts were worthless as the water instantly turned to steam when it made contact with the egg, as it was already searing hot and now almost totally crimson in colour. He dropped the empty pitcher on the floor and took a step back, realising that his attempts to preserve the egg were futile, all the while staring wide eyed at the scene in front of him in sheer terror and panic.

Oran continued to watch in shock as the last of the water that the egg was sat in boiled away, and everything became bone dry. The entire egg was now glowing crimson red and there was the distinct, awful smell of burning. He stood there, rigid with fear, waiting for the Fire Dragon to hatch from the egg and fly out through the hole in the roof, but after a few moments nothing had appeared, and he found himself wondering if something were wrong with it.

At that point, as he stared on in dismay, the uppermost part of the egg started to turn black and smoke started billowing out of the top of it. Within the next few moments, the rest of the egg turned firstly to black, and then to what appeared to be ash, then slowly it began to crumble until there was nothing left on top of the plinth but a small pile of smouldering ashes, but no baby dragon. He was completely speechless and just stood there, staring at the top of the plinth. Thoughts were racing through his head now, about what would happen to him when this came to light.

He didn't have to wait long to find out, as the heavy wooden door to his left swung open violently and an angry looking lean, bearded man in a long leather coat burst into the great room, closely followed by two huge Irish Wolfhounds whose heads were almost level with his shoulders. The man stormed over to the plinth and stared at the ashes in what looked to Oran to be a mixture of complete disbelief, anger and shock. He then swiftly swung his head round and glared directly at Oran, who was now flanked either side by the two wolfhounds.

"Where is the dragon, Oran?" the man demanded angrily.

Oran, who was now shaking with fear, looked at his King and murmured, "I… don't… know… Sire. There… appears to be no dragon, just… ashes."

Just then, Oran began to weep, as fear of what was to come sank in deeper. Seeming to doubt that there was no dragon, King Lugh turned and reached his hand out to the pile of ash and ran his fingers through it, as if hoping to find something in there, but there was, indeed, only ash.

"Tell me what happened, Oran," the King ordered.

"I don't know S… Sire, I… I… I fell asleep… I th… think," Oran stammered through his tears.

The King turned to look at him again, now with an angry scowl across his face.

"What do you mean by, you *think* you fell asleep? You mean you *did* fall asleep, Oran, and that is why this has come to happen… *no*?" Lugh raged, as his mind raced with thoughts of how to overcome the tragedy.

Oran stood with his head hung in shame now, staring at his slippered feet as he continued to weep, not knowing what to say to the King next. Lugh turned to stare at the ash again for a moment, and then turned to Oran again and said, "This will require the immediate attention of the high council, I fear. You have committed a very selfish act, with very severe consequences, against your people - and you have put the safety of all of us in great jeopardy, young man. There is absolutely no time to lose. We must act swiftly."

"But I didn't mean to, my Lord," protested Oran, defiantly.

"Silence now! Stop with your blubbering at once!" Lugh snapped, as he motioned to the two other men who had been waiting silently, just beyond the door. "Men, take him to his quarters where you will watch over him as he gets dressed, and then escort him down to the lowest level of the castle, please. Wait with him in the dark chamber until I summon him."

Oran hung his head in shame again, wondering what awaited him in this mysterious lowest level of the castle. He had never been below ground level and until now, he frankly wasn't even aware that there was any part of the castle that extended below ground. He was now very afraid that he was doomed to spend the rest of his existence locked away in a darkened cell underground - this *dark chamber* which the King spoke of - beneath the castle.

The two men now marched in and approached Oran. They said nothing as they took an arm each and led him off to his quarters to get dressed. Oran did not protest, knowing that it would be pointless.

As the men marched out of the room with him, the King shouted after them, "Have the guards tasked to the walls and turrets immediately, men. We find ourselves vulnerable for the first time in three hundred years. Who knows what's to come of this!"

The King remained in the room for a few moments, alone, staring at the ashes and thinking of his next course of action to protect his people. It was then that he was joined by his champion, Cethen, who strode briskly into the room, having also just discovered the morning's terrible events. Cethen too stared at the pile of ashes for a moment and whispered, calmly, "What of the dragon, my Lord? What shall I do, my Lord?"

"I have given the order to task the entire guard to the walls, to keep watch along with the Shawan sentinels. I need you to release the fireworms into the grounds surrounding the castle as well and have them patrol just below the surface as a precaution. Can you do that for me, Cethen?" Lugh now whispered back to him.

"Yes, of course, my Lord. Right away," Cethen replied, then asked again, "What of the dragon, my Lord?"

"It would appear that three hundred years got the better of it, my friend. Possibly a good thing for all of us," Lugh replied pensively, as he stroked his long beard.

"Probably so, Sire. No telling what could have happened had it hatched and survived. I shall go now and take care of the fireworms and the guard, for I fear that there is no time to lose, my Lord," Cethen said.

He looked briefly toward the hole in the ceiling and then turned and hurried out of the room, leaving the King and his two dogs behind.

King Lugh sat down, in the chair previously occupied by Oran, with a heavy sigh and heavy heart. He hoped desperately that there was a way to fix this before they were discovered by anyone from the outside, enemy or not. No matter what, they could not risk discovery after such a long time hidden from all on the outside. He found some comfort in the knowledge that no-one ever ventured up here really, especially in winter. He also felt reassured by the fact that the exterior walls of the castle were very cleverly designed and fabricated in such a way as to reflect their surroundings like mirrors, so as to give the illusion from a distance that the castle was in fact not there at all. The last thing they needed, he now reminded himself, was discovery by their old enemies, and there certainly weren't enough of the Danu people left to withstand another great battle like the ones fought before they came to this refuge.

Lugh sat there for a few minutes longer, again stroking his long thin beard, as he formed a plan in his head and thought to himself that it may have been good fortune for him and all of his kind that he had bestowed the gift of immortality on the dragon, Rydian. He had had three hundred years to prepare for such a catastrophe and now all he had to do was find her, which would most likely be no easy task, he thought to himself. Asking her to perform the same favour once more by providing another egg would also be no small feat, especially in light of the fact that he didn't have much to bargain with that she might want or, indeed, need.

Just then, an elderly elf in a long white robe walked gracefully into the room alone. He had an extremely long beard and long silver hair that was tied back in a pony-tail and hung almost to the floor at the back. He was known as "Murchad the Wise", and was believed to be the oldest inhabitant of the castle. He walked over to Lugh and stood beside him, at the same time resting a frail, boney hand on his King's shoulder.

"Odd news. We have a visitor, my son. The Shawan have retrieved an outsider found wandering nearby and taken him to the tower, along with his dog," he said, softly.

"What? Already? Does he appear to be any kind of a threat to us, Murchad? Was there anyone else with him, or just the dog?" Lugh enquired with concern.

"It wouldn't seem so. It appears he - a human, no less - was checking his flock of sheep on the slopes nearby when the fuss of the failing time cocoon attracted his attention, or curiosity. He might, however, become a threat if he is released back to his people and talks, obviously," the old elf said thoughtfully, as he too now stroked his long silver beard with his free hand.

"I had better go talk to this man then, I suppose, and try to determine what we should do with him exactly. Thank you, Murchad," Lugh sighed.

"Troubled times ahead, my Lord. You must plan with great care," the old elf warned, cautiously.

Lugh stood up, sighing again, and put his hand on the old mans' shoulder.

"We shall prevail, my old friend," he said, softly, and walked off toward the door with his two dogs following, thinking of Oran and what he would soon be faced with in the chamber of souls. He felt sorry for him in a way. He stopped at the door and turned toward Murchad.

"I may just have a plan that will save us - a plan that will involve a somewhat perilous quest to seek out the last remaining Fire Dragon, if she is indeed still out there somewhere. Let us hope and pray that she is, my old friend, no?"

CHAPTER THREE
First Encounters

Dara tried not to look down as he was carried at alarming speed through the cold morning air by the creature that now held him firmly in its grip, but couldn't help himself and so, looked down anyway. As frightening as this first experience of flight was to him though, something inside him told him that he didn't want to miss this for anything and so he continued to look toward the ground in his newfound amazement. He watched as the castle wall approached swiftly and then, suddenly, there was a gut-wrenching surge upward as the creature shrieked again and climbed directly upward through the air at speed in order to make it safely over the top of the mighty castle wall. As they cleared the wall, Dara could briefly see what lay below within the boundaries of the castle walls, as they flew toward the lofty tower at the centre of its grounds. He didn't wonder where he was being taken, as he knew only too well the answer, but he did wonder, however, where his dear Holly was.

As he was flown over the ramparts, he noticed that the walls themselves were roughly ten or fifteen feet thick, and on the interior of each, it was as though many smaller buildings of a similar size and shape were stacked one on top of the other for about three quarters of the way up the inside, or so. He thought to himself that he'd never seen so many windows in all his life, noticing that they covered almost the entire internal surface of the walls and were stacked five deep, he counted.

Growing over every spare inch of wall where there wasn't a window, or a door was the largest expanse of a blue-green ivy that he had ever seen in his life. It had grown all the way to the tops of the internal walls, and all the way around the interior of the castle. Every building was covered by it. Each window must have represented some type of room, he assumed, and wondered who, or what, occupied them. The great tower he had seen from outside, which they now flew toward, sat directly in the middle of the interior and was surrounded on all sides by numerous different, lesser buildings dotted around it throughout the courtyard, which varied in size, shape and height. A total of four buildings were attached directly to the tower at right angles to each other, two of which stood out from the rest by virtue of their greater size. He could briefly see that both of these larger buildings had stained glass windows and one, strangely, had a small hole in the roof, whereas the other had a spire at one end. This led him to assume that the latter must be their place of worship. All of these buildings were also almost entirely engulfed in the same blue-green ivy.

They were now very close to the tower, circling around it at a slower pace now, level with the glass section at the top, as if waiting for a signal or for something else to happen. On the first circuit, Dara noticed that, on the north side, there was a large arched opening in the glass wall. This appeared to him to be some eight feet high and, from this opening, the floor of the room within continued outward to form a large, stone type balcony which jutted out about ten feet, with a stone balustrade wall around its perimeter. On the second pass, they slowed and landed on the balcony, with a frenzied flapping of wings and yet another loud, ear piercing shriek.

Still restrained by the creature that had brought him here, Dara's thoughts immediately turned to Holly, now that his feet were safely back on something solid again. He looked first to his left, then quickly around to his right and to his relief, there she was, just sitting calmly by his side, looking up at him as usual. She seemed to be unrestrained, strangely, and as far as he could tell, she appeared to be unharmed, of which he was extremely grateful.

As he stood there on the balcony, still held firmly by the Shawan, he peered ahead into the magnificent room that lay ahead of him, dominating the top of the tower. The curved walls seemed to be made from a single expanse of glass for the entirety of their circumference and were almost twice the height of an average man. Dara couldn't help but wonder how they achieved something like this. On the black stone floor inside were scattered a number of large animal skin rugs of various sizes and colours. He could also see numerous pieces of elegant, brightly coloured furniture placed here and there throughout the room, mostly for sitting on. A large round, wooden table dominated the middle of the room, on top of which, placed at its centre, was an ornate vase with the most beautiful and unusual flowers he had ever seen in his life. This struck him as odd in the middle of winter, and he now questioned himself as to where they might have come from.

At the far side of the room, he could just make out what seemed to be a set of stairs providing access to the room from below and where, just now, a bearded man was ascending, turning as he reached the top to walk towards him. The man walked across the room toward Dara slowly, making eye contact with him all the time, with a sort of quizzical, almost puzzled, expression on his face. Dara guessed the man might be aged somewhere in his fifties but couldn't be more wrong - closer to five hundred and fifty was probably more accurate.

The man was followed by two large dogs, neither of which bothered, nor seemed bothered by, Holly in any way. Holly chose to ignore their presence and huddled in close to Dara's leg. Another similarly aged man followed directly behind them and both men came to a halt, and stood side by side just feet in front of Dara, with the two great hounds sat just behind them. It didn't take long for Dara to notice the two men's strangely pointed ears, as well as their diminutive size.

"My name is King Lugh of the people of Danu and this is my champion and right hand, whose name is Cethen," the first man proclaimed, as he gestured toward the fair haired, lean man to his left. He continued by enquiring, "What name are you called by, good sir?"

Dara, at that moment, was still somewhat in awe of his recent experience and simply stammered,

"D - D - Danu?" just then realising what the man had said, then took a deep breath and blurted out, "My name is Dara MacBrien, sir, of the glen below the mountain to the south, Glenarran. I mean you no harm, Sire, I swear of it."

He desperately hoped that his words would keep him safe and free from harm at the hands of his captors.

He was certain that the man talking to him had said the name Danu - or had he just imagined or misheard it. Strange coincidence, he now thought, since he was, just a while earlier, thinking of these very people. Surely not? He hadn't heard that name mentioned since he was a boy. Could these really be the so-called mythical people of Danu whom he'd heard tales of in the past as a child? Surely it couldn't be true, although he'd always hoped it were, in some way.

Nevertheless, here he was now, face to face in this magnificent castle with a man who had just announced that that *was* who he was. If so, however, he worried that there could be no telling how this would turn out for him, as these people were fabled to be capable of all manner of magical feats, not least of which was, until recently, concealing this huge castle. He might well end up being turned into a goat or a sheep, or something much worse if that were possible, he now feared.

"It is unfortunate that you were in the vicinity when the mornings rather... catastrophic... events unfolded, well, Dara MacBrien. Unfortunate for both yourself and us, in all honesty. Perhaps you should not have let your curiosity lead you here so easily, else you would be safe elsewhere now, no?" Lugh pointed out.

Dara was now more concerned for his welfare than ever, on hearing the man say the words *safe elsewhere*. What could he mean by that exactly... was he not safe here? What were this man's intentions for both him and Holly, he wondered? His thoughts suddenly turned to his beloved wife, Mary, and his girls at home. He found comfort in the fact that it was still only late morning and wouldn't be dark for hours yet, and so they would not be expecting him home just yet, as he normally got back just around dusk. Then he thought, *What if these people keep me here until after dark? What if they keep me here forever?* His mind was again racing, with ideas of what was going to happen to him, and of what would become of Mary if he didn't get home to her and his daughters. He was now more worried than he had ever been in his life before, and he was suddenly overcome by sadness.

"This man carries small arms with him, Sire. A bow and arrows, and a hunting knife by his belt," Cethen said, interrupting the brief silence.

"Disarm him please, Cethen," Lugh instructed, with a nod toward Dara.

Cethen stepped forward, and the Shawan that was holding Dara suddenly eased its grip just enough to allow Cethen access to remove Dara's weapons, which he then took into the room and placed on a chair by the large table. He turned and walked back to Lugh's side and stated, "He is now safely unarmed, Sire."

Lugh nodded and said, "Thank you, Cethen. I think it's safe for the Shawan to release him from its grip now. I'm sure he'll do us no harm."

Cethen simply replied, "Aye, Sire, as you wish."

Cethen then spoke, almost whispered, three words to the Shawan in an unusual tongue that Dara had never heard in his life before.

"*Shawan. Callahen lu,*" he said, and no sooner had he uttered the words, than the creature completely released Dara from its grip, took one step back and with another loud shriek and a whoosh of its wings, rose into the air again and flew away from the balcony with its three identical looking companions, all of them vanishing from sight.

Dara immediately felt relieved at this, for at least he could breathe properly now. Then, a sudden thought crept into his mind that he should possibly attempt to make a run for it. But then, just as suddenly, he realised that there was really nowhere he could run to - there was nowhere to go other than somewhere else in this vast castle. Instead, he stood where he was and asked of his captor, "What name is this place called, sir, and what is to become of me, might I ask?"

"That, my friend Dara, is a very good question indeed," replied Lugh. "This *place*, as you call it, has become known to us as home and is called by us simply, the *ivy castle,* for reasons you can clearly see. *You* are now a... a guest, I would say. Yes, a guest... of sorts. Who do you live with at your home? Is there anyone who will be missing you or expecting you home shortly? A wife perhaps?" Lugh continued. "The problem, you see, is that if we allow you to leave to return to your home and your tongue gets the better of you, then we shall have a very serious problem on our hands here, no? We have kept this place a secret for several hundreds of years and I plan to keep it that way at any cost. My people cannot risk exposure, and in that respect, releasing you is a very serious risk indeed."

Dara looked at the stone floor thoughtfully for a moment, and then to Holly by his side. He raised his head back up, staring at Lugh and asked, "What if I promise to keep your secret safe? I could take some kind of oath, and you know now where I live." He paused for a moment, thinking carefully as he continued, "I have a very poorly wife at home and two very young daughters. They desperately need me home to take care of them all, Sire. I beg of you, will you please release me?"

"Hmm, that's as may be, young man, but I have something very important to attend to presently, and so, I will think the matter over whilst I leave you in the charge of my friend, Cethen here. I will give you my answer when I return shortly, Dara MacBrien," Lugh said. He then turned to Cethen and instructed, "Cethen, please take him to the holding area below in the dark chamber, and make sure that he and his dog are both secure. I shall deal with him when I have finished with Oran and the high council."

Lugh then turned and walked back into the tower room and toward the stairs, once again followed by his dogs. As he descended into the stairwell, two much younger looking men dressed somewhat like soldiers or guards appeared and joined Cethen, Dara and Holly on the balcony.

"This way please," Cethen said to Dara, motioning politely towards the stairs where Lugh had just gone. Dara followed the instruction and walked toward the doorway and into the room, followed by Holly, Cethen and the two young men.

In another part of the castle, Oran got dressed in his normal daily attire in his private chamber, while the men who guarded him waited inside, watching closely over him. When Oran had finished dressing himself, one of the men opened the door to the corridor and gestured for Oran to leave the room.

"This way, young master Oran, if you please," said the man, known only as Cathal.

Oran gingerly stepped out into the corridor, with the two men joining him on either side. He was surprised to see that many of the castles' inhabitants had come out to watch as he was led past. No-one said anything to him as he walked past them. They just stared at him as though he had done something terrible and should be ashamed of it. Well, he had done something terrible, or at least had let something terrible happen, for which he *was* ashamed and so, he walked along the corridor and down the stairs with his head down. When they reached the ground floor, the men led him out into the courtyard and across to the large building with the spire, which was attached to the tower at one end.

They reached the entrance a moment later, to find a beautiful young girl wearing an apprehensive expression. Her skin was snow white and she was of roughly the same age as Oran, and stood by the door, facing them. She wore a long, dark green dress and had extremely long black hair, gathered in a pony-tail at the back of her head. She was, in fact, the King's daughter. Her name was Enya and she and Oran had been best friends for as long as they could remember - since childhood, in fact. She moved now and stood in front of them, defiantly blocking the doorway.

"I heard of what happened, Oran, and I wanted you to know that I support you no matter what. You know that, yes?" she said to him. "Whatever happens, I'm here for you, if you need me. I won't allow my father to do anything bad to you."

Oran tried to smile at her and quietly said, "Thank you, Enya. It's going to be fine, I'm sure," trying hard to convince himself, as much as her.

She smiled back at him and asked, "Where are they taking you? Everyone's asking?"

At that point, Cathal said, "He has an urgent audience with your father. Please step aside, Your Highness."

Enya reluctantly moved out of the way with a scowl on her pretty face and said, "Good luck, Oran. Come and find me when you're finished please."

Cathal reached out and pushed the heavy, wooden entrance door open, and the three of them stepped inside the building. He turned and closed the door behind them, leaving Enya outside. It was deathly quiet inside as they quickly ushered Oran along the nave to the far end of the church and past the altar and the huge white statue of the goddess Dana, to the screened off section known as the chancel. Oran had never been in this part of the church before and had always wondered what lay behind the screens.

The chancel was quite large - larger than he had expected - and there were pictures on the walls of what he assumed were previous leaders or rulers of some description. On the very end wall, there were three very old looking doors, separated by about six feet between each, with a wooden sign on each. The one on the left read *Vestry* and the middle one read *Tower,* both in gold lettering, and the one to the right read simply *No Admittance* in red lettering. It was this door that the men now led Oran towards and as they approached, the door mysteriously swung open by itself as if it were expecting them, creaking faintly as it did so.

On the other side of the door was a relatively small, dimly lit room, with a rough stone floor. The room oddly had no windows and only the one door - the door through which they had just come, and which was now closing itself again behind them. There was a small, stone altar in the centre of the room, with half a dozen tiny oil lamps sat on top which provided the only light.

They led Oran to the altar and stopped, facing it, one man either side of him.

"We bring Oran of the people of Danu to face the high council in the chamber of souls," Cathal announced in a loud voice, with his head bowed.

Oran wondered whom he was addressing, as there seemed to be only the three of them present. He also wondered what on earth was *the chamber of souls*. There was an eerie silence for a few seconds, followed by an odd creaking sound, then suddenly, the room began to transform magically before his eyes.

"Stay still now for a moment, master Oran. Don't move," the other man, named Ronan, advised.

At first, as Oran's eyes adjusted to the light, the floor began to extend in front of them as the stone slabs grew and expanded. With this, the room grew longer - much longer - and then taller as well, as the walls stretched upward. A large wooden door magically appeared in the far wall and along each side of the room, rising swiftly up out of the floor, appeared several statues, similar to the ones in the great room except these were larger than life size, probably eight feet tall, and appeared to be made of solid gold. There were, again, six statues in all, of the same people as in the great room, and each one held an object - weapons or instruments of some description. Then, curiously, as Oran watched in awe, each of the statues extended their one free arm with a metallic grinding sound, and gestured toward the newly appeared door at the far end of the room, turning their expressionless faces toward it as a sign for them to approach it.

Oran didn't have time to examine them more closely, as his guard now hastily ushered him to the door at the other end of the room which, again, magically opened itself as they approached. On the other side of the door was a very dark room, a stairwell, containing only a spiral staircase, which Cathal now instructed him to descend. It was an old, stone staircase with a black iron handrail, and it appeared to have had a lot of use over time, in spite of the fact that none of the castle's inhabitants seemed to know of its existence, or so Oran believed anyway, as he'd never heard anyone speak of this place. The centre of each step was well worn in the middle, from what he guessed was hundreds of years of foot traffic - but by whom, he wondered? He guessed it could only be the King, possibly, and wondered what it was that brought him down here so often.

On and on they descended, down the gloomy, dimly lit stairwell for what seemed like ages. Oran guessed he must be at least a hundred feet or more below ground by now and could smell a damp, musty sort of smell and hear water dripping occasionally. He was also very aware of the eerie echo of their footsteps as he descended into the depths of the unknown - unknown to him, at least. Finally, they reached what Oran assumed was the bottom, where the stairs ended and opened out into another large room, or rather cavern, which was again dimly lit by small oil lamps set into niches carved into and along the stone wall on his right. The room had been carved out of the rock that formed the very mountain itself and the moist walls reflected this in their roughness and unevenness.

Oran stopped as he noticed that there was no wall, as such, to his left, but instead a long row of vertical iron bars from the floor to the ceiling, which were spaced about four inches apart, with a sort of similarly forged gate in the middle with a big old-fashioned padlock on it. It was too dark to see what lay behind the bars, apart from the loosely scattered straw on the floor and Oran wondered, sadly, if this was where he would end up after his meeting with the King and the mysterious high council.

The men urged him onward, toward the far end of the room where it narrowed and now, in the dim light, Oran could see that there was another large wooden door set into the rock here - this time with a familiar, yet slightly different, circular ancient Celtic symbol inlaid in gold in the centre of it, which was about the same size as an average dinner plate. Two men stood guard either side of this door, which lay dead centre at the end of the room, though it was really more like a large, tapering cave than a room, to be honest.

As Oran arrived at the door, Cathal announced again, "We bring Oran of the people of Danu to face the high council in the chamber of souls."

The guard to the left of the door nodded as he turned to face it, tapping three times on it with his wooden staff. Within seconds, the symbol began to glow with a brilliant green light. As the symbol glowed, the door swung open slowly by itself, just as the others had done before. Just inside, he was surprised to see King Lugh already stood waiting in the dimly lit room for him, facing the open doorway. The King was dressed differently from normal and now wore a long, dark green robe with intricate gold embroidery of a Celtic nature down both sides at the front and all the way around the bottom. On his head, he wore a small, modest looking crown made of gold with, in its centre, the same Celtic symbol as was on the door. Around the

King's waist was a belt and scabbard in which a sword was sheathed, which worried Oran greatly.

He looked at Oran, smiling, and said, "Come forth, Oran. Please, enter," gesturing with both hands for Oran to walk toward him.

The room was quite dark inside, and Oran could hardly see anything at all, other than the King and the patch of stone floor that lay between them both. He walked slowly and apprehensively forward toward Lugh and once inside, the door swung shut behind him with a loud bang, making him jump. Now it was just him and the King in the darkened room together, alone. He could clearly hear his own heart, beating vigorously in his chest.

"Don't be afraid, Oran. There is nothing for you to fear here. I assure you that you will come to no harm in this place. Now then, none other than I have ever had the privilege of entering here until this day, Oran. You are the first, other than myself," Lugh said quietly, adding proudly, "You are about to witness something seen only by my eyes until this day, and you are extremely fortunate - no, privileged... indeed."

Oran forced a smile as Lugh took a deep breath and said, with a certain sadness in his voice, "It is, however, unfortunate that you arrive here under the given set of very serious circumstances, but I hope for your sake that the outcome of this meeting will be, in some way, favourable for you, my young friend. I have always looked upon you as the son I never had, Oran, ever since the day you were discovered outside the castle all those years ago, and I hope the council have mercy on you now because of this."

Oran was still wondering who this council were exactly but said nothing. He was of the belief that there was only the King and himself here in the room, but truthfully, it was so dark there could easily be any number of other people hidden in here also.

"Come now, Oran. Let us face the high council together," Lugh announced, as he turned his back to Oran. "By my side now, Oran," he instructed, motioning with his left hand to the space beside him, where he wanted Oran to stand.

Oran stepped forward quickly, noticing the impressive symbol which almost covered the back of Lugh's robe which, again, resembled closely the circular Celtic design as before on the door and on Lugh's crown. It was the same Celtic symbol, or similar, used throughout Danu society to represent the status of an individual, or the importance of an area or section of the castle. But this one was different, having the image of a sword placed vertically at its centre - a very unique sword with what he could only imagine was a dragon coiled tightly around its handle.

Until now, Oran had believed there to be only four ranks or positions in the Danu hierarchy. These were awarded based on an individual's skills in the art of magic and were; junior, intermediate, skilled and lastly, master, amongst which Oran held the position of junior, and had only ever seen the King wear that of master... until now. This form of the symbol he had never seen before today, and he felt certain that it must carry very great significance and wondered what it could mean.

He was now very afraid of what was about to happen to him and dug deep in his heart to find some courage. As he reached Lugh's side, the room strangely started to brighten slightly, and he noticed that it was a very large, circular room which appeared to have no ceiling or roof that he could see, seeming to continue upward indefinitely, into complete darkness.

Directly to their front, about thirty feet away, were three large, ornately carved black wooden thrones, which were spaced several feet apart. Immediately in front of them at the centre of the room, laid into the floor where they now stood, was a very large, intricate mosaic which depicted a map of Ireland, again inlaid in gold, with a gold Celtic design like that on Lugh's robe surrounding it entirely in a perfect circle. At the four corners of this map, each inlaid in a different coloured stone, were images of four special objects which Oran instantly recognised, as they were also used on many Danu markings and rank insignia. On the upper left side lay an image of the Cauldron of Dagda and to its right, an image of a spear, the Spear of Lugh. To the lower left side was an image of a rock, the Stone of Fal and lastly, to its right, a strangely glowing sword, the Sword of Light.

He looked up and around the room, suddenly gasping in awe as he now noticed four very large, evenly spaced, reptilian looking skulls mounted around the circumference of the room on the rough stone walls. Each skull was slightly different in size and shape, but each had all manner of horns and boney barbs protruding in various places. He thought to himself that these skulls were so large that he could quite easily fit inside the jaws of one. Although he had never seen one alive, he knew only too well that these could only be the skulls of dragons which had possibly died in battles past and he thought that they must surely have been impressive, formidable creatures in their time. He then felt a sadness at the fact that he had never seen a living dragon - that they had been wiped from existence hundreds of years before his time.

On the floor, directly below each of the skulls, stood a stone plinth, each one just a few feet tall. Just above three of the four plinths, several objects seemed to hover, floating in mid-air, one above each. These objects matched those depicted in the mosaic on the floor. Above one floated the Stone of Fal, the next a cauldron atop it, and the third, a long spear, but nothing on the fourth, strangely. He wondered why for a moment, then realised that it must be the sword hanging from the belt around Lugh's waist - the fabled Sword of Light, an immensely powerful weapon of magic by all accounts, and most likely the same sword depicted in the symbol on the back of the King's robe.

Directly at the centre of the map on the floor stood a small, intricately carved, wooden structure which was several feet tall. It was a stand of sorts, on top of which sat, in a cradle, what he thought to be a small flute or similar musical instrument which the King now reached for. Oran watched intently as Lugh carefully raised the flute up to his pursed lips and blew one long note for several seconds, and then delicately replaced it on its cradle, saying, "Bow your head now, Oran, please. The high council will arrive presently."

Oran obeyed, looking down again as he continued studying the mosaic for a few seconds with his gaze directed toward the floor. He didn't seem to notice what was happening by the thrones off in front of him, until he heard a strange, ethereal voice utter the words, "Welcome, brother Lugh. Welcome, master Oran. Please step forward and face the high council."

Oran snapped his head up quickly, looking in the direction from which the voice had just come. He couldn't quite believe what he was seeing in front of him now, sitting on the three thrones which were just moments ago unoccupied.

CHAPTER FOUR
Incarceration and Inquisition

The back door swung open, letting in a cold breeze, as Mary made her way back inside the house with an armful of logs and some peat for the fire, which she had gathered from the stockpile at the back of the house. She nudged the door closed behind her using her elbow, then leant her back against it and let out a deep sigh. She looked tired - no, exhausted - but the girls were too young to pick up on such things really, and so continued to play happily on the floor near the fire with two old dolls that Mary had sewn together for them using some old rags.

They were joyfully oblivious to the worries and concerns of grown-ups. As Mary approached the fireplace, the girls shuffled to one side a bit, so that she could get to the fire and put the logs and peat on it to keep them warm. She finished tending to the fire, then stood up straight and asked the girls if they would like some tea and something to eat, as it was now late morning, to which they replied, "Yes please," in unison.

A kindly neighbour, known only as the widow Kane, had paid the house a visit earlier in the morning and brought with her some bread and scones that she had baked for them. This was an almost daily occurrence, intended to save Mary from doing the work herself, and also to check on how she was keeping. Various other people in the village often popped in for a visit now and then, family and friends alike, for the very same reasons.

She boiled a kettle on the fire and made tea for all three of them, which she promptly carried to the table. Then, they all sat down and had buttered home baked bread and scones, topped with jam which they had made from the summer crop of blackberries that they had picked themselves.

After they finished their meal, the girls swiftly went back to playing on the floor near the fire. Mary tidied away the leftover food and washed their dishes in the old sink, after which she started to feel particularly weak and unwell, so went to the bedroom to lie down on the bed and rest for a bit. It wasn't until an hour or so later that her eldest daughter, Ellen, began to think it odd that their mother had been asleep for so long, and so got up and went to the bedroom to see if her mother was alright.

As Ellen walked into the room, she could see by the dim light that her mother appeared to be asleep. She could also see, on moving closer to the bed, that her mother's skin looked unusually and oddly pale and moist, which caused her some concern. Ellen walked to the side of the bed and put her hand on her mothers' left shoulder and shook her gently, asking, "Mummy? Are you alright, Mummy?"

There was no response, so Ellen started to panic, shaking her mother's shoulder more vigorously now, repeating her words as she did so.

"Mummy, are you alright? Mummy, wake up, please!"

Slowly, in response, Mary's eyes opened to about halfway and she murmured, "Oh... I'm alright, child, just... a little weary. You... go and play with your sister while... Mummy rests. I'll be... there in a bit, my sweetheart. Daddy will be home soon, hopefully, with something tasty... for this evening's dinner."

With that, Mary closed her eyes again slowly, as she drifted off to a troubled sleep. Ellen walked to the door of the room, head down, then looked back at her mother, thinking, "I wish Daddy would come home right now."

She went back and joined her sister by the fire and resumed playing, but she couldn't stop worrying about her mother's present condition and her unusual behaviour.

Dara had been led down into the dark chamber by his guards via a slightly different route from the one taken by Oran, his route being from the top of the tower, just moments after Oran had entered the chamber of souls. He now found himself sat on the straw covered floor of the barred off area, the cell witnessed by Oran mere moments before as he had passed through. He sat in silence, with his back rested against the hard, stone wall of what he now considered to be his prison cell. Holly lay by his side with her head rested on his left thigh, as Dara stroked her head affectionately.

"Do you think there's any chance we'll be getting out of here soon, Holly girl?" he said quietly to her, as he stroked her soft fur.

Holly raised her eyebrows slightly and looked up at him, as though she knew his question was intended for her, but understandably didn't reply. Dara continued stroking her head and ears, much to Holly's delight, and then began whistling his favourite song again. He didn't at all notice the patch of faint, white mist outside his cell that was gliding slowly across the floor towards them, through the bars and into the cell now, just to his right. Holly noticed it though, or sensed it, and pricked her ears up, aware of something unusual but not quite sure just what.

When he did finally notice it, the mist had come to a halt right in front of his feet, both of which he now suddenly drew in towards himself in fear, dislodging Holly at the same time. He stared at the mist as it swirled slowly in a circular motion, where it now seemed to linger in front of him. Holly had jumped up and was staring at the mist too, letting out a low growl as she did so, but didn't approach, instead staying by Dara's side. As they both watched, just out of sight of the guards, the mist slowly drew itself up into a swirling column about four feet tall and within seconds, took the form of a beautiful young girl in a long green dress. She immediately put her right index finger to her lips.

"Shhh, have no fear," she whispered, then advised in the same hushed voice, "The guards must not know that I am here - we must be quiet. Please, don't be afraid, I mean you no harm. My name is Enya, and I wish to help you."

Enya had overheard the guards talking earlier about Dara and was aware of his plight. She thought it wrong that he be held against his will like this, and so had taken it upon herself to be his saviour. Dara sat and stared at her for a moment, thinking, wondering, then asked her quietly,

"How did you do that? That mist - how on earth? Did I dream it?"

"Ah yes, well, I should explain, as you are human and know nothing of our kind. In this place, we are all of us gifted with magical abilities of various types. It is one of *my* abilities that I can change and manipulate the form of living things, including myself," Enya explained matter-of-factly, as though it were nothing unusual.

It was, however, extremely unusual where Dara was concerned, and he was struggling to take in everything that he was experiencing today. Enya extended her right hand slowly toward Holly in a kindly, beckoning gesture and Holly slowly went to her side and sniffed her outstretched hand cautiously. Enya then stroked Holly on the top of her head and with that, Holly sat down by her feet, content that Enya meant her no harm.

"What is the name of your dog, kind sir?" she asked.

"Her name is Holly, miss... Enya, and my name is Dara - Dara MacBrien. By some chance, do you know what is to become of us?" Dara asked, coming straight to the point.

"I cannot say for certain, as it is my father who will decide your fate, but I will try to influence his decision in your favour," Enya informed him as she moved a little closer to him. "At this moment, I believe that he holds some kind of important meeting concerning the fate of our kind, now that the castle is exposed by this morning's events. Tell me about yourself, Dara. Where are you from, and what were you doing up here that got you brought here to the ivy castle?"

"Firstly, you can tell me what happened earlier. I mean, what was it that happened, exactly? I saw and heard very strange things - lights in the sky and odd noises, and then this huge castle appeared out of nowhere," Dara demanded somewhat sternly, albeit cautiously.

With this, Enya set about explaining to Dara, over the next twenty minutes or so, who they, the people of Danu, were and how they had come to be here on the mountain's summit. She explained to him about the dragon's egg, the dragon crystal, and the power it had held, and about the events of this morning that had led to the demise of the egg and with it, the protection it had afforded them. She finished with the fact that she believed her best friend, Oran, was now in a meeting with her father, who was the King, to decide his fate for permitting this to happen by falling asleep in the course of his duty.

"Now you, Dara MacBrien. Tell me about you... and your dog. Why are you here?" she questioned.

Dara briefly told Enya about his village and his family. He explained that he went out to check his sheep daily and that they had strayed up onto the mountain top in search of food, as the grass on the lower slopes had already been devoured quite early this winter. He went on to explain to Enya that his wife, his beloved Mary, was very ill and needed him home tonight, at all costs.

"Will you give me your hands please, Dara?" Enya requested.

Dara stood up and gingerly extended his hands towards Enya with his palms facing upward, wondering as he did so why she had asked, but complying with her request nonetheless. He was willing to do anything she asked if it would help get him and Holly out of there. Enya was surprised at how tall he was, as she had never actually seen or met a human before this day. She took his hands gently in hers, palm to palm, and closed her eyes, tilting her head back slightly at the same time and then, said nothing as she quietly concentrated.

In her mind's eye, a swirling mist appeared and then cleared to reveal a little thatched house - Dara's house - sat by a stream. *How pretty*, she thought. She was approaching the house now, in her mind, and as she neared the front door, it swung slightly open, gently and silently. She entered inside as the door closed quietly again behind her, then made her way across the room toward the doorway on the other side. She could see two little girls playing on the floor by the fire, but they hadn't noticed the door open slightly and then close again and also couldn't see Enya as she crossed the room, so they continued playing, unaware of her presence. Enya moved silently over to the bedroom door and looked inside the dimly lit room to see a young woman asleep on the bed. The woman's skin was pale and clammy, and she had the appearance of someone who was not at all well.

As Enya moved to the bedside, the woman opened her eyes and mumbled, "Dara... is that you... my dear?"

Enya suddenly released Dara's hands, her vision disappearing as she snapped open her eyes, then said, "I saw your wife. She appears very ill. There is no time to waste, Dara. We must get you out of here and get help to her."

"What did you just do?" asked Dara. "Did you see something? Tell me, please."

"I saw your wife and your lovely children. They are alright for now, but your wife is in dire need of help. I may be able to get that help to her while the castle is in this exposed state, but only while it is so, and I know just the person who can provide such help. He is the only one who *can* help her, as he is the only one with the required magical gift," Enya said, hopefully.

"Help my Mary? You mean make her well again? How? Who can help her, Enya? You must tell me, please, and we must hurry, before it is too late," Dara pleaded, desperately.

"Yes, Dara, I do mean make her well again, and I speak of Oran. Oran is the *only* one amongst us who possesses the gift of healing. It is also believed that he may possibly even be capable of giving life to the lifeless. He has the power to heal the injured and make the sick well again, and so, hopefully, he can also help your wife," Enya replied.

Hearing this made his heart leap for joy. Dara never thought for a second that he would ever hear anyone say these things to him. He lowered his head and in a solemn voice asked, "This Oran - your friend you speak of - do you really think he will help us, Enya? I mean help me and Mary - do you really?

"I'm sure that he will. As long as he is *able* to do so when my father has finished with him, and if my father permits it, of course," she responded.

Oran stood beside Lugh and stared wide-eyed with his mouth slightly open as, on the thrones in front of him now, sat three female figures entirely composed of what appeared to be nothing more than a shimmering blue light. The figure in the middle spoke again.

"Step forward, master Oran. Please, do not be afraid of us, for we mean you no harm. Come closer now, please. Let us see you," one said, in the same spine-tingling voice as before.

Oran obeyed and cautiously stepped forward, Lugh at his side, until he was just a few feet from the one who had spoken, then stopped and lowered his head in fear.

"Do you know who I am, Oran?" the figure enquired. "Rather, do you know who *we* are?"

Oran stood with his head still bowed, not daring to look as he mumbled the words, "I dare not say, my lady, but I believe that I know," having already determined in his mind who it was that now sat before him on the thrones.

"Yes, I think you know only too well, Oran, or at least suspect who we are, but are, perhaps, too afraid to say aloud," came the ethereal voice again. "I will spare you from your misery, my child. I, Oran, am the goddess, Ériu, and these at my sides are my sisters, Banba and Fodla."

Oran immediately dropped down onto his knees, trembling, beside King Lugh on hearing this and continued to bow his head.

"Your humble servant at your service, Your Majesties. I am gratefully at your mercy," he said meekly, his voice also trembling now.

"Please, Oran, rise to your feet," Ériu instructed. "It is not my wish that you cower in front of me like some frightened animal. Now, come closer please, young man... closer."

Oran stood up and stepped forward again until he was just inches away from her. He could feel the tiny hairs on his arms standing on end as he got closer, as though they were somehow charged by some unseen force that attracted them to her.

Ériu looked directly at him and said, "You're a handsome boy, Oran. I hope, for your sake, that your courage is as impressive as your looks."

With this, Oran blushed somewhat. Flattery from a goddess, no less. *Whatever next?* he thought to himself.

"Now, Oran, to the business at hand. It seems you caused some trouble for us, your kinsfolk, this morning by neglecting your duties - very important duties. Is that correct?" Ériu demanded, her tone becoming somewhat sterner now.

"Yes... Your... Majesty, but it was an accident. I... didn't..."

"Stop!" Ériu scolded, cutting him off mid-sentence as she leant forward in her chair, closer to him. "Accident or not, Oran, what has happened has still happened and all because of your neglect. It is a very serious matter indeed - a catastrophe, no less. It should *never* have happened. I'm sure you are well aware of an old Danu saying, *Yours to do, yours to undo.* Have you heard that before, Oran? Do you know what it means?"

"Yes, Your Majesty, I have. It means that if you do something wrong, it is your responsibility alone to undo the harm caused by your actions," Oran answered, swiftly.

"Very good, Oran. Now, here's the thing. Prior to your arrival, my sisters and I have discussed with King Lugh what needs to be done and there appears to be only one option, or solution, to rectify our problem. You alone will have to go on a quest, Oran, to find something of great value, of great importance, which will hopefully undo this damage you have caused. It is *your* duty and *your* responsibility alone," Ériu instructed.

"A quest? But where shall this quest take me, Your Majesties? I've never been beyond the castle's walls. How will I know where to go? Am I really to go alone?" he asked, now growing even more worried about his future.

"We need to replace the egg, Oran, the dragon crystal, to generate a new time cocoon," Ériu began, then went on to explain, "It is the only way known to us whereby we can continue to exist here in peace and safety. It is imperative that we acquire another egg."

"But how can we do that, Your Majesty? There are no longer any dragons that can provide such an egg. There haven't been any dragons for centuries. It's impossible, is it not?" Oran questioned in a bewildered tone, glancing briefly at the huge dragon's skull nearest to him.

"Well, Oran, that's not entirely true," Lugh interrupted, clearing his throat. "If I may, Your Majesty?" to which Ériu nodded consent, so he continued, "There is, Oran you see, still one remaining dragon, we believe - or rather, we hope. The same Fire Dragon who provided the original egg, the mighty and powerful Rydian. Fortunately for us, in return for the egg, she was granted eternal freedom and, mercifully, immortality and thus should still be alive somewhere near Slieve Mish, the old volcano, we hope."

"A... living... dragon," Oran stammered in disbelief, as his master paused for thought.

"Now, what we need is for you to find her, seek her out, then get her to come here so that I can speak with her and bargain with her for another egg," Lugh went on, as he fondly placed a hand on Oran's shoulder. "You will, however, have to go alone, I'm afraid, as the journey may, or rather, will be perilous and we cannot risk the safety of others to join you on this quest. The responsibility lies with you alone, Oran... I'm sorry to say... it is *your* quest and *your* duty, my boy."

Oran's heart sank on hearing this. He lowered his head again, this time in sadness. His mind was racing with thoughts of him possibly never returning to the castle, and possibly of not even surviving this quest. After all, he had no idea what sort of dangers lay ahead of him on his journey across a land he had never seen before - well not since he was an infant, anyway. He found himself wishing that he could have someone accompany him, but he knew that they would not allow such a thing after hearing the King's words.

"When must I set out, Your Majesties?" Oran asked, resigned to the fact that there was no way out of this for him. He now began to wonder, also, if he would ever see Enya again after today.

"You will leave at nightfall this night, Oran. There is no time to lose, I'm afraid," Lugh told him. "Cethen and I will do all that we can to help you prepare between now and the time of your departure. The journey should take only three to four days and we will provide you a map, a horse, and food and other provisions to last you."

"I wish there was another solution, Oran, but there isn't," said Ériu now, sounding remorseful, almost sad. "It is with very heavy hearts that we send you on this quest and place you in mortal danger, but we have no choice. We *must* replace the time cocoon. It is time for Oran the boy to become Oran the man. We wish you good fortune on your journey and hope to see you return... with the mighty Rydian... in a few days' time."

The three sisters then stood up, and in unison said, "May all the gods watch over, favour and protect you on your journey, Oran, and return you safely and swiftly to us. Now, sadly, we must leave you both."

Lugh and Oran watched curiously as the glowing blue figures slowly changed to swirling columns of light, then spiralled upward together into the darkness above and disappeared completely, as the three goddesses returned to wherever they had come from.

With just the two of them left in the room now, Oran turned to Lugh and asked, "What comes next, my King?"

"Let's get you back above ground and do what we can to prepare you before nightfall," Lugh said, encouragingly, as he placed a hand in the small of Oran's back and guided him toward the door.

"In some way, despite being terrified at the prospect of going on this obviously perilous journey alone, I find myself feeling a little... excited in some way, my King," enthused Oran, as he stopped walking and turned to face his King.

"Why would that be then, young Oran?" Lugh asked, somewhat puzzled by the remark.

"Well, I never thought I would ever get to see, or meet, a living dragon - a Fire Dragon, no less, let alone the only living dragon in the land, so I'm excited about that, as long as she doesn't try to kill me, or worse still, eat me, that is," Oran said, trying to lighten the mood.

"Well, Oran, I shall give you something to take with you that will give you protection from her, so to speak. If, and hopefully, when you find her, you must show it to her immediately, without hesitation, so that she does not harm you. She will recognise it as mine and that should be sufficient for her to spare your life, and she will also do your bidding for as long as you possess it," the King advised, sternly.

"What is it, my Lord, that you will give me?" Oran asked, curiously.

Lugh then reached for the sword at his side and pulled it from its scabbard. Holding it by the hilt with the blade pointed toward the floor, he offered it, at arms-length and slightly aloft, to Oran.

"This is the Sword of Light, Oran, as I am sure you well know. It possesses great magic and was the sword of the dragon commanders for hundreds of years past. As long as you hold this in your possession, Rydian shall do you no harm. All dragons are bound by its powers and by its magical laws," Lugh proclaimed, then went on to advise, "When you first confront her, hold the sword up to her as I hold it now, like this, so that she can clearly see it and can recognise it, and say the words, *Rydian, I am Oran, of the Danu. Yield to me.* It is of paramount importance that you say these words to her, at the same time as she is presented with the sword, or she shall not abide by you."

Oran reached out and carefully took the sword from Lugh as he slowly repeated his words,

"Rydian, I am Oran, of the Danu. Yield to me," then quickly asked, "Is that what the emblem on the back of your robe is, my Lord? Dragon commander?"

"Yes, Oran, it is indeed. I only wear this for certain very important ceremonial duties and the like, and this is the first time I've worn it in over two hundred years," Lugh responded, almost regretfully, it seemed.

The sword was quite heavy and measured about two and a half feet long in all. Oran studied the intricate metalwork on the hilt, where a beautifully crafted green dragon was coiled around the solid gold hand grip, with the blade coming out of the dragon's jaws, and its outstretched wings forming the cross guard. At the tip, or pommel end, of the hilt was a large emerald set into the coiled tail of the dragon. *It's beautiful*, he thought to himself, and went to hand it back to Lugh.

"No, no, Oran, it is yours now. *You* must take the sword now and keep it with you at all times for your protection. It must never leave your side," Lugh insisted, as he removed the belt and scabbard from around his waist and handed them to Oran as well. Oran looked at Lugh and smiled from ear to ear.

"Thank you ever so much, my Lord. I shall take the greatest care of it, and I shall guard it with my very life," he said, with a certain seriousness.

"Ha, ha, Oran! 'Tis the other way around, I don't doubt. It will, in fact, be the sword which shall guard and protect you, my boy," the King chortled, as they both turned and walked toward the slowly opening door.

CHAPTER FIVE
A Bargain for Life

Just as she was finishing off telling Dara about Oran and his unique ability to heal and cure, Enya noticed the golden symbol begin to glow green on the door just outside the cell and over to the left of where she and Dara were now stood. Then, the door slowly swung inward. Her father emerged first, then stopped and waited just this side of the door as he was followed immediately by Oran, who appeared to be in unexpectedly good spirits.

She decided right then, despite knowing that the King would be angry with her for coming down here, that she wasn't going to conceal herself from him, regardless of the consequences. She felt that she needed to confront him about Dara's fate and talk him into releasing him. Enya quickly hatched a plan - a very good plan, she thought. She was convinced that her plan would not only buy Dara's silence, but at the same time, would serve to make his beloved Mary well again - simple really.

Now all she had to do was convince her father, Oran and Dara, but she already knew that Dara would agree, as it would greatly benefit him, so it was really just her father and Oran who needed convincing, though she also knew that Oran would be a push-over.

Lugh stopped and turned to Oran just outside the chamber of souls and said to him, "Oran, in the cell over there is an intruder whom we captured this morning, just outside the castle walls - a human intruder, no less - shortly after the time cocoon collapsed. I have to be entirely honest and say that I'm not quite sure what to do with him. I don't know if I should risk releasing him or keep him here. If I release him and he speaks of us to others outside, then we are potentially in grave danger, no?" Thinking carefully for a moment as he stroked his beard, he then glanced toward the darkened cell. "In all honesty, however, if we cannot conceal the castle again, then there is no point in my being concerned over him telling others of our existence when he gets home, as we shall be exposed in time anyway. On the other hand, if we can hide the castle again, then we may need to keep him here... for the sake of our safety... you understand. I really don't know Oran... what to do? Let's go and talk to him, shall we?"

Oran nodded in response to the King and they both walked slowly towards the old iron bars of the cell, Oran peering into the darkness beyond them, wondering what on earth a human actually looked like, as he'd never seen one in his entire life. He had heard stories of humans, of course, and in those stories, he had heard many descriptions of their appearance, but he'd never, ever seen a living, breathing human being in real life - until now, that is. Dara appeared slowly out of the gloom as the pair approached the bars of his prison, standing just a few feet back from them with Holly, as always, at his side. He was looking directly at Oran and the King.

They stopped just a few feet from the bars, not yet aware of Enya stood directly behind Dara, as Lugh said, "Dara MacBrien... now it is time that I decide what I should do with you. I have dwelt on this at great length and am afraid I must now inform you that I believe it to be wise to keep you here until further notice. You will, of course, be treated well and taken care of as best we can, I assure you. Your companion also, of course, will be looked after just as well."

Just as Dara stepped forward and was about to open his mouth to protest his detention to the King, Enya suddenly stepped out from behind him.

"Father, with the greatest respect, I beg of you to release him. He must return to his family at once, please," Enya implored.

"Enya," Lugh bellowed. "What on earth are you doing down here, child? It is forbidden. Really, you must leave this place at once!" he roared.

Oran looked up at Lugh and could see the anger on his face, but thought it wise to say nothing, even though he sided with Enya. He was already in enough trouble, he thought to himself, and had no desire to make his situation any worse than it already was.

"No, you must listen to me, Father," Enya continued in protest. "I know of a way to keep this man's silence regarding our existence. If you can just hear me out, for a moment, I shall explain everything to you," to which Oran raised his eyebrows in surprise at her defiance.

"Don't be foolish, my daughter. There is much too great a risk involved, and it would be terribly unwise of us to trust any human with keeping such a secret. Now, again, I say, you must leave this place," Lugh demanded, as he turned to the guard by the chamber of souls and instructed, "Men, escort my daughter to her quarters immediately please, and stay with her until I arrive."

As two of the guards approached them, Enya quickly blurted out, "Dara swears to keep his silence if Oran rids his wife of that which ails her."

At this, the King raised a hand, out of curiosity as to what she had planned, as a sign for the guards to wait.

The four just stood and looked at each other for a moment, then Lugh, after a moment's thought, asked, "Really, Dara MacBrien? You would swear to keep your silence if I allow Oran to go with you to your home to help your good wife?"

"I would, Your Majesty - there is absolutely no question or doubt. My wife means everything to me. She is my world, my reason for living and without her, I am lost - I am nothing," Dara responded, solemnly.

The King thought for a moment, then asked, "What if I were to ask of you one other favour as part of the bargain, sir?"

"What would that favour be? I cannot truthfully answer without knowing for sure the details, but as you are very much aware, I am not really in a position to refuse, am I?"

Lugh turned and looked at Oran, stroking his beard again, and smiled at him knowingly, whilst at the same time placing a hand fondly on his right shoulder. He knew in his heart that there was a very real chance that Oran may not survive the journey alone, owing to the many dangers that lay beyond the castle walls, not to mention the fact that Oran had never actually been outside the castle and could very well get completely lost.

He turned back to face Dara and began, "My young friend, Oran, here, who is like a son to me, must go on a very perilous journey this night - a quest, if you like - to find something of great importance to us. He must go alone sadly, as I am not prepared to risk the safety of any of the other Danu people, so great is the danger. Alone until now, that is… if you get my meaning."

"What quest? What journey? Where are you sending him, Father?" Enya quickly interrupted, a look of concern spreading across her pretty features.

"Silence, Enya, please, my child. Allow me to finish!" Lugh admonished sternly, still vexed that she had dared to venture down here to this most sacred of places.

"Continue," Dara said, apprehensively. He was fairly certain of what the King was about to say next and was also fairly certain, already, of what his response would be.

Lugh cleared his throat and explained, "I should like you to accompany Oran on his quest, if you would be so kind - as part of our bargain, as it were. I'm sure you have a fairly good knowledge of at least part of the area, and that you can be a great asset to him as a guide and as his protector. There is, of course, safety in numbers, no?"

A smile spread across Oran's face now, as Dara regarded the King thoughtfully for a moment. The prospect of a guide to accompany him on his journey lifted his spirits greatly as he knew very little, if indeed nothing, of the outworld. It mattered not that he knew nothing of this man - a *human* man, no less - he was simply glad not to be going alone. He was certain in his heart that they would get along just fine, and that Dara's company would be of great benefit to him. Suddenly, he wondered what it was that ailed this man's wife and hoped that he *would* actually be able to help her. In times past, he had used the ability to heal on very rare occasions and on those occasions, it was only a very minor injury or ailment in each case, not to mention the fact that he had never tried this magic on a human.

"I accept," Dara said, suddenly, then quickly added, "On the condition that you will provide us with adequate weapons and provisions for the journey, and that we go first to the aid of my wife, then onward on the quest you speak of. Pray tell me, where is it that his quest shall lead us, Sire?"

"You shall guide Oran to the mountain that is called Slieve Mish in the south-east, where you will seek out something very precious to our survival. You will then ensure that both Oran, and it, return safely and swiftly back to the castle for me. Do you know of Slieve Mish, Dara MacBrien? Have you ever been there, or know of its location?"

"Seek out what exactly? And I know of only Slemish mountain in that area, but I believe it is one and the same, if I recall the old tales correctly. And yes, I have a good idea where it lies, although I have never actually been there. I believe that it is about two days' journey from here, if you mean the old volcano, that is?" Dara replied.

"Oran has received his instructions and is very well aware of what he seeks. He shall inform you of the details when you arrive near your destination, as *you* will also need to prepare yourself for what you will face. Besides which, it need not concern you as yet, as you need only guide him safely there and back, my dear friend," the King hastily advised.

Oran looked at the King, a worried expression now spreading across his face, and whispered to him, "Don't you think it wise to tell him now of what he faces, my Lord? It is only fair, I think. He should know the dangers from the outset. I believe that we should tell him about Rydian, now."

"Face what? What dangers, Father? Where on earth are you sending them?" Enya interrupted again, now more worried than ever on overhearing Oran's words, "Oran, what has my father asked of you? Who, or what, is this Rydian you speak of? Tell me, please," she begged of Oran, as her forehead furrowed with great concern.

"Very well," the King sighed, after some long moments thought. "Dara, my friend... Enya, my lovely daughter. Consider what I say now carefully, please. It is with a very heavy heart that I tell you that the only way, unfortunately, to restore the time cocoon that protected both us and the castle from unwanted discovery is for someone to seek out my old friend, Rydian, and ask her for her help. She is the only one who can help us - there is no other way, I am afraid.

"*Who is Rydian, Father?*" Enya butted in sternly, but was ignored by the King as he went on to say,

"We have reason to believe that she will have sought warmth and thus be near, or on, the mountain of Slieve Mish - the old volcano, as Dara has pointed out. To that end, we must send Oran, with the guidance of Dara, to seek her out and bring her here, as the council has decided that it is his responsibility to undo the damage that he alone caused this morning. However, no-one has seen Rydian for three centuries and we can only hope and pray that she can be found and, if so, that she will also agree to help us."

"*Who... is... Rydian?*" Enya pleaded again, growing ever more agitated.

Oran and Lugh looked at each other for a moment, not sure how to say it, and then suddenly, together, "She is the last surviving... er... Fire Dragon," they mumbled.

Horror spread across the faces of both Dara and Enya instantly upon hearing this, and Enya wailed, "*A dragon?* So, you send them to their deaths then, Father? I thought all the dragons were long since gone? You said so in the stories which you, yourself, told us countless times. I thought that name sounded familiar - I should have known."

Dara was speechless. *Dragon?* he thought. *Really, I can't have heard them correctly*. He stood there dumfounded - no, horrified - for a minute. He had only ever heard stories of dragons, but never seen one, obviously, but knew from descriptions in those stories that they were, indeed, the most fearsome of beasts.

Oran and the King said nothing for a moment, then Lugh looked at Enya and said confidently, "Fear not, my child, for he takes with him my sword - the sword of the dragon commanders, the Sword of Light, no less - which will protect them both. When shown to Rydian, she will recognise it and do them no harm, as she, and indeed all dragons, are bound by its very special powers, as I have already explained to Oran. When presented with the sword, she should do his bidding... be at his command. However, it has been a very long time since she was ruled or commanded by anyone, so she may not yield... but she will, I assure you, do them no harm upon seeing it."

"How can you be so sure, Father?" Enya questioned, then insisted, "Oran, you do not have to do this. It is utter madness."

"It will be alright Enya. It is my duty anyway," Oran responded as the King began to say,

"I was dragon commander for many years before your time, my child, through several great battles against our numerous foes, and I know only too well of the power the sword holds over the dragons." He gestured to the sword now hanging from Oran's belt, as he continued, "I fought our enemies astride Rydian's great shoulders, and it was I that gave to her freedom and immortality. We were comrades in arms, friends and companions for a time... a very long time. I give you my solemn word - my promise - as your father and your King, that she will do them no harm. I know her better than anyone."

"I still accept," Dara said, out of the blue, which made Oran smile again. "In spite of the very obvious dangers - a dragon, no less - I still accept. It is worth it to save my beloved wife."

"What is it that ails your wife, sir?" Oran then asked Dara.

It was the first time that Oran had spoken to Dara directly, and also the first time he had looked directly at him throughout this whole encounter. He noticed now, for the first time, just how tall Dara actually was, and also that Dara appeared not to have pointed ears, like the rest of them had. He thought this very peculiar, and that perhaps it was a deformity of some sort, so decided not to remark upon it - at least not for now, anyway.

"My wife is very ill, young sir. A terrible illness or disease grips her," Dara began to explain. "We believe - that is, myself and the good folk of my village believe - that she may not see another year pass; that the Lord may take her before then. This wonderful young lady beside me has kindly informed me that you are in possession of a gift that enables you to make my wife well again, if it pleases you. If you help me - help my wife, that is - then I shall gladly go with you wherever you should need me - to the ends of the earth, if you so wish. Please, master Oran, will you help us?"

Oran looked at Dara thoughtfully for a brief moment and replied, "How can I *not* help you when you are so willing to help I on this most dangerous of journeys - I whom you have never before set eyes upon? It would be the very least I can do to repay your kindness and your bravery, and I pray that I *can* help you, and your good lady wife, of course."

"Thank you so very much, Oran. I am truly forever in your debt," Dara said humbly, as he extended his right hand through the bars, offering it to Oran to seal the bargain they had made. Oran reached out with his right hand and shook Dara's waiting hand, and the deal was sealed. They both smiled and were both also extremely relieved at how fortunate they were to have met on this day. *What strange fortune*, Dara thought.

"Good, it is settled then!" the King exclaimed, as he patted Oran on the back heartily. "We shall go above this instant and prepare you both for your journey, and there shall be a feast this day before your departure. It will be a brief feast, mind, as you must both depart at nightfall. After you leave the castle, you shall firstly both make your way to the dwelling place of this good man, Dara, and make his wife well again, and then set out for Slieve Mish in search of my old friend Rydian," Lugh continued, as he turned to the guard nearest and instructed, "Aedan, please release this man and his companion, his dog, from their confines at once. They are now our guests, not our prisoners."

The man obediently went to the large, heavy padlock on the gate, inserted a big metal key, and opened it swiftly, as Lugh had instructed. As soon as he did so, Dara, Enya and Holly emerged from the cell and joined Lugh and Oran, eager to leave the bowels of the castle and get back above ground again. Dara was both excited, for the sake of Mary and the girls, yet fearful of what dangers lay ahead, but thought to himself that when he had left his humble house earlier that morning, he could never have imagined that events would unfold in the way in which they had done. He thought to himself that no-one in the village would believe him, were he to relate the mornings unbelievable events to them, and that they would probably consider him some kind of lunatic or madman if he did. On thinking this, he quickly pinched his arm to make sure it wasn't just a dream and satisfied himself that it was, in fact, real.

"So... are you both ready for an adventure then, Oran? Dara?" the King asked with raised eyebrows, as he turned and raised his right arm slightly, directing them all towards the stairs.

They made their way across the darkened room and back up the winding stairs, one behind the other, with the King leading the way and Holly at the rear, then through the altar room with the gold statues, back into the chancel once more. Once in the chancel, Lugh went to the door marked with the sign that read *Tower* and opened it, leading them, as he did so, into a large, round room with a spiral staircase, which was actually the base of the lofty tower where Dara had first arrived with the Shawan earlier that morning. He led them straight across to the heavy door opposite, at which he swiftly turned to face them all.

"I had Cethen inform all of the people of the castle earlier of what lay ahead of you Oran, and they decided to lay on a feast for you. Some friends have joined in the great room to see you off. I do hope you are all hungry," Lugh said, smiling, as the others nodded eagerly.

Oran was much loved and greatly respected among those who inhabited the castle. His gift for magic was much more advanced than his peers and he was, indeed, already capable of magical feats that others may never be capable of. Although they could never be truly certain if he was one of their own, even though he looked every part a Danu, the Danu people had always treated him as though he was, since the very day he was discovered outside the castle. To them, he had become a Danu, even if he wasn't born as one. Many were now worried that he may not return and were very concerned that this may be the last they would ever see of him, sadly. While Oran and the King were facing the council, almost everyone else had been busy preparing a surprise for him by turning the great room into a banquet hall and were now gathered inside, patiently awaiting his arrival so they may pay tribute to him and say their farewells.

The King turned to face the door and pushed it open to reveal a very crowded great room inside, with tables laid out in the middle by the stone plinth, where the egg had once sat. The tables were heavily laden with all manner of food and drink. Everyone inside stayed oddly silent and it appeared that the entire population of the castle had, somehow, squeezed into the great room to say goodbye and see Oran off on his journey.

Oran, Enya and Dara stood by the King with stunned expressions on their faces at what they were seeing, not knowing what to say. It was Holly who was first to make her way through the door and into the room, owing to the heavenly smell of food which she found entirely irresistible. As she entered the room, lively music started to play and everyone in the room let out a loud cheer. Oran smiled then and stepped forward past the King into the room, followed closely by Enya, to the applause and cheers of everyone inside. Dara, however, waited by the door, slightly concerned for Holly and himself.

The King, noticing this, turned to him with a smile, and said, "You are most welcome also, my good friend, Dara MacBrien. Please, go inside and eat, and meet my good people... the people of Danu."

Dara smiled at Lugh and gratefully replied, "Thank you, Sire."

He continued to watch the crowded room for a moment, realising then that he was quite unique in this place - unusual, he felt, amongst his new-found company, which made him feel slightly awkward. He thought again of the childhood myths and legends, noticing that everyone in the room was considerably smaller than he, and that all had the same oddly pointed ears as the King, Oran and Enya, understandably of course. *A room full of magical people - people who would no doubt be called elves; the very same elves he'd heard many tales of as a child*, he thought. He brought himself to his senses again and stepped forward gingerly. As he did so, Enya came to his side, to his rescue.

"Don't be scared, Dara. You must come and meet everyone. They will be so excited to talk with you - to learn of you and your ways," Enya insisted, as she led him toward the crowd by the arm.

Over the next two hours, Dara learned an immense amount about the Danu as they, in turn, also learned about him and his family. Enya introduced him to just about everyone in the room, one by one, and explained about their particular magic skills and their standing within the castle's population as she did so. He felt overwhelmed, somewhat, and couldn't help but notice how polite and kind they all were toward him. He almost wished, for a moment, that he and his family could somehow come here to live someday - in the future perhaps.

After a while, and with dusk rapidly approaching, Oran finished saying his good-byes to everyone and came over and sat down between Dara and Enya at their table. He reached down and stroked Holly on top of her head and then looked at Enya with big, sad eyes,

"I will have to go soon, Enya. Will you see me to the gates as I leave?" he asked, hopefully. It was the thought of perhaps never seeing her again which saddened him most and indeed, concerned him deeply. Her company was what he would miss the most, but he kept that fact to himself for now as he waited for her reply.

She reached out and took his hand in hers, smiling falsely as she answered, "Of course I will, dearest Oran. Why ever would I not, silly?"

Dara smiled knowingly at this. *Young love*, he thought to himself. *What a wonderful thing*. He smiled at them both, then offered Holly a scrap of food, which she reluctantly sniffed at, as she was certain of already having eaten far, far too much for her own good.

Just then, the big wooden door burst open and Dara saw only a sea, or rather frenzy, of vivid colours. He thought at first that it was a flock of small, brightly coloured birds which flew into the room and came hurtling toward him. They moved with blinding speed to the space above where he, Oran and Enya were sat, circling above them in a frenzied blur - swirling, darting and diving. As they did so, Dara became aware that they were, in fact, not birds at all. As he watched them circle above Oran, he could make out, much to his amazement, that they were, in reality, tiny people who were only about six inches tall, or thereabouts. He continued to watch in awe as Oran stood up and the tiny people swirled around him in a haze of buzzing colour. Suddenly, they all came to a stop in mid-air, surrounding Oran, and started to laugh and giggle as they hovered there around him.

"Eolande!" Oran beamed, as he addressed the one hovering directly in front of his face. "I was beginning to worry that you wouldn't come to say goodbye to me," he continued, laughing.

"Why, I wouldn't dream of it, my young friend. Don't be so foolish now. We've all of us come to bid you farewell. We're just a little late, that's all, but here for you nonetheless," she responded in a slightly high-pitched voice, as she gestured toward the others of her kind with her small, outstretched arms.

Dara was sat with his mouth wide open, staring in disbelief. He thought these people had no more surprises for him; thought he had met everyone and learned everything about them; but now assumed that he was very wrong indeed. Of all the things to see, he never expected tiny people with wings.

"What on earth?" he mumbled.

"These are the Aos Sí - the fairy people, Dara. Surely you know of the fairies?" Enya pointed out helpfully, albeit matter-of-factly, as if it should be normal to him, and as though everyone knew about fairies.

"Well... ah... only in stories in my childhood, years ago. My mother mentioned them in some old bedtime stories that she told me as a child, but I never, not for a moment, thought that they really existed," he replied, still trying to come to terms with this latest revelation.

"Oh, they certainly do exist, Dara. They are very real indeed, as you can see now," Enya laughed.

Lugh then stood up from where he had been seated, announcing in a commanding voice, "Your attention please, everyone!"

The room fell silent and everyone directed their attention toward the King who was, again, now joined by his two faithful hounds at his sides.

"The time, I'm afraid, has come for Oran and his companion, our new friend Dara, to depart the safety of the castle and set out on their journey. I would ask that any of you who wish to see them off should make your way quickly to the gates, where you may say your final farewells please... as time is of the essence. Thank you, all," Lugh announced, as he began to make his way toward the open door.

Lugh stopped at the door and then turned and directed his attention once more to Oran and Dara. He said to them urgently, "Gentlemen, please, if you would be so kind as to follow me, I shall take you to your horses now. We must hurry please, as there is absolutely no time to lose." He then turned and walked through the door, followed immediately by his two great wolfhounds and then Oran, Dara and lastly, a somewhat overfed Holly.

CHAPTER SIX
Into the Outworld

It was late afternoon now and almost dark outside in the castle courtyard as the last of the elves emerged from the great room, yet still just light enough to see what was going on there. Oran and Dara followed the King closely as he strode across the now crowded courtyard, followed in turn by Holly and Enya. They walked briskly through the crowd toward the huge wooden gates - gates that had remained closed for hundreds of years and which led to the outside world, or outworld as the Danu called it, beyond the safety of the castle.

As Oran got closer to the gates, he once again started to fear this strange outside world, as he gave thought to what lay ahead of him now. He had little or no knowledge of what awaited him - beyond the sealed entrance. The outworld was virtually unknown to him, as he had spent almost his entire life within the safety of the castle's walls. All he really knew of the Ireland beyond the castle walls was the little he had heard about mankind and the country itself from stories told by people like little old Diarmuid, the much-respected castle historian, Murchad the Wise and the King himself, during the many history lessons and tales they had told when he was younger. He had heard that it was a very beautiful land in many, many tales and this he greatly looked forward to seeing for himself, hopefully. It was a welcome thought, which now somewhat lifted his spirits again. He was also cheered up by the well wishes of his fellow elves as he walked through the crowd, and also by the many who reached out and touched his and Dara's shoulder or arm gently as they passed, giving them both a well-meaning smile or nod as they went.

They soon arrived by the gates, where Cethen and Murchad the Wise waited, surrounded by many others, with two majestic black horses. The horses were beautiful, Dara thought, both as black as the night itself. Both horses were already saddled up and had been laden with heavy looking bags that bulged greatly, tied either side of the saddles. The King stopped when he reached Cethen and in turn, Oran and the others stopped directly behind him. Oran was curiously drawn to look upward briefly, owing to the brightness of the full moon that hung in the rapidly darkening sky directly above. Above the horses, he noticed Eolande and the rest of the fairies as they circled and darted about playfully in the cold evening air above. They didn't seem to mind the cold at all, he thought to himself as he watched them.

"The horses have been made ready, Sire," Cethen announced to the King, bowing his head as he spoke.

"Thank you, my good friend," Lugh replied, then paused briefly and turned to Oran and Dara, then said, "Step forward now, Oran and Dara. These will be your mounts for the journey ahead. You will look after them well, no? Now then, both of you, Cethen has information that will, no doubt, be of great value, so please listen to him very closely," he advised them wisely.

At this, Oran and Dara stepped forward to greet Cethen. As they did, Holly sneaked quickly in between them, perhaps for some attention, or perhaps to shelter from the biting cold. They stood directly in front of Cethen now, bowing their heads briefly, then listened to him attentively.

"Oran, Dara, in the saddle bags of each horse is enough food and a supply of drinking water to last you both five or six days safely," Cethen pointed out, as he gestured towards the bags adorning the horse nearest to him. "You will also find in them some extra clothing, should you be in need of it."

He then reached a piece of folded parchment, which he had been holding, to Dara, saying, "This will probably be of more value to you, Dara, as you have some knowledge of the land and where the journey leads you, whereas Oran does not. It is a map, a very old map, I'm afraid, but it should help you both find your way. You should make your way east from your house and find the river that flows to the sea in the north. Follow that river south for a day, where you should then find a crossing. Cross there, and head directly east for another day or so and you will find Slieve Mish. The mountain is easily recognisable as it stands alone on the eastern plain, not far from the coast. I have marked both the route and the rough location of your destination on the map to assist you."

"Thank you, Cethen. I am confident that I can guide Oran safely there. We should have no difficulty in locating the mountain, I hope," Dara said humbly, as he took the map from Cethen.

Murchad the Wise then handed a black sheep-skin jacket, which he had been clutching, to the King who then, in turn, passed it to Oran.

"This was once mine a very long time ago, Oran, but now is yours. I hope that it will fit and help to keep you warm, my boy," Lugh smiled.

"Really? Thank you so much, my King," Oran beamed back at him, eagerly putting the jacket on immediately to show his gratitude. It fit him very well and Lugh was noticeably pleased at this.

Lugh swallowed a lump in his throat and then sternly said, "Mount up gentlemen, please. There is no time to lose, I fear. You must depart at once."

Oran tried to smile at the King, then nodded and turned to walk toward the horses. Dara came to his aid and helped him climb up into his saddle, then patted Holly on the head and said, "Good girl, Holly. Follow us closely now." He quickly mounted the other horse and drew himself alongside Oran.

"Dara MacBrien, one last thing, sir," Lugh called to him.

Dara turned his horse toward the King, who was now holding out to him the weapons confiscated from him upon his arrival in the castle that morning.

"You may have these back as you may be needing them, although I sincerely hope not," Lugh said, as he passed the weapons to Dara, who nodded to him as a gesture of his gratitude. "I hope that we didn't treat you too badly this morning, but I'm sure you understand. I thank you for your patience and for your willingness to accompany Oran," to which Dara nodded again, this time with a smile.

Enya watched silently, all the while, from nearby as all of this took place, not wishing to say good-bye - not wishing to say anything really. She felt her eyes welling up but fought it off and continued to watch as everyone else said their final farewells. As Dara took possession of his belongings, the King turned his head upward toward the guards on the ramparts and bellowed, "Men, open the gates please!"

His command was instantly followed by a loud clanging, clanking noise, then by winching sounds as the huge wooden gates began to swing outward slowly. As they did so, Murchad the Wise went to Oran's side and, placing his frail hand on the horse's flank, looked up at him and said, "Take great care of that sword, young master Oran. It may well mean the difference between life and death for you both. Guard it well and use it wisely, as it wields great power. The success of your quest, your mission and your chances of returning to us safely depend greatly upon it. Remember well everything that I have taught you in magic and use it wisely as it will, no doubt, be invaluable to you both on the outside."

With this, he smiled up at Oran, who simply smiled back, and then patted the horse gently on the flank. "Safe journey men," he added, as he smiled at them both again and turned to walk away.

Oran and Dara turned their attention to the King now, as Oran said reverently, "I promise, my King, to fulfill my quest and return with your old friend Rydian, so undoing the terrible harm I have caused."

"I promise to lead him safely there and back again, Sire," Dara quickly added.

"Good journey men... and good luck on your quest, Oran. Mind the dragon when you find her, as she has great cunning, speed and strength. You will have but a very short window of opportunity to get her attention, to make her yours by use of the sword. You must be swift, or I fear it could end badly. May the gods favour and protect you both," Lugh proclaimed, then took a step backward to give them room to turn the horses. "Go now. Be swift, men, for time is our enemy," he urged.

They nodded respectfully to the King again and obediently turned their horses toward the gates. Oran looked at Dara, with a slight smirk on his face.

"Please sir, lead the way, my newfound friend and companion, Dara MacBrien."

Dara laughed at this and then urged his horse to make its way towards the gates slowly, with Holly, of course, at his side as ever. Oran followed closely behind, but stopped suddenly just before reaching the gates and turned to look for Enya. He had been avoiding getting close to her to say good-bye, as he feared he might upset her and possibly even upset himself by doing so. He found her now, stood alone and to the side of the main crowd, from where she had been watching his departure.

He yelled out to her, "Fear not, my lady Enya! I shall return promptly to you and we shall all have a great feast to mark our success!"

She smiled slightly at this - a forced smile - and raised her hand slowly to wave goodbye to him. Oran waved back eagerly, smiling back at her as he did so, then turned the horse once more to face the gates and rode out after Dara into the night, his heart pounding in his chest with a mixture of fear and excitement. The heavy gates swung slowly closed behind them with a creaking sound and loudly banged shut... Oran and Dara were gone, Enya thought to herself suddenly, and realising the finality of this, she lowered her head in sorrow. Lugh, noticing this, walked to Enya's side and placed a comforting arm around her shoulders.

"You'll worry about him, my dear, no?" the King said to her, softly.

"Yes, of course. Do you really think Oran will ever return, Father. Tell me, honestly, please?"

"Ah yes... of course I do, my child. I believe that it is very likely that we shall see Oran again - I certainly hope we do. He has a strong will and a good heart, my child. His skills in magic are extremely good, which is fortunate for them both and he has the benefit of my sword also. I believe he is, himself, not yet even aware of what he is fully capable of in magic and this quest may very well be an awakening for him... in more ways than one."

On the other side of the gates, just outside the castle's entrance, Oran and Dara stopped side-by-side to take stock and plan the first leg of their journey to Dara's house. Dara reached down and opened the bags by his legs, then rummaged through them to see what was inside. In one, he found all manner of food including bread, fruit and cold meats, at which he grinned. In the other were several flasks, filled with water, he guessed, and some items of clothing, to which he couldn't help but wonder as to whether any of the garments would fit him or not, given the slightly smaller stature of the average Danu male. He closed the bags up again, placing the map inside the one containing the clothing and flasks, saying,

"We shan't be needing that just yet, Oran - not until after we set out from my house, at least. If you're happy to, we'll make our way down the north facing slope of the mountain from here, circle around and approach the house from the north side. That way we shouldn't encounter anyone on our way there, as my house is at the northern-most edge of the village and there is no other house further out in that direction."

"By all means, lead the way, as I have absolutely no knowledge of where your house lies. It's quite cold, Dara. Is it very far from here to your house?" Oran enquired, already shivering from the cold.

"A couple of hours' ride - possibly a little less, I imagine, as we take the long way around for safety really, not to mention the rough terrain and the fact that it is dark."

"We should get going then, I believe - no time to waste. Your wife needs my help... now," Oran stated, ominously.

They looked at the moonlit landscape ahead for a moment, then set off away from the castle and towards the unforested ground on the northern slope of the mountain. Dara was a few feet ahead of Oran as they set out, and when they were only about fifty yards from the castle walls, the ground suddenly erupted off in front and thick, black smoke poured out in several places where large, earthen mounds had appeared just yards ahead of them and to either side of the path they were taking.

"Stop!" Oran shouted. "Fireworms, Dara! They have been summoned to protect the castle from ground intruders - by Lord Cethen, I imagine. Wait there, please."

As Oran said this, five giant fireworms, which glowed bright orange, emerged slowly from the mounds where the ground had just erupted, each of them protruding several feet from the earth - heads pointed skyward. Dara sat and watched, noticing the smoke coming from their skins, thinking that they must be extremely hot for that to happen. The pair sat astride their horses, watching curiously for a moment as the fireworms sat there, motionless, as though waiting for something to happen.

"It's alright, we're fine - they will do us no harm. It is safe to pass now. They have recognised me and will now allow us safe passage onward."

"What? How can you be so sure that they have recognised you?" Dara asked in a slightly alarmed voice, as Holly stood under his horse barking defensively at the incandescent worms.

"Simply because they do not attack us, Dara," Oran stated, matter-of-factly.

With that, Oran now guided his horse slowly past Dara and toward a gap between the fireworms, to show him that it was safe to proceed. Dara cautiously stayed where he was, inwardly refusing to move until Oran was well past the glowing creatures and had reached what he considered relative safety, on the other side of them. He continued to watch as Oran made his way slowly past the fireworms and noticed that, as he did so, they turned what he could only describe as their heads to follow Oran's movement. They did, however, not attack, just as Oran had said they wouldn't.

At this, he breathed a sigh of relief and when Oran was safely through and had turned to face him, Dara squeezed the flanks of his horse with his thighs to encourage it to move forward. The horse obeyed, and Holly swiftly moved out from below as he slowly made his way toward the formidable creatures. Dara could feel his heart beating heavily in his chest as he approached, even though he felt confident that they would not be harmed by the alarming creatures. As he moved between the strange beasts, Dara was uneased by the intense heat which he could feel radiating from the worms' bodies. He was only too happy to get beyond them as quickly as possible.

A moment later, though, he had safely joined Oran at his side, with more than a touch of relief. He smiled at Oran then looked down in search of Holly, but she wasn't there. Quickly, he turned to look back in the direction of the castle and there she was, stood just where he had left her. She let out a high pitched, almost defiant, yelp at him, as he shouted across to her, "Come, Holly! It's alright - come now, girl!"

She stood her ground, however, refusing to move out of uncertainty and more than a hint of fear.

"Holly, come, girl. Come on!" Dara shouted, growing concerned, but still, Holly refused to move and instead, began barking and yelping again.

"I think you will have to go and fetch her," Oran groaned, shivering from the biting cold that penetrated his clothing.

"Hmmph," Dara grumbled, then set off back toward his faithful dog, somewhat reluctantly.

As he reached her, she jumped up toward him excitedly, barking and yelping at the same time. Dara dismounted and stooped to scoop her up in his arms, as she licked his face gratefully. He shoved her up onto the horse's back, just in front of the saddle, where she lay now, draped across it like a coat. Dara quickly climbed back up onto his horse, patted Holly on the head, then placed one hand on her back to secure her as he turned the horse around and made his way back toward Oran. As he passed the fireworms for a third time, he could not only hear, but also feel, Holly let out a low, grumbling, growl at them.

A moment later, he was safely back at Oran's side. He stopped and dismounted, then carefully lifted Holly back down onto terra firma. With her safely back on the ground, he then knelt in front of her and put his arms around her, giving her a fond hug as he said, "There now. That wasn't so bad, was it, girl?" and patted her on her back affectionately. That done, he climbed back up on his horse and looked at Oran.

"Well, I'm glad that's over with," he admitted. "Shall we continue now?"

"Oh, by all means, please do - lead on," Oran said in a slightly smug tone, having been slightly wearied by the dog's stubbornness, and the fact she had kept him waiting in the freezing cold.

They turned to the north and set off carefully, being aware of the rough terrain and the darkness. Thankfully, the full moon was making things easier for them and Dara thought to himself that they were fortunate for that at least. Oran followed closely behind and as they made their way down the slope toward the base of the mountain, he noticed tiny, shimmering lights off in the distance to his right.

"Is that your home over there, Dara?" he asked, pointing in the direction of the distant lights even though Dara was ahead of him, with his back to him, and couldn't see where he was pointing.

Dara turned around in his saddle to look back at Oran and asked, "If you mean the lights in the distance to the east, then yes, that is my village - my home."

He now thought of Mary again and wondered how she was doing.

"Hold on, my love. I'll be there soon. Help is at hand," he said quietly to himself, hoping that Oran didn't hear him.

"How do you plan to explain me to your family when we arrive, may I ask? Have you something in mind to tell them already?" Oran asked him, suddenly.

"I hadn't really given it much thought to be honest - too many other things on my mind, if you get my meaning, with all that has happened to me this day," Dara answered. "Perhaps I'll just tell them the truth, master Oran - that may be the best path to follow. Why lie to them to conceal your true identity when you go there to perform a miracle before their very eyes, no less?" he added.

"That is a very good point, my friend. How do you think your family will handle such a revelation - the existence of a magical being, a being such as myself?" Oran enquired.

"Well, we've all grown up listening to stories and fables of magical and mythical creatures - stories of elves, nymphs, fairies and the like - so perhaps they won't be *that* surprised to find that one really exists after all. Not to mention the fact that you are in my company, which should serve to lessen the shock for them, I should imagine," Dara said, hopefully.

They continued on down the mountain at a steady pace for close to an hour before they reached what could be considered the bottom, or the lower slopes really. All the while, as they progressed, Oran asked Dara questions about his life in the village and his family. He was now very much looking forward to meeting these people he had heard so much about. Dara was eager, Oran had noticed, to discuss his family, so he could tell that he had much love for them and was a very proud husband and father.

"What of your mother and father, Dara? Do they live in the village also?" Oran asked curiously, as he had heard no mention of them at all.

"My parents are gone, Oran. My father passed on a few years back, followed by my dear mother last year, sadly. My family and I now share the house which my father built when he married my mother many years ago," he said, quietly.

"I'm sorry to hear that, Dara - truly sorry," Oran said, solemnly.

Oran had no idea what it was like to lose a parent, as he had never known his parents, for one thing. He had honestly never known anyone to die, or pass on, as Dara called it, as everyone he had ever known were Danu, and were all still alive and would be for who knew how long. Even he himself had been alive for around one hundred years and was still considered a boy to some degree, which wasn't helped by his youthful appearance in any way. His youthful looks were, however, commonplace amongst the Danu though, as they all aged very slowly due to their longevity.

"How old are you, Dara?" Oran suddenly asked, trying to understand the comparatively short lives that these humans seemed to live.

"I will be twenty-five years old on the fourteenth day of this coming July, Oran. Why do you ask?" Dara answered in what seemed a proud manner, as though he believed it were some great achievement.

Oran chuckled at the statement but said nothing. Wondering what was so amusing and with his curiosity again aroused, Dara then asked, "Might I ask, what age are you, Oran?"

Oran hesitated briefly before answering, as he knew the answer would most likely come as a somewhat unwelcome surprise, or even shock, to Dara. He then said, "Well, you may find this rather difficult to believe, and no-one is certain really, as I was not born at the castle, but rather, discovered as an infant and taken in by them. But the closest guess would be - something close to, or around, a rather youthful one hundred, I suppose."

"*What?*" Dara exclaimed suddenly. It was all he could think to say, but then quickly added, "How could you possibly live for so long, Oran? It's unnatural, surely?"

"If you think that's a long time, Dara, then I won't tell you how old the King is, never mind Murchad," Oran stated factually.

"No, no, go on - tell me! I can't wait to hear this!" Dara exclaimed, loudly.

Oran sighed. He detected that Dara would, perhaps, be upset in some way by this information, but decided to tell him anyway, as he knew that he would only keep on asking otherwise.

"King Lugh celebrated his five hundred and fifty-sixth birthday just a few months ago, in October, on the day before All Hallows Eve. As for Murchad, well, again as in my case, no-one knows for sure. He is the oldest of the Danu and is rumoured to be in the region of eight hundred years or more," Oran stated, as though he were reading the facts straight out of a book.

Dara looked at him with a sad expression across his face, then lowered his head briefly. He looked up again, directly at Oran and asked, "Do you know how old my mother was when she passed away last year?"

"I could not possibly know, Dara. Why do you ask?" replied Oran, carefully. He knew Dara was becoming upset and did not wish to say anything that might make him feel worse.

"She was only forty-four, Oran - a brief life to you and your kind no doubt - a blink of an eye. It doesn't seem fair, really. Why do you and your kind get to enjoy such long lives, when we do not? Who decides these things?" Dara said, bitterly, almost angrily.

Oran hung his head and for a moment, felt almost ashamed for some unknown reason. He thought carefully for a minute, then replied, 'Why do many birds and animals only live for a few years, and some insects only for a few days or weeks? It is not I who determines these things, Dara - they are governed by a higher power. I have as much control over how long you live as I do over how long I shall live, and we should be content with what we have for however long we may have it, is that not so? Besides, it is not the number of years we live that matters - it is what we chose to do with them. And also, you should feel fortunate that you knew your parents, however briefly, as I did not have that opportunity."

Dara pondered Oran's statement for a moment before saying, "Wise words. I suppose you're right, my young friend. We should be happy with what we are given and enjoy the time we have, however brief or long it shall be."

Oran was pleased to hear this statement from Dara, but was, at the same time, distracted by a strange sound he could faintly hear coming from the distance in what seemed to be the vicinity of Dara's village, or nearby. He brought his horse to a halt suddenly, in an effort to hear more clearly.

"What is it, Oran? Why have you stopped?

"Shhh... listen," Oran ordered him. "Can you hear that?"

"Hear what?" Dara asked, as he stopped his horse just ahead of Oran and listened carefully.

The two sat there for a moment in silence, Dara trying to hear what Oran was listening to, but could detect nothing. Suddenly, Holly began whining and he wondered if she could hear it too. By this stage, they had been travelling along the side of the stream and were only a few hundred yards from Dara's house, where they had now stopped.

"I can't hear it, Oran. Let's move closer. What does it sound like?" he asked, with growing concern.

"This may sound odd, but it sounds like either a small animal in a lot of pain, or a woman screaming or wailing, if that makes any sense to you," Oran responded, nervously.

Dara let Oran's words sink in for a few seconds, wondering not only why he couldn't hear it too, but also wondering what manner of creature could be making the noise that Oran described. Then, as the sudden realisation swept over him, he roared, "Banshee - it's a banshee! We must go now, right now, Oran... move yourself, quickly! It comes for my Mary, I fear. We must stop it from taking her, Oran! Move!"

Oran had never heard of a banshee before and didn't have time to ask what it was or to reply as, before he could, Dara was off at a gallop toward the house with Holly in pursuit. He yelled out after them, "What's a banshee?" and then set off after them as quickly as he could, the awful wailing noise becoming louder as he neared the house.

CHAPTER SEVEN
The Dance of Light

It was dark inside the old stone house now. Mary had been asleep in her bedroom for most of the afternoon and, sadly, neither of the two young girls knew how to light the old oil lamps, as this was always done by their parents. The fire had almost gone out completely, as it had been neglected also, and the house grew colder and colder by the hour. Mary was oblivious to these things - to all things - as she lay in her bed asleep and near death.

She had drifted in and out of consciousness, for most of the day, since she had gone to bed, only waking briefly when the pain in her breast became intense. During those brief moments of consciousness, she thought only of her beloved children and of Dara, hoping that he would return soon - before it was too late - and found herself vaguely recalling fond memories of the happy times spent with him. She knew, or sensed, that the end was near for her and hoped she could see him, touch him, for one last moment - before her time came.

Ellen had gone to check on her mother periodically and, each time, had found her to be asleep. She had given up trying to rouse her after the first few failed attempts, but she was now growing very concerned that her mother had been asleep for such a long time. She also now wished that her father would return home shortly. She and her sister were sat on the floor near the dwindling fire, amusing themselves with games and singing, when she heard a very unusual noise. To her, it sounded like a wild animal screaming or crying. She found it difficult to describe in her young mind, but it frightened her nonetheless, and she thought it best that she and her sister hide, in case it was coming to the house. She immediately crawled underneath the big wooden table, coaxing her younger sister to follow, then pulled the table cloth down slightly on one side in an effort to conceal them both, as the awful noise outside grew louder and louder.

Dara was approaching the house now, travelling as fast as he could possibly push his horse to carry him. As he neared the back of the house, the sound which Oran had described became horribly, frighteningly evident to him and he was sure that it could only be the terrible thing which he now feared and dreaded most at this very moment in time - a banshee. His heart sank, but also pounded at the same time. He wished he could go faster, could turn back time, could do whatever he needed to do to make things better. He could see no sign of the creature itself and wondered where exactly it was - not that he thought he would recognise it if he saw it anyway. He had never actually seen one, but the elders of the village had described in many tales that the banshee took several forms, seemingly changing at will. Strangely, each tale told of a different form, sadly, with the only consistency in the tales being that it was female - a woman with red, flaming hair, possibly.

All of the old tales he had heard as a boy told of a queen of the banshees, and ruler of some twenty-five others, called Aibell, and he now found himself wondering if it were her who had come to take his precious Mary away. As he jumped down from his horse and bolted to the back door, he sensed the sound was coming from somewhere in the distance, across the field behind him, but not far enough in the distance, alarmingly. He was, at present, more concerned about the fact that his house was, unusually, in complete and utter darkness. Just then, thankfully, Oran suddenly appeared beside him just as, hand on latch, he was about to push the door open. He looked at Oran and hesitated, saying, "Oran, can you please wait here for a moment? I need to somehow prepare my family for your arrival."

"Do I have to? There is little time, I fear. How long will you be?" Oran enquired, worriedly.

"Please, Oran. I need to ensure that everything is alright - before you enter," Dara pleaded.

"Hurry well, if you must. I don't wish to be left here alone with this awful noise and I'm a little afraid, if I must admit."

Dara simply nodded at him, then pushed the door open swiftly and darted inside, the door closing behind him again. Oran stood by the door with his back to it, then realised that he wasn't actually alone. Holly was sat by his feet, thankfully. He knelt down beside her and placed his right hand on her back, for comfort more than anything else, noticing that she was growling as she stared directly ahead into the darkness behind the house, as though she could see something that he couldn't see. He peered into the moonlit field that stretched out behind the house, looking in the same direction as Holly, trying for a moment to see what she could see, if anything. After a moment of scanning the darkness, he noticed it, a hundred yards off or more - a figure that seemed to be moving very slowly toward him and Holly, and toward the house no-less.

His heart began pounding now, as he feared the worst, although he couldn't tell for certain what he saw. He thought at first that it may be a sheep or a pig, due to its shape - but it was too dark to tell, even in the moonlight. Then, as he continued to watch, and his eyes adjusted somewhat to the distance, he realised that it might be a person - a person crawling on their hands and knees, oddly. He suddenly felt a shiver run down his spine, followed by the overwhelming urge to yell out, which he did.

"Dara! Dara, come quickly!"

Ellen and Rosemary were cowering under the table in silence as Dara entered the house through the back door. They had heard the horses outside, which had made them even more frightened now. Ellen tried to peer out from under the table cloth to see who, or what, had entered their home, but couldn't make anything out in the darkness except for the faint glow of the dying fire. Suddenly, mercifully, a familiar voice came.

"Mary, girls, where are you?" Dara called out in panic from near the back door, as he fumbled in the darkness, trying to light the oil lamp on the little table to his right.

"Daddy! Daddy!" Ellen squealed with joy, as she darted out from below the table, quickly pursued by her sister. They both ran straight to him and Dara stooped to scoop them up, one in each arm, having set the now

lit lamp back on the table. He hugged them closely and pressed his face against theirs for a moment, then asked, "Where is your mother, children?"

"Mummy's in bed, asleep. She's been there all afternoon. I tried to... " Ellen started to explain, but she was cut off mid-sentence by her father.

"*MARY!*... " Dara bellowed suddenly, as his heart leapt into his throat at Ellen's words. He feared the worst, as he set the girls down quickly and made a dash for the bedroom. In the dim light, Dara could just make out the shape of Mary lying on top of the bed. He rushed to her side, reaching out and shaking her shoulder, gently.

"Mary? Mary, wake up, my dear. I'm home. Please, wake up," Dara said, softly, yet fearfully.

There was no response, which served only to strike fear into Dara's heart, which was already thumping in his chest. Quickly, he sat down on the edge of the bed beside her and reached for the old lamp on the table next to him, lighting it as swiftly as he could. The light given off was very dim at first, but as it brightened, he studied her for a brief moment and was relieved to see her chest rise and fall slightly, as she breathed in and out. He let out a sigh of relief, as he leant in beside her and pressed his cheek to hers, wrapping his arms around the back of her neck.

"I love you. Please don't leave me," he whispered to her, feeling her move slightly beneath him.

"Dara... you... made it," came Mary's weakened voice, which brought an instant smile to Dara's face.

He sat upright suddenly and replied, "Yes, my love. I'm so glad that you're alright. Made what, my love?" he asked, puzzled by her words, but didn't wait for her answer as he explained, "Mary, please listen carefully to me, as there isn't much time. I've brought a friend to see you - a very special friend. We believe that he can make you well again. He's waiting outside, so I'll go and fetch him now for you."

"That's nice, Dara... A friend?... What's... his name... my darling?" Mary whispered, almost breathlessly, again.

Dara could tell that she was very weak and was worried now as to how long she had left, as he said to her, "His name is Oran, my love. I'll go fetch him inside now and bring him to you."

Dara patted the back of her hand lovingly, then stood up and walked quickly back to where he'd left the girls standing. They were right where he had left them, and Rosemary now covered her little ears with her hands to try to keep out the terrible noise being made by the banshee that must be, by now, very close to their house.

"What makes that awful noise, Daddy?" Ellen asked, loudly.

Dara ignored her question, for there was no time to waste. Instead, he knelt down to eye level with them and took each of their hands in his as he calmly said,

"I have a very special friend waiting outside - a friend named Oran – he is someone very different from you and me, who has come to see Mummy - to help her. So, I want you both to be nice to him and no asking lots of questions, is that understood?"

"Yes, Father," the girls replied simultaneously, as though rehearsed.

Dara stood up again, then reached out and unlatched the door. Oran was directly outside it, knelt beside

Holly with his back to Dara, just the other side of the doorway and so, didn't seem to notice the door open, so intense was his focus on the creature approaching them through the darkness. Dara reached down and tapped Oran on the shoulder lightly, at which the elf jumped visibly, startling Holly also. He let out a slight yelp, as he turned swiftly to face Dara.

He jumped to his feet, exclaiming, "What did you do that for? You scared me half to death, you great fool!"

"Er... sorry," Dara mumbled, ashamedly.

"Speaking of death... look over there! We'd best hurry, I think," Oran stated, ominously, as he pointed toward the figure in the distance that still crawled slowly toward them, wailing all the while.

Dara looked to where Oran was pointing and off in the distance, saw a small, hunched figure. It was hard to make out in the darkness, but was a human figure, he thought. As his eyes adjusted to the gloom, he thought for a just second that its hair appeared to be alight, or glowing, then dragged Oran inside by the arm, urging, "Inside, hurry! Holly, you too, girl! In, now!"

Oran and Holly moved inside, and Dara quickly closed the door behind them, sliding the heavy metal bolt across to secure it. He hoped that it would afford them some protection, or at least buy them some time, perhaps. He moved swiftly to the front door and slid its bolt across too, then turned to the girls and Oran.

"Hello, what's your name?" asked Ellen, almost immediately, her question directed at Oran.

"My name is Oran, young lady. I'm very pleased to meet you," Oran responded, slightly nervously.

"Oran, hurry! This way, please," Dara instructed, as he directed Oran to the room where Mary lay.

"We want to come too, Daddy," Ellen pleaded.

"Alright, but you must stand by the door and stay absolutely quiet, understood? No interfering!" Dara warned, to which both girls nodded their agreement.

He didn't really want the girls to be out of his sight anyway - not while a banshee, of all things, was making its way toward the house from not very far away. Dara guided Oran over to the bedside, then leant over Mary once more and softly said, "Mary, my love. This is the friend whom I told you of - Oran. Can you hear me, Mary?"

She opened her eyes slightly, then winced as pain suddenly raged through her again, but found the strength to say, "Oran? That's a nice... name. A... handsome boy... too. What brings you... here, my... dear?"

"Hello, Mary. Dara brought me here, to help you, of course," Oran replied, as he sat down on the edge of the bed beside her.

Dara put a hand round Oran's upper arm and gestured with a nod for him to move away from Mary. Oran stood up and followed him to the side of the room, a few feet away from the bed, where Dara whispered carefully, "Do you really think you can help, Oran? This spell, this magic of yours won't make matters worse by any chance?"

Oran thought for a moment, choosing his words very carefully, so as not to cause alarm or upset, then replied, "If I'm entirely honest, I do not know if it will work, Dara. I'm sure that you are well aware that the end is very near for Mary, and I've never tried this on anyone who was so close to... er... death, dare I say it. I've also never tried this on a human before, my friend. I hope for both your sakes, however, that it does work, and I shall do my very best to make sure that it does."

Dara lowered his head in sorrow and stared at the floor between them briefly, then looked up again and begged, "Please, Oran. You must try, please. She is my life."

"I shall do my very best, my friend, as I said."

Dara nodded his consent, but didn't speak. Nor did Mary. Oran noticed that Dara had a look of fear mixed with hope and desperation all at the same time, if such a thing were possible, and then turned and said softly to Mary, "Mary, my dear. It is I, Oran. This may feel a little strange for a moment or two, but do not worry and do not try to struggle or fight, whatever you feel and whatever happens, do you understand? Mary? Just stay still for me."

She opened her eyes briefly and whispered, "Yes," before closing them again, slowly, as she drifted back into unconsciousness.

Oran then sat beside her again and leant over her, reaching his hands out toward her head slowly. Placing a palm either side of her forehead, he looked at Dara and softly advised, "Prepare yourself, Dara, and do not interfere, no matter what happens, and no matter what you see or hear."

Dara was unsure as to what Oran meant by this as he stood, apprehensively, by the bed. He watched closely as the elf slowly tilted his head back slightly, then inhaled deeply and closed his eyes - while the Banshee continued to howl and wail outside, nearer now than ever before. Hands placed on Mary's forehead and with his eyes firmly closed, Oran began his magic. He started to recite something in a language that Dara had never heard before, except when being freed from the grasp of the Shawan earlier that day. Dara assumed that it was the old language, of which he knew nothing, as he stood watching, carefully and intently.

"*Altwean de beont, ar tastiel chu seol glantain cuidis,*" Oran began chanting, and Dara could only wonder at what he was saying.

Oran continued chanting, repeating this phrase over and over, as Dara watched and listened carefully. Then, Dara noticed something peculiar - a strange smell in the room, like a faint burning smell, almost. He began to look around the room for the cause, and just as he looked in the direction of the girls, now stood obediently by the door, something akin to a very small bolt of bright blue lightning crackled and snaked its way slowly up the door frame, disappearing at the top. This was followed by another, then another. Suddenly, several more appeared at the four corners of the room and they all, strangely, snaked their way across the floor and walls, converging steadily toward the bed where Oran sat by Mary.

Oran seemed oblivious, or unconcerned, Dara noticed, as he continued the chant with his eyes firmly closed, still holding his palms to Mary's brow. The girls, witnessing this also, now held each other closely, as their father took a step backward from the bed, watching intently all the while. As he stepped backward, Dara looked down at the miniature, bright blue bolts of lightning that were slithering and snaking across his bedroom floor and noticed that they were going into Oran's feet. He began hopping from one foot to the other repeatedly, appearing as though he were performing some type of bizarre dance, in a way, in a concerted effort not to touch, or be touched by, one of the lightning bolts, as he was now extremely concerned as to just what it might do to him.

"Oran!" Dara gasped, still hopping, trying not to touch them. Oran either did not hear, or chose to ignore him, as he continued the chant with a look of extreme concentration, which now seemed to have become more intense, as he appeared to be shaking slightly and sweating visibly.

The little blue lightning bolts had also become more intense and were all hastily finding their way to Oran's feet, and it now appeared that Oran's skin had taken on a somewhat bluish hue as well, particularly the veins in his arms and hands. It became evident to Dara that the lightning bolts were finding their way through Oran and into Mary, through his touch. Dara watched in awe, but the previous events of the day had somewhat prepared him for this, so he did not interfere, trusting Oran instead. The girls, however, were not so calm and as their mother started shaking on the bed in time with Oran's shaking, they both began to sob and cry.

"*Daddy*!" Ellen screamed out, over the crackling noises.

"It's alright, my child! It's alright," her father yelled back.

The buzzing and crackling had become quite loud and chaotic now, as Oran and Mary continued to shake, now somewhat vigorously, in the blue glowing light nearby. Then, suddenly, it all stopped, and the room went dim again. All was quiet, except for the sobbing of the two girls. Oran had stopped chanting and now just sat there with his eyes closed in silence, still holding Mary's head as Dara stood nearby, wondering what had just happened. Suddenly, Oran opened his eyes and removed his hands from Mary's head, the palms of which now glowed the brightest blue, and said, "*Saorie an faol larr*," then closed his eyes again, just as quickly.

Mary lay quite still for a moment, with nothing untoward happening, and Dara feared the worst - feared that it hadn't worked as planned. He felt panic well up inside him and was just about to yell at Oran when she tilted her head back slightly on the pillow and coughed dryly. She coughed again and again, and as she did so, Dara stepped closer, concerned and bewildered, noticing that his beloved wife was coughing up the tiniest blue specks of light that now floated and drifted around the room, before disappearing completely.

"Mary! Oran! Are you both alright?" he cried out.

Mary and Oran both opened their eyes and Oran rose to his feet. At the sound of Dara's voice, Mary turned to look at him saying, "That felt... extremely... odd... my love. I feel a little, no... I feel very... strange. How are you?"

Dara smiled, then laughed at this. He was overjoyed that his wife could simply complete a sentence without sounding like she was in pain. *That's a good sign*, he thought. He sat down on the bedside and took her hand firmly in his, smiling all the while. Oran looked quite tired now - exhausted, almost – so Dara asked again, "Oran, are you alright? How do you feel?"

Oran blinked at him and then yawned a very big yawn.

"Tired, Dara, a little tired. That required more effort than I had expected, to be honest, but it is done, and all seems well. The disease has been expelled from your wife's body," he replied, stifling yet another yawn.

"It worked, Oran?" Dara asked, eagerly.

Oran looked at him for a moment, saying nothing, then smiled as he replied, "Yes, Dara, it worked, I'm pleased to say."

Dara began laughing again, then leant forward and kissed Mary on the forehead, to which she smiled slightly. He jumped up off the bed and ran to the girls by the door, scooping them up in his arms once more, and cheered as he danced, "Mummy's going to be alright, girls! Isn't that wonderful?" to which his daughters both responded with big, smiling faces and laughter.

"Although made well again, your lovely wife needs to rest now, as the magic continues to repair the damage done to her body by the disease that ailed her," Oran interrupted.

"Yes, yes... of course she does, my good friend. I can't - we can't - thank you enough for what you have done here," Dara responded, as he set the girls down again and walked back to Oran's side. He placed his right hand on Oran's shoulder, looked into his big green eyes - the same eyes that were bright blue only a few minutes ago - and solemnly said, "This is truly wonderful, Oran. How can I ever repay you for this?"

"Your company for the next few days and the kindly protection you offer is payment enough sir. I neither need, nor do I wish for, anything else from you and your family - just that you get me home safely to my people when we are finished with the quest," Oran replied, earnestly.

"So, Mary, you're going to rest a bit now and I'll come and see you in a bit. We'll close the bedroom door now to give you peace to sleep a while, my love," Dara then said, directing his gaze at his beloved wife. He made no mention of the awful creature outside, as he had forgotten all about it in his elation, the same creature that had gone quiet for the past few moments.

Mary nodded agreement and managed to reply, "Yes, dear, of course. And Oran... thank you, young man."

Dara moved to her side once more and kissed her on the forehead again, then stood up and walked to the bedroom door, ushering the girls and Oran out into the living room as he closed the door behind him softly, asking, "Cup of tea, anyone? Who's hungry then?" as though what had just taken place in his house during the last half hour were nothing out of the ordinary.

One thing had escaped the attention of all of them though, however, during the healing of Mary and all its excitement. Now, it now suddenly came back to Oran firstly, and swiftly, as they re-entered the living room. The awful wailing noise resumed and now seemed to be coming from just outside the back door - the wailing noise which they had all forgotten about in the chaos and excitement. Suddenly, they heard a loud bang on the back door, followed swiftly by another. Dara looked at Oran in terror, who had turned noticeably pale, and at the same time, the girls screamed and ran for cover under the table again, this time joined by Holly.

"The banshee!" Dara whispered, "We forgot about the banshee, Oran."

Thump, thump, thump, came the terrible, frightening sound on the back door - loudly, very loudly.

CHAPTER EIGHT
The Messenger of Death

As the steady banging on the outside of the heavy old wooden door continued, Dara looked, with a somewhat puzzled expression on his face, at Oran through the dim light cast by the old oil lamp and asked, "Who on earth could that be, do you think?" His voice was noticeably trembling as he stepped slowly backward, trying to distance himself from the door.

"I wouldn't have the faintest idea, but I'm going to guess that it may very well be the not so nice creature that was out in the field behind the house as we came inside. I really hope not though," came Oran's response, as he hastily followed Dara in distancing himself from the door also.

Thump, thump, thump... Again it came, this time even louder. The girls screamed again, louder also.

"What shall we do, Oran?" Dara asked out loud.

"I don't know! How on earth should I know what to do? It's your banshee, after all!" Oran shrieked back at him, now quite afraid.

"*My banshee*? No-one has their *own* banshee, Oran... that's just silly now," Dara declared. "What if we just stay here and ignore it? Maybe it will leave. It might think we're not here if we don't answer and keep quiet, huh?" he whispered, through gritted teeth.

"How will it think we're not here when there is a very good chance it saw us enter the house just a brief while ago, Dara? ... Really now? Not to mention the lamp is lit, as well as the fact that there are two horses tied outside and your two little girls have been endlessly screaming their lungs out, understandably! Now who's silly?" Oran argued back, as he thought to himself, or rather realised, that he'd never actually been in danger in his life before - well, not that he could remember anyway.

The pair stood facing the door with their backs to the dying fire, now nothing more than embers, as the banging on the door continued for several long minutes. In the dim light, it appeared as though, with each hefty bang, the door shook so much that it might come away from its hinges. Suddenly, without warning, the banging stopped and there came an eerie silence for what seemed like an eternity to them both. Oran and Dara looked at each other, wondering what had just happened - had the creature gone away perhaps?

Oran was just about to open his mouth to ask Dara what he thought they should do, when they heard a low, grumbling, growling noise, followed by what sounded like scraping on the other side of the door. They both stared wildly at the door, almost as if trying to see through it, trying to see what was happening on the other side. As they watched, Dara thought the door appeared to be bulging inward slightly - no, it *was* bulging, rather considerably now. *Impossible, it can't be!* he told himself. *Surely, I'm imagining it.*

What came next happened so fast that the pair barely had time to absorb it all. Firstly, the door continued to bulge inward, more and more, to the point where it burst inward and shattered into a thousand pieces with a deafening bang and a brilliant flash of light. The pair shielded their faces with their hands briefly, then lowered them slowly, as the dust settled. They watched in terror as the brief chaos was followed by a ghostly red mist that seemed to linger in the doorway in the ensuing silence.

As the mist began to clear, they could vaguely make out a figure stood in the doorway with a hand placed on each side of the door frame as if for support, or possibly to block their escape. It was staring directly at them both, saying nothing. Without thinking, Dara now instinctively moved to his right and stood in front of the bedroom door, in a defensive stance. As he did, the figure in the doorway turned its malevolent gaze to follow him. He knew, or suspected, what this creature was and he knew only too well why it had come here to his home, if his suspicions were right. His only aim now was to prevent it from gaining access to the bedroom where Mary lay recovering, even if it cost him his life, he told himself. As he stood there guarding the bedroom door, peering into the remnants of the glowing red haze as it cleared, he was somewhat surprised to see a very beautiful young woman dressed in a long, red dress emerge from the clearing veil of mist. Her skin was as white as snow and she had the most stunning long red hair, he observed, red hair that seemed to be glowing or... was strangely... alight. He was briefly mesmerised by what his eyes were seeing, but then quickly came to his senses as he heard Oran yell out, "Dara!"

"What do you want here, evil demon?" Dara called out to the banshee, as he quickly came to his senses and resumed a defensive stance.

He realised at this point that he had never been so scared in his life before, not even when he went flying earlier that same morning. He could feel his arms and legs shaking and noticed that even his voice now trembled. The beautiful young woman, who was now directing her stare at Oran, swiftly turned her head again to look at him and then, in a low, hollow voice said, "Mary MacBrien, *your* time has come. Be with me... now."

"Nooo!" Dara yelled out at the flame-haired woman. "You will *not* take her. It's *not* her time - not any more. Be gone now, I urge you, demon of the night."

With this, the banshee tilted her head back, opening her mouth at the same time and letting out the most ear piercing of wailing noises they had yet to hear. The noise went on for ages, it seemed. The girls started screaming under the table again, adding to the chaos, and Holly joined in and began to howl. The noise was absolutely ear-splitting.

"Oran, use your magic! Do something! Stop her!" Dara yelled to Oran over the terrible racket, as he covered his ears for protection.

Oran mustered all the courage he could find and swiftly responded by taking a pace forward, then knelt facing the banshee, raising both palms toward her as he began to say something which was inaudible over the noise made by the banshee, the girls and Holly. Dara watched in hope as a circle of blue light swiftly appeared around Oran's out-stretched hands and grew to several feet in diameter, then shot off toward the creature in the doorway with amazing speed.

There was another blinding flash, yet another loud bang and then, with horror, Dara regarded what now stood in the doorway where the beautiful young woman had just been. She had transformed into a small, hunched, wizened looking old hag who now stood in the same place where the red headed woman had just been, making the same awful noise as before. She was staring directly at Oran with what could only be described as an expression of utter rage, or contempt, on her face.

"Oran, what happened? Did it not work?" Dara cried out over the wailing, screaming, and howling.

"Maarrryyyyy," the old hag wailed loudly, pointing an outstretched, boney finger in Dara's direction.

"She is too strong, I fear. I believe I may have made her a little angry and I don't know that I can defeat her," Oran yelled back. Suddenly, he remembered the sword and the Kings' words of the magical powers it held. But wait, where was it? He panicked as he suddenly remembered that he'd left it outside with his horse, unthinkably.

"Dara, I need my sword," he cried out desperately, knowing that time was running out quickly for them, as there was no telling what this creature could or would do to them now that he had apparently angered it.

"Yes, use it! Where is it?" Dara called back to him, as he looked around the room for it. "Where did you put it?"

"I... er... left it outside, with my horse... I believe," Oran called out, ashamedly.

"*You did what?*" Dara screamed, but without waiting for a response, bolted to the front door, yelling back to Oran, "I'll back in a moment. Do what you must to keep that thing out of the house and away from my Mary!"

"I shall do my very best, I assure you. Now hurry, please," Oran shouted to him.

Quickly, Dara undid the heavy bolt and lifted the latch, then swung the door open and was gone through the front door and into the chilly night, leaving it open behind him in his haste. He ran as fast as his legs could carry him, around the outside of the house to where they had tied the horses up at the back. As he came around to the back of the house, he could see the horses and also, several yards further along, he could see the banshee standing in the open doorway, with her back to him.

He slowed to a walk, approaching cautiously, noticing that the banshee did not appear to be aware of his presence there and so, continued towards the horses carefully and quietly. Reaching Oran's horse first, thankfully, he quickly began to open the bag nearest to him, by the saddle, all the while watching for any sign that the banshee had noticed him. He was relieved that it took him only seconds to locate the sword, the hilt of which he could see protruding amongst the other items inside. He swiftly removed it from within the bag, then turned and ran back toward the front of the house, as fast as he possibly could. In his mind, he felt as though he had surely been gone for an eternity, although it was, in fact, only the briefest moment.

Oran knelt there on the floor for a moment, his legs trembling under him with fear, thinking that he had better buy Dara some time. He quickly raised his palms again, this time reciting a slightly different spell that created the same blue circle of light, but which, on this occasion, moved or floated slowly toward the wailing banshee and seemed to cover the doorway like a shield or barrier. He glanced quickly over at the girls and Holly under the table, then back again, as he desperately hoped that the spell would work by trapping the banshee where she stood for now, or at least, until Dara returned with the sword. Thankfully, it seemed to be working, as the banshee didn't come any closer, but instead, appeared to be held captive in the blue light surrounding her. Without warning, he suddenly felt a hand on his shoulder and spun around quickly to see Dara, whom he hadn't heard re-enter the house over the still deafening noise. Dara was now standing over him, and mercifully, was holding the sword and scabbard in his right hand.

"Oran, use it now! Quickly," Dara gasped, out of breath, as he pulled the sword from its scabbard and offered it to Oran.

Oran reached for the sword and took it firmly in both hands, then swung round and aimed the gleaming blade directly at the angry, wailing banshee who was still, thankfully, trapped by his spell in the open doorway. He, once again, began reciting his spell, as he held the sword out. Dara stood behind, watching eagerly, as the large emerald in the hilt of the sword began to glow bright green. The same tiny blue lightning bolts as before, emanating from everywhere in the room it seemed, now converged on Oran again, only this time, there were more - many more. A loud buzzing and crackling noise joined the sounds of the banshee's wailing, the girls screaming and, not to be left out, Holly's howling. Dara wondered for a moment if, and how, Mary could possibly be sleeping through all of this, but mercifully, it seemed that she was.

Oran continued reciting his spell with a look of grim determination on his face, as Dara looked on hopefully, wondering why the sword had not yet defeated the awful creature. Suddenly, there was a blinding flash of bright blue-green light and a very loud crackle as a magnificent bolt of blue-green lightning shot out of the blade of the sword and went directly to the banshee. There followed another, louder bang and brighter flash of light, then suddenly, all was dark again except for the tiny lamp near the door. Next came complete and utter silence - eerie silence.

The lamp light illuminated a thick green mist which now hung in the doorway, preventing both Oran and Dara from seeing if the terrifying banshee had been defeated. They continued to stare into the mist as, suddenly, the old hag emerged from within it, toppling forward toward the cold stone floor. Dara couldn't believe what happened next. As the banshee made contact with the hard floor, with a muffled thud, her entire body instantly shattered into thousands of tiny fragments, as if made of glass, that scattered for several feet.

They continued to watch in hope, for a moment, as some of the fragments mysteriously began to gather themselves into a small pile near the open doorway and then, astoundingly, transform themselves into a large cat - an unusually red tabby cat. It now stood looking at them both quietly for a moment, flicking its tail in obvious anger. Suddenly, it opened its jaws wide, hissing angrily at them both, then turned and ran out into the night, growling and hissing as it went. The remaining few fragments of what *had* been the banshee, still scattered across the old stone floor, now floated slowly and gracefully into the air, then swiftly turned to dust and drifted out through the doorway on the breeze and into the night to the sound of a faint, echoing wail.

Oran and Dara stayed where they were for a moment, taking in what had just happened, catching their breath and making certain that the ordeal was over. Dara then reached out and placed a hand gently on Oran's shoulder and calmly said, "You did it, Oran. You defeated the banshee."

Oran lowered his sword, still aimed at the doorway, to the floor and stood up slowly.

Dara could see that he was exhausted and said, "I think you need some rest too, young Oran. It looks like all of that magic has taken a toll on you, my good friend."

"I do feel quite tired, Dara, but a little hungry also, oddly. Is there a possibility of something to eat, perhaps, and a few hours' sleep before we continue on our journey?"

"Of course, of course. You sit down by the table and rest while I just go check on Mary quickly, and then I'll prepare some food for us all," Dara replied heartily, then called out, "Girls, where are you both?"

Ellen and Rosemary did not respond but crawled out from under the table and eagerly ran to their father's open arms, as he knelt down to greet them again. He hugged them both tightly, as Ellen then asked, "Is it over, Daddy? Is the bad monster gone now?"

"Yes, my sweet. The bad monster is gone now," Dara responded, smiling at her as he looked around at the empty space where the banshee had stood. He then turned to Oran and said, "I'll have to find a way to quickly fix that door before we all freeze to death, but first I think it best to get the fire going again as it's freezing in here also," as he released his girls and stood upright again.

"Wait," Oran said, raising a hand to Dara as Holly came to his side with her tail wagging. "I can take care of that, easily. Would these two young ladies like to see some more magic - some *good* magic this time?"

Ellen walked slowly over to Oran who was now sat on one of the chairs by the table, stroking Holly's head. She looked into his bright green eyes and asked, "What's good magic, Oran? Is there a bad magic?"

"Oh yes, child. There is good and bad in everything almost, but good magic is simply when you use magic to do something good, or useful, or helpful. For example, when you use it to create fire or mend something broken, let's say."

"So, what you did to get rid of that monster was good magic then?" Ellen enquired again.

"Yes, well... in a way. Now then, how would you like to see me make the fire grow bright and warm? Actually, I have a better idea. How would you like to *help* me make the fire grow bright and warm, Ellen?"

Ellen turned to look up at her father, and asked, "Can I, Daddy, is it alright? *Pleeeease?*"

Dara looked at her, then at Oran, who was now smiling, and shrugged his shoulders as he responded, "Well, if Oran says it's alright, then I imagine so, my dear."

"Now then, Ellen," Oran instructed, as he stood up and turned the chair to face the fireplace, "You stand just in front of the chair, facing the fireplace, in front of me."

He sat down on the chair again, as Ellen moved in front of him and stood with her back to him.

"Will this hurt?" she twisted round to ask him.

"No, no. Of course not, child. You may feel some sort of a tingling sensation, but it's nothing to worry about.

Raise your palms toward the fire now, young lady, and keep them there," Oran instructed, as he placed his hands on her shoulders and took a deep breath. Ellen obeyed his commands and cautiously raised both palms, aiming them at the dying fire somewhat nervously.

"*Lasaria aradua, lasaria aradua,*" Oran began to recite, repeating it several times. Again, just a few tiny blue charges snaked across the floor and into his feet. "Say the words with me, Ellen... *lasaria aradua.*"

Ellen took a deep breath, as her father and sister looked on in anticipation. She had never heard this language before but found it easy to copy what Oran had said and so repeated his words, saying, "*Lasaria aradua, lasaria aradua.*"

Suddenly, she felt a tingling in her arms and hands, but before she had time to become frightened, a small, bright red ball of fire appeared, hovering in front of her hands for a few brief seconds before shooting off, straight into the fireplace. Ellen shrieked gleefully as the fire immediately sprung to life, flames leaping and licking at the chimney breast.

"I did it, Oran! Look, Daddy!" she screamed with delight as she jumped up and down on the spot.

"How did you do that, Oran?" asked a somewhat bemused Dara.

"It's called channeling. It is used as a teaching tool for young magic students in my world," Oran responded, then continued, "But in this case, I summoned the magic and directed, or channeled it, through your daughter."

"I see, and can you do the same to the door then?" Dara asked of him, pensively.

"Of course I can. That's an easy task, Dara. Would Ellen like to assist me again?"

"Oh, yes please, Oran," Ellen chirped, as she clapped her hands with excitement.

"Alright then, stand facing the doorway this time with your back to me again, please," Oran said, as he turned on the chair to face the doorway once more.

Ellen took her place in front of him, grinning from ear to ear, and said excitedly, "I'm ready, Oran."

Oran and Dara laughed at this, as Oran reached out and placed his hands on her shoulders again. Just then, Rosemary walked over beside her sister and took her right hand in hers, then turned to smile at Oran, saying, "Me too, please, Oran."

Oran looked at Dara for a sign of approval, to which Dara simply responded with a quick nod of his head. He then removed his right hand from Ellen's shoulder and moved it to Rosemary's shoulder, as the two girls stood side by side, holding hands with their backs to him and he began to chant again. The girls didn't need to be told this time and both just copied his words as though it were natural, chanting along with him, palms raised toward the open doorway as their father looked on in awe.

"*Cor anais ain dorais, cor anais ain dorais*," they repeated along with Oran.

Never in all his life did Dara MacBrien think he would ever see the day that both of his daughters would perform magic of all things, but here they both were, doing just that.

Dara continued to watch as the three of them chanted and again, as before, the tiny blue energy bolts found their way, crackling and buzzing, to Oran and the girls. This time there was no single blue bolt that shot out from outstretched hands though. Instead, lots and lots of little lightning bolts rapidly shot from the girls' fingertips and found all the fragments, one after the other, of what had previously been their back door. As this happened, each fragment jumped up off the floor and flew to the opening where it had formerly been. Within moments, the pieces of the door magically knitted back together, and it was soon as it had been before the banshee had destroyed it. Dara walked over to the door and placed the palm of his right hand on it, as though doubting it were real, but it was, and he began to laugh out loud.

"What, may I ask, amuses you, Dara?" Oran asked.

"Is there no end to the wonders this day will bring?" Dara replied, still laughing. He then thought of Mary and added, "I had best check on Mary. It'd be a miracle if she slept through all of that, really," as he moved toward the bedroom door.

Dara opened the door slowly and peered into the dim light for a second. As his eyes adjusted, he could just see his wife asleep in the bed. He crept quietly into the room and walked to her side, just to make sure that she was alright. He watched her sleep for a moment, observing her chest rise and fall, finding comfort in the fact that she seemed to have slept through all the noise. He stood there, watching her for a while longer. He thought that she looked almost as though she was smiling slightly in her sleep and reminded himself that she had good reason to be happy, as did he.

Dara suddenly felt an overwhelming sense of joy as a single tear rolled down his left cheek. He leant over her and kissed her softly on her forehead, then turned and walked back out of the room, closing the door quietly behind him, and went over to his daughters who were talking to, or rather, questioning Oran.

"So, young ladies, have we had enough excitement for one day then? I think so, perhaps, and I think it time you both said goodnight to our guest now and made your way to bed," Dara ordered, as he reached down and took their hands in his.

"But we're hungry too, Daddy! Can we eat with you and Oran before bed, please?" Ellen protested.

"Oh, yes, of course my dear. What on earth was I thinking? You both must be starving. When did you last eat?" her father enquired now.

"Late this morning - a few hours after you left," Ellen informed him.

Dara proceeded to prepare some food for the four of them. When it was ready, he placed it all on the table, while the girls asked Oran questions about where he was from and what his home was like. He then put some scraps in a little ceramic dish and placed it on the floor by the fire for Holly. Holly walked over, gave it a sniff, then lay down and stretched herself out by the fire - *she'd had enough to eat today*, she thought. He took his usual place at the table and they all ate and chatted for a while before Dara put the girls to bed, then re-joined Oran.

"I'll get some spare blankets and you can catch a few hours' sleep on the old couch before we depart. Did you get enough to eat, my friend?" he asked, as he cleared the dishes from the table.

"Yes, I did, thank you," Oran replied, gratefully. "What time shall we leave, do you think?"

"Early morning will be best, before the sun rises. We need to avoid being seen by the other villagers at all costs," Dara advised, as he thought of the questions people would ask were they to catch sight of Oran as they set out on their journey.

Dara went to the bedroom, careful not to disturb Mary as he did so, returning with a couple of thick, heavy blankets in his arms, which he arranged on the couch. He then gestured to Oran that his bed, of sorts, was ready.

"The couch is very comfortable, so you should rest well. I'll be in the next room should you require anything. Sleep well, young master Oran. Wait... I mean *old* master Oran," Dara laughed, then continued, "Your looks belie your true age - I keep forgetting. Forgive me, please."

"Do not concern yourself. I'm well used to it, as I'm amongst the youngest inhabitants of the castle and well accustomed to being referred to in such a manner by most," Oran responded, as he yawned.

"Right, well, sleep then it is," Dara announced, as he walked to the bedroom. "I shall see you in a few hours."

"Yes indeed. Thank you once more," said Oran, as he crawled in under the blankets.

Mary stirred sometime later in the middle of the night to find Dara in his place beside her, but on top of the bed and fully clothed, strangely. She immediately recalled a bizarre dream she'd had where a stranger had come to their home - a young boy who had spoken to her in a strange tongue with which she was unfamiliar. She recalled bright, flashing lights and strange noises.

A sense of thirst overwhelmed her, and she pushed the dream out of her mind as she rose to fetch a drink, trying not to disturb her husband in the process. Guided by the little oil lamp, she went to the old sink to get some water and stared out through the slightly misted window into the darkness outside as she sipped. An image from the dream flashed into her mind again suddenly - the same boy sat beside her on her bed, eyes glowing brightly, and hands pressed against her head. She shook her head, trying to dispel the image in the belief that it was utter nonsense. *Just a silly dream*, she thought, as she turned around and rested her lower back against the sink.

As she stood there trying to recall the previous days' events, wondering why Dara was on top of their bed rather than in it, she realised that she felt much better than she had done for months. In fact, she whispered, "I feel fine. Fantastic, almost."

At that point, as her eyes wandered around the room, she noticed the blankets on the couch. There seemed to be someone underneath them, surely not. But who? Did Dara take in some weary traveler? Had an old friend had too much to drink and been thrown out by his wife? *Who could it possibly be*, she wondered?

She walked slowly and slightly fearfully toward the couch, trying not to make any noise, noticing that whoever lay there had completely covered themselves from head to toe under the blankets. Slowly and carefully, she reached down and took the edges of the blankets between her fingers. She cautiously pulled them back, trying to see who it was that lay there. The back of a head with a long, braided pony tail was all she could see at first, as she peeled the blankets slowly, gently away. Suddenly, having disturbed him, he turned his face to her now as he woke, and she couldn't believe her eyes. It was the same boy from her dream, she was certain. Mary staggered backwards a few paces, in shock at what she now witnessed before her, and stood staring at Oran with her mouth and eyes wide open.

"How can it be so?" she uttered in her confusion. "Aahhhh!" she screamed loudly, waking her sleeping husband in the process.

CHAPTER NINE
The Witch's Forest

Dara woke abruptly to the sound of Mary's screams and leapt off the bed, making a dash for the open door in a panic. As he reached the doorway, he could see Mary stood near the table in the living room, hands clasped to the sides of her face in near shock, staring wide-eyed at Oran, who now lay motionless on the couch, staring back at her. Oran regarded Mary with a somewhat startled, worried look on his face, which appeared to turn quickly to that of relief as soon as he noticed Dara by the bedroom door. By this stage, Holly had woken also, and had chosen to go over and sit by Oran with her back to him, looking up at Mary as if trying to tell her that he was a friend and meant her no harm.

"Who... who are you?" Mary stammered. "Why are you in my house?"

"It is alright, Mary, my dear," Dara answered quickly, before Oran had a chance to say anything. He then added, "He is my good friend - my guest. Come, Mary. Sit by the table with me and I shall endeavour to explain all of this day's strange events to you."

"But it was just a... dream! I dreamt it all, dreamt him... I'm sure of it," Mary now mumbled in confusion through the hand she had since placed over her mouth, still in shock.

"No, Mary. It was no dream, my love. Come, let me explain and all should become clear, clear as the waters in the stream by the house. If you can believe it all, that is," Dara said, comforting her as he placed a hand on her lower back and guided her to a waiting chair.

Mary turned to look at her husband, still wearing a somewhat shocked countenance, as he said this. She moved slowly to the table at his request and sat down at her usual place, uttering the words, "I don't understand. I was sure that I dreamt him. That he - what happened last night - wasn't real. But I do feel strangely well again - like a new person, I must say. I can't explain it for the life of me, Dara. What strangeness has occurred here this night, my love?"

"Don't fret, my dear, for I will endeavour to help you understand everything as best I can. Oran, my friend, will you join us at the table and assist me in my efforts to explain to my good wife the events of the past day, and about your good people?" Dara asked as he took his usual seat opposite his wife at the table, gesturing toward an empty chair to his side where Oran should join them.

Oran slowly peeled away the blankets that covered him, stood up, and walked tentatively to the table, followed closely by Holly. Mary noticed immediately that he was quite a small boy, but didn't notice his peculiar ears - not yet anyway.

"Well, my dog seems to like him," Mary remarked to Dara, with a hint of surprise and raised eyebrows.

"She does that, my dear," Dara responded, as Oran pulled out the chair next to him.

"Hello again, Mary," said Oran shyly, as he nodded to her courteously and took a seat at the end of the table between her and Dara, looking slightly embarrassed now.

"So, my love, you'd best begin, I think. Tell me all, please. How does this young man come to join us this night, and where does my wonderful new feeling of wellbeing come from?" Mary asked, as she leant back in her chair and folded her arms, looking intently at Oran all the while.

"Well now, my love," Dara began with a big sigh, then continued over the course of the next half hour, with some assistance from Oran, to explain the day's wild events to his wife. They firstly told her about the existence of the Danu, of their magical powers and the castle on the mountain where they lived in secrecy, and where he had been captured and held the previous morning. Then, they told her about the bargain he had made with Lugh and Oran that led to his freedom, and to Oran accompanying him here to the house to make Mary well again, telling her simply that he was to guide Oran on a journey as repayment, but did not yet divulge all of its details. By the time they had finished recounting the tale, Mary wore an expression of complete confusion mixed with a hint of disbelief on her face, as she looked at Oran and asked, "So, you're an elf? You can perform magical feats? Well, that would go some way toward explaining those rather unusual ears of yours, at least."

"Yes, Mary, the same magic which I summoned to make you well again. You do feel well again, don't you? Have you noticed?" Oran replied, awkwardly, now feeling somewhat self-conscious about his ears, since she had taken the trouble to point out the fact that she had noticed them.

"Well, yes. I mean, I feel fine, as I said before - fantastic, dare I say it," Mary answered, with a radiant smile directed toward her husband. "I feel wonderfully…

alive, and if it was indeed your doing, then I thank you." She now reached across the table and took one of Dara's hands in hers, squeezing it gently.

Just then Oran had an idea. He felt that he needed to prove himself in order to convince her, felt that Mary was somewhat of a non-believer perhaps and needed some solid evidence of his and Dara's claims. He stood up, saying, "One moment, please," then went to the old sink and picked up a rather tarnished looking old cup, which he brought back to the table with him as Mary and Dara watched and wondered what on earth he could be up to. As he sat down again, he set the empty cup gently in the middle of the table and asked, "You don't mind if I use your cup, do you? Do you like flowers, Mary?"

Mary was a little bewildered by this, as though it were a trick question, perhaps. She didn't understand what her liking of flowers had to do with any of this, but nonetheless answered, "Yes, of course I like flowers, but why?"

"Very good. Any particular variety?" Oran continued.

"Well, roses are my favourite - sweet scented roses, yellow being my favourite colour," she answered again, confused as to where this line of questioning could possibly be leading.

"Very well, sweet scented roses it shall be then," Oran responded, as he reached out and placed his hands either side of the cup, with his palms turned inward to face it and whispered the words, *"Mailas dolath rós."* A blue glowing light quickly appeared and surrounded his hands, then engulfed the old cup.

Mary watched in surprise, speechless, as the cup slowly transformed into a large ornate vase that then filled, one by one, with beautiful roses of all colours, until there were about thirty in all. Oran sat back and placed his hands back in his lap, then looked at Mary and simply smiled. Mary stared in amazement at the vase full of roses for a moment, then cautiously reached out and touched it with her hand, as if she still couldn't believe that it was real.

"My... goodness, it's truly real," she whispered, as she looked at her husband, who now also sat smiling at her. "And oh, how I wish my dear mother were still alive and here to witness this... miracle. She would be so happy," she added, as she then stood up and leant forward to inhale the fragrance of these newly appeared, wonderful roses.

"Mary, there is something else that I - we - need to tell you," Dara quickly interrupted, aware that time was still a very real enemy for them.

"What? More, my love? Surely there cannot be more," she enquired with a puzzled expression, as she sat down again.

"I'm afraid that there is - much more," he advised and then began to explain, in more detail, the nature of his bargain with Oran and Lugh that led to Oran coming here to help her in the first place. He explained about the journey to Slemish and their quest to find a rare and magical artefact and return it to the King, stating that he was bound by oath and debt to accompany Oran as his guide for a few days.

He did, of course, neglect to mention the true nature of the artefact and, in particular, the dragon, on purpose. He knew that if he mentioned Rydian, as well as the potential dangers involved, Mary would most likely become hysterical and do everything she could to prevent him from going at all, so there was no mention of the dragon by him, nor by Oran, who quietly understood the need for secrecy in this respect. Dara could tell that she wasn't best pleased, due to the expression on her face, that he was going away and leaving his family, but nonetheless she understood why and respected the deal which her husband had made with Oran and his King. She knew that her husband was a man of honour who kept his word. After a brief moment's consideration, being extremely grateful for her newfound health and wellbeing, and the fact that she undoubtedly now had a longer life to look forward to as well, Mary regarded him thoughtfully and said, "Very well, my dear. You must, of course, go with him, even though it worries me greatly. I understand that it is your duty and to you, Oran, I am eternally grateful for what you have done for me and my family, and I am forever in your debt."

"There is no debt where you are concerned, dear Mary, and you are most welcome, of course," Oran explained. "Your good husband's company on my quest is repayment enough, I assure you. I would also like to say that it has been my great pleasure and an honour to have met you and your family."

"We should ready ourselves for our departure now. Daylight is approaching, and we should get going - no-one in the village must see Oran," Dara interrupted, gravely.

"Yes, my dear, I understand," Mary said, as she felt a sadness grow inside her now.

Oran stood up and moved to Dara's side, but said nothing except, "Thank you again, Mary, for permitting Dara to accompany me," to which she smiled warmly at him.

"Best not to wake the girls, my love. Will you explain my departure to them later for me, please? I don't wish to disturb them, nor do I really wish to try to explain all of this to them. They have already met Oran earlier this night, but the rest, I fear, they are too young to understand."

"Of course, Dara. You two had best be going now. As much as I don't want to see you go, I also don't want anyone nearby to catch sight of Oran and start asking awkward questions," Mary insisted now, as she moved toward the back door.

Oran and Dara made their way to the door, as Mary undid the bolt and the latch and pulled it open for them slowly. They all stepped outside into the chilly air and Dara helped Oran mount his horse once again, noticing with some concern that the sky was just beginning to turn blue toward the east as he asked, "Are you sure that you have the sword now, Oran? We'll be needing that, no doubt."

"Yes, Dara. I have the sword, don't worry," Oran replied, dryly.

Dara then turned and faced Mary as she walked to him and threw her arms around his neck, pleading, "Stay safe, my dear. Be sure to return home to me and the girls - I'll be waiting, and so will they." She then asked, "Do you both have food to last you your journey?"

"I will, don't fret and yes, we have ample food and water," he said, reassuringly, then let out a loud whistle for Holly to join them from her place of warmth inside the house. Mary released him from her embrace and stepped back slightly, as Holly joined him at his feet. Content that they were ready to set off, Dara climbed up into his saddle as he said to Mary, "Don't worry now. I shall see you in a few days, my love. Take care of yourself and the girls in the meanwhile."

"You too, both of you," she replied, fighting back tears as she thought to herself that he had never before been gone for more than half a day.

Not liking good-byes very much, he gave Mary a final nod as he turned his horse and set off into the still moonlit field at the back of the house, followed closely by Oran and Holly. Mary stood watching from the doorway, as she released the tears which she had been fighting, and they now streamed down her cheeks. Dara painfully resisted the urge to look back, as Mary went inside and closed the door behind her, sobbing as she did so.

As they made their way east across the field in silence, Dara pondered which way to go from here, as there were now only two of three options available to them. They had already ruled out one option of going through the village and via the main routes, owing to the fact that Oran, of course, had to be kept hidden, secret. This left him the choice of either the Glenarran bog or the much-feared Witch's Forest, as it was called by the locals. The bog would be a treacherous choice, especially in the near darkness, as the ground was very soft in many places and there was a very real danger of losing the horses there if they sank in too far, whereas the ground in the forest would be firmer and safer. The forest, however, was the subject of many a chilling tale - tales of strange noises and strange happenings in the night, and even tales of a few people who had ventured in there and mysteriously disappeared, never to be seen or heard from again. As they reached the end of the field, he stopped and turned to Oran, who now drew alongside him with Holly at his side.

"I think it best we make our route through the forest, Oran. It is likely to be safer, I believe - or *safest*," he corrected. Pointing in the direction of the forest off in front, he now thought confidently to himself that Oran's unique abilities would protect them from any form of danger they might encounter whilst they were in there, hopefully.

"Yes, well, I'm completely at your mercy, as I have no idea which way is which, so lead on, good man," Oran declared, as his eyes carefully scanned the dark forest that lay only a few fields length ahead of them now.

"Right then, settled. Let's go," Dara urged, without actually moving.

"Yes, I agree. Let's get going," Oran replied, but also did not move.

"So, let's go then," Dara said again, as he looked at Oran with a nod toward the trees.

"I'm following you, Dara, remember? What's the matter? Are you scared?"

"Not at all. Well... maybe a little - aren't you? I've heard bad stories about this forest - people going in there and not coming back, and the like. The locals call it the Witch's Forest," he answered in somber honesty.

"I'm sure we shall be fine. I have the sword, remember?" Oran reassured him.

Dara looked down at the sword by Oran's side, feeling somehow comforted by its presence, then smiled falsely as he coaxed his horse onward, checking that his knife was also still by his belt. Some time later, as they reached the edge of the forest, they noticed that the trees and shrubs were so densely crowded that there appeared to be no way in and so, without discussion, they turned right and followed the tree line along for a bit. It wasn't long, fortunately, before they discovered a gap in the trees that was large enough to permit them access to the forest, and where they now made their way in cautiously, staying silent as they could be.

They travelled through the woods for a while, to the sounds of branches creaking in the breeze, for what seemed to Oran like ages. They were still saying nothing in an effort not to attract any unwanted attention, when suddenly, an owl cried out, startling Oran.

"What was that?" Oran whispered, in a more than slightly concerned tone.

"Just a wise old owl on the hunt, Oran. Nothing for you to worry about," Dara responded reassuringly, as he continued leading the way, slowly and cautiously through the dense forest ahead. Every now and then, either Dara or Oran would flinch or gasp slightly, as an occasional branch seemed to reach out periodically and stroke either's arm as they passed.

Sunrise was soon upon them, which was, in a way, somewhat of a blessing to them, as they could actually see more clearly where they were going now. Oran noticed that the trees were extremely tall in this area, and obviously very old, as the path which they followed now widened into a fairly large clearing. Dara drew his horse to a halt in the middle of the clearing and Oran rode up beside him.

"Why have we stopped?" Oran enquired, looking slightly puzzled.

"I'm thirsty. I need a drink and I want to get my bearings now that it is getting light," came Dara's answer, as he rummaged in the bags for a flask of water.

"Ah, I see," responded Oran, as he watched Dara eagerly drink from the flask, then offer it to him, with a gasp, when he had finished.

"Would you like some water?" Dara asked, as he held the flask out to Oran and wiped his mouth with his sleeve.

Before Oran had a chance to answer, however, he was taken completely by surprise as a strong gust of wind came out of nowhere, almost dislodging him from his horse, and snatched the flask from Dara's grip, hurling it to the ground. Oran clung to his saddle fiercely, and both he and Dara stared intently as the dead brown leaves, which carpeted the forest floor, lifted into the air and swirled madly around them as the wind grew stronger and began to howl. Holly darted underneath Dara's horse for cover and crouched down on her belly, as the leaves spun around them wildly in a circle, now separating them from the rest of the forest. They sat there in the middle of the clearing, observing the strange circumstance with some concern, and over the noise of the howling wind, Dara yelled out, "This looks bad, Oran... very bad!" to which Oran nodded his head repeatedly in agreement, with a somewhat worried look on his youthful face. He then eased his grip on his saddle somewhat, noticing now that it had become almost completely calm in the middle of this phenomenon, where they currently both sat.

The pair watched on curiously as the leaves continued to circle them at the outer edge of the clearing, forming what seemed to be a rather tall barrier between them and the rest of the forest. Round and round the leaves whizzed, faster than the eye could follow, then suddenly and without warning, came to an abrupt halt and just hung there in mid-air, forming a great wall that surrounded them and stretched some twenty to thirty feet upwards. All fell silent again as Dara gave Oran a bemused look, before cautiously riding over to the wall of leaves and putting the palm of his hand carefully against it. He pushed with all his might, then turned to Oran and gasped.

"It's as solid as stone. We're trapped, Oran!"

Oran, again, did not get a chance to reply, as the leaves that remained on the forest floor within the confines of this new prison now rose slowly into the air and spun themselves into a large, spherical shape. This sphere was slightly taller than his horse and sat just to his front, and a few yards away, revolving slowly. The pair watched in amazement for a moment as the leaves then whizzed and zig-zagged themselves round and round, in and out, before coming to a halt as they miraculously began forming themselves into the shape of a large deer, which then proceeded to be covered in a layer of pine needles to resemble deer hair, it seemed. The leaves, or deer, now took a delicate step toward Oran, then stopped and looked at him silently. It regarded him with big brown eyes, made from two large chestnuts, for a brief moment, before saying in a deep, booming male voice, "I am Arak - forest guardian, keeper and protector of all that you see here. I sense that you are not of mortal man, although he is." It glanced in the direction of Dara, before swinging its great head back to face Oran, and continued, "I should like to ask who is it that you are and where are you come from?

What brings you here, in this forest, my forest? What is your business here?"

"Talking deer now, made of leaves, no less," Dara whispered to himself, shaking his head slowly, as he watched Oran straighten himself up in his saddle in preparation to address the entity now stood in front of him.

"I am Oran of the people of Danu, noble Arak. My friend and I mean you no harm, and we merely seek safe passage through your forest, should you be so kind as to permit it," Oran announced proudly and confidently, hoping all the while that this would end well for himself and, of course, for his companions.

"Nonsense, boy! Danu are all gone, many years since. I do sense magic though, albeit an odd magic, as though there is... a conflict within you... a strange conflict," said Arak, shaking his head, almost as though he believed Oran was lying to him. He then demanded, "No-one has seen Danu for centuries young man, you can't possibly be Danu - all are gone. Who is your leader... sent you hither?"

"King Lugh leads us, as he has done for centuries. We, the Danu, have hidden ourselves on the mountain nearby, to the north, for the past three hundred years. This is why no-one has seen us, but I can assure you that we do exist, and I am here before you as proof now," Oran claimed, as he slowly pulled the sword of light from its scabbard to show it to Arak, holding it aloft as he asked, "What is it that you refer to when you say that you sense a conflict within me?"

Arak chose to ignore the question and immediately bowed his head upon seeing the sword, then looked up and solemnly said to Oran, "'Tis truly the Sword of

Light, sword of the commanders of dragons, wielded by King Lugh himself. I myself fought beside your King Lugh during the last great battle waged against the Danu, all those many years ago. A battle in which he carried that very sword, as my good people went to his aid. Sadly, all was to no avail though, as we all suffered a great many losses and were ultimately defeated. That battle, in fact, is the very reason why I stand here before you now, trapped in this forest for all eternity."

Feeling the need to explain his existence there, he went on to say, "Mortally wounded in battle, you see, and sole survivor of my noble clan, as I endeavoured to make my way home, I fell from my horse here, in this very clearing. As I lay upon this ground, strength ebbing and my blood seeping into the forest floor - dying alone as I thought - a strange woman appeared by my side and whispered to me, *"If you give to me your soul, your services, I will preserve you for all time, here in this place. You shall exist for all eternity, to serve me. I can save you."*

Severely weakened and not wishing to perish, of course, I quickly agreed and she, the witch of the forest as I later learned, cast a spell that took my soul and trapped me here as servant - the servant that guards her forest and all that lies and lives within it. As my mortal body took its last, dying breath, the very last thing I saw as my eyes closed was a magnificent white hart that watched me from nearby. I found it a wondrous and pleasing sight, hence the reason I chose this form to appear before you now, although I may choose any form that I wish. Anyway, enough about me. My sincerest apologies, Sire, for doubting. I am humbly at your service."

"What conflict, Arak?" asked Oran again, slightly impatiently, choosing to almost ignore Arak's tale of how he came to be here, as he was growing more concerned by the remark about the conflict within him.

"Ah, I cannot say as certain. Although, I sense that there is something not quite right, as though two people - two very different personalities or entities - share the same body, your body, that is," Arak tried to explain, as he added, "It is not important, neither here nor there."

Dara observed in silence as the exchange between Oran and Arak took place, not wishing to interrupt or say anything that might endanger this newfound friendship. He beckoned Holly to his side with a muffled *psssttt* and jumped down from his horse to stroke her back, as he continued to watch them.

"How odd. I don't feel such a conflict and, although it causes me some concern at the minute, we have more pressing business to attend to presently. We need safe passage, as I've said, through your forest, my friend. That is all I ask of you, for now. We are on our way to the mountain of Slemish in search of the dragon Rydian. Have you heard of her, perhaps?" Oran now asked.

"Heard of her? But of course I have. As I said before, I fought with Lugh by his side - Rydian was there also. She and Lugh were great allies, great friends," Arak stated proudly.

"Yes, but that was a very long time ago. Have you heard anything of her whereabouts recently though?" Oran enquired, more precisely.

"Ah, recently, well… no. She has not shown herself for many a year, I'm afraid," the great deer responded honestly, realising that Oran held high hopes for confirmation of Rydian's current whereabouts.

Oran lowered his head in disappointment, then said, "We have been instructed by the King that she most probably hides out on the mountain - the old volcano that is called Slemish, in the east. Would you be so kind as to allow us safe passage through your forest, in the direction of the river that runs to the sea in the north? Those are the directions, the instructions, that were given to us by the King."

"Of course, my friend, of course. Do you wish to go now, this minute?" Arak enquired, as though wanting Oran to remain with him for a while.

"We *are* in somewhat of hurry. We seek Rydian with some urgency as we need her help. The King needs her help," Oran urged.

"Oh! What manner of help? What does the King require of her, might I ask?" Arak asked, curiously now.

"I'm afraid that I know not of the details, merely that I have been sent on the orders of the King to find her, and to ask her to come to him," Oran replied carefully, not sure if he could entirely trust this creature that stood before him.

"And what of your companion, the human? How does he come to join you on this mission?" Arak continued to question.

"He is my guide, sought out and tasked by the King to take me safely to Slemish and back," came Oran's thoughtful response, as he was fearful of putting Dara in peril, being more than a little wary of the true purpose of Araks persistent questioning.

Arak looked at Oran thoughtfully for a moment then said, "Very well, my good friend, so be it. Your wish is my bidding. Now, let me think... which way to the river? Ah yes, that way, I'm certain," he said, as he turned his head to look in roughly the same direction in which Oran was currently facing, then proceeded to turn his whole body to face that way also.

Oran sat astride his horse while this took place, marveling at the detail on the deer's body - detail that had been created by nothing more than old, dead leaves and pine needles. Even his very antlers, some eight or nine feet across, were intricately formed with almost immaculate detail. The great stag then stretched his neck out as he raised his snout high into the air and began to emit a low, sort of humming noise for a few seconds, before stopping and closing his eyes briefly. As soon as he stopped making the noise, the wall of leaves which surrounded them simply fell apart, and the leaves fluttered to the ground again, to which Dara breathed an audible sigh of relief and stood up. Dara mounted his horse and drew up by Oran's side saying, "Let's get going, Oran, while we still can."

"Wait! Have not finished yet!" bellowed Arak on hearing this.

Oran and Dara, almost scared to move now by this outburst, watched intently as Arak raised his snout high in the air again and began to emit a similar humming sound, followed by a loud snort from his nostrils. As Arak lowered his head again, still looking to his front, he simply said, "Your pathway awaits, my friends."

Oran and Dara watched intently and quietly, in surprise, as the huge trees ahead of them began to move and glide apart noiselessly, an occasional leaf fluttering silently to the forest floor as they parted. They seemed to slide their roots through the earth, as though they were moving through nothing more than water, as they moved aside slowly to clear a path wide enough for

Oran and Dara to easily pass through, right through the entire forest to its perimeter.

"Impressive magic, my friend Arak," Oran declared, loudly.

"Not so, Oran. You see, the forest is alive, a living thing by all accounts - all of it. As its guardian and protector, I need only ask of it that which I require or need, as I have just now done, and it will do so for me... but *only* for me," Arak explained, as he turned to face Oran once more.

"I should like to say that it was nice to meet you, and thank you for your help, my friend," Oran said politely, as he and Dara prepared to set off again, adding, "Perhaps we shall meet again some other time, and you can explain this conflict which you sense in me - in the future, perhaps."

"Possibly, but not so fast, young Danu, for I shall accompany you and your companions to the forest's edge," Arak insisted, then suddenly, let out a little gasp as he noticed, for the first time, the band adorning Oran's right wrist, enquiring of him, "That bracelet on your right wrist, tell me how it is that you come to possess it? Do you know what it is?"

"It's just an old bracelet. I was found wearing it when I was first discovered by the Danu, outside their castle," Oran told Arak, then continued to briefly explain the history of how and where he was found.

Arak stepped closer, his nose only inches from Oran's face, then advised, "Not just a bracelet. It is one of two talismans - a pair, in fact. The talismans of Ethioné. Together, they enable the wearer to wield unimaginable power - power greater than any magician or sorcerer alive, or who has ever lived - but only together, as a pair.

Their creator, or rather owner, is in possession of the other, if I am not mistaken. I am sure that I am also not mistaken when I say that he has most definitely been searching for the one that is on your arm for as long as you have had it, and that you are in *very* great danger here, as he dwells in a cave on a hillside not far from here, and is someone that you would most definitely not like to meet. I fear I may now know how it is that it comes to be in your possession, but there is no time to explain and we must hurry. You must go now, *immediately*."

"Explain what? Arak, tell me, what is it?" Oran pleaded.

"No time, Oran. You must go if you value your life and the lives of your companions. I will simply say that if Aradone, the talismans' creator and owner, and an extremely malevolent character, senses either your presence or that of the talisman, which I am sure he can, then I am just as sure that he will come for you - for it. If he does come for it, he will stop at nothing to acquire it, killing both you and your companions in the process, no doubt. Now, we *must* go!" Arak roared, as he began strutting toward the cleared pathway which he had made for them.

"You must tell me what you know, Arak, please," Oran begged, as he and Dara urged the horses to follow the large deer, who was now moving at a brisk pace ahead of them.

As they made the journey along the cleared pathway to the edge of the forest, Oran rode alongside Arak in silence, with Dara and Holly close behind. He felt that Arak would stubbornly continue to ignore his pleas for information, should he persist in asking questions about why or how he came to have the talisman, and so, kept silent. It wasn't out of stubbornness, however, that Arak refused to divulge this information, but more in an effort to protect Oran from the knowledge he possessed as to his true origins, and who he suspected Oran really was - that he was not *just* a Danu.

As they reached the forest's edge, Arak stopped and turned to face them, saying, "This, I'm afraid, is as far as I am permitted to go, my friends, as I am bound to stay within the forest. I must say good-bye to you here and wish you all a safe and good journey onward."

"I understand," replied Oran, before asking, "May I ask one last thing of you, Arak?"

"Quickly well, and it depends what you ask," the deer responded, hastily.

"Tell me, what power does this talisman hold on its own, separated from the other?" Oran enquired.

"It holds the power to overcome, or defeat, the spells of others; to shield you; and will slightly enhance the existing powers or abilities of the wearer - you, in this case. You should, by wearing it, be impervious to the spells of others, whether they be good or bad magic. Now, you really must get going - you are in very grave danger hereabouts," Arak advised, urgently.

"One more question, please. It is of great importance," Oran implored.

"Very well. Last question though - time runs out for us," Arak responded, becoming a little frustrated now.

"How do I take it off, or remove it? Others at the castle, in the past, have tried to remove it, but none have succeeded," Oran enquired.

"Ha, ha, Oran, my boy," Arak laughed heartily, before quickly continuing, "As its current wearer, you need only ask it, my dear fellow - that is all. Now, you must go, quickly."

Oran and Dara thanked Arak again and said their goodbyes, as they turned and set off across the field in search of the river. After a few yards, Oran twisted round in his saddle to wave a final farewell to Arak, only to see a large quantity of leaves settling gently to the ground where the great stag had stood just a moment before. He faced to his front again as he rode alongside Dara and Holly, concentrating now on the journey ahead, as he said, "Well, that was a rather interesting experience, I have to say."

Dara didn't answer but simply smiled, feeling that Oran was now somewhat upset by things which he had, or rather, hadn't learned during the encounter with Arak, as they continued away from the trees and toward the morning sun in the east.

Both of them were unaware of the fact that a rather sinister looking figure in a long, black, hooded cloak was now watching them intently, quietly... concealed by the dark shadows just inside the tree line of the forest which they had just left.

CHAPTER TEN
The Veil of Mist

Oran and Dara made their way steadily east, across the field from the forest which they had just left, the forest where they had met a new friend and possibly a new ally in the form of Arak. They fought their way through the thick hedgerow at its end and into the next field, closely followed by Holly who was greatly enjoying this new walk with its new sights and smells, regardless of the many pieces of bramble that were now entangled in her long fur. As they emerged into this next field, Dara slowly raised his head to the sky, looking for the low morning sun. Finding it quickly, he once more set off silently in its direction, toward the east again, with Oran and Holly close behind, in search of the river.

As they made their way across this field, however, a chilly mist began to slowly descend upon them. At first, it caused them no alarm, as it was quite thin and presented no real problem for them, but as they continued onward, the mist grew thicker over time, heavier, becoming so dense over the course of the next thirty minutes or so that they could barely see each other, let alone where they were headed. Dara stopped his horse just ahead of Oran and turned in the saddle to face his companion.

"I think we had best tether ourselves - the horses, I mean - together, lest we get separated in this murk. I can barely see you now when you are but a few feet from me, so I think it may be wise, do you agree?"

"Yes, yes. I think that is an excellent idea and I also think it would be wise to tether Holly to one of the horses also, otherwise we stand a good chance that we may lose her too," Oran advised, as he stopped alongside Dara.

"Yes, of course, that was part of my plan also," Dara quickly responded, as he began to rummage in the bag that hung to the left side of his saddle in search of the rope he had seen there the night before as they were preparing to set off from the castle. He removed the rope from the bag and jumped down from his horse to find Holly by his feet, thankfully. Kneeling beside her, he set the rope on the ground next to her as he placed a hand on her back and rubbed it affectionately, whispering, "Always by my side, eh, girl? What would I do without you? Good girl, eh?"

Holly leaned in close to him and began to lick the side of his face, to which Dara laughed briefly, wiping his cheek with a sleeve that was already dampened by the mist. He put both arms around her and gave her an affectionate hug. Quickly, he grabbed the rope again and stood up as he began to uncoil it, measuring with his feet as he laid it out along the ground. When he had finished measuring, he looked up at Oran and remarked,

"Plenty long enough. I was slightly worried that it wouldn't be. I'll cut it in two and use one half to secure Holly to my horse, and the other half to tether our horses together. That should ensure that we don't get lost - well, separated, at least. We might still get lost in this, but safe to say if one gets lost, we all get lost together, right?"

"True, very true, but hopefully we will not get lost. Let's do that then, and quickly please, as we do need to keep moving," Oran suggested, shivering from the biting cold that was penetrating his clothing by this stage. Not only was he extremely cold now, but his clothes were becoming unpleasantly damp, as the mist continued to adhere and soak into them.

"Yes, yes, right away, of course," Dara responded, eagerly. He worked as fast as he could, having noticed that the mist - or rather, fog - had begun to freeze on the fur near the end of Holly's tail, which now caused him some concern.

With his right hand, he took his hunting knife out of its sheath and reached down for the rope, grasping it about half way along its length. He picked it up and folded the rope over, at its mid-point, into a sort of small loop which he then slid the blade of his knife into and began slicing through eagerly. The blade was keen and, seconds later, the rope became two pieces as he had intended, which he quickly placed back on the ground by his feet. He then slid his knife back into its sheath as he stood upright.

Dara then knelt beside Holly again and, with his right hand, searched through her thick fur for the make-shift collar she always wore, even though she hadn't been on a leash for a couple of years, reaching at the same time for one of the lengths of rope by his knee with his other hand. Finding both simultaneously, he began feeding the end of the rope through Holly's collar and tied it into a secure knot. He then stood up and swiftly secured the other end of the rope, with a similar knot, to his saddle.

"Right then, that's Holly secured. Now for the horses," he announced, somewhat proud of his achievements thus far.

"Quickly, please," was all Oran could say, as his teeth were now chattering from the cold.

Dara nodded and hastily set about tying the horses together with the remaining length of rope. When he was finished, he climbed back up into his saddle and turned to Oran as he said, "Let's get to that river and make camp. We need to make a fire and get you and Holly warmed up before you both freeze to death, my friend. This cursed mist is freezing on her fur already."

"Yes, great idea," Oran murmured through gritted teeth.

As they set off again, Dara glanced skyward. The sun was no longer clearly visible through the thick fog and even though he believed he was headed in the same direction as before - the direction of the rising sun - he was actually now headed in a more south-easterly direction due to the fact that neither himself nor Oran had noticed that his horse had shuffled, or shifted, slightly around to its right as he had worked on securing Holly and the horses together with the ropes.

"Are you sure we are headed in the right direction, Dara? I can't see anything - apart from the back end of your horse, that is," Oran called out, more than a little worried that they were already slightly lost.

"Well, in all honesty, I can only guess that we are, as I believe that I'm heading in the same direction as we were, before we stopped and lost sight of the sun in this mist. I certainly hope we are," Dara called back, as he looked to the sky which was now mostly just a dazzling white haze of illuminated moisture, as the sunlight glared through the dense fog.

Oran did not respond, as he was now so cold that he just wanted to find warmth somewhere - to curl up in a ball somewhere and go to sleep, preferably until this ordeal was over with. He could now feel almost agonising pain in his toes and fingers due to the fierce cold, which he was entirely unaccustomed to and which he very much disliked now. He had never experienced cold like this in his life before, owing to the fact that the ambient temperature inside the time cocoon, due to its magical powers, had never been less than about twenty degrees centigrade, even in winter. This had been the case for all the time that it had been in existence - until yesterday, that was.

He told himself inwardly that, as a direct result of his negligence, the other inhabitants of the castle must also surely be suffering in the winter cold, as he was. Suddenly, he felt an overwhelming sensation of guilt, which was swiftly followed by the sensation of sorrow, and then by remorse. He felt somewhat helpless, as he lowered his head and stared at his reddened fingers which clung to the horn of his saddle, almost weeping from the pain and sorrow he was now experiencing. He had never felt either of these things before today.

They carried on blindly across the thickly shrouded landscape in near silence for several very long hours, regardless of the cold and fog. They crossed an endless number of fields and hedgerows, it seemed, in the desperate hope that they would reach the river at any moment. The veil of mist stayed with them relentlessly as they travelled onward, as much as Dara had hoped that it would lift at some point - but sadly for them, it didn't. And so, heading for what he believed was the brightest part of the sky above, where the sun must surely be, he carried on leading the way, again almost blindly, in the hope that it was the right way - but it wasn't even close to being the right way. For all he knew, they could have been going around in circles all this time, as everything looked almost exactly the same in this dreadful fog.

"We have to stop, Dara!" Oran cried out, suddenly. "I can no longer feel my hands, nor my feet," he almost sobbed in sufferance, for he had reached the point where he was now so cold that he felt nauseous and felt as though he were about to pass out at any moment, to lose all consciousness.

Dara sighed wearily and reluctantly brought his horse to a halt, allowing Oran to come alongside him.

"We need to stop and make a fire, Dara. I can't do this anymore. I'm too cold and I am not accustomed to these temperatures - these conditions. I need warmth and food, now, please," Oran whimpered, desperately.

"Just a little farther, Oran, please. We must keep going, to find the river. Can you last just a while longer, perhaps?" Dara implored.

"How *much* farther, Dara? We've been on the move for hours and there's no sign of a river - not even a stream. We are hopelessly lost, I fear. I think we should take shelter, and make camp 'til this clears. We could be anywhere now, after all - who knows where - do you?" Oran exclaimed.

"To the end of the next field, and if we haven't found the river by then, we'll stop and make camp, yes?" Dara suggested, hopefully.

"The end... of the next... field, no farther. You... give me... your word... on that?" Oran demanded, through chattering teeth.

"Yes, Oran, I promise. You have my word on it," Dara responded, somewhat reluctantly. He wanted to keep going, to get this over with and return home to his beloved family, but he now feared that Oran was becoming ill due to the freezing temperatures, so knew in his mind that it would be best to stop and get him warmed up again. The burden of a sickly companion was more trouble than he needed at this present time, he carefully reminded himself.

"Good, let's get going then. The sooner we... reach the edge... of this field... the happier... I shall be," Oran remarked with some difficulty, as they set off through the long, icy grass again, and towards the next hedgerow.

Some moments later, however, Dara noticed that the horses' hooves sounded oddly as though they were now traversing something akin to gravel, rather than the soft grass which they had been crossing all day up until this point. With mild concern, he looked downward immediately. Below them now, as they headed down a gradual slope, he could just make out in the murk what did, indeed, appear to be a brownish-grey gravel instead of grass.

"Stop!" he exclaimed. "Something is amiss, I fear. Never have I encountered a field where there is only bare gravel under foot. 'Tis rather peculiar, I think. I suggest that we proceed very slowly, and very carefully. I'll lead, of course."

Oran simply nodded his agreement, too cold to speak, and proceeded to slowly follow Dara as he now led on, very cautiously, peering carefully ahead and downward all the while. A moment later and Dara suddenly stopped again, as he said with a tone of excitement, "There's water here, Oran! My horse is standing in water!" He quickly climbed down from his horse to investigate his new findings, feet splashing into the shallow water below.

Dara now found himself, somewhat happily, standing in several inches of water, very cold water, and correctly assumed that they had reached a shoreline or river bank of some description. But which shoreline could it be? Due to the thick fog, he couldn't see much more than ten feet out and at first, he thought - or rather, he desperately hoped - that it might be the river which they sought out. However, he quickly realised, as he watched the water gently lap at the gravel, that these were more likely the still waters of a lake, perhaps. It was obvious that they were not the waters of a fast-flowing river, such as the river they were in search of, as there was also no sound of flowing water that he would expect to hear were he now stood by a fairly large river. This struck him as odd, since even the waters of the little stream just outside his house produced a fair amount of noise as it worked its way past on its journey to wherever. He thought for a minute, without speaking, and then looked up at Oran, who was now regarding him with an expression of apprehension.

"What is it, Dara? What have you found?" Oran asked, hopefully.

"I... er... think we may be a little lost, my friend." Dara forced the answer, knowing only too well that Oran would be more than a little annoyed.

"Well, that comes as no surprise really, all things considered. Nevertheless, my good friend, this will do. We shall make camp here for the night and hopefully this cursed fog will have cleared by morning, whereby we can get our bearings and continue on our way - the correct way, that is," Oran instructed rather confidently, as he climbed down from his horse and began to scour the immediate vicinity in search of a reasonably dry, level area where they could set up camp and spend the night in relative comfort. Dara watched as Oran, now walking somewhat stiffly, hunted around the area in the thick fog for several moments, before turning to Dara and declaring, "Over here is best, I believe. It's far enough from the waters' edge, and fairly level. There is a tree here where we can tether the horses safely. I'll make a fire, shall I?"

"By all means, a fire would be wonderful," Dara enthused, as he untied Holly. "Why are you walking like that, might I ask? You look a little... odd, stiff, dare I say," he then enquired with mild amusement, knowing too well the answer that would come, before continuing eagerly, "I'll gather some wood to help get the fire going."

"Walking like what? Oh! Well, if you must know, my poor backside is somewhat sore from being in that saddle for so long. It's not something that I do very often - horse riding, I mean," Oran remarked with mild embarrassment, vigorously rubbing his rear with both hands, then asked, "Wood? What for?"

"For the fire, of course," Dara declared.

"Now you're thinking like a human again, understandably, and not like a Danu. We don't need wood for this fire, Dara - just a little bit of Danu magic. Now, right there should be just perfect," Oran laughed, as he extended his arms out with the palms of his hands aimed at the spot he had chosen, just a few yards away, where the gravel ended and met the grass, near the tree which he intended to tie the horses to.

"*Altur bakhala, lasaria aradua, lasaria aradua,*" Oran began to chant, as Dara watched in anticipation.

Once again, the all too familiar tiny blue lightning bolts appeared, emanating from his sleeves and snaking and crackling along the backs of his small, frost reddened hands to his fingertips, as Oran concentrated and continued with the spell. He turned the palms of his hands slowly upwards and as he did so, a tiny orange ball of light, approximately the size of an apple, appeared from nowhere and hovered over them, illuminating his face with an orange glow. Dara continued to watch, amazed as ever, as the little lightning bolts seemed to enter the ball of light, and it changed from orange to crimson red in colour. Next, the glowing ball sprouted tiny flames before shooting off toward the gravel covered ground where Oran had directed it to and burst, with a loud whooshing noise, into a roaring fire that reached some two or three feet in height.

"Well now, that ought to keep us warm, no doubt," Dara remarked with some amusement, watching the flames dance as they hovered magically a few inches above the bare gravel, before thoughtfully asking, "Can we cook on that?"

"Certainly, we can, and I fully intend to do so, just as soon as I can feel my fingers and toes again. What would you like to eat, my good friend Dara?" Oran asked, as they both gratefully approached the fire to warm themselves.

Dara didn't respond right away, as he was presently more interested in drying his clothes and heating himself up. It wasn't too long before Holly had worked her way in between them, determined to warm herself up also. She lay down by their feet on the already drying gravel, stretched herself out and yawned sleepily. It had been a long and tiresome day for her and she was now very weary, and very hungry, as she lay basking in the heat of the magical flames that floated strangely in mid-air nearby. She hoped that soon, there might be some food for her, and thought that it was just a matter of time. She need only be patient and wait for her master to provide, as always.

After a brief while spent warming themselves by the fire, having dried their clothes and thawed their frozen fingers and toes, Oran and Dara set about rummaging through the saddle bags in search of food, and something to use as adequate bedding for the night. The fire had done an excellent job of drying out the ground for several yards around it, which was good news for all of them, as no-one relished the thought of having to sleep on cold, wet ground.

They tied their horses to the tree near the fire, then took some furs and blankets from the saddle bags and set about spreading them out on the ground near the fire to form makeshift beds, before sitting down to begin cooking some meats, which they had also taken from one of the bags tethered to Oran's horse. Oran watched in silence as Dara carefully used his hunting knife to hold the meat close enough to the fire to cook slowly. When the first piece was ready, he tore a small part off with finger and thumb, blowing on it briefly, which he then reached to Holly who was waiting anxiously at his side, before turning to offer the remainder of it to Oran, as he said with a smile, "You eat first - I think you are more in need of it than I. I'll have the next piece."

"Are you sure? You don't mind?" Oran asked timidly, reaching gingerly for the piece of meat dangling from the tip of Dara's knife in front of him, a little scared that it might burn his fingers now - fingers that had been nearly frozen just an hour before.

"Hah! Don't worry, Oran. Like I said, I'll have the next piece." He ardently set about impaling another piece of meat on the point of his waiting knife, before offering it to the flames in front of him with a big grin on his face.

When the meat was cooked, he again tore a piece off and offered it to Holly, which she scoffed eagerly in seconds. This made Dara laugh heartily, as he said to her, "Hungry, old girl? You'll feel better now too, I don't doubt. We dine well tonight - venison is a rare treat for you and I."

Holly simply responded by looking at him eagerly, saliva dripping from her tongue, which now dangled from the side of her mouth, as though she wanted more, which, in fact, she did. Oran and Dara continued to eat, savouring every bite in silence for a while longer. When they were finished, Dara stood up and went to his horse to fetch some water, before returning to sit by Oran. As he sat down, he removed the cork and took a healthy swig from the flask. Oran had been very quiet, pensive for some time now, it seemed to Dara. Noticing this, Dara now asked as he reached the flask to him, "What troubles you, master Oran? You've been very quiet, and I feel that something is on your mind. Do you miss your friends and family at the castle?"

Oran looked at Dara momentarily, with bright eyes that reflected the flickering flames of the fire. He took a swig of water and, as he wiped his lips dry, answered thoughtfully, "I miss them, yes, but more importantly, I have many questions since our encounter with Arak in the forest - questions that I must find answers to."

He then stared blankly into the fire as he went on to ask, "What did he mean? Who am I, really? And who is this "malevolent character", Aradone, that he spoke of? Does he know who my parents are, or were? I need to find out somehow, Dara. I must find out who I am, and it seems that he may well know the answers to some, or even all, of these questions."

"Yes, Oran, I can imagine that you must find it very troubling to have been so close to finding answers, but not actually getting any," Dara said with some sympathy, as he stared into the flames while the winter sun began to set behind them.

"When this quest is finished, I must find a way to get back to the forest to find Arak and speak with him again, to get the answers to my questions. It is imperative that I find him again," Oran continued, as he reached out to stroke the top of Holly's head where she lay next to him now.

"It's impossible though, is it not?" Dara frowned, as he added, "Surely once we return to the castle and the time cocoon is re-instated, if we are successful, then neither you nor anyone else will ever be able to leave the castle again, else you will never be able to return to it. That's *my* understanding of how it works, am I wrong?"

Oran looked at him thoughtfully for a second, as though he was uncertain of what he was about to say, then took another gulp of water before placing a hand on Dara's arm, as he said, "I have a theory, Dara - a somewhat wild theory albeit, perhaps. You are most correct in saying that, once one steps outside of the time cocoon, there is certainly no way back in again, but my theory is based on a combination of how I came to be found outside the castle all those years ago, and also, on the limited information provided earlier this day by our new friend Arak, about the bracelet on my arm - this bracelet," setting the flask on the ground and raising his right arm to the light of the fire to show Dara the bracelet, at the same time.

"I'm intrigued - do continue," Dara appealed, with raised eyebrows.

"Well, Arak mentioned that the bracelet allows the wearer - that is me - to overcome the spells or magic of others. What if it were powerful enough to overcome such a magic as the time cocoon which is generated by a dragon crystal? What if that is how I initially came to be within the time cocoon, just outside the castle walls, when I was first discovered by the Danu? No-one has figured this puzzle out before - until now, that is. Surely there is no better explanation?" Oran explained with some excitement, as he continued stroking Holly's soft fur.

Dara looked at him thoughtfully for a few seconds, then asked, "Would you take that risk, Oran? I mean, say that you stepped outside the time cocoon in the belief that the bracelet would allow you to get back in, and it turned out that it didn't. Well, that would be it, no? You'd be stuck forever in a world where you don't really belong, where you don't fit in, with no way to get back to your own people. Would you really take that risk?"

"I think I would, Dara, I really do believe so. It's the only way that I can visit the forest again to speak with Arak and get the answers that I need - to find out who I am, where I came from, and what he meant about a conflict inside me. If worst comes to worst, and I can't get back to the castle, then I could always come and live with you and your family at your house, I suppose," Oran laughed.

"What? Now just hold on a minute. How on earth do you suppose we'd get away with that? What would the locals say?" Dara exclaimed, as he began to stroke his chin thoughtfully. "I suppose, mind you, we could always tell them you're my cousin from far away somewhere - Scotland perhaps. No-one would really know any better and you'd doubtless be very handy to have around, what with your abilities. You'd have to keep those silly ears covered up, mind - they're a bit of dead giveaway!" he grinned.

Oran leant back slightly as he laughed at Dara's jocular comment, then stood up slowly and turned to look at the sunset. The mist had started to lift somewhat, revealing a sky to the west that was now a thousand shades of orange, pink, red and indigo, all mixed together, and he thought that it was the most spectacular thing he had ever witnessed. He stood mesmerised, watching as the sun sank lower, disappearing behind the forest in the distance, appearing to set the silhouetted trees ablaze in a fiery glow as it slowly sank from view. Dara rose to his feet and stood by Oran, as he remarked, "It's truly beautiful, is it not? No two sunsets look the same."

"It is that. Very humbling, also," Oran said softly.

"I hate the winter - it gets dark so early in the day. Too early to go to sleep yet, even though it's almost dark," Dara complained as they watched the sky overhead darken slowly into blackness and fill with a million tiny pinpricks of light that were the stars in the heavens above.

"What do you think lies up there, Dara - out there in the vastness of the heavens?" Oran contemplated, as he gazed upward.

Dara dwelt on the question for a moment, then ruffled his hair with his hand as he answered, "I truthfully have no idea. Does anyone know what lies out there, do you think, Oran? It could be just emptiness, or it could be more - much more. I don't know, honestly."

"Neither do I, Dara. The Danu believe that there are other civilisations out there - worlds that may in some ways be similar to ours, this world. Who knows, indeed?" Oran added, then quickly said, "Anyway, back to my theory about my bracelet."

"Yes, yes, the bracelet," Dara nodded, eagerly. "Do carry on."

"Well, I need to test what Arak said of its protective powers, this... protection of its wearer that he spoke of. That means getting it off me and onto you, my friend," Oran said, guardedly, wondering how Dara might feel about the impending statement. "After we attach it to you, I'll cast some minor spell on you, to find out if the bracelet - or talisman, if we call it by its correct name - does indeed protect the wearer."

"What?" Dara blurted out, as he glared at Oran now with his mouth slightly open and his eyebrows raised. "Cast a spell on me? What spell? You're not going to turn me into something horrible - not a chance! What if it doesn't work - the bracelet, that is - and you then can't undo your own spell? What then? I'll be stuck, that's what. I'm not having it! I won't allow it and I won't be your magical guinea pig. No sir."

"Calm down, Dara. You're overreacting now," Oran assured him. "It will only be something simple like... I'll make it rain on your head, for example, but only on your head. I'm not going to change or alter you in any physical way. Did you think that I was going to turn you into a mouse, or something equally as ridiculous? Come now, please. I'm not a parlour magician."

"You swear to me? No harm?" Dara insisted.

"I swear. No harm will come to you," Oran reassured him, then continued, "But first, I need to figure out what Arak meant about getting the bracelet off me. He said that, as its current wearer, all I need do is ask it. What did he mean exactly, I wonder?"

"I haven't the faintest idea, Oran," Dara said, as he continued gazing at the stars. He then flatly suggested, "Try asking it, just as Arak said."

Oran looked at him briefly, then directed his attention downward to the talisman, as he thought for a second. He raised his right arm, holding the bracelet up to eye level in the glow of the firelight, whilst staring intently at it, and said, "Bracelet off," but nothing happened, and so he continued, "Talisman off," but still, nothing happened.

"Keep trying. Say something different. Maybe you have to use a particular word, or sequence of words," Dara advised, as he turned his attention to Oran and the bracelet now.

Oran then released a string of different commands – "Release ... Release me bracelet, let go of me, free me talisman," and carried on, trying different phrases for what seemed like several minutes, but all to no avail. The bracelet remained firmly attached to his elevated wrist. He lowered his arm back down by his side, released a long sigh, then looked up at the night sky as he said, "Tell me how. How do I make it come off?" as he searched his memory for the name which Arak had said. It came to him swiftly, after just a moment of searching - Ethioné! That was it - Ethioné.

"How do I make the talisman of Ethioné release me, please?" he pleaded to the starlit sky above.

Suddenly, the bracelet glowed with a soft blue light by his side, dimly at first - but Oran hadn't noticed yet. Dara did though, and nudged Oran's arm excitedly, as he almost shouted, "Oran, look! Look at your arm! The bracelet - it's glowing!"

Oran quickly looked down, just as the bracelet unclasped itself and fell to the ground with a muffled sort of clinking sound, as it landed on the bare gravel. He quickly stooped to pick it up, then held it up in front of his face as he stared at it. The bracelet was still unclasped, and he wondered now as to exactly which words had done the trick, as he had said so many different things in his efforts to get it to come off.

"You did it," Dara rejoiced. "But how? What did you say to it exactly? How did you make it come off?"

"I'm not entirely sure," came Oran's murmur as, to Dara, he now seemed a little distracted and somewhat amazed that he had actually succeeded in removing it. "That is the first time that this bracelet has been off my arm in something like a hundred years."

"You almost sound relieved. You need to figure out how you did it though, before you put it on me, otherwise I might be wearing it forever, possibly," Dara advised, before quickly adding, "Think Oran. What was the last thing you said to it?" noticing that the bracelet had now stopped glowing.

"I said..." Oran began, then paused as he thought momentarily, trying to recall his last words. "I said, 'How do I make the talisman of Ethioné release me, please?' That was the very last thing I said, I'm sure of it."

Again, the bracelet glowed, the soft blue light engulfing Oran's hand, as Dara almost shouted at him in his enthusiasm, "Quickly, put it back on your wrist and then try again. We need to be absolutely certain that you've got the words right, Oran. There can be no mistakes - no mistakes at all."

Oran waited a moment until the bracelet stopped glowing again, then looked at Dara apprehensively. Dara regarded him with a mixture of excitement and urgency, then said, "Quickly, Oran. Put it on again, then say the words."

Oran slowly offered the open bracelet up to his wrist and, as it made contact with his skin, it quickly closed and clasped itself shut. They both gasped and stared at the bracelet in awe, as if it were some newfound, magical device. Oran then took a step backwards, away from Dara, as though something bad, or perhaps dangerous, were about to happen.

"Let's test the theory then, shall we?" Oran almost whispered.

"Yes, yes, let's," Dara hurried. "Say the words."

"I think it's just the 'Ethioné release me, please' part that makes it happen," Oran began to say, but no sooner had he uttered the words than the bracelet began to glow again. A few seconds later, it fell off his wrist and onto the gravel once more. He bent down and picked it up again, then gave Dara a big grin.

Dara took a pace toward him and urged, "Again. One more time. We need to be certain, please. This time say only the necessary words - nothing more," Dara insisted, as *he* now took a pace backward, away from Oran.

When the bracelet stopped glowing a moment later, Oran offered it up to his wrist again and, once more, it willingly attached itself to him. He beamed with delight as he looked at Dara, carefully and slowly repeating the words, "Ethioné release me, please."

Dara stared in anticipation, and sure enough, the blue glow appeared again, followed seconds later by the bracelet releasing itself as before, and falling to the ground yet again. Dara began jumping up and down on the spot like an excited child for a moment, then laughed raucously.

"We figured it out - we really did. It appears that Arak knows a thing or two, my young friend - er, *old* friend, I mean."

"Indeed, it would," Oran said, stooping to pick up the bracelet once more, before offering it to Dara. "Your turn now, good fellow."

"Ah... yes. I was worried that you were going to suggest that next. Do we have to, really?" Dara asked, more than a little concerned for his own safety.

"Yes, we do, and you have nothing to fear. You've watched me do it several times now, so you must surely realise that it is perfectly safe. Just take it in one hand like this." He held it out in front of him to demonstrate to Dara, "Then hold the inside of it against your other wrist - simple as that."

Dara reached out gingerly with his right hand and took the bracelet carefully from Oran. It was heavier than he expected - quite a bit heavier. He studied it for a moment, taking in its exquisite detail as Oran watched, then raised it up whilst holding it just as Oran had shown him.

"Go on then - hold the inside of it against your other wrist now, just like I showed you."

"I'm scared. What if we can't get it off again? What if I'm not meant to wear it, and it does something bad to me?"

Oran's patience wore off very quickly now, for he was already growing weary of Dara wasting valuable time. He lunged quickly at Dara, shoving the hand holding the bracelet against his left arm in the process and, as it made contact, the bracelet suddenly closed itself on Dara, just as Oran had hoped and expected that it would. Dara looked, in almost disbelief, at the bracelet which now adorned *his* wrist and not Oran's, then said angrily, "Get it off me! I can't believe you just did that. What were you thinking? I *would* have put it on, you know, in my own time. I just needed a moment to think about it, that's all."

"Hush now. Stop your silly whining. You're perfectly fine, are you not?" Oran scolded, then smiled as he said, "You get it off. You are, after all, its current wearer, are you not? Say the words, Dara. Only you can make it come off now, as *you* are now its wearer."

Dara raised the arm wearing the bracelet to about chest level, then stared at it for a brief moment, before giving Oran a wry smile. "What if I don't want to take it off? What if I wish... to keep it?"

"No you don't. Don't you dare. That's mine and always has been. I need it!" Oran replied, through now gritted teeth.

"Relax, I was jesting with you. Now, what was it that I have to say again?" Dara laughed, looking briefly up at the sky as if for the answer to his question, then back at Oran, who was looking a little nervous presently.

"Ethioné release me, please," Oran instructed. "Just like that, no different," then waited, hopefully.

"Ethioné release me, please," Dara said quickly, not wanting to upset Oran further.

Just as before, and thankfully, as far as both were concerned, the bracelet glowed blue and then came off a few seconds later. Both of them smiled, then laughed heartily at their success in figuring out how to attach and remove the bracelet. Oran stooped once more to pick it up, then offered it to Dara again, as he suggested, "Now we have to see if it will protect you from my spells. I'll do something simple and safe, of course. Don't worry."

Dara didn't waste any time and immediately took the bracelet from Oran, allowing it to attach itself to his left arm once more. He gave Oran an almost frightened look, as he asked, "What are you going to do to me? Don't do anything dangerous, or stupid, yes?"

"Fear not, my friend. You are in safe hands now," Oran chirped, confidently, raising his hands with both palms directed towards Dara.

Dara closed his eyes tight shut and braced himself for what he thought was about to happen to him. He was scared to death, but tried not to show it as Holly came and sat by his side, looking up at him expectantly. He felt Holly lean against his right leg, but ignored her presence for now, keeping his eyes firmly closed. He could hear Oran chanting softly, so quietly that he couldn't make out the words, but he could not feel anything happening to him.

He was completely oblivious to the tiny rain shower that had magically appeared above him now, and had begun to fall just above his head, but which was being deflected by some sort of invisible dome that shrouded and protected him from it. He waited a moment, eyes still firmly shut, for Oran to stop mumbling his chant, then slowly opened his left eye half way. He could see Oran standing directly in front of him, just a few feet away, wearing a huge grin across his face, and asked of him, "What is it that you find so amusing now? Did you do anything yet? Did it work?"

"Ha ha ha," was Oran's response. "Of course it worked - feel Holly's fur."

Dara opened his other eye and, with a puzzled expression, reached down to stroke his dog. He noted that she was wet, very wet, and smiled as he looked up at Oran. He laughed and shook his head, as if in disbelief, as he questioned, "So, you *did* make it rain. I didn't get wet, did I? How?"

"The talisman shielded you and protected you from the spell, if you like?" Oran assured him confidently, before carrying on, "We need to try something... a little more severe next though, to test it properly, I believe."

"Oh no you don't. You didn't say anything about that before - not about anything *severe*," Dara blurted out, but before he had a chance to do or say anything else, Oran was already directing his palms at him again and chanting, rapidly this time.

"*Altur bakhala, lasaria aradua, lasaria aradua.*"

Holly, as though sensing that something bad was about to happen, quickly rose to her feet and fled her master's side, as Dara continued to protest loudly about Oran's intentions. His protestations were of no use, however, as Oran continued chanting, in the process quickly launching a fireball at Dara's feet. Before Dara knew it, he was completely engulfed in flames.

He began to scream and flail his arms about wildly, in a frantic effort to protect or shield himself from the flames. Then, he suddenly realised that he could feel no heat or pain, miraculously. Realising that he was safe, because of the talisman, Dara inhaled deeply, relaxed and stood still, arms by his sides, as he stared at Oran through the orange flames that surrounded him, then laughed loudly,

"It works, hah! It works, Oran! I feel no pain. I can't even feel the warmth of the flames. It is truly amazing - you should try this."

Oran began to laugh, as he made the flames die down and cease to exist. The pair stood and looked at each other, in wonder of the power of the talisman, then Dara scolded, "You could have warned me that you were about to do that to me!"

"You wouldn't have allowed it! You would have moaned and whined like before. You should have seen yourself, though. It was quite amusing, dare I say it, to watch you dancing and flailing about in that way," Oran remarked with a smirk, then added, "Now, time to give it back to its rightful owner, please."

Dara looked at him briefly, with an expression of mild reluctance, then stammered, "Yes... yes. Of... course... Oran." Holding the palm of his right hand under the bracelet to catch it, he recited the words, "Ethioné release me, please."

The bracelet glowed blue again, and dropped into his waiting palm, just as they expected, and once again, the pair laughed loudly. Oran walked over to Dara and took the bracelet from his outstretched palm as he solemnly said, "Thank you, Dara. Thank you for being an honest man and returning the talisman to me. You are a true friend."

"I wouldn't dare dream of trying to take it from you, Oran. That's a ridiculous idea, and I'm not a thief."

"No, no. You misunderstand me. I wasn't suggesting that you were a thief - just that the lure of such power is more enticing than many a mere mortal could resist," Oran apologised, as he put the bracelet back on his right arm and patted Dara on the shoulder.

"I think we should get some sleep now after all of that, don't you?" Dara yawned deeply.

"Yes, certainly. It has been an extremely arduous and wearying day, to say the least. I could use some rest, for we have a long day ahead tomorrow again, no doubt," Oran sympathised.

Dara smiled at Oran, still finding it difficult to see the hundred-year old man, and not the young boy in need of looking after, as they made their way back to the fire and crawled in under the blankets to get some much-needed rest in preparation for the day ahead.

Holly lay down and stretched herself out between Oran and Dara, once again bathing in the luxurious heat of the magical fire that Oran had conjured. As she drifted off to sleep, she dreamt of running through sunny summer fields, chasing after a flock of sheep and the occasional pheasant.

"Goodnight Dara, sleep well," Oran murmured.

"Goodnight, master Oran."

CHAPTER ELEVEN
The Children of the Waters

Dara woke rather abruptly from his somewhat troubled slumber, to the sounds both of Holly's barking and of Oran whistling some strange, yet beautiful melody which Dara was quite sure that he had never heard before. Still laid next to the perpetually roaring fire conjured by Oran the previous day, as he rubbed the sleep from his eyes, he noticed that the mist which had cursed their journey so the previous day had now completely cleared, thankfully, and that he could now see very clearly where they had actually ended up.

As he propped himself up on one elbow in his make-shift bed, he gazed intently, for a moment, at the almost blinding shimmer of a great body of tranquil water that stretched out seemingly endlessly before him in the bright morning sunlight, reasoning to himself that it could, almost certainly, only be Lough Neagh, as it was so vast. He had, of course, never actually been here before, but had heard mention in tales, as a boy, of a great lake or lough that lay to the south, a lough whose expanse was so great that you could not see one shore from the other.

The waters before him were calm and still and although they stretched as far as the eye could see, he was sure that this could not possibly be the ocean, nor indeed the sea, although he could not see the other side - the far shore that he was certain existed off in the distance somewhere. For one thing, there were no waves crashing on the gravel beach nearby - waves that he would certainly expect to see were this the ocean - and he knew in his head and in his heart that they weren't *that* lost, and also knew that they could not possibly have progressed that far - to the coast, that was - after only one day of very troubled travelling.

Oran was at the water's edge nearby, entertaining Holly by throwing an old dead tree branch out into the calm, shallow waters for her to chase and fetch, which she seemed to be enjoying immensely as she barked and yelped at the young elf impatiently and excitedly. Dara watched quietly for a moment, smiling, as Oran hurled the branch out into the water once more, where it landed with a sort of a plop and a splash. Holly keenly bounded out into the shallows after it, splashing water up into the air around her as she went, and Dara couldn't help but notice how the low morning sun illuminated each and every droplet brightly, almost blindingly.

His thoughts then turned, momentarily, to how well he had slept regardless of their present location and of the freezing temperatures, when a vague image slowly entered his mind. It was a hazy image at first... and more than a little disturbing - that of a dark, hooded, or perhaps shrouded, figure which appeared from the depths of his mind, hunched closely over him in the darkness of the cold night. He could not quite see its face in the glow of the flickering firelight but could just make out an open mouth with unusually long teeth bared, as if to bite him. There came the touch of a boney hand, pressing on his chest with razor sharp nails, or claws, that dug slightly into his skin, as the exposed teeth drew nearer.

Suddenly, there came a faint crackling sound, accompanied by a momentary flash of bright green light. At this, the dark figure swiftly recoiled, and seemed to hiss, or growl, angrily, before strangely and swiftly transforming itself into an army of black moths that then fluttered almost silently, but quickly, off into the stillness of the winter night, disappearing from view.

Dara frowned now, as he puzzled over the recollection for a moment, then shrugged it off as nothing more than a bizarre dream, doubtless caused by the miraculous events and revelations of the previous day. He tossed the furs that covered him to one side and rose to his feet, stretching and yawning, then walked briskly down the gravel slope towards Oran and Holly as he boomed heartily, "Good morning to you, master Oran. I trust you slept as well as I." He paused briefly before calling out, "Holly! Come, girl."

Oran wheeled around abruptly where he stood, somewhat startled, as he hadn't heard Dara's approach, while at the same time, Holly ran swiftly and eagerly to Dara's side to greet her master.

"Ah... oh yes... yes, of course. Good morning to you also, Dara. Sorry, you... surprised me a little. I... did not hear you... come toward me, as I was so engrossed in my game with Holly," Oran stammered.

"What a fantastic morning it is! Beautiful sunshine and it is even a little... warm, dare I say it," Dara responded, stooping to pat Holly on the head as she stood next to him with her new toy, vigorously shaking herself dry and spraying his legs with cold water in the process.

Oran said nothing, but looked at Dara thoughtfully for a moment, then downward at the nearby water, up at the sun and then finally back at Dara before asking, "I could do with a wash after our lengthy and arduous journey. How about you, good sir?"

"Wash? I should like to, but how?" Dara now quizzed, before an unsettling realisation forced him to add, "Wait, just a minute now. Surely you don't mean to get into that water for the purpose of bathing, do you?"

"Well..." Oran began, but didn't get a chance to finish his sentence.

"It's freezing! Or certainly, it is very close to freezing, Oran, I'm fairly sure of it. You're mad." Dara warned, shaking his head slowly from side to side.

"You have completely the wrong idea concerning my intentions, good sir. I can *make* warm water for us to bathe in, Dara. Why would I wish to bathe in ice cold water? Your mortal head is not thinking correctly, once again," Oran reassured him, as he immediately began stripping down to his under garments where he stood, in full view of Dara, as though it were a perfectly normal thing to do, then tossed his clothes in a pile on the gravel next to him.

"What on earth are you doing, Oran?" Dara shrieked.

"Why? What do you mean?" Oran asked, as he removed his leggings.

"Your clothes! Put them back on please, at once."

"Why would I do that? I need to remove them so that I may wash myself, do I not?" came Oran's retort.

Dara turned his back now, as Oran stood wearing nothing more than what could only be described as a pair of somewhat worn out, long, white shorts, feeling more than a little embarrassed. He didn't know what to say, or where to look, as he was fairly sure that he had never before seen another male nearly naked - not since he was very young at least, he believed. Oran stood there shivering, staring at Dara's back for a moment before asking, "Are you ashamed of my body? Are you embarrassed, Dara? This is perfectly normal where I come from, you know - getting undressed in front of others to bathe, I mean. We all do it, the Danu, that is."

"It's a bit... unusual for me," Dara answered, uncertainly, still with his back to Oran.

"There is no need to feel either shame *or* embarrassment, Dara. We are all fairly much the same in appearance underneath our garments, gender aside, and even more so under our skins." Oran tried to reassure his companion now as he continued, "Now, enough nonsense. There is absolutely no need for you to turn your gaze away from me and I say it again - there is nothing for either you, or for myself, to feel embarrassed about, yes? It is perfectly normal and, truth be told, I'd be much more concerned were I female. In fact, I would never do this in front of you were I female."

Dara thought for a moment before turning around slowly to find Oran stood with his hands clasped to his front, below his waist.

"So, how then, are you planning to *make* warm water for bathing in, or is that a bit of a pointless question?"

"Aha... yes, it is indeed. You should know by now, really, Dara. You'll like this, I believe," Oran chuckled as he now turned, shivering in his near-nakedness, to face the waters of the great lough and raised his slight arms straight out in front of him, with his palms flattened and facing downward toward the surface of the water just ahead of him.

Dara watched as Oran closed his eyes and began to whisper something softly, in the old language, *"Uiscaihl aradaih, lean téigh le mí."*

Once again, the familiar tiny blue lightning bolts emerged and then converged upon Oran from the ground around him, making their way to his feet and snaking their way up his bare legs and torso to his arms and hands, hands which were now engulfed in a soft blue glow. Dara couldn't help but notice, as he watched the spectacle, how very lithe and perfectly defined Oran's supposedly hundred-year old body was, as though it were crafted by the very gods themselves. He also couldn't help noticing how it appeared as though Oran's extremely pale, white skin seemed almost transparent, as if stretched as tightly as possible over him, to the point where it became almost see through, and that he could almost see every muscle and sinew through it.

He now found himself struggling to process this sight, knowing that the physique before him, which resembled that of a fairly hard-working man in his early twenties perhaps, belonged to a man somewhere in the region of an incredible one hundred years of age, even though he had all the outward appearance of a mere boy who was about thirteen or fourteen years of age when fully clothed. Very confusing indeed, Dara pondered.

His attention was presently diverted, as he became aware of an unusual gurgling, bubbling sound and quickly turned his attention to the water, just in front of Oran. About ten feet out from shore, he observed that the surface of the water was foaming and bubbling slightly, as if disturbed by something unknown, or unseen, beneath it. In the centre of this disturbed patch, a small area of the water appeared to slowly rise and grow, in size and diameter. As it continued to rise upward, it formed into a smooth, dome-like shape which, over the course of the next several minutes, rose completely out of the lough and became a perfect sphere some six or seven feet in diameter, of nothing more than crystal clear water.

The sphere, or globe of water, was now floating in mid-air, under Oran's seemingly effortless control, just above the surface from where it had come. It revolved slowly now, directly in front of Oran's outstretched, glowing blue hands.   Dara continued to watch closely, and with some amusement, as Oran seemed to guide the sphere using subtle hand gestures and barely audible whispers in the old tongue toward the shore, then between them and up the gravel slope toward the still burning fire that he had conjured the previous day. Holly slowly and inquisitively pursued it along its course. It appeared to Dara as though Oran was encouraging it and enticing it, rather than commanding it. He couldn't help but laugh as the sphere of water floated past him silently, having suddenly noticed that there appeared to be at least one average sized fish frantically swimming around inside it as it desperately tried to find its way out, no doubt,

"Hah! You caught a fish, my boy Oran. Our first catch of the day, my friend. Well done," Dara laughed, heartily.

Oran chose to ignore this remark, as he concentrated intently on positioning his water sphere directly over the fire and holding it there. It now became evident to

Dara that the intention was to suspend the water above the flames in order to heat it up - not quite what he had expected, at all. Oran held the water in position with his arms extended toward it as though he was actually physically holding it there, the bottom of the sphere just touching the tips of the flames from the fire, then made a sort of swiping motion from right to left with his right hand.

Dara observed that this caused the water globe to spin slightly more quickly, possibly to speed up the heating process, or perhaps to make it heat more evenly, but he couldn't be certain which. He continued to watch the sight before him in awe, thinking that if anyone were to chance by and see this near naked boy with his body half covered in tiny, bright blue lightning bolts, his long dark tail of hair trailing down his back to his waist, causing this great ball of water to float in mid-air above a fire that wasn't actually real - well, they would most likely scream and then run away. He chuckled quietly to himself at this thought, whilst at the same time hoping that no-one *did* presently arrive to witness the spectacle.

There soon came a faint hissing sound, as steam now began to form and billow out from around the lower portion of the sphere. With that, Oran shouted, "It is ready, I believe," and now guided it gently back to a place on the shore, half way between the fire and the water's edge. He lowered it slowly and gently until it was just touching the ground, then murmured softly, "*Fanasta annan*," before lowering his now normal looking hands back down to his sides as he turned to Dara with a smirk across his face and asked, "Who's going first then - you or I?"

Dara looked at Oran incredulously, then shook his head in dismay as he blurted out, "Think I'm getting in there? There's not a whisper of a chance - never," then, just as swiftly, reconsidered, due to an overwhelming desire to wash himself. He continued, "Well, not until you've gone first and demonstrated that it is safe to do so, at least."

"Very well then, coward. I shall go first."

Without another word, Oran nonchalantly stepped toward the now slowly revolving globe, took a deep breath, and before Dara knew it, had stepped inside the water sphere as though it were the most natural thing in the world to do. Dara puzzled over the sight before him now, staring silently, as Holly cocked her head to one side and began whining at the large ball of water that had just swallowed her most recently acquired friend. He could clearly see Oran inside the water, rubbing his hands vigorously over his body in an attempt to wash himself quickly before he ran out of air. After a minute or two, Oran leapt back out with a gasp for air.

"That felt so good - a little too warm perhaps, but still good. I feel so much better now, Dara – invigorated, dare I say. You really should try it, please - I insist. Oh, this is for you by the way - breakfast. It's partially cooked from the heat already, I believe." He raised his right hand toward Dara.

Dara looked at Oran's outstretched hand, in which he was now holding a freshly caught, sizeable salmon, his fingers inserted in its gills like hooks. He laughed as he reached for and took the fish, then turned and carried it toward the fire. Setting the salmon down on a small rock by the fire, he turned and walked back to Oran as he asked demurely, "How do I do this then - this bathing thing of yours? What do I need to do?"

Oran laughed, then answered, "Well, first, you will need to undress, of course - unless you wish to wear wet clothes for most of the remainder of the day, that is. I wouldn't advise it in this weather, mind."

Dara uttered a disgruntled "hmmph" as he stared at the sphere in front of him. He felt very self-conscious about undressing in front of Oran and was extremely reluctant to do so, but he *did* want to get into the water and wash himself, there was no question about that.

"I shan't look, if it makes you feel more comfortable," Oran stated politely, as he turned his back to Dara and went about getting dressed again.

Dara said nothing as he reluctantly summoned the courage to undress himself, exposing an also quite impressive physique of his own. He threw his clothes on the ground by his feet, and then approached the slowly spinning globe of water cautiously and a little fearfully, in nothing but his under shorts. He glanced around nervously to see if Oran was looking at him and, reassured by the fact that he wasn't, continued until he stood with his face mere inches from the spheres closest point, then hesitated for a moment, summoning more courage perhaps. He told himself that it would be just like when he took his family swimming at the waterfall at Esslan near his home in the summer - just a matter of taking a deep breath and then diving, or in this case, stepping in.

"Take a deep breath and hold it, Dara. Don't forget," Oran called to him.

He hesitated for a moment longer, then inhaled deeply as he reached his right hand out and pushed it carefully into the water in front of him. It felt somehow strange, but also pleasantly warm, as it gently swirled around his hand and wrist - an odd sensation, he thought, but it was all the encouragement he needed to take the final plunge. He exhaled quickly, then took another deep breath and held it as he stepped bravely forward and slowly entered into the sphere, face first. The warm water engulfed him as he immersed himself completely, swirling around his body, bathing and massaging him. He could only think that it felt absolutely luxurious, like nothing he had ever experienced before - it felt wonderful.

Knowing that he only had a minute or so before he ran out of air, Dara began to wash himself vigorously with his hands. As he washed, he could see Holly standing just outside the sphere, looking back at him, and could just make out her muffled barking at him through the water. He stifled the urge to laugh at her, knowing only too well the consequences of doing so with his head under water, as it were. Suddenly, it became apparent that Holly had decided that it would be a good idea to join Dara, as he now observed her head enter the water just below and in front of him. Next came a muffled sort of *woof*, accompanied by a stream of bubbles that drifted up in front of his face, and she was swiftly gone again, having obviously realised the perils of her decision.

A moment later, he exited the water with a gasp for air and was greeted by a rather wet, but excited Holly. Dara stooped briefly to pat her on her rather wet head, gathered his clothes and then turned and walked quickly back to the fireside to dry himself off before he would catch cold. He found Oran by the fire already, as he had gone about preparing the fish while Dara washed. In the morning sun, they sat for a while and dried off by the fire, both of them enjoying a breakfast of freshly caught salmon, which they also shared with Holly, whilst they chatted and laughed about the bathing experience.

"So, Dara, do you plan to sit around half naked all day, or are we going to make a start for that mountain we seek?" Oran remarked, with a smile, after he had finished eating his food.

Dara suddenly realised that he was still undressed and quickly rose to his feet, a little embarrassed, and began to put his clothes back on as quickly as he could. As he dressed, Oran observed something a little odd and commented, "You must have been clawing at your chest in your sleep, Dara - a bad dream perhaps. Those marks look quite fresh."

Dara looked down at his bare chest which, in the middle, bore several faint red scratches. He puzzled for a moment, before recalling the dream of the hooded figure again. Had he somehow scratched himself with his own hand, as he dreamt of being clawed by that creature in the night? *Who knows?* he thought, as he shrugged it off again and continued getting dressed.

"If you'd like to, you can take care of packing up the bedding and getting the horses ready, whilst I take care of the camp fire and return the water sphere to the lough," Oran suggested.

"Of course, of course," Dara agreed as he quickly fastened his jacket closed against the cold winter air.

Dara hurriedly went about gathering up the furs which they had used as makeshift beds and folded them as neatly as he could, before transporting them over to where the horses had been tied up nearby. He turned to watch briefly as Oran firstly went about performing a spell to extinguish the fire that had kept them safe and warm all night, then performed another to return the bathing water to the lough where it had come from - minus the salmon, of course.

These feats of magic were always very special to witness, as far as Dara was concerned, and he would never grow tired of watching Oran perform such spectacles. It was, after all, this very magic and this very magician that had saved the life of his beloved Mary just recently. He would not forget that and would not allow himself to forget that - not ever.

Oran came to Dara's side, as he packed the furs away into the saddle bags, and asked him, "Have you given thought yet as to which direction we must set off in, Dara? We must be certain that we head in the right direction this time."

"I have, Oran, yes," Dara responded, as he turned to point toward the low, early morning sun before continuing, "The sun is to the east, obviously, or east by south east, as it is currently mid-winter. Since this can almost certainly only be Lough Neagh then we must journey north-east, according to our instructions and the information on our very old map."

Taking said map from the saddle bag, Dara now used it to indicate to Oran roughly where he believed they were now situated, and also, the direction in which he believed they must now travel from here. Oran looked at the map, and then thoughtfully at Dara for a moment, before directing a puzzled and bewildered gaze toward the vast lough in front of them as he murmured, "But there is only water in that direction, Dara - water that stretches as far as the eye can see, so how shall we manage that? Do you have a plan?"

"I do, but I'm afraid that it will, perhaps, not please you, my friend, as it means more time journeying than we had anticipated or intended," came Dara's reply.

"I'm not sure that I like the sound of that, Dara. Tell me, please?"

"We shall have to make our way around the lough, Oran. We'll follow the shoreline - there is no other way, I'm afraid," Dara answered, regretfully.

"But that will take longer, Dara - ages perhaps," Oran groaned. "We are already quite some way behind schedule as it is."

"We shall have to move swiftly then. At least the weather is on our side today. Unless, of course, you can conjure up some kind of helpful magical solution to our dilemma, that is," Dara suggested, somewhat hopefully.

"I'm afraid there are limits to what I can conjure. I don't possess the knowledge, nor do I possess the level of power, required to part the waters so that we might walk straight across, if that is what you are suggesting, Dara. Well, anyhow, we are wasting time, as it would appear that we have no choice, so I strongly suggest that we get moving. Need I remind you that time is very much against us? Every moment wasted puts my people in greater danger of being discovered," Oran reminded him, tersely.

"No, you needn't, Oran. I'm very well aware of that fact and I, too, eagerly wish to return to my home and my family, just as you do yours," Dara scolded back, as he prepared to mount his horse, before adding, "You still have the sword, I trust?"

"Fear not. The sword is very safe," Oran replied, as he too prepared to mount his horse.

As they climbed into their saddles, the pair made a final check that they had all of their belongings, as they prepared to set off on the next leg of their journey. Dara beckoned Holly to his horse's side with a whistle, then called down to her, "Stay with us now, Holly. Good girl." He then turned his attention to Oran as he enquired, "Are you ready, master Oran?"

"Ready, Dara. Lead on, please," Oran smirked, finding it difficult to be angry with Dara, especially since none of this was his fault to begin with, and now reminded himself that he should be very grateful for Dara's company.

They turned their horses now, simultaneously, toward the shoreline nearby as they set off. As they did so, they both noticed, in the same instant, something peculiarly striking ahead of them in the water near the shore - something that wasn't there before.

Newly appeared by the water's edge were four beautiful, pristine, white adult swans, who swam side by side, facing them, watching them intently, silently. They neither moved, nor did they make a sound, but instead just sat there, bobbing gently in the water as they regarded both Oran and Dara.

"Aren't they magnificent?" Dara whispered to Oran.

"What are they?" Oran responded, hastily adding, "I mean, I know they're birds of some kind, but which kind?"

"Swans, Oran. They're swans. Haven't you ever seen a swan before?"

"No Dara, I have not. Remind yourself, perhaps, of where I have dwelt for all of my life," Oran stated, factually.

"Yes, of course - how thoughtless of me. My apologies, Oran," Dara replied regretfully, then carried on, "These are swans, Oran. They are the most majestic of all the water fowl, and also the most graceful."

As the conversation took place, the four swans swam slowly to the shoreline, then walked, or rather waddled, almost gracefully up the gravel beach towards Oran and Dara, before coming to a stop just ahead of them. Holly whined and whimpered from under Dara's horse, where she had seemingly taken refuge from the four very large birds as Dara remarked, "I think, perhaps, they are hungry, and that they approach us in search of food."

However, as Dara was saying these words, the four swans reared up to their fullest height and began to honk loudly and to flap their large, now extended wings slightly, which seemed to frighten Holly even more, for she now began to growl softly from where she hid. As the honking and wing flapping continued, the swans appeared to take on a soft, white glow, as if illuminated from within themselves, as Oran and Dara watched on with some degree of concern.

Suddenly, the swans metamorphosed into four young people - three male and one female, each wearing long, brilliant white, hooded gowns that were adorned with the feathers of the swans which they had just been. Oran and Dara were more than a little surprised by this and continued to observe in silence, although Oran was presently reaching slowly for his sword, just in case.

"Careful, Dara, be ready," Oran warned, cautiously.

"Wait," Dara advised, putting a hand on that of Oran's which reached for the sword, whilst all the while keeping his attention fixed firmly on the four young people ahead of them now.

What appeared to be the eldest and tallest of the four now took one step toward Dara as he said softly, "My name is Aodh, and these are my beloved twin brothers,

Fiachra and Conn, and our also beloved sister, Fionnula."
Gesturing to the other three and bowing courteously to
Oran and Dara, he then continued as he stood upright,
"We are the Children of Lir - King Lir. We ask you fear
not, good sirs, for we mean you no harm."

"Surely not! It cannot be," Dara spat out. "The tale
of the Children of Lir was but a myth - a fairytale told
little children as a bedtime story, as I myself was told by
my dear mother when I was but a young boy."

"I assure you, kind sir, that the story is no myth, as
you can clearly see before you now. We are, in fact, very
real," Aodh stated, as he proudly gestured toward his
siblings.

Dara straightened himself up in his saddle and with a
brief glance in Oran's direction, he announced, "My
name is Dara MacBrien, in that case, and this is my
companion and good friend, Oran," gesturing, with a
hand, toward Oran then pausing to look down, in
search of his dog. "And somewhere below is my faithful
dog, Holly," he said, then nodding to Oran with his
head, he added, "It is our great pleasure to make your
acquaintance, Aodh, and also, that of your brothers and
sister." He now nodded politely to the others, who all
remained silent for now.

"Thank you, Dara," Aodh almost whispered. "It is
also *our* pleasure to make your acquaintance on this
most beautiful of days. Indeed, it is almost certainly our
best day for some nine hundred years," as he smiled
warmly at them.

"Nine hundred years!" Dara blurted out, hastily
adding as he and Oran now climbed down from
their horses to greet the foursome properly, "How so,
my friend?"

The four youths now approached Oran and Dara slowly, and they set about greeting each other with hugs and handshakes, as Dara went on to ask, "That's a new trick I've not seen before. How do you do that? Turning yourselves into swans indeed - I've not witnessed that sort of magic before. Very impressive. Can you do that, Oran?"

"I cannot, Dara," Oran stated meekly, then went on to say, "I don't believe it was of their own doing, but rather, a spell - or, dare I say it, a curse; a curse placed upon them by another, as I felt, or was aware of, a very slight presence of the dark arts upon their appearance, hence the reason I was somewhat cautious."

"You are very observant, Oran. Are you of the magical kind yourself?" Aodh asked, inquisitively.

"I am," stated Oran. "I am Oran of the people of Danu, junior elf and servant of King Lugh."

"The Danu, King Lugh? A wonderous people," Aodh remarked. "They had a different king in our time as mortals - Nemed, I believe it was."

"How then were you transformed to swans?" Dara asked of them.

Aodh breathed something of a sigh, and solemnly set about explaining to Oran and Dara, at great length, how they had come to be in the form of swans as a result of the jealousy of their malevolent stepmother, Aoife. He recounted the story of how their real mother, Aoibh, or Eva, had died when they were young, and that their father had taken this second wife, Aoife, to ease his grief. After some time, Aoife grew jealous of the children's love for each other and for their father and so had hatched a plan to get rid of them forever.

He explained how she had taken them to a lake to go swimming one summer, and when all of them were in the water, she cast an evil spell that condemned them to a life as swans for nine hundred years. This evil spell would see them spending the first three hundred years on Lake Derravaragh, then three hundred years on the straits of Moyle, and finally, three hundred years on a lake on the barren and deserted Isle of Inish Glora, where storms had raged almost constantly. Aodh continued that for the first three hundred years, their father came to visit them every day, having learned of their fate, to spend time with them and listen to them sing their haunting melodies. During this time, he also cast a spell, banishing Aoife to the mist for eternity as punishment for what she had done.

Aodh ended his tale by telling Oran and Dara that the curse was ended by them being blessed by a kindly monk, at the ringing of a bell. He explained that this had happened just the previous day and that they were now free again, although they were still able to assume the form of swans at will, deciding to come here to live in peace for the rest of eternity, as it was a particularly beautiful and serene place. He then looked at Dara, and asked, "So, Dara, now that you know all that there is to know about us, please tell us about you and your companions. What brings you to this place - fishing perhaps?" He nodded to his siblings as he continued, "You seem to have packed for a long journey though, judging by those bags. Would you, by any chance, have some food to spare in there?"

"Food? Of course, my friend - yes. We have a little," Dara offered, willingly.

"Might we ask, where is it that you are headed to? What do you seek? Perhaps we can be of some help to you both," Aodh enquired.

Dara now looked to Oran, raising his eyebrows a little, not sure of what response he should give to Aodh's last question.

CHAPTER TWELVE
The Unseen Dragon

Oran stood looking at Dara thoughtfully, albeit somewhat apprehensively, for a moment, not sure of what to say exactly - and even less certain of where to begin, for that matter. He bore a somewhat worried expression on his face, as there was also, of course, the very real danger of making himself look like a complete fool by telling their four new friends - these mystical Children of Lir - the exact details of how he and Dara came to be here. A daunting prospect for him, to say the least.

Dare he honestly tell them the entire story of how he had come to put the safety of the remaining few hundred people of his race in jeopardy, due to his own selfishness... his thoughtlessness and recklessness? But then, on the other hand, of course, there may well be the chance that these new friends could, in fact, be of some help or assistance to them, in some small way or other.

He took a deep breath now, turning to face Aodh and his siblings as he began to tell them all about the Ivy Castle and everything that had gone wrong on the morning before, regarding the dragon crystal and its time cocoon now sadly demised at his hand, and only his hand. Aodh, Fionnula, Fiachra and Conn listened carefully, but said nothing as Oran went on to tell them of the quest to Slemish in search of the Fire Dragon, known as Rydian, upon which King Lugh had sent him in the hope of reinstating the time cocoon as quickly as possible, so as to preserve the safety of their race.

He then paused and took a deep breath as he glanced at Dara and continued by informing them of how Dara and Holly had, thankfully, come to accompany him on this quest in return for a favour, the details of which he did not go into in their entirety. Finally, he ended by telling them of how he and Dara had accidentally ended up here, by the lough, due to getting lost in the fog during the previous day, and that they were now faced with a very long trek around it when they, in fact, needed to go directly across. He pointed across the vast expanse of water that stretched out ahead of him and explained that they had no apparent way of doing so.

The Children of Lir then moved slightly away from Oran and Dara, when Oran had finished telling his tale, and huddled together for a minute or so. They whispered secretly to each other as the duo watched with concern, before turning to face them once more. Now, for the first time since the two parties had met, the twins, Fiachra and Conn, approached and began to speak to Oran. They spoke in some strange unison, or harmony, as if linked somehow, like they were one person in two bodies.

"We should like to be of assistance to you, in your time of need. We believe that we may be able to expedite your journey."

"How so, good friends?" Oran asked, curiously, but at the same time, hopefully.

The twins continued, in the same unified voice, "This past day, we have been very fortunate to have made the acquaintance of a rather special creature - a truly magnificent being that dwells beneath these waters before you, unseen and unknown of by all but ourselves. She tells us that she came to this place a short time ago, from her home in a far-off country to the east, where she had dwelt peacefully for many years in a lake, or lagoon, called Razelm - Limanul Razelm, we believe. Peacefully, that was, until the local human population became aware of her existence and began trying to hunt her down." They then paused briefly, nodding to each other, before continuing, "If you could be so kind as to provide us with some food and the means to warm ourselves, then we should be happy to summon her to shore, and enquire of her if she would be willing to assist you in your endeavours to get across the lough."

"A creature that dwells beneath the water? What manner of creature - a fish, an otter? I would ask how such a creature could be of any help to us?" Dara asked, guardedly now.

"Not a fish, nor an otter, Dara. A water dragon, my friends, or rather, a Balaur, as she informs us, who calls herself by the name Gálin," the twins went on. "She has become friend to us, and we believe that she may be willing to carry or transport you across the lough, to the other side in your time of need."

"Summon her? How?" enquired Oran at this, with a puzzled frown.

"Ah, now, she comes to our singing, simply. She seems to enjoy it, greatly," stated Fiachra and Conn, proudly, in their still synchronised voices.

"How soon can you arrange this meeting, my good friends? We are in somewhat of a hurry, you see - not wishing to sound rude," Oran said, rather excitedly.

"Wait, wait," Dara blurted out, worriedly. "How do we know this water dragon of theirs won't eat us, Oran? Have you considered that, in your blind haste to get ahead? And how, precisely, does she get the two of us, Holly *and* two horses across this lough?"

"The horses are not a problem, Dara, honestly. Those I can take care of easily," Oran said now, before turning back to face the twins, as he said, "Please, would you be so kind as to summon your friend, the water dragon."

"She will not *eat* you, my good friends, for she eats only fish. And yes, certainly, we shall attempt to summon her for you at once," the twins laughed, together, before instructing, "Please, wait here and do not be afraid, no matter what you may see now, for she is rather large - very large." They then turned toward Aodh and Fionnula, as they nodded, but said nothing, as though there was no need for speech between the four of them.

Dara looked at Oran, with more than a hint of fear in his expression now, as he whispered somewhat worriedly, "I've never seen a real dragon, Oran. I'm more than a little afraid, if I'm entirely honest."

"No need to worry. We'll be fine. I'm certain of it," came Oran's strangely confident response.

The Children of Lir then turned and walked to the water's edge, elegantly and silently, as Oran and Dara watched on anxiously, not sure of what to expect now. As the pair continued to observe, the children once again transformed themselves into four beautiful, majestic swans as they stood by the shore. Dara glanced at Oran quickly, with an expression of mild concern mixed with hope, but said nothing, as he returned his attention to the swans ahead of them.

What came next surprised Dara immensely, as the swans began to sing the most haunting, yet enchanting melody, together. It was almost mesmerising - bewitching, he thought - yet he also believed that it was the most beautiful melody he had ever heard in his lifetime. Their singing continued for several minutes, as Oran and Dara watched and listened intently. Holly came and joined Dara from her rummaging in some nearby bushes, sat down by his side, and listened to the swans singing, with her head cocked curiously to one side. Nothing untoward had happened as of yet, and there was no sign of any creature, Oran thought anxiously, as he scanned the vast lough with his keen eyesight.

He was becoming a little despondent when, suddenly, he heard a strange, echoing, sort of hooting sound, whilst off in the distance, he believed he glimpsed a disturbance in the water's surface - a large splash perhaps - a mile or so ahead of them. He grew excited now at this, as he focused his attention on where he had just seen the splash, squinting in the glare of the low sun, whilst at the same time prodding Dara's arm with a finger as he rasped, eagerly, "There, Dara, over there! Look!"

Dara quickly directed his eyesight to where Oran was pointing frantically now, also squinting in the bright sunlight that hurt his eyes, but could see nothing but ripples, or small waves, more accurately, far off in the distance at first. Suddenly, to his utter amazement, as he continued to scan the water's surface ahead, not one, but three great silvery heads on long slender necks rose simultaneously skyward at speed from the calmer water just a little nearer to them, but still some way off. These three huge heads on slender necks were swiftly followed by a long, streamlined silvery body, to which all three were attached, and then an equally long, shimmering tail. Last to emerge from the water was a wide, flattened, crescent shaped tail fin, not unlike that of a dolphin or whale, that sat at the end of the creature's long silvery tail.

Oran and Dara watched in utter astonishment as the great beast now arced its long body, its ascent slowing, and then pointed itself downward and went crashing back to the depths of the lough with a mighty splash and another eerie, echoing, hooting noise. Dara gasped, for he was completely aghast and dumfounded at the sight, as he had never in his life seen a creature so large, so enormous indeed. She was the size of his house - no, larger than his house, he assured himself.

She did not appear again until a few moments later, when she surfaced gradually as she entered the shallower water nearby, at a now much slower pace. Oran and Dara watched in silence and utter awe as the creature's great silvery heads rose slowly and majestically from the still water about a hundred yards or so from the shore directly in front of the swans, who were still singing. The sight was enough to make Holly run for cover by the horses, with a whimper and a defiant *woof*, as Oran and Dara continued taking in the magnificent sight before them.

They took in every detail in complete silence, as the dragon, or Balaur, approached the shoreline slowly, effortlessly gliding through the water, it seemed, until the water became so shallow that she needed to walk on the lough bed below. Her metallic looking heads rose slowly and elegantly, higher from the water, on long, curving and similarly metallic looking necks, as she waded nearer to them.

Her heads were each as big as a horse, almost, and best described as wedge shaped - broad at the rear and narrowing toward the snout, where they almost resembled the tapered, pointed bow of a boat in form. They were somewhat flattened at the sides and had a sort of thin, membranous vertical fin jutting upward in the middle near the rear, on top of all three. Each head was also adorned on either side with a huge yellow reptilian eye, behind each of which protruded two great white, curving horns which were each several feet in length and were swept backwards toward its body upon which, Oran now believed that he noticed, were a pair of cleverly, almost entirely concealed wings.

At the front of each of these heads, at their snouts, were two large, gaping nostrils, one either side, and right at the tip and uppermost point of each snout, a boney horn, or barb, that protruded some two feet in front, curving very slightly upwards and ending in what looked to be an extremely sharp point. There was also on each, naturally, a very large mouth, all of which now opened slightly in unison to reveal several rows of very large teeth, and made the same, but somewhat subdued, hooting noise as before, in greeting to the swans that now stood just below and in front of her. It appeared, to Oran and Dara, that all three heads spoke, if you will, in harmony, also.

The pair watched on eagerly, still saying nothing as the swans continued to sing, although their melody now changed noticeably, and the great water dragon appeared to cock its three mighty heads to one side slightly, as it listened to them for a moment or so longer. Dara observed that the dragon seemed to take no notice of either him, nor indeed Oran, as this took place, and continued to watch as she now appeared to make a subtle nodding gesture, with another subdued and harmonious hoot toward the four swans.

The swans then stopped singing, abruptly, and turned once again to face Oran and Dara, at the same time transforming themselves back to human form once more. The Children of Lir walked over to speak to them now, as the mighty dragon watched on quietly, staying where she was, near the water's edge, with only her legs and tail submerged in the water now. Fionnula now approached closest to them, and spoke to them for the first time since their meeting.

"We have spoken to the water dragon, and we have told her of your plight and that you would greatly appreciate her help and assistance in journeying to the other side of the lough."

Oran regarded Fionnula for a moment, saying nothing. He could only assume, from this statement, that the children communicated with the great beast through song, then replied swiftly, "That is very much appreciated by us both, and we humbly thank you. Might I ask…" He then paused as he raised his eyebrows apprehensively, "What was her response, if any?"

"She informs us that she would be more than happy to assist you, should you be willing to do her a small favour in return, of course," came Fionnula's response.

"What favour?" Oran questioned, then added, "I shall gladly do whatever I can."

As the conversation between Oran and Fionnula took place, Dara slowly moved a few paces to his left in an attempt to get a better look at the magnificent dragon, but, as he noticed one of her great silvery heads tracking his movement, thought better of it and decided to remain where he stood.

Fionnula continued, "She informs us that the lough is barren and devoid of food. She complains that there are very few bradán - or salmon, as you may better know them - and that she is extremely hungry and has been for some weeks now."

Oran rubbed his hairless chin with a thoughtful "hmmm" for a second, then answered, "And if I bring fish - salmon, or bradán, as you prefer - to the waters, she will assist us in our journey? Is that all that she asks of us?"

"It is, Oran. She asks nothing more," Fionnula confidently responded.

"It almost sounds too good to be true, master Oran," Dara butted in suddenly, eyes still affixed on the great beast before him. "Everyone just seems to want feeding today, ha ha."

"True, Dara, very true," Oran began, then somewhat cautiously began walking to the water's edge as he continued, "But we need to get across that lough quickly to make up for time lost yesterday because of the fog, and if that is all that she asks of us, well then, I am happy to fulfil the request."

Dara and the Children of Lir watched on as Oran slowly moved closer to the water, until he stood directly beneath and in front of the mighty creature's three huge heads. Suddenly aware of pressure against his left leg, Dara looked down at his side and was pleased to see that Holly had summoned the courage to rejoin him, then turned his attention back to Oran as he reached down to gently rub her left ear. He knew only too well now what was about to happen next... probably. Oran twisted himself around on the spot, addressing Aodh, "Can you tell the dragon not to be afraid of my impending actions please, Aodh?"

"No need, Oran. She has already informed us that she has sensed, and is aware, of who and what you are, and that she is pleased to be in your company," Aodh called back.

Oran smiled at this as he turned back to face the dragon, who was now looking down at him, all three heads pointed toward him, and gazed directly up at her shiny snouts, where he could see his own slightly blurry reflections. He then softly whispered, "Here we go then, old girl. Let's bring some fish to these waters for you." He then raised his arms slowly out to his sides, parallel to the ground, with his palms facing the lough in front of him and began chanting as he closed his eyes and lowered his head slightly in concentration.

The four children, Dara and Holly watched on raptly as Oran went about conjuring his magic, unable to hear his faint whispers - his chanting. They observed the dozens of tiny blue lightning bolts appear, as if from nowhere, and snake and wriggle across the gravel to his feet. They carried on watching, quietly, as the lightning bolts travelled up Oran's body and worked their way along his arms to his hands and fingertips. Suddenly, after a long moment of chanting, there was a faint crackling sound, which was accompanied by a bright blue flash of light that spread out onto the water's surface behind the dragon, as Oran shouted aloud, "*A lán.*" In the same instant, he quickly jerked his head back up and clapped his hands together in front of him, swiftly.

Dara noticed that the dragon was not in the least perturbed by this event, as she continued to look down at Oran, who now stood smiling, from ear to ear, in front of her. Then, without warning, salmon started leaping out of the water behind her, one after another, after another. There were dozens of them - literally dozens.

"Hah! You did it, Oran!" Dara exclaimed, almost as if he couldn't believe the spectacle before him, despite what he had witnessed over the course of the past two days, almost, as he now walked eagerly down the gravel beach towards his friend and the great, silvery beast.

"Your food awaits you, mighty Gálin," Oran stated, politely, looking up at the dragon and gesturing with a hand toward the many salmon that were jumping and leaping out of the water nearby. She swung two of her large heads around to look behind and, upon witnessing the number of fish that were there, gave Oran a thankful nod with the third, then emitted a loud hoot as she maneuvered her huge body around and headed off in search of a long-awaited meal. Dara smiled, as he now noticed how her silvery skin shone with all the colours of the rainbow when the sunlight hit it at a certain angle, as she turned herself around.

Everyone watched patiently now, as the great beast waded and crashed about through the water noisily, leaping and splashing eagerly, in pursuit of her much-needed food. When, after some ten minutes or so, her hunger was satisfied, she returned gracefully back to the place near the shore where she had first listened to the children sing. She came to a stop and looked directly at the children - Fionnula in particular - and gave another short hoot as she bowed, or nodded, her three great heads slightly. Fionnula then turned to Oran and said, "Gálin thanks you, and states that she is ready now to assist you on your journey onward."

"All that with one sound?" Dara asked, a little uncertainly.

Fionnula simply nodded, in response to Dara's question.

"I'm a little confused," Oran began. "I can see no apparent way for this creature to transport us across the water to the far shore, unless I am missing something obvious."

"Me too," Dara chimed in, then asked, "We surely can't be riding on her back?"

"No, no. Of course not. That wouldn't be at all possible - well, you would probably slip off for one thing, or drown for another," answered Aodh now, advising, "She travels mostly beneath the surface, you see."

"There is a small wooden boat, just big enough for the two of you and your dog, tied to a tree just along the shoreline not far from here," Fionnula informed them, as she pointed roughly in the direction of were the boat was moored.

"We shall fetch the boat here for you, and then Gálin will tow it - with all of you safely on board, of course - across the lough to the other side. It is as easy as that, really," Aodh went on to explain.

"Yes, and when you're safely across, we shall return the boat to its rightful place, and hopefully no-one shall ever notice that we have borrowed it," Fiachra and Conn ended, in unison.

"That sounds like a fantastic idea," Oran beamed, enthusiastically. "Shall we proceed then?"

"What about the horses, Oran?" Dara quizzed, hastily. "Surely you're not thinking that we can get them into that small boat too. Wait, please tell me that you are not planning on leaving them here, and that you and I shall carry out the remainder of our journey on foot? Not a chance, young man... old man, I mean."

"Calm down, Dara. I shall take care of the horses, and don't worry - they *are* coming with us. You shall not have to journey on foot, my friend," Oran said, reassuringly.

"We shall go to fetch the boat for you now while you prepare for the journey, and will return shortly, gentlemen," Aodh now interrupted, as he and his sister turned and walked down the slope toward the water, transforming into swans again as they went.

"Thank you, Aodh," Oran called out to them, as he turned and headed for the old tree where the horses were tied up, with Dara and Holly following on his heels.

"I don't understand, Oran," Dara insisted. "How do you plan to get those two great horses into a little tiny boat?"

"Dara, think for once, my good man," Oran began to say, with some exasperation, and then took a deep breath and calmly continued, "Have you not noticed in all this time that your horse is not of flesh and blood? It is the same as the Shawan, conjured from the very ground beneath us - from the elements, Dara. These are magical beings, not real."

"Really? Well, no, I can't say that I'd paid it that much attention, to be honest, Oran," Dara now stated somewhat gruffly, and then went on, "Mind you, I was beginning to wonder when it was going to eat something, although I wasn't sure if you had fed them in the night, perhaps."

"Really, Dara?" Oran said, as he went about undoing the horses' saddles, adding, "Some help here, please?"

Dara helped Oran take the saddles off the horses and carry them down to the water's edge, where they put them down and then went to fetch the bags and rest of their belongings from where they had made camp for the night, while the dragon, Fiachra and Con watched attentively. They made a last trip to untie and lead the horses down to the water, and by the time they had gathered everything and placed it all together in one pile by the shore, Aodh and Fionnula had returned with the small boat, towing it by means of a length of rope attached to its bow at the breast-hook, and had transformed themselves back to human form.

"So, you're ready then?" Aodh asked of them.

"Not quite," Oran said, as he raised an index finger as a sign for them to wait. "One last thing to take care of, quickly - the horses. Dara, would you be good enough to hold that bag open wide, please - the one there that is almost empty now?" He pointed to the empty saddle bag on the ground, which was closest to Dara.

Dara immediately crouched down and grabbed the bag which had been indicated by Oran, pulling its mouth open as wide as he could. As he did this, Oran went to the horse nearest to him and seemed to whisper something in its ear softly, and rather briefly. No sooner had he done so than the horse almost immediately disappeared with a muffled sort of pop, replaced now by a small, shiny black ball about the same size as an apple that hung, or floated in mid-air, effortlessly.

He then went to the other horse and repeated the process, whispering in its ear also. Another pop, and soon there were two shiny black balls floating side-by-side in the air near Oran, as everyone watched on with mild amusement. Holly now, wrongly got the idea that these balls were, in fact, toys for her amusement.

She quickly lunged at the one closest to her, but before she even got near it, they both darted off with an odd whizzing noise, into the bag that Dara was presently holding open, and vanished from sight.

"Too slow, girl," Dara laughed, as he closed the bag and tied it firmly, whilst he said, "Now I know about the horses," chuckling to himself, quietly.

Oran chuckled as well, and they then set about loading their things into the little wooden boat. Dara called Holly to his side and, as he stooped to pick her up, said, "Ready for your first ever boat ride, girl?" Lifting her carefully into the boat, he added, "Sit now, girl. Stay. Good girl," as he ruffled the fur on her back, affectionately. Holly looked excitedly at him, wagging her tail, eager for the next leg of the adventure.

Oran walked quickly back to where they had camped for the night and conjured a new fire using the same spell as before, then returned to the boat, where he reached for one of the bags and then turned and held it out to Aodh.

"Your food as promised, my friend. It's not much, I'm afraid, but I hope it helps." He then smiled as Aodh gratefully took it from him, and added, as he climbed back into the boat, "That fire will burn forever, I imagine, without the need for fuel or tending."

Once all three of them were settled in the boat with their belongings, Dara at the back facing forward with Holly by his feet, and Oran in front facing the rear, Aodh stooped to pick up the loose end of the rope which was still tethered at its other end to the breast-hook of the boat. He proceeded to tie a big knot in it and then offered it up to Gálin. She lowered one of her huge heads gracefully and took the knotted end of the rope in her mouth carefully, as Aodh held it for her and said to her, "You know what to do, girl," taking a pace backwards as Gálin straightened up again.

Gálin gave Aodh a knowing, gentle nod and then slowly began to turn herself, being careful not to hit the boat and upset it and its occupants, toward the open, deep water. She moved slowly at first, taking up the slack in the long rope as she headed for deeper water. The tiny boat with Oran, Dara and Holly turned slowly to follow her, ten yards or so behind her three necks and heads that were all that now showed of her above the water's surface. As the dragon towed the boat away from the shore, Aodh and his siblings once again transformed themselves into swans and began flapping their great, outstretched wings. Making a run toward the water, the four great birds took to the air gracefully, in pursuit of the dragon, the boat and its three new occupants, as they headed for the open and relatively calm water ahead.

Dara looked at Oran excitedly, yet apprehensively, hugging Holly tightly as they moved slowly out onto the lough.

"This is fun. Do you think it's safe, Oran? What if something goes wrong? What if we spring a leak?" Then, looking behind as something caught his eye, he added excitedly, "They're following us, the swans. Look, Oran!"

Oran was just about to answer Dara when Gálin let out an unexpected, loud hoot and, in his surprise, he swung his head around swiftly to see if she was alright, just in time to catch sight of her heads plunging into the water ahead and disappear completely from view with a mighty splash. In the next instant, there came an almighty surge forward as the little boat sped up dramatically - very dramatically - as Gálin accelerated below the surface. Within seconds, they were travelling at an almost alarming speed, and Oran braved a look over the bow, hanging on tightly to the wooden side rail. He could clearly make out the long silvery body of Gálin shimmering in the water below them, just beneath the surface. He stared in amazement as he noticed how her now outstretched wings and broad tail swept gracefully up and down, propelling her forward, as he managed the words, "My goodness, Dara. She can move at quite a speed!"

Dara said nothing in response, but just sat there with a rather alarmed expression on his face, hanging on to the side of the boat with one reddened hand, whilst keeping a firm hold of Holly with the other. He and Oran spent the rest of the twenty-minute boat ride in silence, as the four swans flew gracefully alongside them to the other side of the lough. As they drew near to the other shore and the water became shallower, Gálin slowed and then surfaced again as she made her approach to a low, nearby grassy bank. This was a sure sign that Dara could now ease his grip on both Holly and the boat, as he scanned the shore ahead for any signs of danger.

"It looks deserted, thankfully," he called to Oran, who now had his back turned to Dara, as he too studied the shore ahead.

"I'm rather relieved at that, to say the least. I dread to think what anyone might think, or do, should they witness our arrival like this," Oran said, collectedly.

Gálin slowly drew the boat in as close to the bank as she could, nudging it gently against the overhanging grass with one of her heads, whilst that which had held the rope now dropped it onto the grassy shore next to the little boat. Presently, the four swans landed nearby on a grassy slope and reverted to human form again. Oran and Dara quickly went about the business of removing the bags from the boat, as Holly leapt out and began sniffing her way around this new territory. When they had everything placed carefully onto the grass bank, Oran crouched down onto one knee and went about untying the bag with the two magical black balls inside it. Dara watched on as Oran then put his face into the open bag and whispered something that he couldn't quite make out, or understand, then removed his face and stood upright. A few seconds later, the two black balls flew out of the bag with their familiar whizzing sound, and floated in mid-air, just a few yards from Oran.

"*Beithíoch*," Oran announced, and no sooner had he said it, that the two balls made a strange popping sound and quickly turned back into the horses that they had been prior to their boat trip.

"Well, all back to normal then," Dara stated with some relief, then sarcastically added, "If anyone would call this normal, that is."

"You may as well get used to it, Dara," Oran advised. "This may well be what normal is to you for the rest of your life now. Now that you're a part of all of this, that is to say."

"I thought I'd be going back to my family and a normal life, after all of this is over in a few days, no?" Dara remarked now.

"Perhaps," Oran said, quietly, without looking at Dara directly, as he went about putting his saddle back on his horse.

Dara approached Oran now from behind and placed a hand on his shoulder. Oran looked around quickly, as Dara almost demanded, "What are you saying, Oran? What do you mean, exactly?"

"I'm just saying that there's more to life than that which you had been experiencing up until two days ago," Oran responded, calmly, then added, "Perhaps there may be a place for you and your good family at the castle, when this is all over with. A better life, and certainly, a longer life. That's all I'm saying."

Dara looked at Oran with incredulity, at first, as he was shocked by the statement. His head spun with the possibilities, as he dwelt on it for a moment, then slowly said, "That's a very kind offer. I'm very grateful to you, but you must understand that I should talk it over with my Mary, firstly." He squeezed Oran's shoulder gently as a sign of his gratitude.

"Well don't be too hasty," Oran insisted. "It was merely a thought, but I'll need to get the permission of King Lugh first, of course."

During this exchange, the Children of Lir had come to stand nearby as they listened but did not interrupt. Having sensed that the conversation between Oran and Dara was now at an end, as such, Aodh stepped forward toward Oran, and said, "The time has come for us to bid you farewell, my friends. We must return the boat quickly, before anyone notices that it is missing, and send Gálin back to the depths before any should become aware of her existence, also." He gestured toward the great dragon, who had been watching them all, silently, before continuing, "It has been our great honour to have met you both, and as a parting gesture of good will, and of our friendship, we should like to give to Dara a gift... if it is deemed fitting and acceptable."

"A gift?" asked Dara. "How very kind of you, but there is truly no need."

"Oh, there is indeed need, my friend. You see, you are but mortal, and therefore, we should like to be of some small service to you - to help you in some small way," Aodh offered as he turned to Oran, before adding, "You, Oran, of course, do not need our help, as you already possess your own very unique skills in magic, you understand."

"I do, Aodh," Oran smiled.

"This gift you speak of then - what might it be?" Dara now asked, curiously.

"We wish to bestow upon you a small gift that we call *the sight*, Dara. It will help you in your times of need, if be," Aodh responded, simply.

Dara looked to Oran for some kind of inspiration, or approval, and Oran simply nodded back to him as a sign for him to accept the gift that Aodh offered, to which he announced, "I gratefully accept your gift, in that case."

"Very good, Dara. Please stand just where you are for a moment," Aodh instructed now, as he and his siblings moved to form a close circle around Dara where he currently stood, then continued, "This will not hurt at all, and will take but a few seconds."

Dara smiled anxiously, unsure of what to expect, or of what was about to happen to him. The four stood around him and placed their right palms on his chest and back as Aodh began chanting something unintelligible, sounding to Dara as though he was talking backwards. While Aodh chanted, his siblings began to sing to Dara, a haunting melody, in a language he had never heard before. He felt awkward and embarrassed at first, and then suddenly, a warming sensation travelled through their hands and into his body, briefly. Suddenly, the chanting and singing stopped, and the children removed their hands and stepped a pace back, and away from Dara, as Fionnula announced, "It is done. You are empowered with *the sight*, Dara."

"I don't feel any different," Dara thought aloud. "How do I use this new gift then?" he then asked.

"You need do nothing, Dara," Fionnula stated. "As Aodh has said, it will come to you in your time of need. You will experience *knowledge* at a time when you need it most - that is all, simply."

Dara looked a little bewildered, if not somewhat disappointed. He wondered what use he could have for a magical gift that he had no control over, but decided not to complain and instead, simply said, "Thank you, my friends. I am forever in your debt. Now then, Oran and I must, sadly, also get going, so we must bid you all farewell, I'm afraid."

"Yes, farewell, and thank you all so very much," Oran added, as he climbed up into his saddle with a knowing, smug sort of smile directed toward Dara.

"Should either of you ever have need of us, you know where to find us," Aodh called out to them, as they turned to leave.

As Dara climbed onto his horse, the Children of Lir once again became swans, which now flapped their great wings once more as they ran toward the water's edge and lifted gracefully into the air. Gálin's heads tracked the swans' paths briefly, before turning to look at Oran and Dara as she nodded to them - almost bowed, it seemed - elegantly, with a final hoot, before turning away slowly as she began to swim after the swans, the tiny boat in tow behind her. Oran and Dara watched from their horses, somewhat sadly, as the great beast's three silvery heads soon plunged dramatically into the depths again in the distance, leaving a small wooden boat that oddly appeared to be propelling itself, somehow, at great speed across the open water.

A few moments later, when the swans and the little boat were all but out of sight, Oran turned to Dara and said, "So, mister *I don't think much of this gift*, which way are we headed now then?"

Dara gave him a slightly embarrassed look as he answered, "Was I that obvious?"

"Yes, you were."

"That way," Dara said, meekly, with a nodding gesture, feeling ashamed now. "North-eastwards, to the mountain."

"I'm jesting - you weren't that obvious," Oran reassured him. "It's a good gift. You'll find out, someday, possibly."

"Holly, come girl," Dara called, as he and Oran urged their horses forward in the direction he had just indicated. Dara told himself inwardly, as they rode off, that he wasn't entirely sure that he ever wanted to be in a position where he would be required to make use of his new gift if it was, indeed, intended for times of need.

CHAPTER THIRTEEN
The Boy Changeling

It was already well into late morning as Oran and Dara headed steadily, yet somewhat forlornly, away from the lough and the both pleasing and welcome new acquaintances and experiences which it had brought to them. They travelled on steadfastly towards the northeast in their continuing search for the mountain, where they hoped to find the dragon known as Rydian. Holly, as though leading the way, darted about busily through the yellowing grass and occasional bushes just in front of them, as if she was scouting the way ahead to make sure it was safe for them to proceed. Oran and Dara were, of course, mindful to stay out of sight of others at all costs, avoiding any villages or other signs of human habitation as they made their way across country, using frequent copses, hedgerows and the like for cover where possible.

The sky above them had, meanwhile, turned an unwelcome dark grey, as dense cloud rolled in from the Atlantic Ocean to the west. The thick layer of cloud now blocked out what little warmth the winter sunshine had offered them, as well as removing Dara's navigational aide in the form of the the sun, bringing with it something more than a stiff breeze as the wind picked up and buffeted them from behind. Dara braced himself against the chill of this new foe, as he turned to Oran and said in a low voice, "We'll have to navigate by guesswork again, Oran, now that we've lost sight of the sun." Giving his friend a sort of hopeful grimace, he added, "I'm fairly certain we're headed in the right direction, mind. No need to worry - I'm sure we'll be just fine. We can use the clouds' movement as our guide - they generally travel west to east, you know. Well, they do most of the time anyhow, so we should keep heading this way." He pointed directly ahead of them as he said this.

"That sounds oddly and worryingly familiar, Dara," came Oran's retort. "I'm equally concerned, mind you, that it might start raining soon. The sky grows worryingly darker by the minute, it seems. I'm fearful that a storm may be on the way."

"Rain? Let's hope not, Oran," he said, as he looked up at the sky briefly, with a frown, and then ahead again as he continued more chirpily, "I'm a little thirsty, how about you? Would you like something to drink from the bag here?" He pushed his hand blindly into the large leather bag that was hanging from the right side of his saddle and began to rummage for a flask that he knew was there, somewhere.

"A little, perhaps," Oran replied, with what seemed to be uncertainty, as though his mind was elsewhere presently. He was, in fact, hoping desperately that they would find the mountain soon, and that Rydian would be easily tracked down and agreeable to his, or rather, Lugh's request. Dara, sensing something was amiss with the elf, guessed wrongly at his behaviour, believing that he was just concerned about the inclement weather, probably.

A moment later, after some more rummaging, Dara produced a quite ornate looking silver flask, which he hadn't noticed in the bag previously, as he announced, "Yes! You're mine now, you little beauty."

He gave it a slight shake to make sure that it was full, then held it aloft as he looked at it with a somewhat pleasantly surprised expression, before lowering it again as he proceeded to carefully remove the cork from its neck. He held, or rather, offered the flask at arms-length, toward Oran.

"Would you care for first sip?"

"No, no, you first. I insist," Oran stated, politely.

Dara grinned widely as he complied, and eagerly raised the flask up to his waiting mouth. Just as he was about to take a swig from it, his nose detected a strong but not altogether unpleasant smell, at which he recoiled a little as he announced with some surprise, "This isn't water! There's whiskey in this flask - I'm sure of it!"

"It's more likely to be poitín, home brewed at the castle by Murchad the Wise," Oran remarked a little off-handedly, knowingly adding, "Rather than whiskey, if I know anything."

"Well, it's alcohol, whichever it is - that much I'm quite certain of," Dara assured him.

"It will serve to warm you up - keep the cold at bay, if you will," Oran told him.

"Aye, it will that," Dara laughed now, and carefully raised the flask to his mouth again.

He sampled the contents of the flask cautiously at first, not sure if he would like the taste that much or not. He had never been much of a drinker and had always preferred to stay at home with his family rather than frequent the local tavern most evenings, like many of his fellow male villagers of Glenarran. Lowering the flask again slowly, and looking at Oran with something of a grin, he said, "I must say that I do quite like this. It burns a little, but in a pleasant way, if you get my meaning?"

"I did say that it would warm you, and be careful with that, Dara. That poitín is renowned throughout the castle's population for its extreme potency. It has a bite that sneaks up on you," Oran advised, wisely, then asked, "Are you planning on drinking the whole thing yourself now, then?" as he reached for the flask.

"We should be careful - you're absolutely right," Dara agreed, taking another eager sip, or rather swig, before passing the flask to Oran's waiting hand. "We need to keep our wits about us, and that means not getting drunk – so, in moderation, if you please, my friend."

Oran smiled at him and then raised the flask to his mouth, taking what appeared to Dara to be a very healthy swig, then lowering the flask again as he let out a gasp of what Dara assumed to be relief - or maybe it was just pleasure from the taste. Dara couldn't be sure which, as Oran passed the flask back to him with a smile, and decided to have another little sip himself - just one more couldn't do any harm after all, he told himself. The pair rode on as they, over the course of the next half hour, merrily and blissfully drained the small silver flask of its contents entirely. Dara had just taken the last mouthful, and now looked regretfully at Oran as he tipped the flask upside down, shaking it to demonstrate the fact that it was now completely and utterly empty.

"Oh dear," Oran said, as he feigned disappointment.

"Oh dear, indeed," responded Dara, somewhat despondently.

"Probably a good thing, to be honest," advised Oran. "I was beginning to enjoy the drink quite a bit, worryingly."

"Aye, true, very true," Dara now seemed to mumble, then hiccoughed suddenly, as he brought his horse to a halt.

"Are you alright, Dara?" Oran laughed, as he too brought his horse to a stop alongside Dara's. "Will you be able to continue leading the way? Can you see alright? See clearly, I mean?"

"Yes, I'm fine," Dara mumbled again, feeling a little tipsy, or dizzy, then looked at the ground below and back up at the way ahead. "Let's get going then, old fellow."

"Enough with the old," Oran admonished.

Dara urged his horse forward again, saying nothing of the fact that he felt slightly inebriated, closely followed by a mildly concerned Oran and an oblivious Holly as he began singing loudly and merrily about someone - a girl, Oran surmised, called Ginny. *Who could this person be?* Oran wondered, *this Ginny that Dara sang of,* as they travelled on in what they hoped and believed to be the direction of Slieve Mish. He also wondered where Dara had learned to sing so awfully, as he now changed the name in the song to Mary, unsurprisingly.

A few painfully sung renditions later, they came upon a rather large woodland on a gentle, upwardly sloping hillside, which, after some deliberation, they decided to risk going directly through, rather than the longer way around. This, they agreed, would serve several purposes - firstly, by saving them time and secondly, by providing some shelter from the harsh wind, as well as protecting them from unwanted and unwelcome discovery, they hoped.

As they entered, it was clear to both that this was a very ancient pine forest. The tall trees were very large and looked very old, and were well-spaced, so the going was quite easy although slightly, but not worryingly, uphill for the foreseeable future. The vast forest floor was covered almost entirely in a thick amber-brown carpet of fallen pine needles that must have taken many decades to accumulate, and which felt decidedly soft and spongey underfoot, as it became apparent that the horses were almost struggling to walk through it.

Dara looked down to see his horse's hooves sinking some six inches into the bed of pine needles with each step but knew that this was normal and nothing to be concerned over, so persisted onward. He had stopped singing now, and this brought Oran to notice how eerily quiet it was in the forest, the only sound being that of the tree branches brushing together in the winds aloft as they caressed each other gently. He found now that he almost wished that Dara had continued with his singing and was about to suggest to him that he did so, but immediately thought better of it out of concern for his hearing.

Dara was presently focused on the path ahead, as he rode steadily but slowly onward, looking upward occasionally through the trees to get his bearings from the direction in which the clouds were moving overhead. He reached down to his side and took the old map from the saddle bag as he rode, studying it for a moment thoughtfully, before turning to Oran and stating confidently, "I'm fairly certain, according to this map which we possess, that we are presently just a few miles east of the village of Na Cealla. If I'm correct and such *is* the case, then we are getting close, my friend. A further half day's travel, perhaps."

Oran simply nodded agreement, with a half-smile, whilst Dara shoved the map back into the bag, as they continued onward through the forest. Dara smiled too, as he watched Holly darting and weaving about ahead of them, sniffing almost every inch of the ground keenly as she went, when suddenly he felt his stomach rumble. He realised, as he gave it some thought, that he hadn't eaten much today, apart from the little salmon he had shared with Oran and Holly that morning at the lough side. He wondered now if Oran, too, might possibly be a little hungry and so, turned to him and enquired, "Are you in need of something to eat, Oran? I'm a little peckish, and it's surely around noon, time for some lunch?"

"Well," Oran began, placing the palm of his hand on his stomach, as he continued, "Now that you mention it, I *could* eat something - something light perhaps - but not too much." He hastily added, "I don't wish to stop again though. Let's eat on the move, yes? We can't afford to lose any more time, Dara. We really must make it to the mountain by this nightfall if we are to stay on schedule. We should remind ourselves that the castle still lies exposed for as long as we are out here on this quest, no?"

Dara wasted no time and moved his attention now to the bag that hung from the left side of his saddle, opening it quickly. As he shoved his hand fervently inside, looking down to his left as he did, he couldn't help noticing that Holly was walking directly between him and Oran now, or rather between their horses, and that she appeared to be chewing on a small piece of raw meat, wherever she had gotten it from, oddly. He brushed it off quickly, in the belief that she had found it by chance, somewhere nearby - perhaps the unwanted remnants of some wild animal's prey. Then, just as suddenly, he realised that he was quite certain he had just seen her off in front of them mere seconds ago, so how did she get there so quickly, walking between them now?

He glanced up swiftly with some concern, looking to the front again and incredibly, there was Holly, just where he had seen her a moment before, walking some ten yards ahead of them. He swung his gaze back down in alarm and disbelief, now to find no sign of the Holly he'd just seen there between the horses. *How could this be?* he asked himself inwardly. He had failed to notice, however, that she was actually now directly underneath his horse, just out of his line of sight.

Must have been the alcohol, he now assured himself, as he sat in his saddle feeling slightly foolish for having possibly drunk too much.

"Are you alright, Dara?" Oran asked, noticing Dara's odd actions and concerned expression. "You look a little confused... bewildered. Is everything well with you?"

"Yes, yes, of course it is," Dara responded, as he confessed, "I think that the drink, the poitín, may have caused me to hallucinate somewhat, maybe."

"How so?" Oran chuckled, finding Dara's plight mildly amusing.

"I believe that I'm seeing double, is how so. I seemed to have two dogs, just now, instead of only the one," he nervously laughed.

"Don't be silly, man. She's right there between us, where she's been for the past five minutes or so. I've seen no other dog," Oran insisted, as he now considered the prospect that Dara might have become more than a little intoxicated by the alcohol.

Dara knew that Oran's statement surely couldn't be true, however, and quickly looked to his front again, where he could clearly see his faithful dog, Holly. He then glanced downward quickly, looking between the horses, and sure enough, saw her there as well, as she had now reappeared from underneath his horse. He sat bolt upright in alarm, taking a deep breath through his nostrils as he shook his head quickly, desperately trying to clear his mind and vision, then assured Oran, "I'm still seeing two of her... help me, man! I think I'm losing my faculties."

Oran looked at Dara with a bemused expression, then looked down, briefly, at the Holly that walked between them, before lifting his head casually, certain that Dara was imagining this second dog, and looking directly ahead. What he saw now, however, alarmed him greatly also, for there, several yards in front of them, was Holly - another, second Holly - sure enough. His expression quickly turned to one of alarm, as he knew that it was virtually impossible for both he and Dara to share the same hallucination - particularly in the same instant.

"It's not just you, Dara!" Oran exclaimed in panic. "I can see two of her as well. Something is not right here - not right at all. There's some kind of sorcery at play here, I'm sure of it!"

"Holly!" Dara now yelled, and as he did so, the Holly off to their front stopped and turned her head round to face them briefly, before returning eagerly to her scouting and sniffing. At this, they both drew their horses to an abrupt and simultaneous halt as they regarded each other with some confusion, and then looked down between their horses in unison.

The Holly that walked between them carried on walking for a few seconds, as Oran's and Dara's eyes followed her carefully, before stopping and turning also, as she, or it, realised that the horses had stopped behind her, and that their occupants were now paying her a great deal of unwelcome attention. Oran and Dara stared at this second Holly momentarily, then back at the other Holly who had gone back to sniffing the ground far ahead, and who was oblivious to what was taking place behind her, as the occupants of the horses tried to comprehend what they were seeing. They regarded the nearer dog in silent confusion for a moment when, suddenly and without warning, it bolted toward and in between their now stationary horses.

What developed next happened so quickly that Oran and Dara could hardly believe their eyes. It seemed as though, in the mere blink of an eye, the *other* Holly - the imposter, it would seem - firstly transformed into a young boy as it, or he, swiftly approached Oran's horse with almost inhuman speed. Amazingly, and just as swiftly, as the boy touched the horse's shoulder with his outstretched right hand, he then almost instantaneously transformed himself into what appeared to be an exact duplicate of Oran's horse, which then continued running, or galloping, off in the direction from which they had come. It was all just a blur really - one almost fluid movement, occurring in mere seconds. Dara wasted no time in shaking off any fear or concern and swiftly reacted by turning and giving chase, despite his alarm and confusion at what he had just witnessed, with Oran and what they were now certain was the real Holly in pursuit not far behind.

"You there! Stop! Get back here now!" he yelled at the rider-less horse, as he galloped furiously after it through the trees. "Stop, who are you?" he yelled again.

He frantically pursued the horse for several minutes through the forest at breakneck speed, with Oran and Holly not far behind him. Suddenly, the fleeing horse seemed to lose its footing as it tried to change direction swiftly in an attempt to shake Dara, no doubt, sliding in the soft bed of pine needles and then crashing to the ground before rolling and colliding with a huge tree trunk, its legs flailing wildly in the air.

Dara seized his opportunity and was upon the stricken animal in seconds. He quickly leapt down from his horse and drew his blade, as he carefully approached the horse which now lay motionless on its right side, staring up at him with big dark eyes and snorting heavily through its nostrils, seemingly injured. As he drew cautiously nearer, however, the horse once again transformed into a very slim, pale, and sparsely clothed young boy with long, unkempt, dark hair, who now curled into a ball on his right side as he raised his hands to cover his face, and tearfully whimpered, "Please, sir... no harm, no harm! I was hungry... not eaten for days. Aghh, my leg!" He cried out in pain, reaching down to touch a rather large graze on his left shin.

Dara halted a few steps from the boy on hearing this, as Oran and Holly joined him. All three stood side-by-side, regarding the scruffy looking boy with some perplexity. Dara's countenance softened slightly now on hearing the boy's pleas. Holly was the first to make contact, as she soon wandered over to him cautiously, tail tucked between her back legs, and began to sniff at the animal furs tied around him. The boy seemed somewhat afraid of her, drawing himself into a tighter ball as Oran now approached him slowly, and asked softly, "Who are you? What is your name, child?" He then comforted him, "You need not be afraid of us, as we, also, mean *you* no harm. My name is Oran, of the good people of Danu and this, to my left, is my trusted companion and guide, Dara MacBrien. The dog, who now pays you careful attention, is named Holly."

The boy, on hearing this, slowly removed his hands to reveal a rather dirty, youthful face. He then gingerly extended a hand toward Holly as a gesture of friendship, whilst remaining curled up on his side. Oran watched as Holly tentatively sniffed at the boy's outstretched, trembling hand, then noticed how the boy's pale, yellow eyes shifted constantly between himself and Dara. He could sense that the boy was, indeed, very frightened by them.

"I ask again, what are you called, child? Do you have a name?" Oran enquired once more, speaking softly in an effort not to frighten the boy further.

The boy looked directly at Oran for a moment, as though searching for words and then almost whispered, "Name is Tarnée, good sir... Tarnée."

"Tarnée?" Dara interjected, with a frown. "That's not an Irish name - not one that I know of, well. Where are you from then... Tarnée?"

"Come here from Scotland - well, was sent. Banished for my curse - curse of being a shape shifter. Changeling, they call me," the boy began to explain in a timid voice, before continuing as, with apparent difficulty owing to his injury, he sat himself upright, "Everyone called me Obblob though - nickname from childhood. Say it is first thing I ever said, as an infant."

"*Oddlob*?" Dara asked, quizzically. "A strange name, indeed."

"No... *Obb... lob*. Nickname, as said, but you may call me by either," the boy explained again, in his odd, somewhat broken vocabulary.

"Ah, well then, Obblob it is," Dara laughed heartily, as Oran approached the boy and knelt directly in front of him.

"Why are you here in the forest? All alone, I mean? Where is your family, where are your parents?" Oran asked.

"I was banished here some time ago, told you that. Well, not here, exactly, island off the coast, but managed to sneak onto a fishing boat. Brought me to this land a few months ago. Took form of a rat, I did, for the whole journey. To hide, you see, was nasty nasty," the boy continued to explain to Oran, then asked suddenly, "Where is *here* exactly? What land's this? Is this Ireland... you, mister... said Irish name?" as he looked directly up toward Dara.

"It is that, yes," Oran confirmed, then asked again, "What of your family?"

The boy looked at them both for a minute, thoughtfully, before speaking. He was still quite concerned for his safety and, after all, had no idea what the intentions of Oran and Dara might be. Perhaps they planned to kidnap and imprison him, or perhaps, something worse. He took a deep breath, sighed as he looked at Oran, and then answered, "My father is Formorian prince, name of Alkan and my mother a gypsy traveller, from lands far away in the east. Her name was Raylsha. Was she who gave me the curse, if you like - changeling she was too." He then paused for a moment, as Oran and Dara waited patiently for more, in obvious apprehension, then continued, "When I came of age and my true nature - my ability - became known, Formorian leaders had my mother put to death, executed. Father was stripped of his title and locked away in a dungeon for life. Obblob was not executed, but banished, owing to my young age."

"That's terrible for someone so young," Dara interrupted. "How old are you, boy?"

"I have fifteen years, I believe," Obblob answered with some uncertainty.

"So, are you all alone here in Ireland then?" Oran continued to question.

"Well, yes, of course I am," Obblob replied, sadly, then added in a hopeful tone, "But now I have company, yourselves. Nicey nicey," now referring to Holly as he sat stroking her ears affectionately, which she was obviously enjoying, as her eyes were now almost fully closed.

"Wow, wow, wow. Now no-one said anything about us being your companions, yet," Dara said, gruffly.

The boy looked up at him with an expression of great disappointment, which Oran noticed clearly, and so stood up and walked over to Dara, whispering, "A word please, Dara."

He took Dara gently by the arm and led him over to the horses, as he called back to Obblob, "Wait there just a moment please, young man, if you'd be so kind."

"What troubles you, Oran?" Dara asked.

"The boy is all alone, Dara. He has no-one. I think that we should take him along with us on our quest, don't you agree?" Oran pointed out, now adding, "At least he'll be with people who understand him, in a way. People of a similar kind, in some respect."

"Well, how do we know that he won't give us trouble?" Dara warned Oran. "What if he steals all of our food, then makes off with the horses in the night while we are both asleep. Have you thought about that possibility, Oran? He's already stolen from us once! Then there's the small fact that he's also half Formorian - sworn enemy of the Danu, your people, no?"

"Yes, half Formorian, but only half, and on that basis, I'm willing to take the risk. After all, he may be of use to us with his unique ability - his talent," Oran said, toying with his bracelet thoughtfully, then adding, "I also think that King Lugh will be interested to meet the boy, and to learn from him, perhaps, the whereabouts of the Formorians upon our return to the castle. Don't you agree?"

"Well, yes, I suppose so. Do I have a choice?" Dara asked, curtly.

Oran chose not to answer the question as he turned and walked back to the boy and again, knelt in front of him where he sat now, still stroking Holly affectionately. The boy seemed more interested in Holly and didn't even appear to notice Oran, knelt directly in front of him now. Oran reached out and touched him on his shoulder gently to get his attention, startling him slightly, as he asked, "Tarnée, how do you feel about your people after how they have treated you and your parents? How do you feel about the Formorian people, I mean?"

"Nasty nasty. I hate them all... nasty, evil people," he responded, angrily.

"Really? You really hate them, all of them?" Oran searched.

"Yes, really, really hate them all... for what they have done to me, and my family. Loved my parents dearly, miss them, miss my home," the boy assured him.

"Very well then. How would you like to come with us on our journey in that case?" Now, looking round at Dara, Oran tried to gauge his reaction to this suggestion. No reaction came, however, as Dara watched and listened in silence, and so, Oran enquired, "Dara, are you content with this arrangement? If not, speak now please."

Obblob certainly wasted no time in accepting the offer and blurted out eagerly, "Come with you, really? Yes, yes. Likey likey."

Dara looked at the ground pensively for a moment, as he aimlessly created a small pile of pine needles using his right foot, then looked back up at Oran, and then at the boy as he answered gravely, "If you're happy, then I'm happy, master Oran. It's your quest, after all. You're in charge, and *you* are responsible for him."

Oran smiled at Dara, then turned back to the boy, rising to his feet as he announced, "It's settled then. You're coming with us, Tarnée... sorry, I meant Obblob."

The boy pulled himself painfully up onto his feet, his injured leg still smarting from the earlier fall, and enquired, "Where, might I ask, is it that we are going exactly?"

Dara looked at the boy and began to laugh as he informed him, "Oh, we're just out looking for a dragon - a big dragon... a Fire Dragon no less. That's all."

"A what!" the boy yelped, in wide-eyed terror.

CHAPTER FOURTEEN
Behold! Slieve Mish

The three of them stood there, in the depths of the ancient forest, looking silently at each other for a minute. Obblob was still stood next to Holly, staring wide-eyed and in complete disbelief at what he had just heard Dara say, then suddenly demanded, "Explain *looking for a dragon,* please?"

"It's very simple really, Obblob," Dara began, as he turned to Oran and proposed, "Master Oran, would you care to explain the exact nature of our quest to this young man?" gesturing now toward the boy, with an outstretched right arm.

Oran looked at Dara momentarily, a little lost for words at first. He wondered how best to explain things to the frightened looking youth that stood some yards away from him without going into too much detail, then looked down at the ground and back up at the boy again, trying to think of a way to subdue his obvious fear. If truth be told, he now realised, he too, was also afraid of the dragon to some degree, but decided that he should keep that fact to himself. He took a few paces closer to Obblob, and then offered, "I need the help of a particular dragon to fix something that I, shall we say, broke a few days ago, and only the dragon that we seek out can help me, no other." He then turned and gestured toward the object that was just visible, protruding from the bag that hung from his saddle, as he continued, "You need not be afraid of her, as I have in my possession the Sword of Light, an enchanted sword that was carried by dragon commanders - Danu leaders - who rode on the backs of mighty dragons in battles of old. This sword will empower and permit me, as it did them, to tame and command the dragon as I wish. She will not do any of us any form of harm, I give you my word as a Danu... my solemn promise."

The boy took a step toward Oran and began to ask, meekly, "So you know of this dragon then? Know where to find it, where to look?"

"Yes, we know of her. Her name is Rydian, and she served faithfully under our King, King Lugh, in the last great battle fought by the Danu, after which she was granted her freedom and also, immortality. I must say, however, that the mere fact that we know of her is by no means a guarantee that we shall be able to locate her. We have, however, been given certain information as to her most likely whereabouts and thus, have good reason to believe that our search leads us in the right direction, if she *is* to be found."

"Rydian, you say?" Obblob began, then stated almost matter-of-factly, "Can't say I've ever heard that name in any stories or tales of dragons that *I've* been told."

"Ah, well now, you see, she hasn't been seen by *our* people for some three hundred years or thereabouts - quite possibly not by anyone, in fact." He then paused for a second, before advising, "I almost hope, in fact, that no-one *has* seen her, as that would, no doubt, serve to put her in probable danger, I fear. As I already said, we don't even really know for sure that we shall find her, as she may very well have gone into hiding underground, you see. But, we certainly hope that we do find her, as we are very much in need of her help - our very lives may depend upon it."

Obblob spent a moment allowing Oran's most recent statements to sink in, then cheekily enquired, "What you break, Oran?"

"Ah, that's a rather difficult thing to explain, but suffice to say that we need one of the dragon's unhatched eggs - a very rare and precious object known as a dragon crystal, in order to put things right," Oran curtly answered, not wishing to go into a long and detailed explanation of the recent events surrounding the demise of the time cocoon. Besides, he was very eager to get on the move again, and so enquired rather abruptly of the boy now, "Are you coming with us or not, young master Obblob? We need to be on the move again as time is very much against us, as always."

Obblob looked at Oran pensively for a moment, then at Dara, who was now stood just behind Oran, but said nothing in response at first. He stooped as he reached down and patted Holly on the head briefly and then, as he stood upright again, replied, "Never heard of dragon crystal, but certainly, I will join you. Obblob will make good company for your dog, I think."

Oran and Dara glanced at each other briefly, as they laughed at the changeling's strange comment. Oran then said, "Very well, it's settled then. Oh, and speaking of putting things right... would you like me to tend to that injury on your leg?" He then smiled at the boy as he pointed at the nasty graze on his leg.

"Well, it does hurt quite a bit. What can you do though?" the changeling asked, as if doubting that there was anything that either Oran or Dara could do to ease the pain and suffering caused by his injury.

"Well, I can do this," Oran stated confidently, as he knelt in front of Obblob and placed his right hand just above the wound on his leg.

Obblob looked down and watched apprehensively as Oran closed his eyes and began to whisper. He stood motionless as Dara observed quietly from behind Oran. Dara was well aware of what was about to happen next. A moment later, Oran stood up again as the faint blue glow of his healing spell faded from his hand, announcing with a grin, "There you go - all better now."

Obblob no longer felt any pain. He looked down at his leg, amazed to find no sign of the wound that was there just a moment ago, then smiled as he said, "Thank you, Oran," before nonchalantly reaching down to touch Holly again, as he quipped, "Well, let's get going then, what are you both waiting for?"

Oran and Dara laughed again at the boy's blatant impudence for such a young person, then both raised their eyebrows simultaneously as they watched him once again shape-shift into an exact copy of Holly upon touching her flank with his hand. They laughed and shook their heads in near disbelief, as they both turned and walked towards their horses, and the two dogs began play-fighting behind them. A few moments later, they were both saddled up and Oran, once again, asked of Dara, "Lead the way, good sir."

Dara nodded with a smile, as he swiftly complied with his friend's request by commanding his horse to move off, beckoning Holly and Obblob to follow them. Glad that the ill effects of the alcohol had completely worn off now, he set off in the direction which he felt sure in his head and heart to be the right way, briefly looking upward to check the direction of the cloud travel above, just as he'd done before. They travelled cautiously onwards through the forest for an hour or so, with Holly scouting the way, just in front as usual, and the canine Obblob shadowing her every move.

Eventually, they arrived at the forest's edge and could once more, with now unobstructed views, see clearly what lay ahead of them in the distance. They came to a halt just beyond the tree line, atop a hillside that sloped gently downward in front of them and then levelled out in the distance. Oran and Dara allowed their eyes time to adjust to the brighter light beyond the reasonably dense, evergreen forest canopy. Sharing a feeling that they must be close to their destination by now, they both began scanning the distant, relatively flat landscape for signs of the mountain they sought.

"Behold! Over there, Dara!" Oran soon exclaimed, pointing excitedly ahead of them. "That bump on the horizon, way over there - look! It has to be Slieve Mish, no?"

Dara scanned the horizon for a moment in the direction which Oran had just signified, still squinting slightly, as the dogs played in the grass nearby. He had found that he couldn't tell which one was the real Holly by just appearance alone, except for when he caught a glimpse of her old collar under her fur, which troubled him slightly. Then he saw it - far off in the distance - a small rounded bump on the otherwise flat horizon, almost directly ahead of them now. He recalled the description he had been given by Cethen on the night that they had departed the castle, and now agreed that the mountain did, indeed, stand alone on a flat plain, just as he had said.

"Told you that I would get you there, didn't I?" Dara said smugly, with a big grin.

"Ah! Not so hasty, my friend. We're not *there* yet, are we?" Oran retorted.

"True, my good man, very true. But at least we can see exactly where it is that we are headed now. That is a good thing, yes?"

"I just realised something," Oran began, as his stomach rumbled loudly. "We never did get around to having some food earlier, due to all the excitement of meeting our new friend, Obblob, there. I'm actually starving now - what about you, Dara?"

"Well, I knew that we had to get going, and we had already lost more time due to our young shape-shifting friend here, so I didn't want to say anything," Dara responded, honestly.

"Well, let's eat something now then, shall we," Oran suggested with a smile.

"Of course," Dara agreed. "We can still eat on the move if you prefer. I don't mind at all."

"Agreed, let's do that then," the boyish looking elf said, as he began to rummage in the bags for something to eat.

Dara also began rummaging in one of the bags attached to his saddle and, having both found something satisfactory to eat, they set off again, down the hillside in the direction of the now visible Slieve Mish. They rode along at their usual steady pace, eating as they went and briefly discussing Dara's life as a husband, father and farmer when, as they were just finishing their food, Oran made a rather strange suggestion.

"I think we should make a run for it, Dara, now that we can see where we are headed to - the mountain, I mean. We can't get lost now - no chance of it. How long can Holly maintain a swift pace for, do you think? What I mean to say is, how long would she last, with the horses at a gallop? Do you think she could keep up with us?"

Dara pondered Oran's strange line of questioning for a second or two, before answering, "Don't really know, if I'm honest," then paused for a moment, before continuing, "She's never had to do a lot of running. I mean, maybe five or ten minutes here and there while she was rounding up the sheep, but certainly nothing more, and I honestly doubt that she could keep up with them for long... why do you ask, Oran?"

"The horses will never tire out, you see, Dara. They could gallop at full speed from here to that mountain, easily," Oran explained, rather enthusiastically. He sat in his saddle staring at the mountain in the distance for a moment, thinking, and then made another suggestion. "If you could get Holly up into the saddle with you, and Obblob can ride with me, then we'd certainly be at the mountain by nightfall if the horses ran at full speed - there's no doubt in my mind."

"I could give it a try, I suppose - don't know how she'll react to it though, at speed," Dara replied, with some apprehension, then advised, "Can you get down and lift her up to me though? It's a bit of a struggle trying to do it on my own."

"Done!" Oran chirped, as he eagerly dismounted from his horse, calling Holly to his side and remarking to her, "First time on a boat today, and now first time on a horse, eh girl? Quite the adventurer, aren't you?" He ruffled the fur at the back of her neck affectionately, before bending down to scoop her up in his arms. He then carried her over to Dara's waiting hands, while the other dog, Obblob, watched them curiously from nearby.

"Memory playing up on you, eh, old timer? Holly was on horseback but two days ago, the evening we departed the castle... remember?" Dara quizzed mockingly, as he regarded Oran with a frown, then reminded him confidently, "To get her past the fireworms, yes? It is her second time on a horse... isn't it now?"

Oran gave him a bemused look, then muttered, "Oh, yes, how foolish of me. Like I haven't got anything more important to concern myself with presently."

Dara then turned slightly in his saddle and called to the changeling, "Obblob, you need to change back to yourself, to human form again. You're going on horseback with Oran for a while."

Obblob complied with Dara's request and, as he quickly shape-shifted back to his natural form, Oran and Dara wrestled a somewhat nervous Holly up into the saddle between Dara's legs. With Holly now in place between Dara's knees, and seemingly content, Oran turned and called over to the boy, now stood waiting by his horse.

"Look in the bags on my horse and find yourself some warmer, more suitable clothing. You're about the same size as me, after all. We don't want you to freeze to death on the back of my horse, in those furs that barely cover you."

"I can't fathom how he hasn't already frozen to death, dressed like that," Dara remarked, off-handedly.

Having heard Dara's remark, Obblob simply responded by saying, "Easy enough to become an animal that can deal with the cold, like a rabbit or a fox."

Dara scratched the top of his head as he responded, "Silly me - didn't think about that for some reason."

As the boy changeling went about his search through Oran's saddle bags for some warmer clothing, Dara suggested to Oran, "Can you shorten my stirrups a little please, Oran? Raise them up a bit, I mean? That way, my knees will be raised higher, and I can use them to help keep Holly safely in place."

"Yes, certainly," Oran replied, as he fastidiously set about tying loops in the leather straps that Dara's stirrups hung from, then proudly stood back and announced, "There you go, my good man. Job done... how's that for length?"

Dara placed his feet back in the stirrups, testing the position of his knees relative to Holly and, with a confident nod, responded, "Perfect - that should do the trick. Well then, all you need to do now is get yourself and the boy mounted up, and we're ready to get going."

"Yes," Oran said, as he walked off toward the boy changeling, who was still stood by the horse and now also wearing some of Oran's clothes. As the elf neared the boy, he instructed, "Right then Obblob, get yourself up in that saddle - nearest the back end if you will, please."

The changeling nodded agreement, as he turned and pulled himself up onto the horse and shuffled his bottom toward the rear of the saddle as much as he could. Oran was swiftly up after him and sat directly in front of him. He reached down and took hold of the reins, before twisting round to the boy to advise, "Put your arms around my waist, Obblob. Hang on tightly and don't let go for any reason, do you understand me?" Then, as the boy did as he was instructed, Oran turned to Dara and called out, "These horses are a little faster than any horse you may have encountered before, Dara. Hang on to Holly tightly, yes? Now, bring yourself alongside me, please. I need to command the horses simultaneously, otherwise one of them might run off without the other, and we don't want that to happen, do we?"

Dara, with Holly positioned between his knees and sitting with her back to him, guided his horse over to and in beside Oran's and watched as Oran leant as far forward as he could manage. The elf then whispered something inaudible to them, before sitting back and instructing, "Everyone hold on tight now!" He then shouted the command to the horses, *"An súarra!"*

In an instant, the horses set off together at a reasonably brisk pace - but not unusually fast though, Dara noticed. He held the reins tightly with one hand, whilst maintaining a firm hold of Holly's collar with the other, at the same time keeping her confined between his raised knees. As he glanced over toward Oran and Obblob briefly, he found the changeling with his face pressed against Oran's back, eyes firmly shut, clinging to Oran around his waist as though his very life depended on it. The horses were only two or three feet apart and didn't yet seem to him to be travelling at anything near the speed Oran had suggested, when suddenly, Oran called out again, *"An falcúla!"*

Worryingly for Dara, the horses suddenly surged forward, accelerating rapidly, gaining more and more speed. It reminded him of how the little boat had sped up that same morning, as the water dragon had submerged and gathered speed with himself, Oran and

Holly in tow behind it. He now clung on as tightly as he could to both Holly and the reins, but still felt somewhat fearful of falling off. The grass and shrubs below them passed in a blur as he now held on for dear life. He noticed that his face gradually began to feel strange, as though his skin and flesh were loosening and wobbling, as it was buffeted by the rapidly approaching cold air ahead. Making a concerted effort not to fall off, he turned his head to face Oran, and yelled out, "I think... my face... is coming loose!"

Oran merely turned to face him and smiled somewhat awkwardly, Dara immediately noticing how Oran's cheeks had taken on the ridiculous appearance of ripples in water, to some extent. He thought that his own face must surely look equally as comical, which was probably why Oran had smiled at him. He shrugged it off as they hurtled past some low flying pigeons that were headed in roughly the same direction as they were, startling and scattering the birds everywhere as they sped past them. *We're travelling faster than the pigeons*, Dara laughed inwardly to himself, then called out with some difficulty, "Hold on tight, Holly!"

Holly seemed to ignore him. She had her head tucked down as low as possible behind the horse's head and neck, her ears flapping madly in the wind, which Dara thought was quite clever of her. This position was, no doubt, offering her some protection from the oncoming wind, he assumed. They rode on across the thankfully open grassland at this incredible speed - for a horse, that is - for half an hour or so, Slieve Mish looming rapidly closer all the while, growing larger and larger in front of them. As they neared the base of the mountain, Dara thought he could hear Oran shout something over the noise of the wind that was assaulting his ears also, but was unable to discern what it was. Suddenly, the horses slowed to their normal canter. Dara sat upright in his saddle again and breathed a big sigh of relief as he patted Holly on her back, easing his grip on her at the same time.

"Is everyone alright?" Oran called out.

"Only just, I think," came Dara's mumbled response. His face still felt very odd indeed – quite numb and almost painful, in fact.

"I'm fine," Obblob stated, as he removed his arms from around Oran's slender waist, taking hold of the sides of his jacket now, instead.

As they arrived near the base of Slemish and came to an eventual halt, Oran jumped down from his horse and went over to assist Dara with getting a rather relieved looking Holly back onto firm ground. Obblob stayed where he was for a moment and watched them struggle with the now flailing dog that couldn't wait to get off Dara's horse and back onto her own four feet, chuckling quietly to himself. With Holly eventually lifted down from his horse, Dara began to massage his cheeks with his reddened hands, at which point Oran assured him, "Your face will feel normal in a little while, don't worry."

"Well, I hope so. I wouldn't want to feel like this for the rest of my life," Dara mumbled again.

"We still have an hour or two of daylight left," Oran advised, quickly changing the subject, more pressing matters on his mind presently. "I think we should start by skirting around the base of the mountain, to see if we can find the easiest way up to the summit, as the sides look quite steep here. Let's just hope that Rydian is somewhere up there. We're so close now, Dara."

"Well," responded Dara, feeling returning to his face now, "Perhaps the beast is somewhere up there, watching us this very instant." He turned his gaze upward, at the barren looking, rocky mountain-side.

Meanwhile, Obblob had dismounted from Oran's horse and had rejoined Holly in his role as a dog - frolicking with her, nearby. Oran noticed this but thought little of it as it now seemed normal to him. He went back to his horse and climbed up into the saddle, saying, "Let's get going then. Agreed?"

"Agreed," answered Dara.

They set off again and rode along for an hour or so, Holly and Obblob in front once more, trekking around the base of the mountain in search of a path or trail that might lead to the top, but found nothing of the kind. The sides of the mountain were steep and rocky, and there appeared to be no easy path to the top. Dara looked up, momentarily, to see that the skies above were still overcast and threatening, but, thus far, there had come no rain, fortunately for them. The lack of any evident trail, Oran believed, was probably a very good indication that no-one else had been up here recently, nor up onto the mountain, and so assured himself that no-one else was - until now, at least - aware of Rydian's presence, or indeed, her existence.

This, he assured himself, could only increase the chances of her still being here - that she had been undisturbed, thus far, by any. He desperately hoped that he was right. As they made their way along, Oran felt a strange mixture of emotions - excitement, fear and worry - to name but a few. This all made it very difficult for him to concentrate on the task at hand and so, as nightfall was rapidly approaching, he turned to his companion and advised, "I think we should call it a night here, Dara. The ground is reasonably level here and we can shelter under those trees just over there." He indicated towards the trees he spoke of, with a nodding gesture. "It's going to be dark soon anyway, so best to prepare camp while there is still enough daylight to do so by."

"Yes, of course, Oran. We should all get a decent meal and some rest, in preparation for tomorrow," Dara said, then paused before adding, "Tomorrow could be a very eventful day for all of us, especially if this dragon of yours - this Rydian - actually materialises."

"I can only pray that she does," Oran said, hopefully.

They spent the next hour preparing their camp and eating a hot meal, which Dara had cooked by a small fire that was, once again, conveniently conjured by Oran's skills in magic. They talked about the day ahead as they ate, and the conversation eventually focused on Obblob's shape-shifting ability, with Oran posing the question, "So, Obblob... can you become any creature that you wish, or are there limits to your ability?"

"Yes, well, I can assume the form of any creature, just so long as I can get close enough to touch or make physical contact," the changeling answered with a mouthful of food.

"I can imagine that getting close enough is not always easy. I mean, how do you sneak up on a wild animal without scaring it off? That would require quite some skill, I don't doubt," Dara contributed, as they carried on eating their food and the conversation turned to the probability of rain during the night.

Concerned about this and the possibility of unwelcome discovery by potential night predators such as wolves, perhaps, Oran also felt it wise to conjure a form of protective dome, or shield, over their camp, to keep them safe as they all slept. He worked his magic once again and, after the shield was in place, they all bedded down around the fire for the night, falling asleep quite quickly after their somewhat arduous day.

Predators never came, though... nor did any rain. What did come, however, as they slept peacefully next the warm fire, was a heavy snowfall during the night - a snowfall that lasted for almost six hours.

CHAPTER FIFTEEN
The Ascent

It was early morning as King Lugh and Cethen stood looking in frustration at a large, firmly shut and locked wooden door in the old stone passageway on the highest level of the castle - the private royal quarters. The well-worn stone floor beneath the two men's feet showed clear evidence of the several hundreds of years of foot traffic it had witnessed. The smooth, grey walls on either side were adorned with numerous large tapestries and gold framed paintings that depicted both present and past royalty, with an occasional wall sconce providing meagre lighting.

Presently, the two men were positioned just a few feet from, and facing, the heavy solid oak door that served as the entrance to Enya's private chambers. Both men were bathed from behind, from the waist up, in the multi-coloured sunlight that filtered softly through a nearby stained-glass window, as the previous night's snow storm cleared slowly toward the east. They had grown ever more concerned, over the past twenty-four hours, that Enya had, just as she had threatened to, locked herself away in her chambers. She had taken this decision shortly, but not lightly, after Oran's departure almost three days earlier and no-one had seen her, nor had they spoken with her, since.

It was a well-known fact, throughout the castle, that she had done so in protest at Oran being sent to the outlands on the quest to find the dragon, Rydian. Visibly distraught, Enya had sternly told her father, on that evening of Oran's departure, that she fully intended to do so and would come out of her quarters *only* upon his safe return. She ran off in tears directly after the altercation, witnessed by all who were present in the courtyard at the time - the castle's entire population, no less.

Her father had, now, after some three days, become gravely concerned that she had apparently not eaten anything in all that time, so he was now quite desperate to get her attention and, also quite eager to get her out of her room. He reached out slowly with his right hand and banged on the pointed-top door with the flat of his open palm. Hearing this, the two Irish wolfhounds, that lay sprawled on their sides on a green rug that lay on the floor nearby, now lifted their heads briefly to look in his direction, before lowering them again and returning to their slumbers with indifference.

"Enya! This is your father speaking! Please, answer me, my child!" Lugh seemed to implore of the closed door. "Enya, please, my dear child. For goodness sake, answer me!"

"I fear that she will not, as she stated, respond until the return of Oran, my King," Cethen said, forlornly, after some moments waiting for a response, as he looked despairingly at the King.

"Open this door at once, Enya!" Lugh bellowed now, stubbornly ignoring Cethen's comment, whilst frowning and shaking his head at him in frustration at the same time.

"Perhaps we should give her more time, my Lord," Cethen suggested, cautiously, not wishing to further anger his King.

Cethen was, quite rightly, growing more and more concerned that the King would soon completely lose his temper and have the door forced in, perhaps. He knew quite well that doing such a thing would only serve to upset Enya even more, which he believed not to be the best course of action for them - not the best course of action for anyone, really. Suddenly, an idea came to him - an idea that might hold the King's anger at bay, for the time being, at least.

"Perhaps she will respond, more willingly, to her friend Orla, my Lord. They are very close, after all." Placing a hand gently on the King's right arm, he went on, "We should go and fetch her - what do you say, my Lord?"

The King slowly lowered his hand away from the door in silent agreement, and then looked briefly, woefully, at the floor before turning to face Cethen with an expression of renewed hopefulness.

"Yes, yes. Perhaps you are right, my good fellow. Shall we go and ask her, now? You know where to find her - find Orla, that is?"

"Certainly - of course I do. Let's give it a try, my Lord. I imagine that it can't do any harm, after all. Well, certainly no more harm than has been done already."

"Oh, I almost forgot to ask, with this nonsense of Enya's," Lugh declared suddenly. "Have the sentinels reported any more intruders - any new visitors since the arrival of our foolhardy friend, Dara MacBrien?"

"None, my Lord. We remain undiscovered and safe for now, it would seem."

"Hmmm…" the King mused. "Let us hope that young Oran returns to us soon, bringing with him, of course, my dear friend, Rydian."

The two men turned and walked off briskly along the old corridor, to fetch Enya's friend. Noticing their departure, the two lethargic wolfhounds rose slowly to their feet, yawning widely, and slunk off after them - their beloved master and his most trusted friend.

Meanwhile, some fifty miles to the east - as the crow flies - near the base of a snow covered Slieve Mish, the changeling was first to awaken. As the boy lay curled on his side in the near darkness, snuggled under a large sheepskin and facing toward the small fire, he slowly opened his pale, yellow eyes, believing that it was still night. He instantly wondered, noticing by the dim light of the fire that the others had not yet stirred, what time of night, or early morning, it must be. He suddenly felt a need to answer the call of nature, as he rolled onto his back to gaze upward at the night sky. To his surprise, or alarm, rather, there was no night sky, but instead what appeared in the glow of the firelight to be a large, curved white dome, which had somehow been placed over them and now surrounded their camp, reaching some fifteen feet upwards. At the very top of this dome, he observed what looked like a small hole, or opening, merely a foot or so in diameter, through which he thought he could just make out daylight. He immediately panicked.

"Dara, Oran! Wake up, *now*! Oran, Dara!" he called out in alarm to the still sleeping others, as he jumped to his feet.

Oran and Dara bolted upright at Obblob's disturbing and alarming cries as Holly, at the same time, rolled over toward him and pricked her ears up. All three of them were startled and confused as to what could be the matter with the boy, as they stared at him in dismay. Oran was first to notice, however, before Dara even had the chance to speak, exactly what was the matter. He sat there looking about him for a moment, and then almost whispered, "I believe that it must have snowed while we all slept." He then looked at Obblob, as he went on to explain in his normal tone, "The protective dome which I created has kept the snow out, and it has settled on the outside of it, I fear. You can see, at the very top, where the heat of the fire has caused it to melt slightly, it would seem."

"Looks quite spectacular, really," Dara mumbled, sleepily, as he looked at the anomaly surrounding them. "How do we get out of here now, though?"

"That's easy," Oran responded, quickly, as he rose to his feet. "I'll just make the shield disappear and the snow will collapse and fall to the ground - simple as that."

"Fall on us, you mean - fool!" Dara babbled, in obvious annoyance at the prospect of being covered in snow.

"You have a better suggestion?" Oran immediately demanded.

"Er... no. Not really," came his friend's sheepish response.

"I think it's a good idea. I like it - I need to go," Obblob now contributed to the debate, clutching his groin and wincing in obvious discomfort.

"Need to go where?" the other two asked, simultaneously.

"Need to go. Just... *go*. You know what I mean," he said, as he pointed with his right hand toward his lower regions, in mild embarrassment.

"Ah... right... yes. I see what you mean now," Dara nodded, as he now realised that the changeling meant that he needed to empty his bladder.

Oran thought for a moment how best to go about the task of removing the protective dome without burying everyone in the snow, then looked at the boy and smiled, as he uttered, "I'll have it down in no time - shan't take long, Obblob." He then went about reciting a quick spell to make the fire disappear. After he'd done this, he instructed Dara and Obblob to stand directly in the middle, where the fire had just been, as there was less chance of being covered in snow there, which Dara hastily complied with.

Obblob simply said, "Thank you," as he stretched his arms above his head and yawned the words, "Sleepy sleepy." Moving swiftly toward the centre of the dome, he stood next to Dara.

Dara next called Holly to his side, being somewhat fearful of just how much snow was about to come crashing down on them, as Oran went about reciting the spell to make the dome disappear again, whispering the words, "*Carana adoúa, Carana adoúa.*"

The dome glowed faintly blue for a few seconds as they all watched in eager anticipation. Then, as nothing else seemed to happen, and the snow remained in place, Oran stepped cautiously toward it as he explained to the others, "It must be frozen solid, since the dome which supported it is now gone. It appears to be supporting itself, and not falling in on us as we believed it would."

"We'll have to break our way through it then, somehow," Dara suggested, confidently, as he suddenly came up with an ingenious idea. He carefully walked toward the curving wall of snow, slowly drawing his knife. "Hopefully my blade is long enough, and I can simply cut a doorway for us."

"Certainly, give it a try," Oran agreed.

"Hurry. Need to go badly, now!" Obblob moaned impatiently, holding his belly in apparent discomfort.

Dara pushed his hunting knife easily into the smooth wall of snow in front of him at around waist height, and steadily began to carve a rudimentary doorway, large enough to fit not only themselves, but also the horses. It was done in a few minutes and, content with his efforts, he took one step back, placed both hands against it firmly, and gave it a mighty push where he had cut the doorway.

Oran and Obblob watched hopefully, as the snow easily gave way and Dara tumbled outward with it as it went, losing his balance and landing face down on top of the snow outside with a muffled thud and a grunt. Holly quickly ran to his side, shoving her nose in his face with a playful *woof*, as Oran and Obblob stood inside, laughing at his misfortune. Obblob was next out through the newly made doorway, desperately trudging past the still prone Dara, through the fresh snow, in search of a bush or tree where he could relieve himself in relative privacy. Oran followed next through the opening, closely behind Obblob, leading the horses outside as Dara swiftly pulled himself to his feet and brushed the snow from his clothes with his bare hands.

As they gathered outside to prepare for the next leg of the journey, the ascent of Slieve Mish, Oran turned to look at the large snow dome standing behind them now, with its crudely cut-out doorway, and commented wryly, "That should serve to give anyone, should they chance by and witness it, something to ponder over, no?"

"Certainly, it would, master Oran. I don't doubt it, at all," Dara laughed, heartily.

"The snow doesn't appear to be too deep hereabouts - perhaps a foot or so - so the going shouldn't be too bad I think. For the horses, I mean," Oran remarked, confidently, as he climbed up into his saddle.

Obblob quickly appeared at Oran's side and asked of him, "Might I ride with you again, Oran, please? I'd rather not walk in this snow."

"Yes Obblob, of course you may and actually, I was just about to suggest that to you." Reaching down with his right arm to pull the boy up, he called over to Dara, "I think you ought to put Holly in the saddle with you again too, Dara. With her size, I fear that she may find it quite difficult to walk in this."

"Yes," Dara agreed, somewhat tersely now. "But you will need to get down again and help me with her. I can't do it by myself, as I said before, just yesterday. You should, perhaps, have thought of that before climbing onto your horse, no?"

Oran quickly complied, as Dara pulled himself up into his saddle, swinging his leg forward and up over the horse's neck. He jumped down into the slightly frozen snow, with a crunching sound, leaving Obblob in the saddle alone, momentarily. He then called to Holly and, as she obediently came to him, bent down to take hold of her and heaved her up to Dara's waiting arms with a grunt, remarking, "Oh, I think she may have gained a little weight, owing to the snow that has already stuck to her fur on her underside. Either that, or we've been over-feeding her," he added, as Holly cautiously clambered up into the saddle and sat between Dara's knees again.

Oran then turned and made his way back through the snow to his waiting horse - the blackest black against the freshly fallen, white snow. He took hold of the reins in his right hand, then pulled himself up into his saddle using his left, being careful not to kick Obblob as he swung his left leg over. As this took place, Dara pushed his already near frozen feet carefully into his still shortened stirrups and pressed his legs gently, but firmly, against Holly's sides to secure her in place, as he patted her on the head affectionately.

"Ready!" Dara announced.

"Ready!" Oran concurred. "That way... east. We'll continue our search around the base, in the hope of finding a trail that will take us to the summit. I'll lead now," indicating in a direction beyond the snow dome with an index finger, as Dara raised his eyebrows in mild surprise at the elf's newfound confidence as leader.

They set off together in single file now, with Oran in front, in an easterly direction around the north facing side of the base of the mountain. Dara rode along with Holly, closely behind Oran and Obblob, for a short while, thinking to himself that he, thankfully, didn't feel quite so cold now. He was busy admiring the beauty of the surrounding landscape in its freshly fallen coat of pristine snow, when Oran slowly brought his horse to a halt just ahead of him, and called back, "The side of the mountain is more gently sloping here - it does not rise so steeply." He then turned his horse to face the slope, as he continued, "This depression here - the shallow ravine here, in front of me now - may serve as our best way to ascend the mountain."

Dara looked toward the mountainside at the area where Oran was now facing and noticed, just as Oran had stated, a shallow ravine. It had become buried under the snow, but was still quite obvious and appeared to progress, as he looked upward, all the way up the side of the mountain as far as he could see. He looked back toward Oran, and asked, "Shall we go that way then?"

"Yes. I believe that we should, my friend." He thought for a moment, then added, "If we can expedite a path to the summit this way, then good. If we arrive there, and still haven't found any sign of the dragon, then I suggest we split up and scour the mountainside as two teams, separately. We will cover more ground that way. It will serve to speed up our search, agreed?"

Dara became instantly alarmed at the suggestion of splitting up, insisting, "No, no! We stay together! Safety in numbers and all that." He glared at Oran sternly, then babbled, "What if you're on one side of the mountain, and I'm all the way around the other side, and one of us chances upon the beast? How could I possibly let you know that I had found her, if I did find her, if you were some way round on the opposite side of this mountain? That would be extremely dangerous, don't you think? There's only one Sword of Light, after all, and you would be the one carrying it, which would mean that I would be completely powerless against her. I'd be a dead man, for sure. No, I say again, it's a ludicrous idea."

Oran thought for a moment then answered, remorsefully, "True... I wasn't thinking really, was I? I'm just eager to find her and get back home, as I'm sure you are too. My apologies for being so thoughtless, Dara. We shall remain together for safety, as you say."

They presently agreed on following the ravine to the summit, and so, set off in single file once more, upwards through the undisturbed snow. The trek to the top took them several arduous hours, with more than a few slips and falls on the way. Fortunately, no-one had gotten hurt, owing to the soft snow, on each occasion where one of the horses had fallen and, eventually, they arrived safely on the summit, much to their delight. As the horses came to a halt just over the crest, and the last of the dark cloud drifted away to the east, the sun came out for the first time since the previous morning. The intrepid travelers sat there on their horses, looking around them for a moment, squinting against the bright sunlight and the glare of the snow as it almost blinded them, taking in the breathtaking views. Oran turned his horse around slightly, to face west, and sat staring into the distance for a moment, quietly.

"Look over there, Dara. It's Faltanragh - I'm sure of it! Look, to the north-west - that sloping bump with a peak at the end, on the horizon... home," Oran uttered, somewhat dolefully.

Dara turned and peered into the distance with obvious concentration, for a moment, before saying, "Yes, I can see *your* home, but I can't see my little cottage. It might as well be a thousand miles away," Dara acknowledged, dejectedly.

"You'll get home soon. We're almost there, Dara," Oran then beamed, in an attempt to lift his friend's spirits, as he turned to Obblob and added, "That's where you shall live soon, my young friend. Well, as long as the King is agreeable, which I'm sure he will be - and as long as you behave yourself, of course."

Obblob avidly stared into the distance, over Oran's shoulder, at the far away mountain range and quietly murmured, "Home... safe."

"You are a man of very few words, Obblob," Dara laughed briefly, as they all turned again to face the mountain's peak.

Ahead of them now, however, the summit of Slieve Mish had no obvious, defined peak to speak of. They observed that it was more flattish, and spread out like a giant, round, saucer shaped depression, some several hundred feet across. It was almost perfectly round and looked to be around twenty or thirty feet lower at its centre, in relation to where they were currently situated at the rim. It was also, like everything else around them, entirely buried in the snow.

This had been the caldera, long since filled in by rocks and other debris over eons, of the now long extinct volcano. As he looked ahead at the blinding snow that completely covered the crater, Oran now found himself hoping, desperately, that the great dragon he sought out lay somewhere hidden from view not far beneath it - perhaps in some hidden away cave or cavern, below the surface. However, the obvious absence of any animal tracks, prints or other signs of any disturbance in the untouched snow caused him to feel somewhat fearful that she had not been here recently, at all. He now worried that she had not been here for a very long time, perhaps - if indeed, ever.

"Let's begin our search, shall we?" Dara enthused, having noticed Oran's facial expression change to one of dejection. "I think we should head straight across the middle, to begin with."

Oran simply nodded in agreement, forcing a half-hearted smile, as they set off together into the vast, shallow crater to look for signs of the dragon. They spent several hours trekking back and forth across its huge expanse, covering almost every square inch of terrain and stopping only briefly to eat, before pressing on with their search. Subsequently, they circumnavigated the entire rim of the crater in their continuing hunt for her, drawing to a halt as they finally arrived back at the point where they had first arrived on the summit earlier that very morning, as the sun now began to sink lower in the sky above, toward the west. Oran looked at Dara with a sense of hopelessness, as he released a heavy sigh, then suddenly yelled out in frustration at the top of his voice, "*Rydian, where... are... you?*"

The three of them sat there on the horses, in complete silence, for a moment as, understandably and quite expectedly, no response came to Oran's plea. Holly had, meanwhile, wandered off a little further along the rim by herself. She was poking her nose in the snow occasionally, sniffing and snorting, as though she was trying to find something - but what? Dara thought nothing of it, as he kept a close eye on her, believing that it was probably just a rabbit's scent, or something of the kind.

"It's going to be dark in a couple of hours," Dara warned, taking his eye off Holly for a moment to look at Oran. "Are you alright, master Oran? You look rather down-spirited."

"Yes, Dara. I'm fine," Oran replied, adding thoughtfully, "We should make camp for the night, then resume our search in the morning, at first light. There's still the rest of the mountain to cover, but there's no point in tackling it this late in the day. I'll create a fire. I'm sure everyone would like to get warmed up."

"Warm, yes, good," Obblob whimpered from behind Oran, where he'd been clinging to him tightly for warmth.

"There seems to be a flatter, more level spot just over there, close to where Holly is," Dara advised. "Looks like the snow has drifted into a long ridge, just inside of the rim."

"Good idea. Let's make camp there then," Oran responded, as he and Obblob moved off in the direction of Holly.

Dara followed closely behind them, and in a few moments, they had all arrived at the point which he had spoken of. The snow here had, indeed, formed into a long, odd shaped drift, just inside the rim of the crater. Such was the way that it seemed to have formed, that the top of it was wide and almost flat - or reasonably level - unlike the gently sloping area that surrounded it.

They dismounted from their horses and Oran wasted no time in conjuring a fire by which to warm themselves, as Dara and the changeling went to the bags in search of something to cook for supper. A short time later, having cooked and eaten the food, and warmed themselves satisfactorily, Obblob got up and wandered off a little way, but not far, down into the crater, as he proceeded to play a game of fetch with Holly. He had fashioned a toy for her using a short length of rope, in which he had tied several large knots, and which she seemed to be enjoying greatly, much to Dara's amusement.

Meanwhile, Oran had gone to his horse to fetch the sword for the purpose of cleaning it, sitting on the snow drift beside Dara upon his return. The two men sat near and with their backs to the fire, discussing their, so far, fruitless search for Rydian, as Oran wiped the blade diligently.

As they talked on, Dara noticed Oran becoming more and more frustrated at the fact that they had not yet found the dragon, frowning ever more heavily, as he now wiped the blade of the sword more vigorously - almost angrily, it appeared. At the same time, he also watched Obblob, directly to his front, throw the knotted rope for Holly to chase. The rope landed in the snow, nearby, about twenty feet to the right of where Oran and Dara were currently sat, near the end of the oddly shaped snow drift. Holly found the toy quickly, where it lay in the snow, but then seemed to lose interest in it almost immediately. She now began to dig and bark at the snow next to it, in a kind of excited frenzy. This concerned Dara, somewhat, as he firstly wondered what she had found, then stood up and began to walk briskly toward her.

As Dara walked off, Oran lost interest in cleaning the sword. In his frustration and anger, he plunged it forcefully into the snow beside him with all his might, burying it right up to the pommel. In the same instant, as he walked away, an image quickly flashed through Dara's mind. It was a vague, blurry image, of what he could only describe as an enormous dark green beast, buried under what seemed to be a layer of snow, seemingly asleep. He shook his head vigorously and shrugged it off as some weird, momentary hallucination, blaming tiredness and the cold. He was completely unaware of what he had actually just seen, in his mind's eye, as he trudged on toward Holly.

Oran was still sat there in the snow, with his head down and his face buried in his hands, almost wanting to weep, when he suddenly thought that he felt the ground move below him slightly. Dara felt it too, as he reached Holly, then spun around and looked back toward Oran to see that a large crack had newly appeared in the frozen surface of the snow, stretching almost the entire distance between himself and his companion. Oran swiftly lifted his face from his hands, fearfully, feeling the ground shudder and shift beneath him yet again, then looked down to his side, immediately noticing that the patch of snow where he had just plunged the sword had now turned to crimson red. Dara yelled out to him in panic, "*Oran, move! Move now!*" He now had the sudden realisation as to what his vision meant, and that he may well have just had his first experience of *the sight,* the gift bestowed upon him by the Children of Lir. "*Get off there! Run! Nowwwww!*"

It was too late though, as the snow, with Oran still sat on it, and the conjured fire just behind him, all surged upward violently and simultaneously. Oran had no idea, at first, what was happening to him... but Dara did. Dara could see quite clearly, from where he stood, as the huge, dark green beast from his brief vision very quickly unearthed itself from beneath the snow, where it had obviously slept until just a moment ago, sending the camp fire hurtling bizarrely through the air and over the side of the mountain, as it carried Oran upward with it. He watched in horror as its great, long tail now waved about slowly, just feet in front of him, observing how the tip was shaped like a giant arrow-head, as it waved from side to side, just feet from his face.

Oran presently felt himself being hoisted swiftly upward, as he looked down to briefly see Dara and Obblob looking back up at him in terror - the same terror that he, also, now felt. He glanced to his side in panic, as he continued to rise skyward, to see his sword sticking, or rather, hanging out of what now appeared to be a massive green wing which was bleeding from where he had inadvertently stabbed it. He desperately tried to reach for the sword now, his fingertips just falling short, and felt utterly helpless at this point, but still, managed to yell out, "Dara, *help meeee!*"

The huge claw at the elbow joint, mid-way along the wing, the same wing upon which Oran and Dara had been unwittingly sitting just moments ago, and from which the sword now dislodged itself and began falling back toward the ground, had hooked itself on Oran's sheepskin jacket as the creature stirred, carrying him upward with it. It all happened so fast that Oran didn't even have time to think of a spell with which to defend or protect himself, let alone conjure one.

Dara continued to watch, frozen in place by absolute horror, as the huge creature now stood fully upright on its robust hind legs, facing away from him and raising itself to its full height. It emitted a ferocious, deafening cry, spreading its enormous wings to their fullest span at the same time. In the process, Oran was catapulted, wailing and screaming, over the rim of the crater after the camp fire, and hurtled down the mountainside and out of sight.

"Rydian?" Dara gasped, staring fearfully up at the terrifying beast before him. Holly stood next to him, oddly silent for now as she glared at the creature, with her ears flattened against her head. Dara grabbed Obblob's arm, then reached down to take hold of Holly's collar and began walking slowly and cautiously backwards, his only desire being that of wishing to get himself, Holly and the boy as far away from it - from her - as he could. He was unable to find any other words now, as he watched his good friend vanish from view with a wail. He instantly wondered if Oran was safe - would he survive the fall? The next thought to spring into his mind was that this monster, he thought, was easily almost half as big again as the water dragon, Gálin - it was enormous.

Dara kept his eyes fixed to his front while he carried on walking backwards, his heart pounding in his chest, as the dragon shook the last of the snow from her body and let out another ear-piercing cry at the sky above, seemingly unaware of the presence of himself, Obblob and Holly behind her. Suddenly, she flapped her huge wings and launched herself over the edge of the crater, clearly in pursuit of Oran - her latest quarry.

"Oh... my! The... dragon," Obblob stammered, as he lay half buried in the snow nearby, where he was now attempting to conceal himself from view, staring wildly at where Oran and the dragon had just been, moments before.

"Orannnn!" Dara cried out, then ran off frantically in the direction of where he had last seen his friend.

CHAPTER SIXTEEN
Rydian Versus Rydian?

Oran flailed his arms and legs wildly, all to no avail, as he flew through the cold air and then landed hard on his back on the steep hillside below. He felt himself helplessly rolling and slipping down the near vertical slope, tumbling over and over for what felt like ages, before sliding to a gradual halt at the bottom, at the point where the terrain levelled out again. He lay there spread-eagled on his back in the freezing snow for a moment, dazed and motionless, staring up at the blue sky above him as he tried to get his bearings and attempted to comprehend what had just happened to him.

Then, it hit him... *Rydian*... he suddenly realised to himself, as his senses slowly returned to him. At that same instant, as a great dark shadow loomed over him, the blue sky above all but disappeared. He gasped as he lay there, quite still, rigid with fear and not daring to move.

Dara, meanwhile, had already reached the rim of the crater, having mostly sprinted across the near snowless area where Rydian had just slept, to expedite his pursuit of Oran. Obblob and Holly arrived by his sides within the next moment, as he stood there looking down at where Oran now lay motionless some way below them, at the bottom of the very steep slope. He had an expression of sheer terror on his face, mixed with incredulity, as he took in the scene that was currently unfolding below.

Fifty feet beneath them, where Oran now lay immobile, the mountain levelled out to a large, and fairly level, shelf like feature, which was approximately one third the size of the crater at its summit. It then dropped off again steeply in the distance. Oran was lying face up, a little way beyond the point where the steep slope met the level area, with Rydian now approaching him rapidly from the distance. She glided silently and effortlessly toward him, wings fully extended, then landed just beyond him. The terrifying beast was coming in for the kill, Dara feared.

"Orannnn!" Dara yelled at the top of his voice, hoping that his friend would get up and run - run for his life.

He was just about to make a dash down the slope, as the beast loomed over his friend below, when he heard something rather unbelievable, incredible, he thought. A female voice, just behind him now, urged, *"Dara! The sword - take the sword to him!"*

Dara wheeled round immediately to find, astoundingly, that Enya was now, somehow, stood directly behind him, offering the Sword of Light to him in her pale, outstretched hand. He was utterly confused at this point, believing her to be some kind of apparition, as he mumbled, "Enya? The sword... yes, of course. But... how?"

"There's no time to explain now, Dara. Take the sword and run with it to Oran - run as though your very lives depend upon it, for they may." Dara snatched the sword from her as she said this, and swiftly turned toward Oran as she then confessed, "I've been with you all the way, but I'll explain later. Now, *runnnn!*" But he was already gone, vanished before she had even finished the sentence.

He was already sliding, speeding down the steep slope on his bottom, almost half way down and clutching the sword tightly to his breast, hoping that he would get there in time to help his friend - to help Oran. Enya, Obblob and Holly watched from the rim above, Holly barking wildly at the scene below, as Enya and Obblob watched in desperate hope that Dara would reach Oran with the sword in time.

He didn't get there in time, however, still sliding downward, watching helplessly as Rydian loomed directly over Oran. She was now staring down at Oran, malevolently, as she made a guttural, growling noise and deftly placed her heavily clawed right front foot on his still spread-eagled body, pinning him to the ground and effortlessly piercing his fragile chest with one huge, razor sharp claw. There came an awful, sickening, crunching sound as Oran's body succumbed to the stress.

Oran had felt mesmerised, frozen in place by complete and utter fear at the sheer size of the dragon as she stood over him, growling, towering above him and bringing her immense foot toward him, and then setting it down on him. He screamed out in agony as he felt the excruciating, burning sensation in his lower chest, abdomen and legs, then fell deathly quiet as the air was forced from his lungs and his world turned to one of complete darkness... and silence. He lay quite still now, staring upward, unblinking and motionless.

Time suddenly, and strangely, seemed to slow down for Dara at this instant, upon witnessing this, this most terrible tragedy, as he neared Oran and the formidable beast that still stood over him. As he continued his descent, he watched on in some surreal form of slow-motion as, firstly, two Hollys overtook him and then headed straight for the dragon's left flank as it slowly lowered its great spiny head toward Oran's lifeless body. As he drew closer still, he observed that one Holly became Obblob, briefly, approaching the dragon from the side in an arcing, slow-motion run as he transformed, mercifully un-noticed by her, and then touched the beast on its left hind leg.

Almost instantly, as the changeling made physical contact, there appeared a second Rydian - a second Rydian that seemed to be slightly larger than the original. This second dragon, Obblob, now lunged with his full force and weight at the Rydian that still stood over Oran, displacing her with a violent head butt and a mighty thud, as Dara came to a gradual halt several feet from his seemingly lifeless friend, and the ground shook around them.

Rydian quickly righted herself and aggressively lunged back at Obblob, forcing him backwards as he lost his balance, thankfully taking the fight away from Oran and Dara. The dragons fought and struggled violently, with Rydian repeatedly dousing Obblob in great puffs of black smoke as they exchanged blows and swipes of their deadly tails. Their mighty wings flapped noisily all the while as they fought, continuing to battle their way gradually around toward the farthest reach of the shelf, as snow and earth flew into the air around them. At some stages in their duel, Rydian clearly had the advantage, whilst at others, it seemed evident that Obblob was the dominant, mercifully. Whichever of the two was currently winning, it was, however, undoubtedly beneficial that they were, at least, a safe distance from Oran and the others... for now.

Dara just sat there, stunned and not moving, in shock at what he now saw before him. He heard Enya wail Oran's name from somewhere just behind him, but did not look round. He continued to stare, numbly, at Oran's body and the crisp, white snow around it that was now slowly turning to crimson red as Oran's blood seeped into it.

"Oran," he whimpered, a tear rolling down his cheek and falling quietly onto the snow below, as Holly returned to his side and sat by him, dutifully.

Enya moved gracefully past Dara and appeared in front of him now, slowly draping herself over Oran, whilst yelling something unintelligible back to him, all in the same bizarre slow-motion as everything else that he was seeing, as she then began weeping uncontrollably over the lifeless body. Dara remained still, staring wildly in horror, hearing only muffled sobs and muffled roars and thuds as sound now seemed to play tricks on him also. Everything had slowed down now as he observed Oran's body to his front, Enya crying helplessly over it, and the snow around him as it grew still redder. The two great dragons fought on relentlessly, just beyond them, in the background. The ground continued to shake all around as Dara looked on hopelessly, great clumps of earth and snow flying slowly, as though almost weightless, into the air around the dragons as they struggled, everything in the same slow-motion view. He watched silently with Holly now by his side, as she whimpered and whined mournfully for Oran.

"It's my fault," he murmured, distractedly. "I should have realised that it was *the sight* - the vision that I had. I could have prevented this, Holly."

It was at this point that Dara shook himself to his senses, coming back to reality, and time suddenly returned to its normal speed for him. Enya now lifted her head from Oran's crushed chest and looked directly at Dara as she screamed, *"The sword, Dara! Go to her now! Command her, before it's too late... for all of us!"*

Dara glanced down at the sword, which he was still clutching tightly to his chest, then pulled himself quickly to his feet as her words sunk in. He quickly realised how right Enya was, and that if he didn't do something to take control of Rydian *now*, they might all very well perish here on this mountain, today. He looked at the battling dragons, now near the edge of the shelf, and took a deep breath.

"Enya, you have to save Oran," he ordered, with a glance at her, and began to run toward the dragons with the sword held high, dodging clumps of falling earth and snow as he went, and screaming aloud, *"Arggghhh!"*

As he neared the dragons, he noticed the larger one, Obblob, get the upper hand in the fight and take hold of Rydian in his jaws, at the uppermost part of her neck, forcing her to the ground in one fluid movement. There was a mighty thud, accompanied by the roar of a now slightly wounded Rydian, as earth and snow once again went flying into the air and the ground shuddered beneath them once more. Dara slowed to a brisk walk now, less than thirty feet from them, as he continued to watch Obblob subdue Rydian, straddling her and pinning her to the ground with all four legs whilst maintaining his grip on her neck with his incredibly powerful jaws. Rydian lay on her belly now, with her head pressed on its right side into the snow, struggling desperately to free herself, but to no avail. Obblob was clearly not only bigger and heavier, but also stronger than her. She was trapped for the moment, it appeared.

Dara became aware, as he approached yet closer to the pair, that Obblob's pale yellow eyes were shifting back and forth, looking directly at him and then at Rydian's head alternately, as though urging him to act, and so moved cautiously closer to Rydian, raising the sword aloft for her to see clearly. As he drew nearer, he noticed that the emerald in the pommel of the sword began to glow bright green and knew that this could only be a sign - a good sign for himself and the others, giving him new hope and courage. Moving slowly toward her as she lay struggling, still pinned on her underside and pressed firmly against the snow by Obblob, Dara now, for the first time, was able to see her head and face in all their magnificent detail. He warned the changeling, "Don't kill her, Obblob. We need her alive," as he bravely positioned himself several feet from her snout.

He stared at her for a minute, saying nothing as he took in the incredible sight before him, still holding the sword aloft, the emerald shining brightly. Her head, which was long and tapered, or pointed, toward the front and almost twice the size of his horse, was a dusky, dark green in colour, with all manner of boney, glossy black barbs protruding from her cheeks, snout, forehead and indeed, the top of her head also. Her eyes, now staring directly at him, were blood red in colour and behind her ears, which were merely small holes or openings, one each side, were two great black horns that swept upward and backward for some eight to ten feet. The horns curved as they went, and terminated in extremely sharp points, one of which was currently very close to Obblob's cheek. There was also a shiny black barb which protruded downward, some two feet long, from the point of her lower jaw and either side of her mouth were two large, white tusks, jutting forward, which were also approximately two feet long. There was no question in Dara's mind, upon seeing all of this, that this creature would be capable of inflicting heavy damage upon anything it attacked, with all of this weaponry. Suddenly, using her large, powerful legs, she attempted to lunge forward, under Obblob's heavy bulk, toward a now startled Dara.

As Dara leapt backward in alarm to evade her, relieved that she had failed to reach him, she opened her huge mouth slightly to reveal some extremely dangerous looking teeth, blowing a puff of black smoke, or soot, at him as she did so. Dara remained there for a moment, eyes closed and holding his breath, and his resolve, till he thought the smoke had cleared again. A terrible stench had filled his nostrils and while he stood there, waiting for the thick, acrid smoke to clear, he chanced opening his eyes again slowly. To his relief, the smoke had all but vanished, as he took a deep breath and then moved one pace closer, again, toward her formidable head, shaking the sword at her in defiance. What came next shocked him greatly.

"Say the words, bearer of the sword," came an authoritative, female voice.

Dara was bewildered. Did the dragon just speak to him? Surely not?

"Say the words, bearer of the sword," Rydian commanded once more, as she once again dragged herself inches closer to him, under the burden of Obblob's weight, using her front feet and claws.

Dara shook his head from side to side briefly, came to his senses again, and asked of her in frustration, "What words? What words?" He thought momentarily and then stammered, in hope, "Dragon... I... command thee!"

"Say the words, bearer of the sword," came her reply, simply, at Dara's failed attempt.

"Dragon... heed my... bidding," Dara stammered again, in despair now.

Again, the dragon simply held him in her gaze, repeating the phrase, "Say the words, bearer of the sword."

"But I don't know which words to say! Only Oran knows, and *you... killed... him!*" Dara protested, then angrily roared at her, *"Look what you have done!"* He wheeled round to point toward Oran's body as he shouted, "I should have my good friend, Obblob," then turned quickly back to face her whilst gesturing toward the other dragon with a brief pause and a nod, and continued, "Finish you where you lie, as punishment."

As he had turned to point at Oran, however, he had noticed something odd - something very peculiar. He turned to look again, doubting his eyes. Oran's body presently seemed to float several feet above the blood-soaked snow, where he had recently perished, with Enya and Holly stood to his side. There was now, also, a strange woman stood by Oran's feet, with her back to Dara. Dara shook his head again, thinking that it might be another hallucination or premonition, then quickly yelled out to Enya, *"Enya! What's happening?"*

"Don't worry, Dara. Everything will be fine. Keep the dragon, Rydian, restrained," Enya called back to him.

Dara spun round to face the dragons again as he ordered, "Obblob, you heard her! Keep Rydian exactly where she is, please."

Obblob did not answer, but simply held Rydian in place as instructed, squeezing her neck a little more tightly with his strong jaws. Dara held his position too, with the sword raised high, gazed fixed upon Rydian, waiting.

As Enya had wept over Oran's lifeless body, while Dara and Obblob dealt with Rydian a little way off, she had desperately tried to think of ways to save him - to bring him back. Unfortunately, however, she neither knew how, nor was she skilled in the necessary fields of magic. Sadly, for all of them, Oran was the only one who possessed the necessary powers and abilities to perform this kind of sorcery. As she continued to weep helplessly, she thought that she heard a voice whisper something almost inaudible to her, but it was so faint at first that she passed it off as the mountain breeze playing tricks on her in her grief. She heard it again now - louder this time, clearer. It was a female voice, she was sure of it, but she still found it difficult to make out what it was saying. She lifted her head from Oran's chest again and turned to look in the direction from which she thought the voice came, toward Oran's feet.

As she turned, she noticed that the snow just beyond Oran's feet had risen, forming into a perfect column some four feet in height and around a foot in diameter. Enya remained still and said nothing as, over the course of the next minute or so, the column took the shape of a woman, while she watched closely. The woman was beautiful, Enya noted - raven-haired with the palest skin and dressed in a long white gown that flowed and fluttered in the breeze. The woman looked down at Oran, sadly it seemed, and spoke softly, "Oran, my son. I have missed you so very much. You have grown into a very handsome young man, I see."

Enya was utterly confused by this. Oran had never known his parents - had never even known their names. This, surely, couldn't somehow be his mother. Enya rose to her feet and bravely addressed the woman.

"I am Oran's friend. My name is Enya," she said, then bowed slightly, in anticipation of what response might come.

"My name is Ethioné, of the Danu. I am Oran's mother," the woman stated as she smiled warmly at Enya.

"His... mother? But... how?" Enya stammered.

"There is no time to explain, my child, for I must act quickly if I am to save him - to return him to you," Ethioné advised.

"You can save him? But how? He's gone... look!" Enya declared in her confusion at the woman's bold statement, pointing tearfully at Oran's crushed and lifeless body.

"Fear not, my child. I believe that there may still be time... time to save him, that is. There are many things which you do not yet fully understand," Ethioné said, patiently. "Now, child, you should move aside slightly, I think." She then raised her arms out to her front, toward her beloved son.

Enya did as she was asked and moved back a few paces away from Oran, calling Holly to her side as she watched the woman begin to recite a spell.

"*Oran... aradua, Oran... aradua,*" Ethioné chanted, over and over.

As his mother recited the first part of the spell, Oran's body lifted from where he lay and rose to several feet above the snow, floating there, motionless and still lifeless. Ethioné now spread her fingers to their farthest extent, as though reaching, grasping for something that wasn't there, and began to recite a different incantation, "*Tahain ar mí, Tahain ar mí.*"

Enya watched intently as the bracelet now glowed and then magically detached itself from Oran's wrist, before floating through the air to Ethioné's waiting hand. The bracelet slowly clasped onto her right wrist as she again changed the incantation, reciting more sternly, more forcefully now, "*Altwean de beont, ar tastiel chu seol Oran cuidis, Altwean de beont, ar tastiel chu seol Oran cuidis.*"

As Ethioné recited these words, a dense blue mist appeared, swirling around and engulfing Oran's crushed and broken body. Oran now almost disappeared entirely from Enya's view, as Ethioné continued chanting intensely. As the blue mist continued to swirl about him, his broken ribs, legs and pelvis were mended first, followed swiftly by the complete repair of his crushed organs. Next, the mist - the magic conjured by Ethioné - forced air into his lungs and caused his heart to begin pumping rhythmically again. He opened his eyes slowly as he struggled to take in what was happening to him.

The mist dispersed as Oran settled slowly back toward the ground below him, and his mother ceased chanting, lowering her arms and clasping her hands to her front, with a smile directed at Enya. Oran immediately sat up, looked around for a moment in confusion, then asked the strange woman in front of him, "What happened? Who are you, and where did all this blood come from? Is someone hurt?"

Before Ethioné could answer him, Enya rushed to his side with excitement and knelt by him, as she blurted out, "Oran, I'm so happy you're alive!" throwing her arms around him and giving him a tight hug as she went on to explain urgently, "Forget about us, for now. You need to go to Dara... *at once*. He needs your help! *Hurry*."

Oran looked to his front with a puzzled expression, at the unknown woman in the white dress who stood smiling down at him now, holding his bracelet out to him in her left hand. He rose to his feet and took it from her, gently. "Thank you," he said, then gazed past her as he urgently placed the bracelet back on his own wrist, noticing Dara in the distance and not one, but two dragons, incredibly. He smiled at Enya and the strange woman briefly, then ran off in Dara's direction, shouting back to them as he went, "I'll be back soon!"

A brief moment later, he arrived unnoticed by and directly behind Dara, who was still holding the sword aloft, facing the two enormous dragons. Oran stood there for a moment, taking in the scene before him, suddenly realising why there were two dragons, and quickly figuring out which of them was Rydian and which was Obblob. It was the eyes, he told himself - the eyes gave it away. Who could forget Obblob's pale yellow eyes? He looked up at Obblob and gave him a confident nod, then lightly tapped Dara on the shoulder as he taunted, "Ahem. Since you don't know what you are doing there, might I have my sword back, please?"

Dara wore an utterly stunned expression across his face, or perhaps it was one of sheer disbelief, as he spun around to find Oran, miraculously, stood just behind him. He struggled to comprehend the sight before him - was he dreaming again, or had he gone completely insane? He reached out with his hand and prodded Oran's arm gingerly.

"You're... real. You're... alive!"

"Hah! Of course I am real, Dara. Now, the sword, please?" Oran laughed. "There's work to be done here."

"Yes, yes, here, take it," Dara babbled, eagerly thrusting the sword into Oran's waiting hand with a huge grin on his face, then asking, "But how, Oran? I watched that beast, that monster... I watched her kill you. It was terrible."

"I'll try to explain later, if I can. But, first of all, we need to deal with our friend Rydian here," Oran asserted, looking directly past Dara at the subdued dragon that lay helpless and motionless in the snow before him, as she stared back at him in silence, with her unblinking, blood red eyes.

Dara nodded, eagerly in agreement, as he was joined by Enya, Ethioné and Holly at his sides. They all watched on expectantly and silently, as Oran stepped cautiously toward Rydian, raising the Sword of Light up at arm's length in front of her, uncertain of what to expect now. With the emerald still glowing brightly in its pommel, he spoke to her, at long last.

CHAPTER SEVENTEEN
The Joining

It was late afternoon and Mary was currently hunched over the old stone sink, at the little window that faced east at the rear of the house, near the back door where the banshee had been defeated by Oran just three nights previously. She was diligently washing her daughters' clothes in some soapy water - water which she had fetched, ice cold, from the stream outside and then carefully heated, using a large pot, on the big open fire nearby. Ellen and Rosemary were sat on the floor a few yards away in front of the crackling fire, playing with an old wooden box as they laughed and giggled, oblivious to their mother's toils.

Mary stopped scrubbing for a moment and peered out through the tiny window that looked out over the field at the back of the house, letting out a long, quiet sigh as she rested her hands on the edge of the sink. She stood there, gazing into the far distance for several minutes, hoping to catch sight of her greatly missed husband whom she had now not seen for more than two days, as he returned to her. There was sadly, however, no sign of him, as she scanned the empty field, while the sun sank lower and the daylight began to fade. She lowered her head, looking down at the water in the sink, and whispered quietly and comfortingly to herself,

"He'll be back soon. Don't worry, dear," unaware that he was, presently, many miles away from her on the snow-covered Slemish mountain, face to face with untold danger in the form of a Fire Dragon, no less.

She slowly put her hands back into the water and continued with her labours when, unexpectedly, there came a faint rapping on the back door, nearby, to her left. Mary jerked her head up, startled, then around at the girls, who had now stopped playing and laughing as they both stared at the door, wide-eyed and silent. Mary leant carefully forward, over the sink, craning her head to the side in an attempt to see who could be there. She couldn't quite tell though, seeing only the hind quarters of a black horse, as her view was mostly obstructed by the thick stone reveal around the window, on the outside. She turned slowly around to face her daughters again, and asked, curiously, "Whoever could that be now, this late in the day?" Slowly and carefully, she took a big carving knife, from the sparse but neat collection of utensils by the sink, in her right hand, and ordered, "You two, go and hide in the bedroom, now... and stay quiet." She pointed a finger at them as she picked up an old towel that hung next to the sink and quickly dried both her hands and the knife with it, walking slowly toward the back door at the same time.

As the girls went into the bedroom and closed the door behind them, their mother's thoughts turned to a wild story that she had heard earlier that day - the tale of a young girl in the village who had mysteriously disappeared in the night and completely vanished from existence. This tale now caused Mary more concern than it had when she had first heard of it, given the current situation.

The bearer of this story had been Ronan Osgard, Mary's first cousin on her mother's side, who had come to visit Mary that lunch time, mainly to check on her state of health, but also to warn her of the recent strange events in Esslan. Ronan had babbled almost nonsensically as he told Mary the peculiar tale of the young woman, named Bronagh Rankin, who had been *taken* during the previous night - taken from her very bed as she slept, it appeared, leaving no trace at all. He had seemed very frightened, as well as extremely concerned for the wellbeing of Mary and her family, worriedly enquiring as to Dara's whereabouts, to which Mary replied that he had gone hunting and to check on the flock, as always, and would return soon, she expected.

Ronan went on about the disappearance, frantically, for some moments. He seemed obsessed, claiming that there was some kind of witchcraft or sorcery at play and warning Mary to lock all of her doors and windows, before excusing himself and leaving in a hurry to return to the relative safety of his own home.

Mary carefully contemplated her own safety now, and that of her children, as she stood by the door for a moment, then nervously called out, "Who is it?"

She was immediately answered by yet another knock at the door, and called out again, "Who's there? Who is it?" She pressed her right ear to the door and listened carefully.

"My name is Cethen of the Danu, good lady. I am a friend of Oran and of your husband, Dara," came the softly spoken male voice from the other side of the door, unexpectedly.

Mary paused for a moment, reassured by the mention of her husband and of Oran. She quickly convinced herself that this could only be a friend on the other side of the door, if he did, as he claimed to, know both Dara and Oran. She assumed correctly that the only way someone could possibly know of Oran was for them to be one of his own kind. She reached out and slowly drew back the heavy iron bolt, lifted the latch, and cracked the door open a few inches - just enough that she could see who was there.

On the old, worn out, stone step outside, in the dwindling daylight, she found a strange man whom she had never before seen. He was a lean man and small in stature - shorter than her, in fact - wearing a neat beard and with long, blond hair that was combed neatly back and braided into a long pony tail. He also had oddly pointed ears, somewhat comfortingly for her.

Oh no! she immediately feared, placing a hand over her mouth, with a gasp. A terrible realisation hit her, and she suddenly suspected the worst, as she stood staring at him in silence now.

Lugh and Cethen returned later in the day with Enya's friend, Orla, having spent some hours searching the castle's vastness for her. As they arrived at the door leading to Enya's private chambers, they came to a halt, bidding Orla to approach the door. Fearing the worst, they had also brought Cathal and Ronan on the off-chance that their might would be needed. They were now, once again, stood impatiently by the heavy door as Orla knocked on it, pleading, for the fifth time, "Enya, it is I, Orla. You must open this door at once, please!"

Again, there came no response, just as expected. Lugh glared at the door in obvious frustration, before turning to his friend and growling, "Enough of this nonsense, I say. Time to break it in - I'm concerned for my dear daughter's wellbeing." He turned quickly to Cathal and Ronan, who were stood just behind him, and instructed, "Gentleman, the door, please... if you will?"

Cathal and Ronan stepped forward immediately, with a courteous nod, then swiftly lunged at the door with all of their might, using their shoulders as battering rams. The door gave instantly, under the force, and the two men stumbled - almost fell, in fact - into the dimly lit room as the door flew inwards, swinging round and hitting the wall inside with a loud bang. Lugh wasted no time and swiftly stormed into the room, past them, then called out, "Enya! Where are you, my child?"

There came no response to his question - no sound at all - as he stood near the centre of the room, looking about him frantically, with a bewildered expression spreading across his face, noticing that there was no sign of his cherished daughter anywhere.

"Search her quarters! Find my daughter... *now*!" he bellowed.

Cethen and the other two men hurriedly went about scouring the chambers for Enya, as Lugh waited hopefully and patiently. After several minutes spent searching the various rooms, they returned to where the King stood, wearing perplexed expressions on their faces. Cethen looked at the King regretfully now, as he said, almost apologetically, "We can find no trace of your daughter anywhere, Sire - no sign of her, at all."

Lugh regarded his friend with some confusion, stroking his beard thoughtfully for a minute, then looked toward the window nearby, to his left, as he muttered, "I fear that I may very well know exactly where she is - or rather, where she has gone. I believe that she may have sneaked out of the castle in the night and followed Oran and Dara." He then turned back to Cethen to add, "What to do, Cethen? I can't risk sending people after her - it's much too dangerous. It would be extremely selfish of me to do so, no? But I can't leave her out there on her own... if she is, indeed, alone. She's my only child, after all."

"What shall I do, Sire?" Cethen offered, obediently. "You need only ask of me, my Lord."

Lugh looked at his dearest friend for a moment, as his two enormous Irish Wolfhounds sauntered into the room and lay down by his feet, thinking carefully over the worrying situation at hand. He knew that he couldn't risk sending a search party after his beloved daughter, and now, dearly hoped that she was, indeed, in the safe company of Oran and Dara, wherever they may be, and that she would soon return safely with them. His thoughts then turned to how long they had been gone for, telling himself that it had now been the best part of three days. He regarded Cethen with a frown, then strangely asked, "Do you believe they *will* succeed, Cethen? Do you think they *shall* return to us, with Rydian, of course?"

Cethen looked at Lugh in surprise, surprise at the despairing words that he knew to be decidedly uncharacteristic of his King. He knew that the King needed, and deserved, his support at this moment and quickly responded, "But of course they will return. I have every confidence in them, Sire."

Lugh, however, detected now that Cethen's voice faltered slightly, as though he himself also had doubts as to whether or not Oran would ever make it back to the castle safely. He walked slowly over to the window nearest to him and stared out into the distance, saying nothing for a short moment. The window faced eastward and from this elevation, he could just make out the grey plumes of chimney smoke rising from the village of Glenarran far below in the distance, although he could not quite see any of the houses, as the distant edge of the summit blocked his view. Suddenly, a thought came to him - a reminder of something he had considered, occasionally, during the past few days. He turned around slowly and faced Cethen, pointing toward the window next to him as he ordered, "I want you to take Cathal and Ronan and go down to that village at dusk." He then asked, "What did Dara say was the name of his wife?"

"Mary, I believe. Yes, Mary, Sire," Cethen replied, with some confidence. He wondered, with deep concern, what might be coming next.

"Mary, very good - yes," Lugh mused, stroking his beard again, "I want you to go there and find Mary MacBrien, and her children, and bring them here to the castle, quickly. You understand me, yes?"

"To the castle, my Lord?" Cethen enquired.

"Yes, Cethen, to the castle," Lugh said, rather impatiently this time.

"A-ah, yes. Very good, Sire. A-as you wish," he said, his voice faltering again somewhat at the belief that he may have slightly irritated his King by his questioning.

"I have been giving it some thought over the past few days, Cethen - the wellbeing of Dara's young family should he not return to us safely, that is," Lugh began to explain, adding, as Cethen listened intently, "Should he *not* return... well, it would serve to make their lives extremely difficult, with no husband or father there to provide for them, no? Since that loss would, essentially, be at *my* bidding, it is, I believe, *my* duty and *my* responsibility to provide for them - to see that they have a decent future, as such. I have, therefore, taken the somewhat difficult decision that they shall come here, to the castle, to live with us - the Danu."

Wasting no time, Cethen turned to Cathal and Ronan when Lugh had finished speaking, and quickly instructed, "Go now and prepare the horses, men. We leave soon, before the sunset."

The two men nodded, without speaking, and quickly left the room to carry out Cethen's orders. Cethen turned to face the King again, and enquired, "What if she will not come, Sire? What then?"

"You shall do your very best to persuade her, my good fellow. Make it very clear to her that she may be in great peril if she and her children were to remain in that house," Lugh answered, simply, then went on, "Go now - bring them here at once, Cethen."

Cethen bowed to his King, silently, then turned and rushed out of the room, leaving Lugh behind. The King moved back to the window and looked out again over the snow-covered landscape into the distance, as he placed a hand gently on the glass and said softly, "Where are you, my child? Be safe. Get home swiftly to us."

At that moment, Murchad the Wise walked slowly and graciously into the room and came to stand behind Lugh, placing a hand, fondly and comfortingly, on the King's shoulder, as he uttered in his frail, ancient voice,

"Lugh, my son," he said, squeezing the King's shoulder with his boney fingers. "We need to think about taking the castle underground for safety's sake - out of sight. We are running out of time, my boy. We must act soon."

Lugh then turned around to face Murchad, with a heavy sigh and a knowing nod, whilst at the same time, Cethen made his way quickly down to the courtyard, as the daylight began to fade. Cethen found Cathal and Ronan already there, mounted on horseback and patiently awaiting his arrival. He marched urgently toward his horse, taking its reins from Cathal's outstretched hand as he climbed up into his saddle, then nodded. "Let's get going," he said, as he looked upward toward the top of the ramparts, and called out, "Open the gates, men!"

The mechanism that controlled the only access to the castle clanged and clanked loudly, as the heavy wooden gates slowly opened, and the three men set off on horseback, leaving the safety of the castle - of their home - behind them. They made their way away from the castle, cautiously crossing through the barrier formed by the ever-watchful fireworms, and down the mountain toward Esslan, at the edge of the village of Glenarran.

Cethen was confident - or rather, certain - that he could find Dara's house simply by tracking Oran's distinctive magical aura - something that all Danu possessed, fortunately for him now. He concentrated deeply as he led the way, following a faint, bluish, wispy trail that was sparsely dotted with the smallest specks of bright blue light, which hung in the air ahead and showed the path that Oran and Dara had taken. He changed his focus, briefly, now noticing a similar, but this time, greenish coloured trail with yellow specks of light, which confirmed to him that Enya had, indeed, come this way also... just as her father had suspected.

He grunted knowingly as he quickly switched his focus back to Oran's trail and they carried on, carefully and quietly, toward Dara's quaint little cottage.

Under the cover of near darkness now, and still unseen, the three men followed Oran's slowly fading aura as they made their way around to the rear of the tiny, thatched cottage. Cethen slowly dismounted from his horse, approaching the back door, somewhat hesitantly, on foot. He could hear the sounds of children laughing from inside the house, as he reached out and knocked softly on the door with his knuckles. He then took a pace back, away from the door, and waited anxiously for a response. After a moment, he heard a faint voice call out from inside the house - that of a young woman, he surmised - say something which he couldn't quite make out, so stepped forward and knocked once more. Again, the woman's voice came through the door, more clearly this time, and which he believed to be saying, *"Who's there? Who is it?"*

His immediate and prudent reaction was to attempt to gain the trust and confidence of the woman, whom he believed to be on the other side of the door. He then announced clearly who he was, including, cleverly, the names of her husband and of Oran, to further secure her trust.

Next came a moment's silence as he waited, followed then, just after, by the sounds of a bolt and a latch being undone. The door opened slowly, ever so slightly, before him with a creaking sound, to reveal a young, dark haired woman in a long, grey, somewhat tattered dress. The young woman immediately gasped as she placed a hand over her mouth in apparent shock at what, or rather whom, she now saw before her.

"Fear not, my good lady, for I am friend. My name is Cethen, of the Danu," he announced again, urgently, concerned that she might scream out in fear. He then continued in a slightly more relaxed tone, as he bowed, "I am, as I said, a friend of your good husband, Dara... and of Oran, whom I am certain that you will have met recently." Cethen then noticed, peering past her, that he could see signs of Oran's aura within the house, thankfully.

Mary removed her hand from her mouth and slowly lowered it to her side, as she stood there staring at him blankly, thinking for a moment. As Ellen and Rosemary emerged from the bedroom and came to her side, she began to fear the worst, realising that this man must surely have brought terrible news - that her husband was not to return to her alive. She began to weep, as she continued to gaze out through the open door at him, then sobbed, "Is ... my... Dara... alright?"

Cethen took a pace toward Mary, gesturing hastily with flattened palms raised toward her, as he answered, "No, no, you misunderstand! Yes, yes! I mean, of course, your husband is fine... we believe," realising instantly that she was of the mistaken belief that he had brought news of her husband's untimely demise.

Mary raised the towel that she was still holding in her hand, pressed it to her face and dabbed at the tears that ran down her reddened cheeks. As she stopped sobbing, Cethen explained, "The King - King Lugh of the Danu, that is - has requested that I come here to find you, and that I escort you and your children immediately to the castle, where you shall await the return of your husband in safety."

Mary looked at him quizzically, then asked, distraughtly, "Go to what castle? You mean now, right away?"

"Yes, my dear lady, right now," Cethen replied, earnestly, then went on to say, "The King fears that you are, all three, in certain danger if you remain here, and also believes that you would be most pleased at the opportunity to see your husband all the sooner - upon his return to the castle with Oran, of course."

Mary thought for a moment, somewhat enticed by the prospect of seeing both the castle and its mystical inhabitants, glanced briefly down at her daughters, who were now clinging onto her dress, then looked back at Cethen as she responded with uncertainty, "All three of us - we're all invited, yes?"

"Yes, yes, of course. But we must leave now, right away, this instant," Cethen urged now, growing ever more concerned that some friend of the MacBriens might happen to chance by for an evening visit, thus discovering him and his companions in the process. *That would never do*, he thought.

"But... I need to pack... some things, clothes... and the like," Mary stammered, taken completely off guard now.

"I'm afraid that there is no time for such things, dearest Mary," Cethen insisted. "We must leave now, before we are discovered. No-one must know of our existence, of the Danu, you see."

"You know my name?" Mary asked, curiously. "What else do you know of me... of us?"

"I do, dear lady. Your husband spoke of you at great length," Cethen replied with a smile, "And with great love, also. Now then, we really must get going... just as you are. If you are agreeable, of course, and would be kind enough to don some warmer clothing, quickly though."

"Well... yes, I suppose. If you insist," Mary agreed, wisely, remembering the tales that her cousin had told her, then suddenly thought of something else, as she demanded, "There's one thing I'm not willing to leave behind though - our cat. She's coming with us too."

"What, might I ask, is a... *cat*?" Cethen enquired, somewhat addled by her last statement. "I don't believe that I've ever had the good fortune to come across one of those."

Mary laughed at this, as she turned and pointed toward the big, grey and black tabby cat that was stretched out, fast asleep, on the hearth in front of the fire place.

"That lazy animal, asleep there by the fire, is Lucy... our cat, of course," she declared.

Cethen looked past Mary, to where she was pointing, then raised his eyebrows as he realised, "Ah, we call that a felis where I am from... now I understand." With a brief laugh, he then looked back at Mary, as he quickly added, "Of course, bring her by all means, but we must go now, urgently."

Mary nodded in agreement, without saying a word, then swiftly returned the knife and the cloth to where she had taken them from, by the old sink. She then fetched and hastily went about putting some warmer clothes on herself, Ellen and Rosemary, before walking briskly over to the hearth and picking Lucy up in her arms. The cat let out a sleepy, protesting meow as Mary carried her from her much-loved place of warmth, took her outside into the cold night air, and lowered her into a big saddle bag which Cathal held kindly open, which was then buckled closed to keep her in. She hurried back into the house and quickly doused the fire with water from the sink and extinguished the oil lamp on the table. Then, as she emerged again with her children, she closed the back door, bolting it firmly shut behind her.

Mother and daughters then climbed nervously up onto the horses - Mary behind Cethen, Ellen and Rosemary in front of Cathal and Ronan, respectively - and set off into the cold night air together. As they rode off, Mary glanced back briefly, worriedly, at her little house - her home, the home that she was now leaving behind for the first time ever, since she had married Dara. She and her children clung on tightly to whomever or whatever they could, as they galloped at full speed away from the village. They were, all three, wondering what lay ahead of them now, as they moved swiftly in the darkness toward Faltanragh and the Ivy Castle, which they had never seen, even though it had stood there on the mountain for all of their lives. None of them noticed, however, the unusual swarm of large black moths that passed high above them, heading silently in the opposite direction - in the direction of Esslan.

Dara had wondered what Rydian had meant by *Say the words, bearer of the sword.* But now he knew, at last, as Oran stood there in front of them in his blood-soaked clothes with his back turned to them, holding the Sword of Light up to Rydian with its brightly glowing emerald for her to see. Standing mere feet away from her snout, he said confidently and optimistically, "Rydian, I am Oran, of the Danu. Yield to me."

They all watched and listened in hope, as nothing seemed to happen at first, and Rydian neither said nor did anything, for a moment. Then, Oran noticed her eyes slowly change colour, from blood red to vivid green, and a contented smile spread across his youthful face. As he stood there smiling from ear to ear, Rydian began to speak to him for the first time, saying, "Oran of the Danu. Greetings, dragon commander. I am called Rydian. I am your humble servant and yours to command," and the bond between the two - the joining, as it was known - was made, for all eternity.

Oran continued to stand where he was for a moment, delighting the sight before him, still smiling – no, grinning now. He then looked up at Obblob and curtly advised, "I think you can get off her now, Obblob." He then asked with feigned uncertainty, "That is you, Obblob, no?"

"Why yes," came Obblob's rather louder than usual voice, as he struggled to speak with his jaws still clamped around Rydian's neck. He immediately released Rydian from his grip and stated factually, "Of course it is I."

Obblob then, slowly and carefully, climbed off Rydian's back, stepping down onto the snow beside her. She immediately seized the opportunity to take a swipe at him with her tail, but missed, mercifully, as he suddenly shrank in size whilst transforming back to his normal self again and stood next to her, beaming. He gave her a somewhat mocking smile and then walked over to where everyone else now stood, in front of her barbed and horned head.

Rydian said nothing else at first, simply blinked briefly, then lifted her head up off the ground and shook it vigorously, like a wet dog trying to dry itself. She pulled herself up out of the snow and onto her feet, stretching her enormous wings out to their limits and at the same time, raising her head aloft, pointed directly upward, as she released a huge puff of black smoke and soot at the sky above. She shook her head again, folded her wings back in, and then looked down at Oran and his friends, lowering her head to his eye level, slowly and gracefully. She then stated in a husky voice, "Master Oran, since you had the gall to, albeit unwittingly, wake me from my peaceful slumber, you may atone for your actions by mending something for me... with your magic? There is no fire in my breath, as you can see. I've not used it for such a long time that it seems to have extinguished itself, somehow." She clawed lightly at her throat with her front left foot, to indicate where the problem seemed to be.

Oran gazed at her for a moment, then briefly around at his friends, before turning back to Rydian as he said, meekly, "I apologize for the rude awakening, Rydian. It was an accident that I stabbed you with my sword, believe me. As for your fire, I do believe that I *can* help you, but you'll have to get down on your belly though. I can't reach up there, and I must lay my hands on you for the magic to work. May I?" He gestured toward the afflicted area, ten or more feet above him, with a hand and walked toward her, pushing the sword back into its scabbard as he drew closer.

"You may, of course," she responded, eagerly, with a gentle nod of her formidable looking head.

She slowly lowered herself down onto her underside, into the snow again, adopting a position that resembled how a cat might sit, so that Oran might be able to reach her. Now within easy touching distance of him, Oran slowly extended his arms out to his front and placed his palms on her throat, tentatively at first, as she looked down at him. The others watched on from behind, anxiously. Holly instantly began to whine, concerned for Oran's safety, no doubt, as Dara looked down at her and said, "Shhh, Holly! Be good."

Oran then began to whisper something, something completely inaudible to the others, except for Holly, but the tiny blue lightning bolts that snaked up his body and onto Rydian's neck made it obvious, to Dara and Enya at least, that he was performing a healing spell of some kind. After a moment or so of whispering, or chanting, Oran removed his hands from Rydian's throat. The lightning bolts swiftly vanished, and he stepped back a few paces and looked up at her with a smile, then wailed loudly at her, "*Wai, eeese.*" Rydian's throat glowed briefly red where he had had his hands just a moment before, then returned to normal as Oran recommended to her, "Try to breath your fire now, old girl, but do direct it somewhere safe, if you don't mind, please."

Rydian once again nodded at him in acknowledgement, silently, then lifted her spiny head upward, to the fullest extent of her long neck, and tilted her snout skyward again. She took a deep breath, as everyone watched from below, then stupendously exhaled a plume of flames that must have reached fifty feet into the air above, as the sun neared the horizon behind her. She looked quickly back down at them, as they all gasped loudly, Dara and Enya wearing stunned expressions now, and laughed loudly. As she lowered her head back down to near Oran's level again, she said, "Thank you, Oran. How can I ever repay you?"

Oran stared thoughtfully at her for a second, then humbly stated, "Well, there is one thing you could do for me - for all of us, now that you mention it."

"You need only ask, my young friend," Rydian answered, respectfully.

"Well," Oran began, "Do you remember the egg - the dragon crystal - that you gave to King Lugh some three hundred years ago as part of a bargain which you made with him?"

Rydian stared at him blankly for a moment, as if trying to recollect, then answered, "Why, yes - of course I remember. How could I forget a dear friend such as King Lugh?"

"Well... ahem... I... destroyed it... destroyed the egg, sort of... kind of, yes... I destroyed it... by accident... of course," Oran stammered worriedly, afraid of the possibility of incurring her wrath, then took a deep breath and continued with his explanation, "I was charged with watching over it, tending to it, but I fell asleep and it... well... it incinerated itself. We lost the time cocoon in the process and the Ivy Castle lies exposed now because of me. King Lugh and the high council have tasked me to come here to find you and to ask if you would be kind enough to return to the castle with us and provide a replacement egg before we are discovered by our enemies. It's all my fault - I am truly sorry."

Rydian regarded the young elf, thoughtfully, for a moment, then stated, "You destroyed the egg. Well now, that was clever of you." Rising to her feet again with a subdued growl, she went on to compliment him, "You are, though, a very brave young man to come all this way with your few friends here, in the hopes of finding me - not even knowing for sure that I would be here. You are certainly very fortunate, there is no doubt."

"I am that, yes," Oran answered, apprehensively, then pleaded, "Will you help me - help us - Rydian? Please?" He looked at her for a moment and then cheekily added, with a boyish grin, "You owe me a favour... for killing me, no?"

Rydian looked back at him as he tried to read her expression - *no easy task with a dragon*, he thought - then admonished, "You attacked first with that sword, remember? I claim self-defence. All in the past, dear boy." She then softened her tone as she went on, "Well now, how can I not help you? Of course I will. One thing though - I am not willing to spend an eternity back here on this mountain, in solitude, when it is done. I should like to remain at the castle, where I belong."

Oran pondered over her demand for a moment, then remarked, "I'm sure that the King will agree to that. We need the egg, after all." He then beamed the biggest smile as he turned around to his friends behind him, who were now smiling back at him, and suddenly remembered his mother, who was stood smiling back at him, also. He excused himself as he walked over to her, still beaming, and whispered excitedly to her, "Mother? You're my mother... yes?" He then reached out to take her hand, but found, disappointingly, that he couldn't - that she was simply an apparition and was not real, as he went on, "I... don't... understand. Where have you been? Why can I see, but not touch you?"

The woman looked at him and smiled sadly now, it seemed, as she answered, "My dear son, I am truly sorry. I left my mortal body soon after I placed you near the castle that morning, all those years ago, you see. I was executed for my actions - kidnapping you, as it were - at the hands of your evil father. I knew of his cruel plans for you and knew also that I had to get you away from him - to hide you from him. The Ivy Castle was the best place to conceal you, before it was too late. I left my bracelet, which I see you still wear, with you... to protect you. You must never lose that bracelet, Oran, and you must certainly *never* allow it to get into the hands of your malicious father."

"But *who* is my father?" Oran interrupted.

"There is no more time to explain, my son. I have but a limited time here with you and sadly, I must go now. I can be with you only in your times of great need, and you now no longer need me here," his mother answered, as her image began to fade in front of him.

"But... mother... what is your name? *Mother...* I do... need you!" Oran cried in exasperation.

"Ethioné. My name is Ethioné, Oran," came the fading answer, as his mother vanished from view, and he looked sadly, mournfully, at the snow where she had just stood.

Enya came quickly to his side, taking his hand in hers as a tear rolled slowly down his cheek, attempting to lift his spirits. "We should get going, Oran - back to the castle - before it is too late. I'm sure your mother will return someday." She then smiled at him reassuringly, as she squeezed his hand in hers.

"Yes, of course... you're right, Enya." He then frowned at her as a sudden realisation hit him, and asked, "How did *you* get here?"

"It's a long story," she laughed. "I'll tell you later. Now, let's prepare for our journey back to the castle, heh?"

Oran nodded at her in agreement, as Holly came to his side, then looked at Dara, Obblob and Rydian in turn, before announcing, "Homeward then, my friends, yes?"

CHAPTER EIGHTEEN
Homeward

Mary was still clinging on tightly to Cethen's jacket with both hands, decidedly cold hands, as they arrived on the snow-covered summit, galloping single file. The great white castle loomed into view in the distance, ahead of them, at last. The moon was in the waning gibbous stage, having been full just three nights earlier, and was illuminating the castle's exterior clearly for her to see over Cethen's shoulder as she stared ahead, wide-eyed and awestruck. She kept her gaze fixed on the impressive structure as they drew swiftly nearer it, distracted momentarily by the strange, incandescent objects that were dotted either side of their path just ahead, protruding several feet from the snow-covered ground and swaying rhythmically as they rode past them. The smell of burning grass, mixed with peat and dirt, filled her nostrils briefly - *a not altogether unpleasant smell*, she thought. She spoke loudly into Cethen's ear for the first time since leaving her house, over the thunderous noise of the horses' hooves, "What were those - those orange things, burning and smouldering in the ground?"

"Fireworms. They guard the castle perimeter from unwanted intruders," he called back to her, without taking his eyes off the slowly opening gates just ahead of them now.

The entrance to the castle was already open as the horses charged through and sped into the courtyard, all of them coming to a halt as the gates immediately began to close again behind them. The mechanism clanked loudly until the heavy gates came together with a loud bang and the castle was, again, sealed shut. Lugh was already there, standing patiently in the courtyard with Murchad the Wise at his side, waiting for them. He walked toward Cethen's horse and then stopped a few feet away, as he bowed gracefully, stood straight again, and announced, "Mary MacBrien, welcome to the Ivy Castle, home of the Danu. My name is King Lugh and it is my great pleasure - an honour - to meet you."

Mary studied the distinguished looking man from where she sat for a moment, noticing his long, neat beard and long hair, like the all others... *and* his pointed ears, like all the others. She then glanced briefly at the other, much older man, incorrectly thinking that he must be the King's father. She inadvertently ignored him as she quickly looked around for her daughters, finding them behind her and calling out, "Ellen, Rosemary... are you both alright?"

"Yes, Mummy," Ellen called back. Rosemary merely nodded in agreement with her sister, alarmed into silence by so many strangers and the unfamiliar surroundings that she now found herself in.

Mary turned back to face Lugh, then climbed down carefully from Cethen's horse and approached him, asking hopefully, "Is there any news of my dear husband, kind sir?"

Lugh regarded her thoughtfully for a second, fearful of upsetting her further, having already taken both her and her children from their home rather abruptly. He then turned his thoughts briefly to his missing daughter, Enya, as he declared truthfully, "We expect that Oran and your husband shall return to us no later than tomorrow, my dear."

"Tomorrow, you say? I can only pray that you are right, good sir," Mary responded, forlornly, standing directly before him now.

"Might I ask, dear lady… was there also a young girl with Oran on the night that he first came to your home?" Lugh asked, hopefully, as he looked up at her.

"Why, no, there was not. It was just my husband and Oran, no-one else," Mary answered, curiously, wondering who he meant, as she went on to enquire, "Why do you ask? Is someone missing?"

Lugh sighed deeply, as he looked at her and stated, "Yes, my only child, my daughter, Enya. She has been missing since shortly after Oran and Dara left - missing for several days now. I fear that she may have followed them, foolishly. She and Oran are very close friends, you see."

"We shall pray together then for the safe return of our loved ones," Mary answered, encouragingly.

"Yes, we shall," Lugh affirmed, before enquiring, "It's a chilly evening, my dear Mary. May I call you Mary? Might I show you and your dear children to your private quarters, good lady?" hoping to diffuse a situation that might, otherwise, become awkward.

"Private quarters?" Mary asked in surprise, then nodded, as she politely smiled and added, "Of course, wonderful. Please do, and by all means, call me Mary." She was eager to get herself and her daughters indoors, away from the cold night air.

"Excellent. This way then, if you please," Lugh announced, with a gesture of his right arm toward a large, brightly lit doorway at the far side of the courtyard, adding as he marched off, "We shall get you settled in firstly, and then you can join us for dinner and meet everyone."

Ellen and Rosemary had, meanwhile, been helped down from the horses by Cathal and Ronan during the brief exchange between their mother and the King. They now stood obediently by her side, Ellen clutching Lucy tightly in her arms, having collected her from the saddle bag, both waiting patiently in the freezing air for their mother's instruction. Mary took Rosemary's cold little hand in hers, then placed her other hand in the small of Ellen's back, and guided them off across the courtyard after Lugh. All three of them followed closely behind the King toward the lighted doorway, looking around in wonder at the castle's ivy covered interior as they went.

Dara walked over to Oran and eagerly threw his arms around him, giving him an affectionate hug as he enthused, "I'm so glad you're here, Oran. With us... er, alive... I mean."

"Where else would I be?" Oran demanded, grimacing and patting Dara on the back with both hands, before stating, "That's more than enough - you can let go of me now, Dara. Ugh, you're smothering me."

"I'm just *so happy* to see you," he said, as he released Oran from his embrace and leant back slightly, his hands now moving to Oran's shoulders. He then continued with a smile, "Can I not show my appreciation? I'm so glad you're still with us, really. You must explain what happened. I'm eager to know how - as are both Enya and Obblob, I'm sure."

"More importantly, let's set up camp for the night, firstly," Oran advised, glancing toward Rydian. "And we need to discuss our plan for the journey home come first light, also."

"Yes, yes, but of course," Dara agreed, as he turned to Enya and insisted, "And you, young lady, can explain how you got here, as well."

Enya gave him a wry smile as she remarked, "As I said before, I have been with you both for the entire journey," continuing factually, "I witnessed the banshee at your house, Arak the deer in the forest, the three-headed dragon and the Children of Lir at the lough, *and* our young friend Obblob here. I witnessed all of it... everything." She then laughed as she walked off in the direction of Rydian, with Obblob following her.

Oran and Dara exchanged looks of surprise at Enya's revelation, then smiled and laughed at each other as Oran suggested, "I think this is as good a place as any to make camp. I'll make a fire for us to keep ourselves warm through the night." He then realised suddenly that the horses were missing, asking, "Where are the horses?"

"Errr... where we left them, of course, in the chaos... up on the summit," came Dara's matter-of-fact response.

"Well, we'll have to go up there and fetch them now, in the dark, won't we, Dara?" Oran demanded.

Dara had the sudden suspicion that by *we*, Oran actually meant *he*. This didn't sit well with him and he immediately blurted out, "I'm not going up there alone! You'll come with me, and I'm not asking."

"Hah! Giving orders now, are you?" Oran laughed. "Don't worry, I'll go with you. Let me get the fire going first though, so the others can get warmed."

"Yes, fine, of course," Dara grumbled, as he bent down to stroke Holly at his side, then urged, "Just be quick about it, please. I'm cold too, and extremely hungry. It's been quite a day, really."

Oran briefly nodded at him in response and then went about the business of preparing their camp for the night, conjuring a fire in his usual way so that the others could get comfortable. As Dara waited with Holly, Oran walked over to the others and explained that he and Dara had to go back up to the summit to fetch the horses and the provisions, and that they would return soon, at which point they could all eat supper together. He then looked up at Rydian and asked, "Would you like to accompany us, mighty dragon? You can light the way for us with your fiery breath."

"Dragon has a name. That name is called Rydian, as you very well know, young man," she admonished, then politely continued, "And yes, of course. I would be happy to accompany you."

Oran smiled up at her, then turned and briskly set off toward a path that he had noticed earlier - a trail which led back up to the summit - with Dara and Rydian following closely behind as Enya, Obblob and Holly awaited their return, warming themselves by the fire. They soon arrived at, and followed, the shallower path, which had, no doubt, been created by sheep or goats that scoured the mountain in search of food, back up to the caldera. This was certainly a much easier path, Dara thought, than the near vertical one which had brought them here earlier that day - that being much too steep for them to climb back up, obviously.

Somewhere nearer home, in the deepest, darkest and dampest reaches of a very old and somewhat dilapidated castle, not many miles from Glenarran, Bronagh Rankin opened her eyes. She did so slowly at first, just as the sun disappeared below the horizon outside, taking in her dimly lit and unfamiliar surroundings. As she lay there, quite still, in what seemed to be a shallow earthen pit, peering around her in the sparse light cast by the few flaming torches that hung on the walls of the seemingly large room, she could hear a strange fluttering, then shuffling, noise nearby. The sound drew closer, as she stared directly upward into the near darkness above her, but she did not feel fear, oddly - she did not feel anything, in fact. She continued to lie there, gazing upward, motionless, as a gravelly, male voice came to her through the darkness, from somewhere very close by.

"Ah, my child… you are risen, I see."

It was already dark by the time Oran, Dara and Rydian arrived back on the summit, Rydian illuminating the way ahead for them occasionally by breathing great plumes of flame, although there was no real need for her to do so, as the moon brightly illuminated the snowy caldera clearly for them to see. Soon, thanks to Rydian's fire breathing and to the brightness of the moonlight, they found the horses and the remainder of their belongings, just where they had left them.

They quickly mounted up and set off back the way they had come, with Rydian leading the way again, descending carefully toward the camp site which was clearly visible below, thanks to Oran's magical fire. Soon, they arrived back at the camp to find Enya and Obblob chatting and laughing by the glow of the fire, with Holly stretched out by their feet, fast asleep. The pair were getting along famously, it seemed, which brought a smile to Oran's face as he enquired, "So, what have you two been talking about then? Pray tell, what is it that is so amusing?"

"Oh, not much," Enya replied with a kind of coy smile, looking directly up at him, then admitted with a giggle, "I was just telling my young friend here about your... erm, bathing experience... by the lough yesterday morning, that's all."

Oran blushed slightly at the thought that she had seen him undressed, near naked, but thankfully, the glow of the fire hid his embarrassment from everyone, as he climbed down from his horse, bravely asking her, "And were you pleased by what you saw?"

"Well..." Enya responded vaguely, diverting her gaze to the flames in front, in reluctance to continue the conversation now, feeling somewhat embarrassed herself.

Oran, also not wishing to pursue this sensitive topic, and Dara, quickly went about rummaging through the saddle bags for some food, finding that they had just enough left to feed everyone. Together, they all sat around the fire as they prepared and ate dinner, chatting about the events of the past few days, with Enya finally divulging the details of how she had used a concealment spell to follow them all the way there, undetected.

They briefly discussed the sensitive topic of Oran's death and resurrection, with Enya explaining how she had watched Oran's mother use her skills - magic which Enya had never seen before - to bring him back to life. The conversation moved on swiftly and, at one point, Enya began to tell the story of how she had kept a watch over them - hidden from sight, of course - as they slept by the fire at the lough side. She recounted how a strange, dark being had materialised from nowhere in the middle of the night, and then crouched over Dara as he slept, as though to attack him.

"I thought I dreamt that!" Dara blurted out, almost choking on his food. "You mean to tell me that it was real?"

"Yes... very real," Enya stated, sternly, as she reached out and placed her hand on his arm. "But have no fear, for I scared it off with a banishment spell. It can never touch you again, or harm you, for as long as you may live."

"Well that is certainly good to know, but what was it, that creature?" Dara enquired, still gravely concerned.

"I'm not entirely sure as to what, or indeed, who it was," Enya began, "But of one thing I am quite certain - that his intentions were not good."

"I thank you, Enya, from the very depths of my heart," Dara said, as he looked directly into her eyes and patted the back of her hand with his. "I believe that you may very well have saved my life. Thank you, again."

Dara stared into the flames as he wondered what this creature might be, and what evil intentions it might have had. His thoughts turned quickly to where it might be now, as he said to the rest of them, "When this is done - when the quest is finished, that is..." He paused for thought briefly, before looking hopefully at Oran, as he continued, "I think, perhaps, that we should find this evil being and destroy it, before it harms someone else. Who knows, even, that it hasn't already done so?"

Oran looked at Dara for a moment, as he pondered his words, then advised, "That may not be an easy task, Dara. We cannot leave the castle once the time cocoon is re-instated, else we will never be able to return to our people."

Dara laughed loudly at this, then pointed at Oran's wrist, declaring, "I think that, perhaps, your death earlier today has somewhat affected your memory, Oran. The bracelet - your mother's talisman - should allow you to come and go as you wish, if I am not mistaken."

Oran looked down at the bracelet around his wrist and then smiled as he acknowledged, "Oh yes, of course. How silly of me - it *has* been a rather wearisome day."

Enya and Obblob joined in and laughed as well, while Rydian, lying curled up in the snow just behind them, simply opened one glowing green eye in response to the noise of their laughter. She raised her head from the snow and turned to face them as she asked, "So then, all of you, what are your plans for the journey home tomorrow morning?"

They all regarded her silently at first, realising immediately that they had not, so far as yet, discussed any real plans for the trip back to Faltanragh and the castle, as they had been too busy eating, chatting and reminiscing, somewhat, over the events of the past few days. Oran was first to speak, as he cleared his throat and suggested, "We four and Holly shall make the journey home on horseback while, I believe it best, Rydian, that you make your way there under cover of night. Then, we shall meet you there in two days' time, back at the castle." He then paused briefly, before asking curiously, "You shall fly there, I presume?"

Rydian did not answer immediately, instead pulling herself to her feet and then lowering her barbed head down to near Oran's level, before stating in her elegant voice, "I may have a better plan... to expedite our journey. If you are interested in returning to the castle sooner, that is?"

Oran looked at her, wide-eyed and hopeful. Any plan she may have that might get them back to the castle more safely and more quickly was certainly a much better plan than his, as far as he was concerned. He stood up, intrigued by her statement, and looked her directly in the eye nearest him - a bright green eye not unlike his - and calmly said, "Continue, please."

"I have a plan that will see all of you safely back at the castle by late morning tomorrow," Rydian advised, confidently.

"How so?" Oran questioned, with a now puzzled expression on his young-looking face, but at the same time, excited by the prospect of getting home all the sooner.

"Your young friend there - the boy changeling," she said, with a brief nod toward Obblob, before turning back to Oran as she went on, "He can make himself to be like me at will - a dragon, correct?"

"He can that. We have all witnessed that feat," pausing briefly, then asking, "Where, exactly, are you going with this, Rydian?" as he grew ever more concerned as to what her plan might hold for him and his friends.

The others continued to listen to the exchange between Oran and his dragon, patiently, all of them also now growing concerned as to her intentions, when she suddenly announced, "We all fly - it is that simple, really. We would be at the castle in a matter of hours, instead of days."

"Huh... fly?" Oran stammered, turning to look at the others, who were all now wearing rather stunned expressions on their faces, faces that were reddened by the heat of the fire nearby.

Rydian then began to explain her plan at length, in the hope of relieving any sense of panic or fear among her new companions, as Oran turned back to face her, stating clearly to them, "Firstly, the changeling shall transform himself once more into my form... that of a dragon. You will then secure the saddles from the horses to our backs at the base of our necks, where they should fit comfortably and where it should be possible for you to secure the straps properly and safely. Two of you shall then mount up on the saddle on my back, with the other two mounting the saddle upon the changeling's back, at which point we shall fly together back to the castle. It will be much quicker."

Oran looked around at his friends briefly, all of them still silent and bewildered, then back at Rydian, as he nervously admitted, "None of us have ever flown before. I'm a little worried, if I'm to be completely honest. And a little scared, no less."

"I've flown!" Dara quickly interrupted, as he jumped to his feet. "It's quite... exhilarating, I think, is the best way to describe it."

"Really?" asked Oran, raising his eyebrows, "When, exactly?"

"The morning that I was captured outside your castle, a few hours before I met you," pausing as he tried to remember the name that Lugh had used to call the creatures by, then suddenly found it and continued, "Those Schawan creatures that flew me to the castle, from where they found me outside - yes, exhilarating."

Oran shook his head in disbelief at the fact that Dara had flown only once, for a few minutes, and found it to be exciting, as he demanded, "Will we be safe?" directing the question at both Rydian and Dara.

Dara answered first, and thoughtlessly, with, "You will - just as long as you don't fall off. That would be a bad thing to do, really."

"It is perfectly safe, master Oran," Rydian interjected quickly, giving Dara an angry, disapproving glance as she blew a small puff of soot at him. "We shall take every precaution to ensure the safety of everyone before we take to the air. As long as the changeling gets the hang of flying quickly, which he should, then everyone will be fine. It should come naturally to him - once he assumes my form, of course."

Obblob stood up quickly, as Dara coughed and wiped the soot from his face with his sleeve, then walked over and stood beside Oran as he asked of Rydian, "Will you teach me to fly, Rydian, in the morning before we set off, please?"

"Of course I will, young man," Rydian assured him.

"Enya, what about you? Are you happy with this plan?" Oran now enquired of his oldest friend.

"Yes, Oran, I'm fine with it. I believe it is an excellent idea," she said, as she now also rose to her feet to join the group that stood before Rydian in the glow of the fire. She politely asked of the dragon, "Who shall ride with you, dear Rydian?"

"Since Oran is dragon commander, it is fitting that he shall ride with me. You may ride with him, also, if you so wish, Enya," Rydian answered respectfully, to which Enya smiled.

"Well then, since that's all settled and arranged, apparently, I think we had best get some sleep," Oran advised everyone, then remarked, "Exciting day ahead tomorrow. I'll create a shield to protect us for the night, shall I?"

"No need, master Oran," Rydian chortled, "You have me for protection, remember?"

Oran smiled as he looked at her, nodding his agreement, then walked over to the horses, beckoning Dara to follow and hold one of the saddle bags open for him. He then proceeded to recite the spell that made the horses turn back into little black balls of matter which, once again, disappeared into the bag held open by Dara, with their familiar whizzing sound. Soon after, they all went about preparing their beds for the night, using some furs which Dara had retrieved from the bags, placing them near and around the fire, as Obblob walked back over to Rydian and asked, "I'll transform now, if you don't mind?" as he smiled up at her, adding, "Keep you company, help dragon keep watch through the night, if that is alright with you?"

Rydian regarded him thoughtfully for a moment, then consentingly answered, "Of course it is, young man. Of course."

As Oran, Dara and Enya bedded down around the floating fire for the night, beside an already slumbering Holly, Obblob reached out and gently touched Rydian's front left leg. A few moments later, two great dragons sat silently together in the moonlit snow, watchfully guarding over their companions as they drifted off to sleep.

Morning came to the castle, the morning of the fourth day since the departure of Oran and Dara, as Mary was woken by the bright sunlight that shone in through the east facing window of her new home for the night - her *private quarters* at the Ivy Castle, no less. She hadn't slept particularly well, partly because the bed was quite small - elf sized, indeed - partly due to worrying about Dara, and partly because of her very unfamiliar surroundings. She wondered how the girls had slept, since she could hear no sound from them in the next room, and was about to sit up in her bed and call out to them when she heard a knock at the door.

"Mrs. MacBrien, will you be joining us for breakfast, with your dear children?" a male voice enquired from the other side of the locked door. It was the same voice that had called to her through her own back door the previous night - that of Cethen, a very pleasant and courteous young man, she thought.

"Er... just a moment please, Cethen. We need a minute or two to get dressed," Mary called back, as she climbed out of the bed wearing only her night gown, and rushed into the next room in almost panic at the unwelcome and unusual silence of her children.

There, peacefully fast asleep under the heavy woollen blankets on the tiny bed in front of her, lay her cherished daughters. It was apparent that they had both slept much better than she had, and were still enjoying that sleep, blissfully unaware of the man at the door who was requesting their presence at the breakfast table. Mary reached out and put her hand tenderly on Ellen's arm, shaking her gently as she said softly, "Girls... Ellen, Rosemary. It's time to wake up now. We have to go for breakfast. Quickly now."

Ellen's eyes opened slowly, then Rosemary's, as they both woke to their new surroundings. Ellen smiled and then yawned, as she asked her mother, "Will Daddy be coming home today, Mummy?"

"Yes, yes, I'm sure that he will, my sweet," her mother reassured her, as she went on to urge them,

"Now, let's get dressed and then we can go down and have breakfast with our new friends. You liked the fairies last night, didn't you Rosemary? Such fun you had. The one called Eolande is your new best friend now, I don't doubt."

Rosemary simply smiled, sleepily, as she and her sister obediently climbed out of the bed.

As daybreak arrived on the ancient volcano, Dara was rudely awakened by the sound of a strange and rather loud flapping noise. This *noise* was accompanied by stern instructions which were being issued, very loudly, by Rydian, whom he could see now, stood some fifty feet away. She was looking up at the greying sky above her, Holly sat at her side, their eyes fastidiously tracking the path of something moving in the air, overhead.

"Slowly now, turn, turn," Rydian called upward, continuing, "Back toward me now. That's it, yes."

Dara crawled out from under his furs and stood up slowly, stretching his clenched fists up and out to the sky as he yawned and looked around for Oran and Enya, who were also just waking up nearby, he noticed.

There was an almighty *whoosh* overhead, which caused Dara to duck and then look up, just as Obblob soared past at a most alarming speed, toward the steep hillside in the distance.

"Now turn again, tightly. Come back to me and land. Remember now, flare and flap, flare and flap, good boy," Rydian enthused.

Dara watched in awe, as Obblob banked and turned his huge form gracefully, almost effortlessly, now making his final approach, great wings flapping thunderously against the dense air as he slowed himself so as to soften his landing next to his mentor. As Obblob touched down next to Rydian, he pointed his head skyward and scorched the air above them with a plume of flames in celebration of his success. Dara ran over to them immediately, followed closely by Oran and Enya, who were now laughing joyously at Obblob's achievement.

As he reached the dragons, he looked up at Obblob and called out to him with an excited laugh, "So you can fly now... heh? Well done!"

The dragon with the pale-yellow eyes slowly lowered his head down to near Dara's level and said in a rather loud voice, "Yes, I certainly can, luckily for you... because you and Holly will be riding with me."

Dara gave him a disapproving frown, as Oran now approached Rydian and enquired, "Is he ready, Rydian? Well done, Obblob, by the way," glancing at Obblob with a grin, then back at Rydian to ask, "Can we get going now? I'd like to set off as soon as possible. We mustn't forget, the people of Danu still need us."

"Yes, of course, Oran, I understand. And yes... he is ready," Rydian answered, confidently, as she glanced at her protégé and winked one eye at him.

"Right then," Oran pressed on, looking round at Enya and Dara. "Let's get them both saddled up. This way please, people and dragons." He briskly marched off toward the camp to retrieve the saddles.

Over the course of the next half an hour, Oran, Dara and Enya secured the saddles to both Rydian's and Obblob's backs at the base of their necks, just as Rydian had instructed. They made good use of the ropes from the bags to fashion harnesses that would hold them all safely in place, effectively tethering themselves to the saddles as they made the flight homeward. Dara made a special harness that would serve to keep Holly safe, then hoisted her up onto Obblob and lovingly secured her in place, rubbing her ears affectionately when he had finished and kissing her on the forehead as he advised, "You hang on tight now, girl. I don't want to lose you."

As Dara climbed up behind her and began tying himself into the saddle, he heard Oran call out to him, "We're both secured and ready over here, Dara. Are you ready?"

"Almost... one minute, please," Dara shouted back, as he tied the last knot and took a firm hold of Holly's collar in his left hand, then wound the rope, which was tied to his saddle, around his right wrist and forearm several times for added peace of mind. "Ready now!" he called out to Oran, as he patted Obblob on his neck and urged, "No funny business now, and whatever you do, and for goodness sake, do not transform back to yourself in mid-air, please."

Obblob swung his head round to face a concerned looking Dara and tauntingly laughed the words, "Scary, scary."

"We'll fly side by side during the journey homeward, agreed?" Oran instructed, adding, "Rydian, I think it best that we take a coastal route. It's longer, I know, but I believe that there is less chance that we will be seen by others." Then, as an afterthought, he enquired, "You remember where the castle lies, of course, yes?"

"Agreed, master Oran - very wise - and yes, I remember." As she looked up at the sky, which was now more than fifty percent overcast directly above and to the east, Rydian cautioned, "Be warned, though - there will be a near vertical ascent as we set off, so that we may climb above the clouds and make use of them to conceal ourselves from view. When we reach the east coast, we may have to fly nearer sea level, depending upon the cloud cover when we get there."

"Carefully, mind," Oran called out. "Nothing too dangerous or frightening please, if you will. We should all like to arrive back at the castle safely."

"Understood, master," Rydian acknowledged, obediently, before turning her attention to Obblob to give some last-minute advice. "Stick close to me, young man. It's quite calm here on the ground, but the winds will change as we climb aloft, and you may experience sudden, unexpected gusts. Remember well what I have taught you. Keep your head and all will be fine."

"Understood," Obblob nodded.

"Everyone ready? Call out one by one, please," Oran ordered.

"Ready," came Enya's voice from behind him, as she wrapped her arms tightly around his waist.

"Ready as I'll ever be," shouted Dara, performing last-minute checks on Holly's harness.

"Rydian, let's go," Oran commanded with a firm nod, tightening his grip on the ropes attached to his saddle.

Rydian nodded back at him, then at Obblob, before turning her head quickly toward her front, as she and Obblob simultaneously extended and began flapping their huge wings and then suddenly began to run toward the precipice at the edge of the shelf. Dara clung on tightly to Holly as they surged forward, a slight grimace spreading across his face as they lurched across the snowy ground and began to lift into the air, rising slowly at first, then feeling himself tilt backward dramatically as Obblob began his ascent.

They climbed steeply, matching Rydians course as they headed for cover in the clouds just above. He glanced to his left and saw Oran clinging desperately to his saddle, head down with Enya behind, holding onto him tightly, her face pressed against his back, then looked down at the ground that was rapidly disappearing below as they crossed the edge of the shelf and the mountain dropped away beneath them. This was already a lot higher than he had flown with the Schawan a few days ago - a lot higher, he worried. *Perhaps this wasn't such a good idea after all*, he suddenly told himself.

Moments later and they were passing through the dense cloud layer - still climbing, but not quite as steeply now. Dara felt this was a blessing, as he could no longer see the ground below and, more importantly, could not tell how high they currently were above it. He felt cold moisture on his face as they passed through the clouds, and suddenly, feeling the urge to check on Holly, shouted, "Are you alright, Holly girl?"

Holly turned her head slightly to look at him, very briefly, ears flapping wildly in the wind as they broke through the clouds and the sky turned blue all around them again. Dara looked over toward Oran again, who was currently looking back at him, smiling, and smiled back as Oran yelled out, "I could get to like this, I really could - it is truly amazing!"

Dara just smiled again in response. It was too cold up here, he thought, for idle chatter. As they flew onward, Dara marvelled at the sight below him as an almost smooth blanket of pristine white cloud stretched out before them in the bright sunlight. He had never imagined that it could look so beautiful from the other side.

It wasn't long - fifteen minutes, Dara thought - before they made a left turn and the early morning sun swung around to their right side as they headed north, and the cloud cover beneath all but disappeared ahead of them.

"Hang on tightly, everyone," Dara heard Rydian call out, as they began a relatively steep dive now. They descended toward the coastline several thousand feet below, much to Dara's alarm, as they picked up considerable speed in the process. He soon found himself struggling to breath against the force of the oncoming wind.

Down and down they went, for what seemed like too long, descending below scattered wisps of cloud as they neared sea level now. The dragons slowed down slightly as they levelled off where they passed the small bay at Cushendun, racing along just ten or fifteen feet above the blue-green Irish Sea about half a mile out from the shore. Dara relaxed slightly now, trying to enjoy the dramatic scenery - scenery that he had never seen before in his life and, until now, had thought that he would probably never see.

Soon, there was another left turn, into the prevailing wind now. They headed west to follow the dramatic coastline as they passed the near vertical, six-hundred-foot high dolerite cliffs of Robogdion. Shortly after, there were deserted sandy beaches on their left, with Rathlin island off to their right. They carried on at speed, passing intriguing rock formations where ancient volcanic eruptions and the subsequent lava flows had formed strange hexagonal columns of stone, where the hot lava had cooled as it merged with the cold waters of the North Atlantic Ocean. It was truly breath-taking, Dara thought, wishing now that Mary could be here to witness it.

Oran, meanwhile, couldn't believe just how many beautiful, golden sandy beaches there were, dotted along the north coast, as they made their way steadily along in silence, all but for the noise of the wind rushing past them. They carried on against the strong headwind for the best part of an hour, westward, eventually passing over small islands known as the Skerries, as the Inishowen Peninsula now loomed ahead in the distance. This was a welcome sight, which Dara clearly recognised from his time on the summit of Faltanragh recently - a sign that they were almost home, thankfully.

"There's no cloud cover to conceal us," Rydian called out. "We'll just have to hope that we aren't seen." She made a final left turn just before the sandy point on the northern plain, as they neared the mouth of Lough Foyle and headed south on the last leg of their journey home.

With the sun to their left now, Rydian and Obblob ascended again, steeply, to clear the tall cliffs at Binevenagh. As they flew over the edge of the cliffs, still climbing, the mountain range that was home came into view ahead of them, just below and stretching off into the distance. Oran excitedly called over to Dara now, with some difficulty due to the cold, "Dara! I think... I can... see... home!"

Dara nodded back to him, forcing a smile. He knew full well that the wind and the cold made it very difficult to have a conversation up here, for his face was near frozen now. He turned to his front again as he peered, eyes streaming from the biting wind, into the distance beyond Obblob's barbed neck and head, which bobbed up and down gracefully in front of him in synchronisation with his beating wings. Far off in the distance, right on top of a snow-covered mountain directly ahead, sat what from here appeared to be a tiny, white stone structure with a tall tower at its centre, which shone brightly as it reflected the morning sunlight. They were almost home, he told himself thankfully, and smiled again... but it wasn't forced this time.

It was late morning in the castle and most of the Danu were going about their daily business as usual, despite the very unwelcome cold. Everyone except for Lugh, Cethen and Murchad the Wise, that was. The three men were stood in the glass walled section at the top of the tower and had been busily planning what to do if Oran, Enya and Dara did not return to the castle with Rydian by nightfall that night, heatedly discussing their few alternatives to a new dragon crystal.

"It's settled then," Lugh sighed, gruffly. "If there's no sign of them by dusk, we go underground - all of us. But, we give them until dusk."

"Let us hope that it doesn't come to that, my Lord," Cethen comforted, as he placed a hand gently on Lugh's shoulder.

"We have no choice!" Murchad the Wise scolded, hoarsely. "We must protect ourselves! We *cannot* remain exposed like this indefinitely. Who can say that our enemies have not gotten wind of our presence here already? Next there'll be another war, and that's the last thing we want."

"Easy for you to say, old man," Lugh responded, angrily. "It is not your child that is missing, after all."

Murchad recoiled at the King's anger, stammering, "My sincere apologies... my... King, I did not... wish to offend you." Composing himself, he added, "Let us hope that they return soon - there is still time, my son."

"Yes, old man, there is still time," Lugh replied, hopefully.

As the three stood silently, facing the sun to the east, none of them noticed the two tiny black specks in the sky toward the north - specks that grew larger by the minute; specks that were two dragons, with riders upon their backs.

Below them in the courtyard, many of the castle's inhabitants were milling about, trudging through snow and slush, oblivious to the discussion being held above, in the tower, by their King and his two closest friends. Mary and the children were there in the courtyard also, being shown around by Enya's friend, Orla. As they wandered through the castle grounds in the bright morning sunlight, greeting people as they went, the sky suddenly seemed to darken slightly above them.

A shadow was suddenly cast across the snow-covered ground where they stood, accompanied by a strange, thunderous noise, as everyone stopped what they were doing and stood still, frozen in place by fear. Mary looked slowly upward, gasping in shock, firstly. Her expression quickly changed to that of puzzlement, though, as she took in the completely unexpected spectacle of her beloved husband and her dog sat astride a huge dragon as it crossed over the north-west ramparts in front of and above her. She was dumbstruck, frozen in place, watching in awe as they flew slowly over the wall, heading directly toward some open ground nearby to where she currently stood.

Oran began laughing now, looking down at everyone in the courtyard below, as Rydian and Obblob flapped their great wings furiously to cushion their landing. Dara spotted Mary right away, calling down to her, "Mary, my love! What are *you* doing here?"

Everyone gasped as they realised what was happening, moving swiftly back out of the way, as they cleared an area large enough for the majestic beasts to land. Mary grabbed her daughters' hands excitedly, declaring, "Ellen, Rosemary! It's Daddy... look!"

Ellen and Rosemary squealed with delight as they looked up and recognised their father sat atop the dragon nearest them.

Within moments, the dragons and their riders were safely on the ground and everyone in the courtyard gave a loud, rapturous cheer, gathering around the great beasts excitedly as Oran, Dara and Enya dismounted their saddles. Dara quickly freed Holly from her restraints, lifting her carefully down onto the ground, then turned to his wife and children with arms outstretched, a huge smile across his face,

"Well? Come and give me a hug then," he beamed.

Mary and the girls rushed into his arms, squealing and sobbing with joy, as everyone in the courtyard went about welcoming the adventurers back, with fond hugs, smiles and handshakes. It wasn't long before someone sent news of their return to Lugh, and he and Cethen hurried down to the courtyard to greet them also, leaving the frail Murchad to make his way down at his own pace. The King stormed across the courtyard and found Enya quickly, stood in the crowd, smiling and talking to Orla. He halted several paces from her, regarding her with a scowl, as everyone else fell silent around them. Enya looked sheepishly at the King as she murmured, "Forgive me, Father," lowering her head in shame.

Lugh did not respond at first, still scowling at her, then suddenly laughed as he held his arms out to his sides and beamed, "Enya, my child! It is so good to see you again. Come here, my child."

Enya rushed into her father's arms and wept, "I'm sorry, Father... I had to go after them."

"I understand, child. You're home safe now... that is all that matters," Lugh said, calmly, then slowly removed himself from her embrace as he declared, "Now then, to urgent business."

He trudged over to Oran, eagerly, a smile spreading across his face as he looked up at the dragons. He turned back to Oran, placing his hands upon his shoulders, and chortled, "You did it, my boy," quickly adding, "But you brought two dragons back - how so?"

Before Oran could answer, however, Rydian lowered her head down to Lugh's level and said softly, "Long time, old friend. You look well."

"Long time indeed, old friend," Lugh responded, as he turned slowly to face her and fondly enquired, "How have you been, Rydian?"

"Lonely, very lonely," came Rydian's swift and deliberate reply.

"No doubt, yes," Lugh agreed. "But, I see you have found company," nodding toward Obblob as he reached out to stroke the side of her jaw, continuing, "Oran has explained why I have summoned you here, no?"

"He has that, yes," Rydian agreed, adding firmly, "I am agreeable to your request, on the condition that I may remain here on this mountain... and that my new companion stays with me, also."

"But of course, of course," Lugh smiled at her again, without hesitation, as he declared, "That's wonderful news. We must hurry, though, if you don't mind - time is, as always, against us."

"No doubt," Rydian agreed, asking, "Shall we proceed? Where should you like me to place the egg?"

"Well, here will be just fine," Lugh answered. "We can carry it from here, carefully, to its rightful resting place in the great room."

The entire population of the castle had gathered around them as they talked, avidly watching now as Rydian went about the task of laying a replacement egg, which was, on this occasion, fertilised by Obblob, avoiding the need to transform Rydian to a male dragon. The crowd looked on eagerly as the newly fertilised egg sat there, upright in the snow, and soon began to glow bright blue - the first stage of the impending time cocoon.

"Everyone back now!" Lugh shouted, as the egg began to emit a loud buzzing sound - the second stage of the developing time cocoon.

As they all moved back, safely away from the brightly glowing egg, there came a loud crackling noise as a bolt of bright, white light shot straight up several hundred feet into the sky above. Everyone looked upward, observing now as the welcome ring of blue mist spread slowly outward across the sky high above them, descending slowly and increasing in diameter as it engulfed the castle and all within it. The bolt of light disappeared as the egg fell silent again, still glowing brightly where it sat in the snow. As egg then became dragon crystal, and the third and final stage was completed, the time cocoon secreted the castle and its inhabitants from the outside world once more.

Lugh breathed a sigh of relief then announced, "A feast, to celebrate, I think," to which everyone cheered loudly.

Over the coming hours, after the dragon crystal was taken to its rightful place in the great room where it was immediately tended to by one of Oran's peers, a junior elf named Eldris, there was much celebration, feasting and drinking. Oran, Dara and Enya recounted the details of their exciting adventures to an enrapt audience, going into as much detail as possible as the feast went on. Lugh carefully hid his concern when they told the story of the appearance of Oran's mother, stealing off to speak to Rydian privately, with the intention of discussing the matter further with Oran later that evening.

As the afternoon went on, Mary explained to Dara how she and the girls had been summoned to the castle by Lugh the previous night. She also explained that she was now very worried about their house and possessions, at which Dara went to Oran and said, sadly, "Well, my young friend…" He sighed deeply as he struggled to find the words. "It's been… quite an adventure."

"It has that," Oran agreed, knowing in his heart what Dara was about to say next, as the celebrations continued around them.

Dara swallowed a sizeable lump in his throat, as he fought to get the words to come out of his mouth, "It has been… a pleasure… to have met you… and your good people. My life will never be the same."

"You won't stay, then?" Oran simply asked now, raising his eyebrows as he stood up.

"We should really get back home, where we belong, to our friends and family, you understand? My livestock, and our way of life, too," Dara apologised.

"I understand, no need to explain," Oran soothed.

"Will you see us to the gates?" Dara asked, looking round at Mary and the girls.

"Of course, Dara, gladly," Oran replied, being the one now forcing a smile.

Dara and Mary spent the next half hour saying their good-byes to everyone, as they gradually made their way through the crowd. They found Lugh waiting at the gates, stood next to a magnificent black horse, staring at them oddly.

"Are you leaving us, Dara?" he enquired.

"Yes, I'm afraid so, Sire," Dara answered solemnly, glancing at Oran as he added, "Oran will explain, I'm sure."

"Well, that is truly a shame," Lugh replied, with a hint of surprise mixed with disappointment. "There is always a place here for you and your family. Nonetheless, Dara, I should wish to thank you for what you have done for us - for Oran. I would like you to take this horse as my gift of gratitude to you. It is the horse which you have ridden for the past few days and is now yours to keep."

"Why thank you, Sire. You are most welcome. Thank you, again," Dara humbly responded, as he took the reins from Lugh.

Dara lastly said his final, sad goodbyes to Enya, Rydian and Obblob, who had also joined them by the heavy entrance gates, which were now slowly opening.

As they walked to the outside of the castle entrance, Oran placed his hand firmly on Dara's arm and said, "Wait! Before you go, I want you to have something." He then looked down at his wrist as he commanded, "Ethioné, release me, please."

He took the bracelet from his wrist and held it out to Dara in his hand, advising, "A way back, should you ever be in need of us - the *only* way back." He then added, "I also need a favour of you."

"But Oran, I couldn't," Dara said in shock.

"I insist," Oran ordered, forcing the talisman into Dara's hand.

Dara smiled as he agreed and took the talisman, attaching it to his wrist, then asked, "What favour do you need? Ask and it shall be done, my friend."

"Will you return to the Witch's forest and seek out Arak for me? Find out all that he knows of me and my parents, then bring that information back to me, please?" Oran almost begged.

"Well, yes, of course... *if* I can find him," Dara answered.

"I imagine that you won't need to look for him and that he, in fact, will find you," Oran laughed now.

"Very well. I'll see you soon then, in that case," Dara smiled, then laughed, "Goodbye, for now, my *old* friend."

"Goodbye, Dara," Oran mumbled, as he lunged at Dara and threw his arms around him, then whispered, "Thank you for your help, and for your friendship."

Dara patted Oran on the back, then removed himself from his embrace as he said, "I'm sure that we shall see each other soon - in a few days perhaps."

"Yes," Oran grinned.

Dara gave Oran a last smile as he turned and set off with his family, Holly, Lucy and the horse away from the castle, as the sun sank lower behind them. A few minutes later, as they walked across the summit in the direction of home, Dara felt an odd, tingling sensation pass through his entire body. He stopped and turned to look back at the castle. The castle was gone, however - no longer visible, as they had just crossed the barrier of the time cocoon. He looked at Mary and said,

"It's gone - look, Mary."

Mary turned and searched the summit for the castle and, not finding it, simply said, "Incredible, my love."

"I need to test something, quickly. Walk with me, please," Dara urged, then instructed his daughters, "Wait here, girls. Don't be scared, we'll be right back." He began walking slowly back in the direction they had just come from, gaze fixed on the empty space ahead, with Mary at his side. After a few paces, he felt the tingling sensation once again, and the castle miraculously reappeared in front of him, shimmering into view. He stopped and stood staring at it, with a grin on his face as he turned to Mary and asked, "Can you see the castle, Mary?"

"Why, no... I can't," she replied in confusion.

"Hah! It works, Mary. I can see it because of the bracelet, but you cannot - it truly works. I can come back," Dara laughed loudly, then exclaimed, "Quickly, take my hand!"

Mary reached out and took Dara's hand. As soon as she touched him, the castle appeared to her again."

"I can see it now, too!" she said in surprise.

They smiled at each other and hugged, smothering Lucy, whom Mary had been carrying, in the process.

Dara and Mary then walked back to the children and took them by their hands as they turned and set off again, across the summit toward Glenarran and home, with Holly leading the way and the horse following closely behind - a robin now perched on its rump, singing cheerfully, strangely.

As they walked away, laughing and talking, all of them were oblivious to the fact that a rather sinister looking figure in a long, black, hooded cloak was now watching them intently, quietly, concealed by the dark shadows just inside the tree line of the forest nearby. The figure quickly diverted his attention away from Dara and his family, looking to the now barren summit where the castle had been recently visible, and whispered quietly, "So, now I know where to find you."

Next in the series...

ORAN

and the
Vampire King

By

A.J. Clinton